THE
HUNGER GAMES

SCHOLASTIC INC.
New York Toronto London Auckland
Sydney Mexico City New Delhi Hong Kong

SUZANNE COLLINS

THE HUNGER GAMES

No part of this publication may be reproduced, stored in a retrieval system, or
transmitted in any form or by any means, electronic, mechanical, photocopying,
recording, or otherwise, without written permission of the publisher.
For information regarding permission, write to Scholastic Inc., Attention:
Permissions Department, 557 Broadway, New York, NY 10012.

This book was originally published in hardcover by Scholastic Press in 2008.

ISBN-13: 978-0-439-02352-8
ISBN-10: 0-439-02352-1

12 11 10 9 8 7 6 5 4 3 2 1   11 12 13 14/0

Printed in Jiaxing, China   68
First Scholastic paperback printing, September 2009

The text type was set in Adobe Garamond Pro
Book design by Phil Falco

For James Proimos

PART I
"THE TRIBUTES"

When I wake up, the other side of the bed is cold. My fingers stretch out, seeking Prim's warmth but finding only the rough canvas cover of the mattress. She must have had bad dreams and climbed in with our mother. Of course, she did. This is the day of the reaping.

I prop myself up on one elbow. There's enough light in the bedroom to see them. My little sister, Prim, curled up on her side, cocooned in my mother's body, their cheeks pressed together. In sleep, my mother looks younger, still worn but not so beaten-down. Prim's face is as fresh as a raindrop, as lovely as the primrose for which she was named. My mother was very beautiful once, too. Or so they tell me.

Sitting at Prim's knees, guarding her, is the world's ugliest cat. Mashed-in nose, half of one ear missing, eyes the color of rotting squash. Prim named him Buttercup, insisting that his muddy yellow coat matched the bright flower. He hates me. Or at least distrusts me. Even though it was years ago, I think he still remembers how I tried to drown him in a bucket when Prim brought him home. Scrawny kitten, belly swollen with worms, crawling with fleas. The last thing I needed was another mouth to feed. But Prim begged so hard, cried even, I had to let him stay. It turned out okay. My mother got rid of the vermin and he's a born mouser. Even catches the occasional rat. Sometimes, when I clean a kill, I feed Buttercup the entrails. He has stopped hissing at me.

Entrails. No hissing. This is the closest we will ever come to love.

I swing my legs off the bed and slide into my hunting boots. Supple leather that has molded to my feet. I pull on trousers, a shirt, tuck my long dark braid up into a cap, and grab my forage bag. On the table, under a wooden bowl to protect it from hungry rats and cats alike, sits a perfect little goat cheese wrapped in basil leaves. Prim's gift to me on reaping day. I put the cheese carefully in my pocket as I slip outside.

Our part of District 12, nicknamed the Seam, is usually crawling with coal miners heading out to the morning shift at this hour. Men and women with hunched shoulders, swollen knuckles, many who have long since stopped trying to scrub the coal dust out of their broken nails, the lines of their sunken faces. But today the black cinder streets are empty. Shutters on the squat gray houses are closed. The reaping isn't until two. May as well sleep in. If you can.

Our house is almost at the edge of the Seam. I only have to pass a few gates to reach the scruffy field called the Meadow. Separating the Meadow from the woods, in fact enclosing all of District 12, is a high chain-link fence topped with barbed-wire loops. In theory, it's supposed to be electrified twenty-four hours a day as a deterrent to the predators that live in the woods — packs of wild dogs, lone cougars, bears — that used to threaten our streets. But since we're lucky to get two or three hours of electricity in the evenings, it's usually safe to touch. Even so, I always take a moment to listen carefully for the hum that means the fence is live. Right now, it's silent as a stone. Concealed by a clump of bushes, I flatten out on my belly and slide under a two-foot stretch that's been loose for years. There are several other weak spots in the fence, but this one is so close to home I almost always enter the woods here.

As soon as I'm in the trees, I retrieve a bow and sheath of arrows from a hollow log. Electrified or not, the fence has been successful at keeping the flesh-eaters out of District 12. Inside the woods they roam freely, and there are added concerns like venomous snakes, rabid animals, and no real paths to follow. But there's also food if you know how to find it. My father knew and he taught me some before he was blown to bits in a mine explosion. There was nothing even to bury. I was eleven then. Five years later, I still wake up screaming for him to run.

Even though trespassing in the woods is illegal and poaching carries the severest of penalties, more people would risk it if they had weapons. But most are not bold enough to venture out with just a knife. My bow is a rarity, crafted by my father along with a few others that I keep well hidden in the woods, carefully wrapped in waterproof covers. My father could have made good money selling them, but if the officials found out he would have been publicly executed for inciting a rebellion. Most of the Peacekeepers turn a blind eye to the few of us who hunt because they're as hungry for fresh meat as anybody is. In fact, they're among our best customers. But the idea that someone might be arming the Seam would never have been allowed.

In the fall, a few brave souls sneak into the woods to harvest apples. But always in sight of the Meadow. Always close enough to run back to the safety of District 12 if trouble arises. "District Twelve. Where you can starve to death in safety," I mutter. Then I glance quickly over my shoulder. Even here, even in the middle of nowhere, you worry someone might overhear you.

When I was younger, I scared my mother to death, the things I would blurt out about District 12, about the people who rule our country, Panem, from the far-off city called the Capitol. Eventually I understood this would only lead us to more trouble. So I learned to hold my tongue and to turn my features into an indifferent mask so that no one could ever read my thoughts. Do my work quietly in school. Make only polite small talk in the public market. Discuss little more than trades in the Hob, which is the black market where I make most of my money. Even at home, where I am less pleasant, I avoid discussing tricky topics. Like the reaping, or food shortages, or the Hunger Games. Prim might begin to repeat my words and then where would we be?

In the woods waits the only person with whom I can be myself. Gale. I can feel the muscles in my face relaxing, my pace quickening as I climb the hills to our place, a rock ledge overlooking a valley. A thicket of berry bushes protects it from unwanted eyes. The sight of him waiting there brings on a smile. Gale says I never smile except in the woods.

"Hey, Catnip," says Gale. My real name is Katniss, but when I first told him, I had barely whispered it. So he thought I'd said Catnip. Then when this crazy lynx started following me around the woods looking for handouts, it became his official nickname for me. I finally had to kill the lynx because he scared off game. I almost regretted it because he wasn't bad company. But I got a decent price for his pelt.

"Look what I shot." Gale holds up a loaf of bread with an arrow stuck in it, and I laugh. It's real bakery bread, not the flat, dense loaves we make from our grain rations. I take it in my hands, pull out the arrow, and hold the puncture in the crust to my nose, inhaling the fragrance that makes my mouth flood with saliva. Fine bread like this is for special occasions.

"Mm, still warm," I say. He must have been at the bakery at the crack of dawn to trade for it. "What did it cost you?"

"Just a squirrel. Think the old man was feeling sentimental this morning," says Gale. "Even wished me luck."

"Well, we all feel a little closer today, don't we?" I say, not even bothering to roll my eyes. "Prim left us a cheese." I pull it out.

His expression brightens at the treat. "Thank you, Prim. We'll have a real feast." Suddenly he falls into a Capitol accent as he mimics Effie Trinket, the maniacally upbeat woman who arrives once a year to read out the names at the reaping. "I almost forgot! Happy Hunger Games!" He plucks a few blackberries from the bushes around us. "And may the odds —" He tosses a berry in a high arc toward me.

I catch it in my mouth and break the delicate skin with my teeth. The sweet tartness explodes across my tongue. "— be *ever* in your favor!" I finish with equal verve. We have to joke about it because the alternative is to be scared out of your wits. Besides, the Capitol accent is so affected, almost anything sounds funny in it.

I watch as Gale pulls out his knife and slices the bread. He could be my brother. Straight black hair, olive skin, we even have the same gray eyes. But we're not related, at least not closely. Most of the families who work the mines resemble one another this way.

That's why my mother and Prim, with their light hair and blue eyes, always look out of place. They are. My mother's parents were part of the small merchant class that caters to officials, Peacekeepers, and the occasional Seam customer. They ran an apothecary shop in the nicer part of District 12. Since almost no one can afford doctors, apothecaries are our healers. My father got to know my mother because on his hunts he would sometimes collect medicinal herbs and sell them to her shop to be brewed into remedies. She must have really loved him to leave her home for the Seam. I try to remember that when all I can see is the woman who sat by, blank and unreachable, while her children turned to skin and bones. I try to forgive her for my father's sake. But to be honest, I'm not the forgiving type.

Gale spreads the bread slices with the soft goat cheese, carefully placing a basil leaf on each while I strip the bushes of their berries. We settle back in a nook in the rocks. From this place, we are invisible but have a clear view of the valley, which is teeming with summer life, greens to gather, roots to dig, fish iridescent in the sunlight. The day is glorious, with a blue sky and soft breeze. The food's wonderful, with the cheese seeping into the warm bread and the berries bursting in our mouths. Everything would be perfect if this really was a holiday, if all the day off meant was roaming the mountains with Gale, hunting for tonight's supper. But instead we have to be standing in the square at two o'clock waiting for the names to be called out.

"We could do it, you know," Gale says quietly.

"What?" I ask.

"Leave the district. Run off. Live in the woods. You and I, we could make it," says Gale.

I don't know how to respond. The idea is so preposterous.

"If we didn't have so many kids," he adds quickly.

They're not our kids, of course. But they might as well be. Gale's two little brothers and a sister. Prim. And you may as well throw in our mothers, too, because how would they live without us? Who would fill those mouths that are always asking for more? With both of us hunting daily, there are still nights when game has to be swapped for lard or shoelaces or wool, still nights when we go to bed with our stomachs growling.

"I never want to have kids," I say.

"I might. If I didn't live here," says Gale.

"But you do," I say, irritated.

"Forget it," he snaps back.

The conversation feels all wrong. Leave? How could I leave Prim, who is the only person in the world I'm certain I love? And Gale is devoted to his family. We can't leave, so why bother talking about it? And even if we did . . . even if we did . . . where did this stuff about having kids come from? There's never been anything romantic between Gale and me. When we met, I was a skinny twelve-year-old, and although he was only two years older, he already looked like a man. It took a long time for us to even become friends, to stop haggling over every trade and begin helping each other out.

Besides, if he wants kids, Gale won't have any trouble finding a wife. He's good-looking, he's strong enough to handle the work in the mines, and he can hunt. You can tell by the way the girls whisper about him when he walks by in school that they want him. It makes me jealous but not for the reason people would think. Good hunting partners are hard to find.

"What do you want to do?" I ask. We can hunt, fish, or gather.

"Let's fish at the lake. We can leave our poles and gather in the woods. Get something nice for tonight," he says.

Tonight. After the reaping, everyone is supposed to celebrate. And a lot of people do, out of relief that their children have been spared for another year. But at least two families will pull their shutters, lock their doors, and try to figure out how they will survive the painful weeks to come.

We make out well. The predators ignore us on a day when easier, tastier prey abounds. By late morning, we have a dozen fish, a bag of greens and, best of all, a gallon of strawberries. I found the patch a few years ago, but Gale had the idea to string mesh nets around it to keep out the animals.

On the way home, we swing by the Hob, the black market that operates in an abandoned warehouse that once held coal. When they came up with a more efficient system that transported the coal directly from the mines to the trains, the Hob gradually took over the space. Most businesses are closed by this time on reaping day, but the black market's still fairly busy. We easily trade six of the fish for good bread, the other two for salt. Greasy Sae, the bony old woman who sells bowls of hot soup from a large kettle, takes half the greens off our hands in exchange for a couple of chunks of paraffin. We might do a tad better elsewhere, but we make an effort to keep on good terms with Greasy Sae. She's the only one who can consistently be counted on to buy wild dog. We don't hunt them on purpose, but if you're attacked and you take out a dog or two, well, meat is meat. "Once it's in the soup, I'll call it beef," Greasy Sae says with a wink. No one in the Seam would turn up their nose at a good leg of wild dog, but the Peacekeepers who come to the Hob can afford to be a little choosier.

When we finish our business at the market, we go to the back door of the mayor's house to sell half the strawberries, knowing he has a particular fondness for them and can afford our price. The mayor's daughter, Madge, opens the door. She's in my year at school. Being the mayor's daughter, you'd expect her to be a snob, but she's all right. She just keeps to herself. Like me. Since neither of us really has a group of friends, we seem to end up together a lot at school. Eating lunch, sitting next to each other at assemblies, partnering for sports activities. We rarely talk, which suits us both just fine.

Today her drab school outfit has been replaced by an expensive white dress, and her blonde hair is done up with a pink ribbon. Reaping clothes.

"Pretty dress," says Gale.

Madge shoots him a look, trying to see if it's a genuine compliment or if he's just being ironic. It *is* a pretty dress, but she would never be wearing it ordinarily. She presses her lips together and then smiles. "Well, if I end up going to the Capitol, I want to look nice, don't I?"

Now it's Gale's turn to be confused. Does she mean it? Or is she messing with him? I'm guessing the second.

"You won't be going to the Capitol," says Gale coolly. His eyes land on a small, circular pin that adorns her dress. Real gold. Beautifully crafted. It could keep a family in bread for months. "What can you have? Five entries? I had six when I was just twelve years old."

"That's not her fault," I say.

"No, it's no one's fault. Just the way it is," says Gale.

Madge's face has become closed off. She puts the money for the berries in my hand. "Good luck, Katniss."

"You, too," I say, and the door closes.

We walk toward the Seam in silence. I don't like that Gale took a dig at Madge, but he's right, of course. The reaping system is unfair, with the poor getting the worst of it. You become eligible for the reaping the day you turn twelve. That year, your name is entered once. At thirteen, twice. And so on and so on until you reach the age of eighteen, the final year of eligibility, when your name goes into the pool seven times. That's true for every citizen in all twelve districts in the entire country of Panem.

But here's the catch. Say you are poor and starving as we were. You can opt to add your name more times in exchange for tesserae. Each tessera is worth a meager year's supply of grain and oil for one person. You may do this for each of your family members as well. So, at the age of twelve, I had my name entered four times. Once, because I had to, and three times for tesserae for grain and oil for myself, Prim, and my mother. In fact, every year I have needed to do this. And the entries are cumulative. So now, at the age of sixteen, my name will be in the reaping twenty times. Gale, who is eighteen and has been either helping or single-handedly feeding a family of five for seven years, will have his name in forty-two times.

You can see why someone like Madge, who has never been at risk of needing a tessera, can set him off. The chance of her name being drawn is very slim compared to those of us who live in the Seam. Not impossible, but slim. And even though the rules were set up by the Capitol, not the districts, certainly not Madge's family, it's hard not to resent those who don't have to sign up for tesserae.

Gale knows his anger at Madge is misdirected. On other days, deep in the woods, I've listened to him rant about how the tesserae are just another tool to cause misery in our district. A way to plant hatred between the starving workers of the Seam and those who can generally count on supper and thereby ensure we will never trust one another. "It's to the Capitol's advantage to have us divided among ourselves," he might say if there were no ears to hear but mine. If it wasn't reaping day. If a girl with a gold pin and no tesserae had not made what I'm sure she thought was a harmless comment.

As we walk, I glance over at Gale's face, still smoldering underneath his stony expression. His rages seem pointless to me, although I never say so. It's not that I don't agree with him. I do. But what good is yelling about the Capitol in the middle of the woods? It doesn't change anything. It doesn't make things fair. It doesn't fill our stomachs. In fact, it scares off the nearby game. I let him yell though. Better he does it in the woods than in the district.

Gale and I divide our spoils, leaving two fish, a couple of loaves of good bread, greens, a quart of strawberries, salt, paraffin, and a bit of money for each.

"See you in the square," I say.

"Wear something pretty," he says flatly.

At home, I find my mother and sister are ready to go. My mother wears a fine dress from her apothecary days. Prim is in my first reaping outfit, a skirt and ruffled blouse. It's a bit big on her, but my mother has made it stay with pins. Even so, she's having trouble keeping the blouse tucked in at the back.

A tub of warm water waits for me. I scrub off the dirt and sweat from the woods and even wash my hair. To my surprise, my mother has laid out one of her own lovely dresses for me. A soft blue thing with matching shoes.

"Are you sure?" I ask. I'm trying to get past rejecting offers of help from her. For a while, I was so angry, I wouldn't allow her to do anything for me. And this is something special. Her clothes from her past are very precious to her.

"Of course. Let's put your hair up, too," she says. I let her towel-dry it and braid it up on my head. I can hardly recognize myself in the cracked mirror that leans against the wall.

"You look beautiful," says Prim in a hushed voice.

"And nothing like myself," I say. I hug her, because I know these next few hours will be terrible for her. Her first reaping. She's about as safe as you can get, since she's only entered once. I wouldn't let her take out any tesserae. But she's worried about me. That the unthinkable might happen.

I protect Prim in every way I can, but I'm powerless against the reaping. The anguish I always feel when she's in pain wells up in my chest and threatens to register on my face. I notice her blouse has pulled out of her skirt in the back again and force myself to stay calm. "Tuck your tail in, little duck," I say, smoothing the blouse back in place.

Prim giggles and gives me a small "Quack."

"Quack yourself," I say with a light laugh. The kind only Prim can draw out of me. "Come on, let's eat," I say and plant a quick kiss on the top of her head.

The fish and greens are already cooking in a stew, but that will be for supper. We decide to save the strawberries and bakery bread for this evening's meal, to make it special we say. Instead we drink milk from Prim's goat, Lady, and eat the rough bread made from the tessera grain, although no one has much appetite anyway.

At one o'clock, we head for the square. Attendance is mandatory unless you are on death's door. This evening, officials will come around and check to see if this is the case. If not, you'll be imprisoned.

It's too bad, really, that they hold the reaping in the square — one of the few places in District 12 that can be pleasant. The square's surrounded by shops, and on public market days, especially if there's good weather, it has a holiday feel to it. But today, despite the bright banners hanging on the buildings, there's an air of grimness. The camera crews, perched like buzzards on rooftops, only add to the effect.

People file in silently and sign in. The reaping is a good opportunity for the Capitol to keep tabs on the population as well. Twelve- through eighteen-year-olds are herded into roped areas marked off by ages, the oldest in the front, the young ones, like Prim, toward the back. Family members line up around the perimeter, holding tightly to one another's hands. But there are others, too, who have no one they love at stake, or who no longer care, who slip among the crowd, taking bets on the two kids whose names will be drawn. Odds are given on their ages, whether they're Seam or merchant, if they will break down and weep. Most refuse dealing with the racketeers but carefully, carefully. These same people tend to be informers, and who hasn't broken the law? I could be shot on a daily basis for hunting, but the appetites of those in charge protect me. Not everyone can claim the same.

Anyway, Gale and I agree that if we have to choose between dying of hunger and a bullet in the head, the bullet would be much quicker.

The space gets tighter, more claustrophobic as people arrive. The square's quite large, but not enough to hold District 12's population of about eight thousand. Latecomers are directed to the adjacent streets, where they can watch the event on screens as it's televised live by the state.

I find myself standing in a clump of sixteens from the Seam. We all exchange terse nods then focus our attention on the temporary stage that is set up before the Justice Building. It holds three chairs, a podium, and two large glass balls, one for the boys and one for the girls. I stare at the paper slips in the girls' ball. Twenty of them have Katniss Everdeen written on them in careful handwriting.

Two of the three chairs fill with Madge's father, Mayor Undersee, who's a tall, balding man, and Effie Trinket, District 12's escort, fresh from the Capitol with her scary white grin, pinkish hair, and spring green suit. They murmur to each other and then look with concern at the empty seat.

Just as the town clock strikes two, the mayor steps up to the podium and begins to read. It's the same story every year. He tells of the history of Panem, the country that rose up out of the ashes of a place that was once called North America. He lists the disasters, the droughts, the storms, the fires, the encroaching seas that swallowed up so much of the land, the brutal war for what little sustenance remained. The result was Panem, a shining Capitol ringed by thirteen districts, which brought peace and prosperity to its citizens. Then came the Dark Days, the uprising of the districts against the Capitol. Twelve were defeated, the thirteenth obliterated. The Treaty of Treason gave us the new laws to guarantee peace and, as our yearly reminder that the Dark Days must never be repeated, it gave us the Hunger Games.

The rules of the Hunger Games are simple. In punishment for the uprising, each of the twelve districts must provide one girl and one boy, called tributes, to participate. The twenty-four tributes will be imprisoned in a vast outdoor arena that could hold anything from a burning desert to a frozen wasteland. Over a period of several weeks, the competitors must fight to the death. The last tribute standing wins.

Taking the kids from our districts, forcing them to kill one another while we watch — this is the Capitol's way of reminding us how totally we are at their mercy. How little chance we would stand of surviving another rebellion.

Whatever words they use, the real message is clear. "Look how we take your children and sacrifice them and there's nothing you can do. If you lift a finger, we will destroy every last one of you. Just as we did in District Thirteen."

To make it humiliating as well as torturous, the Capitol requires us to treat the Hunger Games as a festivity, a sporting event pitting every district against the others. The last tribute alive receives a life of ease back home, and their district will be showered with prizes, largely consisting of food. All year, the Capitol will show the winning district gifts of grain and oil and even delicacies like sugar while the rest of us battle starvation.

"It is both a time for repentance and a time for thanks," intones the mayor.

Then he reads the list of past District 12 victors. In seventy-four years, we have had exactly two. Only one is still alive. Haymitch Abernathy, a paunchy, middle-aged man, who at this moment appears hollering something unintelligible, staggers onto the stage, and falls into the third chair. He's drunk. Very. The crowd responds with its token applause, but he's confused and tries to give Effie Trinket a big hug, which she barely manages to fend off.

The mayor looks distressed. Since all of this is being televised, right now District 12 is the laughingstock of Panem, and he knows it. He quickly tries to pull the attention back to the reaping by introducing Effie Trinket.

Bright and bubbly as ever, Effie Trinket trots to the podium and gives her signature, "Happy Hunger Games! And may the odds be *ever* in your favor!" Her pink hair must be a wig because her curls have shifted slightly off-center since her encounter with Haymitch. She goes on a bit about what an honor it is to be here, although everyone knows she's just aching to get bumped up to a better district where they have proper victors, not drunks who molest you in front of the entire nation.

Through the crowd, I spot Gale looking back at me with a ghost of a smile. As reapings go, this one at least has a slight entertainment factor. But suddenly I am thinking of Gale and his forty-two names in that big glass ball and how the odds are not in his favor. Not compared to a lot of the boys. And maybe he's thinking the same thing about me because his face darkens and he turns away. "But there are still thousands of slips," I wish I could whisper to him.

It's time for the drawing. Effie Trinket says as she always does, "Ladies first!" and crosses to the glass ball with the girls' names. She reaches in, digs her hand deep into the ball, and pulls out a slip of paper. The crowd draws in a collective breath and then you can hear a pin drop, and I'm feeling nauseous and so desperately hoping that it's not me, that it's not me, that it's not me.

Effie Trinket crosses back to the podium, smoothes the slip of paper, and reads out the name in a clear voice. And it's not me.

It's Primrose Everdeen.

One time, when I was in a blind in a tree, waiting motionless for game to wander by, I dozed off and fell ten feet to the ground, landing on my back. It was as if the impact had knocked every wisp of air from my lungs, and I lay there struggling to inhale, to exhale, to do anything.

That's how I feel now, trying to remember how to breathe, unable to speak, totally stunned as the name bounces around the inside of my skull. Someone is gripping my arm, a boy from the Seam, and I think maybe I started to fall and he caught me.

There must have been some mistake. This can't be happening. Prim was one slip of paper in thousands! Her chances of being chosen so remote that I'd not even bothered to worry about her. Hadn't I done everything? Taken the tesserae, refused to let her do the same? One slip. One slip in thousands. The odds had been entirely in her favor. But it hadn't mattered.

Somewhere far away, I can hear the crowd murmuring unhappily as they always do when a twelve-year-old gets chosen because no one thinks this is fair. And then I see her, the blood drained from her face, hands clenched in fists at her sides, walking with stiff, small steps up toward the stage, passing me, and I see the back of her blouse has become untucked and hangs out over her skirt. It's this detail, the untucked blouse forming a ducktail, that brings me back to myself.

"Prim!" The strangled cry comes out of my throat, and my muscles begin to move again. "Prim!" I don't need to shove through the crowd. The other kids make way immediately allowing me a straight path to the stage. I reach her just as she is about to mount the steps. With one sweep of my arm, I push her behind me.

"I volunteer!" I gasp. "I volunteer as tribute!"

There's some confusion on the stage. District 12 hasn't had a volunteer in decades and the protocol has become rusty. The rule is that once a tribute's name has been pulled from the ball, another eligible boy, if a boy's name has been read, or girl, if a girl's name has been read, can step forward to take his or her place. In some districts, in which winning the reaping is such a great honor, people are eager to risk their lives, the volunteering is complicated. But in District 12, where the word *tribute* is pretty much synonymous with the word *corpse*, volunteers are all but extinct.

"Lovely!" says Effie Trinket. "But I believe there's a small matter of introducing the reaping winner and then asking for volunteers, and if one does come forth then we, um . . ." she trails off, unsure herself.

"What does it matter?" says the mayor. He's looking at me with a pained expression on his face. He doesn't know me really, but there's a faint recognition there. I am the girl who brings the strawberries. The girl his daughter might have spoken of on occasion. The girl who five years ago stood huddled with her mother and sister, as he presented her, the oldest child, with a medal of valor. A medal for her father, vaporized in the mines. Does he remember that? "What does it matter?" he repeats gruffly. "Let her come forward."

Prim is screaming hysterically behind me. She's wrapped her skinny arms around me like a vice. "No, Katniss! No! You can't go!"

"Prim, let go," I say harshly, because this is upsetting me and I don't want to cry. When they televise the replay of the reapings tonight, everyone will make note of my tears, and I'll be marked as an easy target. A weakling. I will give no one that satisfaction. "Let go!"

I can feel someone pulling her from my back. I turn and see Gale has lifted Prim off the ground and she's thrashing in his arms. "Up you go, Catnip," he says, in a voice he's fighting to keep steady, and then he carries Prim off toward my mother. I steel myself and climb the steps.

"Well, bravo!" gushes Effie Trinket. "That's the spirit of the Games!" She's pleased to finally have a district with a little action going on in it. "What's your name?"

I swallow hard. "Katniss Everdeen," I say.

"I bet my buttons that was your sister. Don't want her to steal all the glory, do we? Come on, everybody! Let's give a big round of applause to our newest tribute!" trills Effie Trinket.

To the everlasting credit of the people of District 12, not one person claps. Not even the ones holding betting slips, the ones who are usually beyond caring. Possibly because they know me from the Hob, or knew my father, or have encountered Prim, who no one can help loving. So instead of acknowledging applause, I stand there unmoving while they take part in the boldest form of dissent they can manage. Silence. Which says we do not agree. We do not condone. All of this is wrong.

Then something unexpected happens. At least, I don't expect it because I don't think of District 12 as a place that cares about me. But a shift has occurred since I stepped up to take Prim's place, and now it seems I have become someone precious. At first one, then another, then almost every member of the crowd touches the three middle fingers of their left hand to their lips and holds it out to me. It is an old and rarely used gesture of our district, occasionally seen at funerals. It means thanks, it means admiration, it means good-bye to someone you love.

Now I am truly in danger of crying, but fortunately Haymitch chooses this time to come staggering across the stage to congratulate me. "Look at her. Look at this one!" he hollers, throwing an arm around my shoulders. He's surprisingly strong for such a wreck. "I like her!" His breath reeks of liquor and it's been a long time since he's bathed. "Lots of . . . " He can't think of the word for a while. "Spunk!" he says triumphantly. "More than you!" he releases me and starts for the front of the stage. "More than you!" he shouts, pointing directly into a camera.

Is he addressing the audience or is he so drunk he might actually be taunting the Capitol? I'll never know because just as he's opening his mouth to continue, Haymitch plummets off the stage and knocks himself unconscious.

He's disgusting, but I'm grateful. With every camera gleefully trained on him, I have just enough time to release the small, choked sound in my throat and compose myself. I put my hands behind my back and stare into the distance. I can see the hills I climbed this morning with Gale. For a moment, I yearn for something . . . the idea of us leaving the district . . . making our way in the woods . . . but I know I was right about not running off. Because who else would have volunteered for Prim?

Haymitch is whisked away on a stretcher, and Effie Trinket is trying to get the ball rolling again. "What an exciting day!" she warbles as she attempts to straighten her wig, which has listed severely to the right. "But more excitement to come! It's time to choose our boy tribute!" Clearly hoping to contain her tenuous hair situation, she plants one hand on her head as she crosses to the ball that contains the boys' names and grabs the first slip she encounters. She zips back to the podium, and I don't even have time to wish for Gale's safety when she's reading the name. "Peeta Mellark."

Peeta Mellark!

Oh, no, I think. *Not him.* Because I recognize this name, although I have never spoken directly to its owner. Peeta Mellark.

No, the odds are not in my favor today.

I watch him as he makes his way toward the stage. Medium height, stocky build, ashy blond hair that falls in waves over his forehead. The shock of the moment is registering on his face, you can see his struggle to remain emotionless, but his blue eyes show the alarm I've seen so often in prey. Yet he climbs steadily onto the stage and takes his place.

Effie Trinket asks for volunteers, but no one steps forward. He has two older brothers, I know, I've seen them in the bakery, but one is probably too old now to volunteer and the other won't. This is standard. Family devotion only goes so far for most people on reaping day. What I did was the radical thing.

The mayor begins to read the long, dull Treaty of Treason as he does every year at this point — it's required — but I'm not listening to a word.

Why him? I think. Then I try to convince myself it doesn't matter. Peeta Mellark and I are not friends. Not even neighbors. We don't speak. Our only real interaction happened years ago. He's probably forgotten it. But I haven't and I know I never will. . . .

It was during the worst time. My father had been killed in the mine accident three months earlier in the bitterest January anyone could remember. The numbness of his loss had passed, and the pain would hit me out of nowhere, doubling me over, racking my body with sobs. *Where are you?* I would cry out in my mind. *Where have you gone?* Of course, there was never any answer.

The district had given us a small amount of money as compensation for his death, enough to cover one month of grieving at which time my mother would be expected to get a job. Only she didn't. She didn't do anything but sit propped up in a chair or, more often, huddled under the blankets on her bed, eyes fixed on some point in the distance. Once in a while, she'd stir, get up as if moved by some urgent purpose, only to then collapse back into stillness. No amount of pleading from Prim seemed to affect her.

I was terrified. I suppose now that my mother was locked in some dark world of sadness, but at the time, all I knew was that I had lost not only a father, but a mother as well. At eleven years old, with Prim just seven, I took over as head of the family. There was no choice. I bought our food at the market and cooked it as best I could and tried to keep Prim and myself looking presentable. Because if it had become known that my mother could no longer care for us, the district would have taken us away from her and placed us in the community home. I'd grown up seeing those home kids at school. The sadness, the marks of angry hands on their faces, the hopelessness that curled their shoulders forward. I could never let that happen to Prim. Sweet, tiny Prim who cried when I cried before she even knew the reason, who brushed and plaited my mother's hair before we left for school, who still polished my father's shaving mirror each night because he'd hated the layer of coal dust that settled on everything in the Seam. The community home would crush her like a bug. So I kept our predicament a secret.

But the money ran out and we were slowly starving to death. There's no other way to put it. I kept telling myself if I could only hold out until May, just May 8th, I would turn twelve and be able to sign up for the tesserae and get that precious grain and oil to feed us. Only there were still several weeks to go. We could well be dead by then.

Starvation's not an uncommon fate in District 12. Who hasn't seen the victims? Older people who can't work. Children from a family with too many to feed. Those injured in the mines. Straggling through the streets. And one day, you come upon them sitting motionless against a wall or lying in the Meadow, you hear the wails from a house, and the Peacekeepers are called in to retrieve the body. Starvation is never the cause of death officially. It's always the flu, or exposure, or pneumonia. But that fools no one.

On the afternoon of my encounter with Peeta Mellark, the rain was falling in relentless icy sheets. I had been in town, trying to trade some threadbare old baby clothes of Prim's in the public market, but there were no takers. Although I had been to the Hob on several occasions with my father, I was too frightened to venture into that rough, gritty place alone. The rain had soaked through my father's hunting jacket, leaving me chilled to the bone. For three days, we'd had nothing but boiled water with some old dried mint leaves I'd found in the back of a cupboard. By the time the market closed, I was shaking so hard I dropped my bundle of baby clothes in a mud puddle. I didn't pick it up for fear I would keel over and be unable to regain my feet. Besides, no one wanted those clothes.

I couldn't go home. Because at home was my mother with her dead eyes and my little sister, with her hollow cheeks and cracked lips. I couldn't walk into that room with the smoky fire from the damp branches I had scavenged at the edge of the woods after the coal had run out, my hands empty of any hope.

I found myself stumbling along a muddy lane behind the shops that serve the wealthiest townspeople. The merchants live above their businesses, so I was essentially in their backyards. I remember the outlines of garden beds not yet planted for the spring, a goat or two in a pen, one sodden dog tied to a post, hunched defeated in the muck.

All forms of stealing are forbidden in District 12. Punishable by death. But it crossed my mind that there might be something in the trash bins, and those were fair game. Perhaps a bone at the butcher's or rotted vegetables at the grocer's, something no one but my family was desperate enough to eat. Unfortunately, the bins had just been emptied.

When I passed the baker's, the smell of fresh bread was so overwhelming I felt dizzy. The ovens were in the back, and a golden glow spilled out the open kitchen door. I stood mesmerized by the heat and the luscious scent until the rain interfered, running its icy fingers down my back, forcing me back to life. I lifted the lid to the baker's trash bin and found it spotlessly, heartlessly bare.

Suddenly a voice was screaming at me and I looked up to see the baker's wife, telling me to move on and did I want her to call the Peacekeepers and how sick she was of having those brats from the Seam pawing through her trash. The words were ugly and I had no defense. As I carefully replaced the lid and backed away, I noticed him, a boy with blond hair peering out from behind his mother's back. I'd seen him at school. He was in my year, but I didn't know his name. He stuck with the town kids, so how would I? His mother went back into the bakery, grumbling, but he must have been watching me as I made my way behind the pen that held their pig and leaned against the far side of an old apple tree. The realization that I'd have nothing to take home had finally sunk in. My knees buckled and I slid down the tree trunk to its roots. It was too much. I was too sick and weak and tired, oh, so tired. *Let them call the Peacekeepers and take us to the community home,* I thought. *Or better yet, let me die right here in the rain.*

There was a clatter in the bakery and I heard the woman screaming again and the sound of a blow, and I vaguely wondered what was going on. Feet sloshed toward me through the mud and I thought, *It's her. She's coming to drive me away with a stick.* But it wasn't her. It was the boy. In his arms, he carried two large loaves of bread that must have fallen into the fire because the crusts were scorched black.

His mother was yelling, "Feed it to the pig, you stupid creature! Why not? No one decent will buy burned bread!"

He began to tear off chunks from the burned parts and toss them into the trough, and the front bakery bell rung and the mother disappeared to help a customer.

The boy never even glanced my way, but I was watching him. Because of the bread, because of the red weal that stood out on his cheekbone. What had she hit him with?

My parents never hit us. I couldn't even imagine it. The boy took one look back to the bakery as if checking that the coast was clear, then, his attention back on the pig, he threw a loaf of bread in my direction. The second quickly followed, and he sloshed back to the bakery, closing the kitchen door tightly behind him.

I stared at the loaves in disbelief. They were fine, perfect really, except for the burned areas. Did he mean for me to have them? He must have. Because there they were at my feet. Before anyone could witness what had happened I shoved the loaves up under my shirt, wrapped the hunting jacket tightly about me, and walked swiftly away. The heat of the bread burned into my skin, but I clutched it tighter, clinging to life.

By the time I reached home, the loaves had cooled somewhat, but the insides were still warm. When I dropped them on the table, Prim's hands reached to tear off a chunk, but I made her sit, forced my mother to join us at the table, and poured warm tea. I scraped off the black stuff and sliced the bread. We ate an entire loaf, slice by slice. It was good hearty bread, filled with raisins and nuts.

I put my clothes to dry at the fire, crawled into bed, and fell into a dreamless sleep. It didn't occur to me until the next morning that the boy might have burned the bread on purpose. Might have dropped the loaves into the flames, knowing it meant being punished, and then delivered them to me. But I dismissed this. It must have been an accident. Why would he have done it? He didn't even know me. Still, just throwing me the bread was an enormous kindness that would have surely resulted in a beating if discovered. I couldn't explain his actions.

We ate slices of bread for breakfast and headed to school. It was as if spring had come overnight. Warm sweet air. Fluffy clouds. At school, I passed the boy in the hall, his cheek had swelled up and his eye had blackened. He was with his friends and didn't acknowledge me in any way. But as I collected Prim and started for home that afternoon, I found him staring at me from across the school yard. Our eyes met for only a second, then he turned his head away. I dropped my gaze, embarrassed, and that's when I saw it. The first dandelion of the year. A bell went off in my head. I thought of the hours spent in the woods with my father and I knew how we were going to survive.

To this day, I can never shake the connection between this boy, Peeta Mellark, and the bread that gave me hope, and the dandelion that reminded me that I was not doomed. And more than once, I have turned in the school hallway and caught his eyes trained on me, only to quickly flit away. I feel like I owe him something, and I hate owing people. Maybe if I had thanked him at some point, I'd be feeling less conflicted now. I thought about it a couple of times, but the opportunity never seemed to present itself. And now it never will. Because we're going to be thrown into an arena to fight to the death. Exactly how am I supposed to work in a thank-you in there? Somehow it just won't seem sincere if I'm trying to slit his throat.

The mayor finishes the dreary Treaty of Treason and motions for Peeta and me to shake hands. His are as solid and warm as those loaves of bread. Peeta looks me right in the eye and gives my hand what I think is meant to be a reassuring squeeze. Maybe it's just a nervous spasm.

We turn back to face the crowd as the anthem of Panem plays.

Oh, well, I think. *There will be twenty-four of us. Odds are someone else will kill him before I do.*

Of course, the odds have not been very dependable of late.

The moment the anthem ends, we are taken into custody. I don't mean we're handcuffed or anything, but a group of Peacekeepers marches us through the front door of the Justice Building. Maybe tributes have tried to escape in the past. I've never seen that happen though.

Once inside, I'm conducted to a room and left alone. It's the richest place I've ever been in, with thick, deep carpets and a velvet couch and chairs. I know velvet because my mother has a dress with a collar made of the stuff. When I sit on the couch, I can't help running my fingers over the fabric repeatedly. It helps to calm me as I try to prepare for the next hour. The time allotted for the tributes to say good-bye to their loved ones. I cannot afford to get upset, to leave this room with puffy eyes and a red nose. Crying is not an option. There will be more cameras at the train station.

My sister and my mother come first. I reach out to Prim and she climbs on my lap, her arms around my neck, head on my shoulder, just like she did when she was a toddler. My mother sits beside me and wraps her arms around us. For a few minutes, we say nothing. Then I start telling them all the things they must remember to do, now that I will not be there to do them for them.

Prim is not to take any tesserae. They can get by, if

they're careful, on selling Prim's goat milk and cheese and the small apothecary business my mother now runs for the people in the Seam. Gale will get her the herbs she doesn't grow herself, but she must be very careful to describe them because he's not as familiar with them as I am. He'll also bring them game — he and I made a pact about this a year or so ago — and will probably not ask for compensation, but they should thank him with some kind of trade, like milk or medicine.

I don't bother suggesting Prim learn to hunt. I tried to teach her a couple of times and it was disastrous. The woods terrified her, and whenever I shot something, she'd get teary and talk about how we might be able to heal it if we got it home soon enough. But she makes out well with her goat, so I concentrate on that.

When I am done with instructions about fuel, and trading, and staying in school, I turn to my mother and grip her arm, hard. "Listen to me. Are you listening to me?" She nods, alarmed by my intensity. She must know what's coming. "You can't leave again," I say.

My mother's eyes find the floor. "I know. I won't. I couldn't help what —"

"Well, you have to help it this time. You can't clock out and leave Prim on her own. There's no me now to keep you both alive. It doesn't matter what happens. Whatever you see on the screen. You have to promise me you'll fight through it!" My voice has risen to a shout. In it is all the anger, all the fear I felt at her abandonment.

She pulls her arm from my grasp, moved to anger herself

now. "I was ill. I could have treated myself if I'd had the medicine I have now."

That part about her being ill might be true. I've seen her bring back people suffering from immobilizing sadness since. Perhaps it is a sickness, but it's one we can't afford.

"Then take it. And take care of her!" I say.

"I'll be all right, Katniss," says Prim, clasping my face in her hands. "But you have to take care, too. You're so fast and brave. Maybe you can win."

I can't win. Prim must know that in her heart. The competition will be far beyond my abilities. Kids from wealthier districts, where winning is a huge honor, who've been trained their whole lives for this. Boys who are two to three times my size. Girls who know twenty different ways to kill you with a knife. Oh, there'll be people like me, too. People to weed out before the real fun begins.

"Maybe," I say, because I can hardly tell my mother to carry on if I've already given up myself. Besides, it isn't in my nature to go down without a fight, even when things seem insurmountable. "Then we'd be rich as Haymitch."

"I don't care if we're rich. I just want you to come home. You will try, won't you? Really, really try?" asks Prim.

"Really, really try. I swear it," I say. And I know, because of Prim, I'll have to.

And then the Peacekeeper is at the door, signaling our time is up, and we're all hugging one another so hard it hurts and all I'm saying is "I love you. I love you both." And they're saying it back and then the Peacekeeper orders them out and the door closes. I bury my head in one of the velvet pillows as if this can block the whole thing out.

Someone else enters the room, and when I look up, I'm surprised to see it's the baker, Peeta Mellark's father. I can't believe he's come to visit me. After all, I'll be trying to kill his son soon. But we do know each other a bit, and he knows Prim even better. When she sells her goat cheeses at the Hob, she puts two of them aside for him and he gives her a generous amount of bread in return. We always wait to trade with him when his witch of a wife isn't around because he's so much nicer. I feel certain he would never have hit his son the way she did over the burned bread. But why has he come to see me?

The baker sits awkwardly on the edge of one of the plush chairs. He's a big, broad-shouldered man with burn scars from years at the ovens. He must have just said good-bye to his son.

He pulls a white paper package from his jacket pocket and holds it out to me. I open it and find cookies. These are a luxury we can never afford.

"Thank you," I say. The baker's not a very talkative man in the best of times, and today he has no words at all. "I had some of your bread this morning. My friend Gale gave you a squirrel for it." He nods, as if remembering the squirrel. "Not your best trade," I say. He shrugs as if it couldn't possibly matter.

Then I can't think of anything else, so we sit in silence until a Peacemaker summons him. He rises and coughs to clear his throat. "I'll keep an eye on the little girl. Make sure she's eating."

I feel some of the pressure in my chest lighten at his words. People deal with me, but they are genuinely fond of Prim. Maybe there will be enough fondness to keep her alive.

My next guest is also unexpected. Madge walks straight to me. She is not weepy or evasive, instead there's an urgency about her tone that surprises me. "They let you wear one thing from your district in the arena. One thing to remind you of home. Will you wear this?" She holds out the circular gold pin that was on her dress earlier. I hadn't paid much attention to it before, but now I see it's a small bird in flight.

"Your pin?" I say. Wearing a token from my district is about the last thing on my mind.

"Here, I'll put it on your dress, all right?" Madge doesn't wait for an answer, she just leans in and fixes the bird to my dress. "Promise you'll wear it into the arena, Katniss?" she asks. "Promise?"

"Yes," I say. Cookies. A pin. I'm getting all kinds of gifts today. Madge gives me one more. A kiss on the cheek. Then she's gone and I'm left thinking that maybe Madge really has been my friend all along.

Finally, Gale is here and maybe there is nothing romantic between us, but when he opens his arms I don't hesitate to go into them. His body is familiar to me — the way it moves, the smell of wood smoke, even the sound of his heart beating I know from quiet moments on a hunt — but this is the first time I really feel it, lean and hard-muscled against my own.

"Listen," he says. "Getting a knife should be pretty easy, but you've got to get your hands on a bow. That's your best chance."

"They don't always have bows," I say, thinking of the year there were only horrible spiked maces that the tributes had to bludgeon one another to death with.

"Then make one," says Gale. "Even a weak bow is better than no bow at all."

I have tried copying my father's bows with poor results. It's not that easy. Even he had to scrap his own work sometimes.

"I don't even know if there'll be wood," I say. Another year, they tossed everybody into a landscape of nothing but boulders and sand and scruffy bushes. I particularly hated that year. Many contestants were bitten by venomous snakes or went insane from thirst.

"There's almost always some wood," Gale says. "Since that year half of them died of cold. Not much entertainment in that."

It's true. We spent one Hunger Games watching the players freeze to death at night. You could hardly see them because they were just huddled in balls and had no wood for fires or torches or anything. It was considered very anti-climactic in the Capitol, all those quiet, bloodless deaths. Since then, there's usually been wood to make fires.

"Yes, there's usually some," I say.

"Katniss, it's just hunting. You're the best hunter I know," says Gale.

"It's not just hunting. They're armed. They think," I say.

"So do you. And you've had more practice. Real practice," he says. "You know how to kill."

"Not people," I say.

"How different can it be, really?" says Gale grimly.

The awful thing is that if I can forget they're people, it will be no different at all.

The Peacekeepers are back too soon and Gale asks for more time, but they're taking him away and I start to panic. "Don't let them starve!" I cry out, clinging to his hand.

"I won't! You know I won't! Katniss, remember I —" he says, and they yank us apart and slam the door and I'll never know what it was he wanted me to remember.

It's a short ride from the Justice Building to the train station. I've never been in a car before. Rarely even ridden in wagons. In the Seam, we travel on foot.

I've been right not to cry. The station is swarming with reporters with their insectlike cameras trained directly on my face. But I've had a lot of practice at wiping my face clean of emotions and I do this now. I catch a glimpse of myself on the television screen on the wall that's airing my arrival live and feel gratified that I appear almost bored.

Peeta Mellark, on the other hand, has obviously been crying and interestingly enough does not seem to be trying to cover it up. I immediately wonder if this will be his strategy in the Games. To appear weak and frightened, to reassure the other tributes that he is no competition at all, and then come out fighting. This worked very well for a girl, Johanna Mason, from District 7 a few years back. She seemed like such a sniveling, cowardly fool that no one bothered about her until there were only a handful of contestants left. It turned out she could kill viciously. Pretty clever, the way she played it. But this seems an odd strategy for Peeta Mellark because he's a baker's son. All those years of having enough to eat and hauling bread trays around have made him broad-shouldered and strong. It will take an awful lot of weeping to convince anyone to overlook him.

We have to stand for a few minutes in the doorway of the train while the cameras gobble up our images, then we're allowed inside and the doors close mercifully behind us. The train begins to move at once.

The speed initially takes my breath away. Of course, I've never been on a train, as travel between the districts is forbidden except for officially sanctioned duties. For us, that's mainly transporting coal. But this is no ordinary coal train. It's one of the high-speed Capitol models that average 250 miles per hour. Our journey to the Capitol will take less than a day.

In school, they tell us the Capitol was built in a place once called the Rockies. District 12 was in a region known as Appalachia. Even hundreds of years ago, they mined coal here. Which is why our miners have to dig so deep.

Somehow it all comes back to coal at school. Besides basic reading and math most of our instruction is coal-related. Except for the weekly lecture on the history of Panem. It's mostly a lot of blather about what we owe the Capitol. I know there must be more than they're telling us, an actual account of what happened during the rebellion. But I don't spend much time thinking about it. Whatever the truth is, I don't see how it will help me get food on the table.

The tribute train is fancier than even the room in the Justice Building. We are each given our own chambers that have a bedroom, a dressing area, and a private bathroom with hot and cold running water. We don't have hot water at home, unless we boil it.

There are drawers filled with fine clothes, and Effie Trinket tells me to do anything I want, wear anything I want, everything is at my disposal. Just be ready for supper in an hour. I peel off my mother's blue dress and take a hot shower. I've never had a shower before. It's like being in a summer rain, only warmer. I dress in a dark green shirt and pants.

At the last minute, I remember Madge's little gold pin. For the first time, I get a good look at it. It's as if someone fashioned a small golden bird and then attached a ring around it. The bird is connected to the ring only by its wing tips. I suddenly recognize it. A mockingjay.

They're funny birds and something of a slap in the face to the Capitol. During the rebellion, the Capitol bred a series of genetically altered animals as weapons. The common term for them was *muttations*, or sometimes *mutts* for short. One was a special bird called a jabberjay that had the ability to memorize and repeat whole human conversations. They were homing birds, exclusively male, that were released into regions where the Capitol's enemies were known to be hiding. After the birds gathered words, they'd fly back to centers to be recorded. It took people awhile to realize what was going on in the districts, how private conversations were being transmitted. Then, of course, the rebels fed the Capitol endless lies, and the joke was on it. So the centers were shut down and the birds were abandoned to die off in the wild.

Only they didn't die off. Instead, the jabberjays mated with female mockingbirds, creating a whole new species that could replicate both bird whistles and human melodies. They had lost the ability to enunciate words but could still mimic a range of human vocal sounds, from a child's high-pitched warble to a man's deep tones. And they could re-create songs. Not just a few notes, but whole songs with multiple verses, if you had the patience to sing them and if they liked your voice.

My father was particularly fond of mockingjays. When we went hunting, he would whistle or sing complicated songs to them and, after a polite pause, they'd always sing back. Not everyone is treated with such respect. But whenever my father sang, all the birds in the area would fall silent and listen. His voice was that beautiful, high and clear and so filled with life it made you want to laugh and cry at the same time. I could never bring myself to continue the practice after he was gone. Still, there's something comforting about the little bird. It's like having a piece of my father with me, protecting me. I fasten the pin onto my shirt, and with the dark green fabric as a background, I can almost imagine the mockingjay flying through the trees.

Effie Trinket comes to collect me for supper. I follow her through the narrow, rocking corridor into a dining room with polished paneled walls. There's a table where all the dishes are highly breakable. Peeta Mellark sits waiting for us, the chair next to him empty.

"Where's Haymitch?" asks Effie Trinket brightly.

"Last time I saw him, he said he was going to take a nap," says Peeta.

"Well, it's been an exhausting day," says Effie Trinket. I think she's relieved by Haymitch's absence, and who can blame her?

The supper comes in courses. A thick carrot soup, green salad, lamb chops and mashed potatoes, cheese and fruit, a chocolate cake. Throughout the meal, Effie Trinket keeps reminding us to save space because there's more to come. But I'm stuffing myself because I've never had food like this, so good and so much, and because probably the best thing I can do between now and the Games is put on a few pounds.

"At least, you two have decent manners," says Effie as we're finishing the main course. "The pair last year ate everything with their hands like a couple of savages. It completely upset my digestion."

The pair last year were two kids from the Seam who'd never, not one day of their lives, had enough to eat. And when they did have food, table manners were surely the last thing on their minds. Peeta's a baker's son. My mother taught Prim and me to eat properly, so yes, I can handle a fork and knife. But I hate Effie Trinket's comment so much I make a point of eating the rest of my meal with my fingers. Then I wipe my hands on the tablecloth. This makes her purse her lips tightly together.

Now that the meal's over, I'm fighting to keep the food down. I can see Peeta's looking a little green, too. Neither of our stomachs is used to such rich fare. But if I can hold down Greasy Sae's concoction of mice meat, pig entrails, and tree bark — a winter specialty — I'm determined to hang on to this.

We go to another compartment to watch the recap of the reapings across Panem. They try to stagger them throughout the day so a person could conceivably watch the whole thing live, but only people in the Capitol could really do that, since none of them have to attend reapings themselves.

One by one, we see the other reapings, the names called, the volunteers stepping forward or, more often, not. We examine the faces of the kids who will be our competition. A few stand out in my mind. A monstrous boy who lunges forward to volunteer from District 2. A fox-faced girl with sleek red hair from District 5. A boy with a crippled foot from District 10. And most hauntingly, a twelve-year-old girl from District 11. She has dark brown skin and eyes, but other than that, she's very like Prim in size and demeanor. Only when she mounts the stage and they ask for volunteers, all you can hear is the wind whistling through the decrepit buildings around her. There's no one willing to take her place.

Last of all, they show District 12. Prim being called, me running forward to volunteer. You can't miss the desperation in my voice as I shove Prim behind me, as if I'm afraid no one will hear and they'll take Prim away. But, of course, they do hear. I see Gale pulling her off me and watch myself mount the stage. The commentators are not sure what to say about the crowd's refusal to applaud. The silent salute. One says that District 12 has always been a bit backward but that local customs can be charming. As if on cue, Haymitch falls off the stage, and they groan comically. Peeta's name is drawn, and he quietly takes his place. We shake hands. They cut to the anthem again, and the program ends.

Effie Trinket is disgruntled about the state her wig was in. "Your mentor has a lot to learn about presentation. A lot about televised behavior."

Peeta unexpectedly laughs. "He was drunk," says Peeta. "He's drunk every year."

"Every day," I add. I can't help smirking a little. Effie Trinket makes it sound like Haymitch just has somewhat rough manners that could be corrected with a few tips from her.

"Yes," hisses Effie Trinket. "How odd you two find it amusing. You know your mentor is your lifeline to the world in these Games. The one who advises you, lines up your sponsors, and dictates the presentation of any gifts.

Haymitch can well be the difference between your life and your death!"

Just then, Haymitch staggers into the compartment. "I miss supper?" he says in a slurred voice. Then he vomits all over the expensive carpet and falls in the mess.

"So laugh away!" says Effie Trinket. She hops in her pointy shoes around the pool of vomit and flees the room.

For a few moments, Peeta and I take in the scene of our mentor trying to rise out of the slippery vile stuff from his stomach. The reek of vomit and raw spirits almost brings my dinner up. We exchange a glance. Obviously Haymitch isn't much, but Effie Trinket is right about one thing, once we're in the arena he's all we've got. As if by some unspoken agreement, Peeta and I each take one of Haymitch's arms and help him to his feet.

"I tripped?" Haymitch asks. "Smells bad." He wipes his hand on his nose, smearing his face with vomit.

"Let's get you back to your room," says Peeta. "Clean you up a bit."

We half-lead half-carry Haymitch back to his compartment. Since we can't exactly set him down on the embroidered bedspread, we haul him into the bathtub and turn the shower on him. He hardly notices.

"It's okay," Peeta says to me. "I'll take it from here."

I can't help feeling a little grateful since the last thing I want to do is strip down Haymitch, wash the vomit out of his chest hair, and tuck him into bed. Possibly Peeta is trying to make a good impression on him, to be his favorite once the Games begin. But judging by the state he's in, Haymitch will have no memory of this tomorrow.

"All right," I say. "I can send one of the Capitol people to help you." There's any number on the train. Cooking for us. Waiting on us. Guarding us. Taking care of us is their job.

"No. I don't want them," says Peeta.

I nod and head to my own room. I understand how Peeta feels. I can't stand the sight of the Capitol people myself. But making them deal with Haymitch might be a small form of revenge. So I'm pondering the reason why he insists on taking care of Haymitch and all of a sudden I think, *It's because he's being kind. Just as he was kind to give me the bread.*

The idea pulls me up short. A kind Peeta Mellark is far more dangerous to me than an unkind one. Kind people have a way of working their way inside me and rooting there. And I can't let Peeta do this. Not where we're going. So I decide, from this moment on, to have as little as possible to do with the baker's son.

When I get back to my room, the train is pausing at a platform to refuel. I quickly open the window, toss the cookies Peeta's father gave me out of the train, and slam the glass shut. No more. No more of either of them.

Unfortunately, the packet of cookies hits the ground and bursts open in a patch of dandelions by the track. I only see the image for a moment, because the train is off again, but it's enough. Enough to remind me of that other dandelion in the school yard years ago . . .

I had just turned away from Peeta Mellark's bruised face when I saw the dandelion and I knew hope wasn't lost. I plucked it carefully and hurried home. I grabbed a bucket and Prim's hand and headed to the Meadow and yes, it was dotted with the golden-headed weeds. After we'd harvested those, we scrounged along inside the fence for probably a mile until we'd filled the bucket with the dandelion greens, stems, and flowers. That night, we gorged ourselves on dandelion salad and the rest of the bakery bread.

"What else?" Prim asked me. "What other food can we find?"

"All kinds of things," I promised her. "I just have to remember them."

My mother had a book she'd brought with her from the apothecary shop. The pages were made of old parchment and covered in ink drawings of plants. Neat handwritten blocks told their names, where to gather them, when they came in bloom, their medical uses. But my father added other entries to the book. Plants for eating, not healing. Dandelions, pokeweed, wild onions, pines. Prim and I spent the rest of the night poring over those pages.

The next day, we were off school. For a while I hung around the edges of the Meadow, but finally I worked up the courage to go under the fence. It was the first time I'd been there alone, without my father's weapons to protect me. But I retrieved the small bow and arrows he'd made me from a hollow tree. I probably didn't go more than twenty yards into the woods that day. Most of the time, I perched up in the branches of an old oak, hoping for game to come by. After several hours, I had the good luck to kill a rabbit.

I'd shot a few rabbits before, with my father's guidance. But this I'd done on my own.

We hadn't had meat in months. The sight of the rabbit seemed to stir something in my mother. She roused herself, skinned the carcass, and made a stew with the meat and some more greens Prim had gathered. Then she acted confused and went back to bed, but when the stew was done, we made her eat a bowl.

The woods became our savior, and each day I went a bit farther into its arms. It was slow-going at first, but I was determined to feed us. I stole eggs from nests, caught fish in nets, sometimes managed to shoot a squirrel or rabbit for stew, and gathered the various plants that sprung up beneath my feet. Plants are tricky. Many are edible, but one false mouthful and you're dead. I checked and double-checked the plants I harvested with my father's pictures. I kept us alive.

Any sign of danger, a distant howl, the inexplicable break of a branch, sent me flying back to the fence at first. Then I began to risk climbing trees to escape the wild dogs that quickly got bored and moved on. Bears and cats lived deeper in, perhaps disliking the sooty reek of our district.

On May 8th, I went to the Justice Building, signed up for my tesserae, and pulled home my first batch of grain and oil in Prim's toy wagon. On the eighth of every month, I was entitled to do the same. I couldn't stop hunting and gathering, of course. The grain was not enough to live on, and there were other things to buy, soap and milk and thread. What we didn't absolutely have to eat, I began to trade at the Hob. It was frightening to enter that place without my father at my side, but people had respected him, and they accepted me. Game was game after all, no matter who'd shot it. I also sold at the back doors of the wealthier clients in town, trying to remember what my father had told me and learning a few new tricks as well. The butcher would buy my rabbits but not squirrels. The baker enjoyed squirrel but would only trade for one if his wife wasn't around. The Head Peacekeeper loved wild turkey. The mayor had a passion for strawberries.

In late summer, I was washing up in a pond when I noticed the plants growing around me. Tall with leaves like arrowheads. Blossoms with three white petals. I knelt down in the water, my fingers digging into the soft mud, and I pulled up handfuls of the roots. Small, bluish tubers that don't look like much but boiled or baked are as good as any potato. "Katniss," I said aloud. It's the plant I was named for. And I heard my father's voice joking, "As long as you can find yourself, you'll never starve." I spent hours stirring up the pond bed with my toes and a stick, gathering the tubers that floated to the top. That night, we feasted on fish and katniss roots until we were all, for the first time in months, full.

Slowly, my mother returned to us. She began to clean and cook and preserve some of the food I brought in for winter. People traded us or paid money for her medical remedies. One day, I heard her singing.

Prim was thrilled to have her back, but I kept watching, waiting for her to disappear on us again. I didn't trust her. And some small gnarled place inside me hated her for her weakness, for her neglect, for the months she had put us through. Prim forgave her, but I had taken a step back from my mother, put up a wall to protect myself from needing her, and nothing was ever the same between us again.

Now I was going to die without that ever being set right. I thought of how I had yelled at her today in the Justice Building. I had told her I loved her, too, though. So maybe it would all balance out.

For a while I stand staring out the train window, wishing I could open it again, but unsure of what would happen at such high speed. In the distance, I see the lights of another district. 7? 10? I don't know. I think about the people in their houses, settling in for bed. I imagine my home, with its shutters drawn tight. What are they doing now, my mother and Prim? Were they able to eat supper? The fish stew and the strawberries? Or did it lie untouched on their plates? Did they watch the recap of the day's events on the battered old TV that sits on the table against the wall? Surely, there were more tears. Is my mother holding up, being strong for Prim? Or has she already started to slip away, leaving the weight of the world on my sister's fragile shoulders?

Prim will undoubtedly sleep with my mother tonight. The thought of that scruffy old Buttercup posting himself on the bed to watch over Prim comforts me. If she cries, he will nose his way into her arms and curl up there until she calms down and falls asleep. I'm so glad I didn't drown him.

Imagining my home makes me ache with loneliness. This day has been endless. Could Gale and I have been eating blackberries only this morning? It seems like a lifetime ago. Like a long dream that deteriorated into a nightmare. Maybe, if I go to sleep, I will wake up back in District 12, where I belong.

Probably the drawers hold any number of nightgowns, but I just strip off my shirt and pants and climb into bed in my underwear. The sheets are made of soft, silky fabric. A thick fluffy comforter gives immediate warmth.

If I'm going to cry, now is the time to do it. By morning, I'll be able to wash the damage done by the tears from my face. But no tears come. I'm too tired or too numb to cry. The only thing I feel is a desire to be somewhere else. So I let the train rock me into oblivion.

Gray light is leaking through the curtains when the rapping rouses me. I hear Effie Trinket's voice, calling me to rise. "Up, up, up! It's going to be a big, big, big day!" I try and imagine, for a moment, what it must be like inside that woman's head. What thoughts fill her waking hours? What dreams come to her at night? I have no idea.

I put the green outfit back on since it's not really dirty, just slightly crumpled from spending the night on the floor. My fingers trace the circle around the little gold mockingjay and I think of the woods, and of my father, and of my mother and Prim waking up, having to get on with things.

I slept in the elaborate braided hair my mother did for the reaping and it doesn't look too bad, so I just leave it up. It doesn't matter. We can't be far from the Capitol now. And once we reach the city, my stylist will dictate my look for the opening ceremonies tonight anyway. I just hope I get one who doesn't think nudity is the last word in fashion.

As I enter the dining car, Effie Trinket brushes by me with a cup of black coffee. She's muttering obscenities under her breath. Haymitch, his face puffy and red from the previous day's indulgences, is chuckling. Peeta holds a roll and looks somewhat embarrassed.

"Sit down! Sit down!" says Haymitch, waving me over. The moment I slide into my chair I'm served an enormous platter of food. Eggs, ham, piles of fried potatoes. A tureen of fruit sits in ice to keep it chilled. The basket of rolls they set before me would keep my family going for a week. There's an elegant glass of orange juice. At least, I think it's orange juice. I've only even tasted an orange once, at New Year's when my father bought one as a special treat. A cup of coffee. My mother adores coffee, which we could almost never afford, but it only tastes bitter and thin to me. A rich brown cup of something I've never seen.

"They call it hot chocolate," says Peeta. "It's good."

I take a sip of the hot, sweet, creamy liquid and a shudder runs through me. Even though the rest of the meal beckons, I ignore it until I've drained my cup. Then I stuff down every mouthful I can hold, which is a substantial amount, being careful to not overdo it on the richest stuff. One time, my mother told me that I always eat like I'll never see food again. And I said, "I won't unless I bring it home." That shut her up.

When my stomach feels like it's about to split open, I lean back and take in my breakfast companions. Peeta is still eating, breaking off bits of roll and dipping them in hot chocolate. Haymitch hasn't paid much attention to his platter, but he's knocking back a glass of red juice that he keeps thinning with a clear liquid from a bottle. Judging by the fumes, it's some kind of spirit. I don't know Haymitch, but I've seen him often enough in the Hob, tossing handfuls of money on the counter of the woman who sells white liquor. He'll be incoherent by the time we reach the Capitol.

I realize I detest Haymitch. No wonder the District 12 tributes never stand a chance. It isn't just that we've been underfed and lack training. Some of our tributes have still been strong enough to make a go of it. But we rarely get sponsors and he's a big part of the reason why. The rich people who back tributes — either because they're betting on them or simply for the bragging rights of picking a winner — expect someone classier than Haymitch to deal with.

"So, you're supposed to give us advice," I say to Haymitch.

"Here's some advice. Stay alive," says Haymitch, and then bursts out laughing. I exchange a look with Peeta before I remember I'm having nothing more to do with him. I'm surprised to see the hardness in his eyes. He generally seems so mild.

"That's very funny," says Peeta. Suddenly he lashes out at the glass in Haymitch's hand. It shatters on the floor, sending the bloodred liquid running toward the back of the train. "Only not to us."

Haymitch considers this a moment, then punches Peeta in the jaw, knocking him from his chair. When he turns back to reach for the spirits, I drive my knife into the table between his hand and the bottle, barely missing his fingers. I brace myself to deflect his hit, but it doesn't come. Instead he sits back and squints at us.

"Well, what's this?" says Haymitch. "Did I actually get a pair of fighters this year?"

Peeta rises from the floor and scoops up a handful of ice from under the fruit tureen. He starts to raise it to the red mark on his jaw.

"No," says Haymitch, stopping him. "Let the bruise show. The audience will think you've mixed it up with another tribute before you've even made it to the arena."

"That's against the rules," says Peeta.

"Only if they catch you. That bruise will say you fought, you weren't caught, even better," says Haymitch. He turns to me. "Can you hit anything with that knife besides a table?"

The bow and arrow is my weapon. But I've spent a fair amount of time throwing knives as well. Sometimes, if I've wounded an animal with an arrow, it's better to get a knife into it, too, before I approach it. I realize that if I want Haymitch's attention, this is my moment to make an impression. I yank the knife out of the table, get a grip on the blade, and then throw it into the wall across the room. I was actually just hoping to get a good solid stick, but it lodges in the seam between two panels, making me look a lot better than I am.

"Stand over here. Both of you," says Haymitch, nodding to the middle of the room. We obey and he circles us, prodding us like animals at times, checking our muscles, examining our faces. "Well, you're not entirely hopeless. Seem fit. And once the stylists get hold of you, you'll be attractive enough."

Peeta and I don't question this. The Hunger Games aren't a beauty contest, but the best-looking tributes always seem to pull more sponsors.

"All right, I'll make a deal with you. You don't interfere with my drinking, and I'll stay sober enough to help you," says Haymitch. "But you have to do exactly what I say."

It's not much of a deal but still a giant step forward from ten minutes ago when we had no guide at all.

"Fine," says Peeta.

"So help us," I say. "When we get to the arena, what's the best strategy at the Cornucopia for someone —"

"One thing at a time. In a few minutes, we'll be pulling into the station. You'll be put in the hands of your stylists. You're not going to like what they do to you. But no matter what it is, don't resist," says Haymitch.

"But —" I begin.

"No buts. Don't resist," says Haymitch. He takes the bottle of spirits from the table and leaves the car. As the door swings shut behind him, the car goes dark. There are still a few lights inside, but outside it's as if night has fallen again. I realize we must be in the tunnel that runs up through the mountains into the Capitol. The mountains form a natural barrier between the Capitol and the eastern districts. It is almost impossible to enter from the east except through the tunnels. This geographical advantage was a major factor in the districts losing the war that led to my being a tribute today. Since the rebels had to scale the mountains, they were easy targets for the Capitol's air forces.

Peeta Mellark and I stand in silence as the train speeds along. The tunnel goes on and on and I think of the tons of rock separating me from the sky, and my chest tightens. I hate being encased in stone this way. It reminds me of the mines and my father, trapped, unable to reach sunlight, buried forever in the darkness.

The train finally begins to slow and suddenly bright light floods the compartment. We can't help it. Both Peeta and I run to the window to see what we've only seen on television, the Capitol, the ruling city of Panem. The cameras haven't lied about its grandeur. If anything, they have not quite captured the magnificence of the glistening buildings in a rainbow of hues that tower into the air, the shiny cars that roll down the wide paved streets, the oddly dressed people with bizarre hair and painted faces who have never missed a meal. All the colors seem artificial, the pinks too deep, the greens too bright, the yellows painful to the eyes, like the flat round disks of hard candy we can never afford to buy at the tiny sweet shop in District 12.

The people begin to point at us eagerly as they recognize a tribute train rolling into the city. I step away from the window, sickened by their excitement, knowing they can't wait to watch us die. But Peeta holds his ground, actually waving and smiling at the gawking crowd. He only stops when the train pulls into the station, blocking us from their view.

He sees me staring at him and shrugs. "Who knows?" he says. "One of them may be rich."

I have misjudged him. I think of his actions since the reaping began. The friendly squeeze of my hand. His father showing up with the cookies and promising to feed Prim . . . did Peeta put him up to that? His tears at the station. Volunteering to wash Haymitch but then challenging him this morning when apparently the nice-guy approach had failed. And now the waving at the window, already trying to win the crowd.

All of the pieces are still fitting together, but I sense he has a plan forming. He hasn't accepted his death. He is already fighting hard to stay alive. Which also means that kind Peeta Mellark, the boy who gave me the bread, is fighting hard to kill me.

5

R-i-i-i-p! I grit my teeth as Venia, a woman with aqua hair and gold tattoos above her eyebrows, yanks a strip of fabric from my leg, tearing out the hair beneath it. "Sorry!" she pipes in her silly Capitol accent. "You're just so hairy!"

Why do these people speak in such a high pitch? Why do their jaws barely open when they talk? Why do the ends of their sentences go up as if they're asking a question? Odd vowels, clipped words, and always a hiss on the letter *s* . . . no wonder it's impossible not to mimic them.

Venia makes what's supposed to be a sympathetic face. "Good news, though. This is the last one. Ready?" I get a grip on the edges of the table I'm seated on and nod. The final swathe of my leg hair is uprooted in a painful jerk.

I've been in the Remake Center for more than three hours and I still haven't met my stylist. Apparently he has no interest in seeing me until Venia and the other members of my prep team have addressed some obvious problems. This has included scrubbing down my body with a gritty foam that has removed not only dirt but at least three layers of skin, turning my nails into uniform shapes, and primarily, ridding my body of hair. My legs, arms, torso, underarms, and parts of my eyebrows have been stripped of the stuff, leaving me like a plucked bird, ready for roasting. I don't like it. My skin feels sore and tingling and intensely vulnerable. But I have kept my side of the bargain with Haymitch, and no objection has crossed my lips.

"You're doing very well," says some guy named Flavius. He gives his orange corkscrew locks a shake and applies a fresh coat of purple lipstick to his mouth. "If there's one thing we can't stand, it's a whiner. Grease her down!"

Venia and Octavia, a plump woman whose entire body has been dyed a pale shade of pea green, rub me down with a lotion that first stings but then soothes my raw skin. Then they pull me from the table, removing the thin robe I've been allowed to wear off and on. I stand there, completely naked, as the three circle me, wielding tweezers to remove any last bits of hair. I know I should be embarrassed, but they're so unlike people that I'm no more self-conscious than if a trio of oddly colored birds were pecking around my feet.

The three step back and admire their work. "Excellent! You almost look like a human being now!" says Flavius, and they all laugh.

I force my lips up into a smile to show how grateful I am. "Thank you," I say sweetly. "We don't have much cause to look nice in District Twelve."

This wins them over completely. "Of course, you don't, you poor darling!" says Octavia clasping her hands together in distress for me.

"But don't worry," says Venia. "By the time Cinna is through with you, you're going to be absolutely gorgeous!"

"We promise! You know, now that we've gotten rid of all the hair and filth, you're not horrible at all!" says Flavius encouragingly. "Let's call Cinna!"

They dart out of the room. It's hard to hate my prep team. They're such total idiots. And yet, in an odd way, I know they're sincerely trying to help me.

I look at the cold white walls and floor and resist the impulse to retrieve my robe. But this Cinna, my stylist, will surely make me remove it at once. Instead my hands go to my hairdo, the one area of my body my prep team had been told to leave alone. My fingers stroke the silky braids my mother so carefully arranged. My mother. I left her blue dress and shoes on the floor of my train car, never thinking about retrieving them, of trying to hold on to a piece of her, of home. Now I wish I had.

The door opens and a young man who must be Cinna enters. I'm taken aback by how normal he looks. Most of the stylists they interview on television are so dyed, stenciled, and surgically altered they're grotesque. But Cinna's close-cropped hair appears to be its natural shade of brown. He's in a simple black shirt and pants. The only concession to self-alteration seems to be metallic gold eyeliner that has been applied with a light hand. It brings out the flecks of gold in his green eyes. And, despite my disgust with the Capitol and their hideous fashions, I can't help thinking how attractive it looks.

"Hello, Katniss. I'm Cinna, your stylist," he says in a quiet voice somewhat lacking in the Capitol's affectations.

"Hello," I venture cautiously.

"Just give me a moment, all right?" he asks. He walks around my naked body, not touching me, but taking in every inch of it with his eyes. I resist the impulse to cross my arms over my chest. "Who did your hair?"

"My mother," I say.

"It's beautiful. Classic really. And in almost perfect balance with your profile. She has very clever fingers," he says.

I had expected someone flamboyant, someone older trying desperately to look young, someone who viewed me as a piece of meat to be prepared for a platter. Cinna has met none of these expectations.

"You're new, aren't you? I don't think I've seen you before," I say. Most of the stylists are familiar, constants in the ever-changing pool of tributes. Some have been around my whole life.

"Yes, this is my first year in the Games," says Cinna.

"So they gave you District Twelve," I say. Newcomers generally end up with us, the least desirable district.

"I asked for District Twelve," he says without further explanation. "Why don't you put on your robe and we'll have a chat."

Pulling on my robe, I follow him through a door into a sitting room. Two red couches face off over a low table. Three walls are blank, the fourth is entirely glass, providing a window to the city. I can see by the light that it must be around noon, although the sunny sky has turned overcast. Cinna invites me to sit on one of the couches and takes his place across from me. He presses a button on the side of the table. The top splits and from below rises a second tabletop that holds our lunch. Chicken and chunks of oranges cooked in a creamy sauce laid on a bed of pearly white grain, tiny green peas and onions, rolls shaped like flowers, and for dessert, a pudding the color of honey.

I try to imagine assembling this meal myself back home. Chickens are too expensive, but I could make do with a wild turkey. I'd need to shoot a second turkey to trade for an orange. Goat's milk would have to substitute for cream. We can grow peas in the garden. I'd have to get wild onions from the woods. I don't recognize the grain, our own tessera ration cooks down to an unattractive brown mush. Fancy rolls would mean another trade with the baker, perhaps for two or three squirrels. As for the pudding, I can't even guess what's in it. Days of hunting and gathering for this one meal and even then it would be a poor substitution for the Capitol version.

What must it be like, I wonder, to live in a world where food appears at the press of a button? How would I spend the hours I now commit to combing the woods for sustenance if it were so easy to come by? What do they do all day, these people in the Capitol, besides decorating their bodies and waiting around for a new shipment of tributes to roll in and die for their entertainment?

I look up and find Cinna's eyes trained on mine. "How despicable we must seem to you," he says.

Has he seen this in my face or somehow read my thoughts? He's right, though. The whole rotten lot of them is despicable.

"No matter," says Cinna. "So, Katniss, about your costume for the opening ceremonies. My partner, Portia, is the stylist for your fellow tribute, Peeta. And our current thought is to dress you in complementary costumes," says Cinna. "As you know, it's customary to reflect the flavor of the district."

For the opening ceremonies, you're supposed to wear something that suggests your district's principal industry. District 11, agriculture. District 4, fishing. District 3, factories. This means that coming from District 12, Peeta and I will be in some kind of coal miner's getup. Since the baggy miner's jumpsuits are not particularly becoming, our tributes usually end up in skimpy outfits and hats with headlamps. One year, our tributes were stark naked and covered in black powder to represent coal dust. It's always dreadful and does nothing to win favor with the crowd. I prepare myself for the worst.

"So, I'll be in a coal miner outfit?" I ask, hoping it won't be indecent.

"Not exactly. You see, Portia and I think that coal miner thing's very overdone. No one will remember you in that. And we both see it as our job to make the District Twelve tributes unforgettable," says Cinna.

I'll be naked for sure, I think.

"So rather than focus on the coal mining itself, we're going to focus on the coal," says Cinna.

Naked and covered in black dust, I think.

"And what do we do with coal? We burn it," says Cinna.

"You're not afraid of fire, are you, Katniss?" He sees my expression and grins.

A few hours later, I am dressed in what will either be the most sensational or the deadliest costume in the opening ceremonies. I'm in a simple black unitard that covers me from ankle to neck. Shiny leather boots lace up to my knees. But it's the fluttering cape made of streams of orange, yellow, and red and the matching headpiece that define this costume. Cinna plans to light them on fire just before our chariot rolls into the streets.

"It's not real flame, of course, just a little synthetic fire Portia and I came up with. You'll be perfectly safe," he says. But I'm not convinced I won't be perfectly barbecued by the time we reach the city's center.

My face is relatively clear of makeup, just a bit of highlighting here and there. My hair has been brushed out and then braided down my back in my usual style. "I want the audience to recognize you when you're in the arena," says Cinna dreamily. "Katniss, the girl who was on fire."

It crosses my mind that Cinna's calm and normal demeanor masks a complete madman.

Despite this morning's revelation about Peeta's character, I'm actually relieved when he shows up, dressed in an identical costume. He should know about fire, being a baker's son and all. His stylist, Portia, and her team accompany him, and everyone is absolutely giddy with excitement over what a splash we'll make. Except Cinna. He just seems a bit weary as he accepts congratulations.

We're whisked down to the bottom level of the Remake Center, which is essentially a gigantic stable. The opening ceremonies are about to start. Pairs of tributes are being loaded into chariots pulled by teams of four horses. Ours are coal black. The animals are so well trained, no one even needs to guide their reins. Cinna and Portia direct us into the chariot and carefully arrange our body positions, the drape of our capes, before moving off to consult with each other.

"What do you think?" I whisper to Peeta. "About the fire?"

"I'll rip off your cape if you'll rip off mine," he says through gritted teeth.

"Deal," I say. Maybe, if we can get them off soon enough, we'll avoid the worst burns. It's bad though. They'll throw us into the arena no matter what condition we're in. "I know we promised Haymitch we'd do exactly what they said, but I don't think he considered this angle."

"Where is Haymitch, anyway? Isn't he supposed to protect us from this sort of thing?" says Peeta.

"With all that alcohol in him, it's probably not advisable to have him around an open flame," I say.

And suddenly we're both laughing. I guess we're both so nervous about the Games and more pressingly, petrified of being turned into human torches, we're not acting sensibly.

The opening music begins. It's easy to hear, blasted around the Capitol. Massive doors slide open revealing the crowd-lined streets. The ride lasts about twenty minutes and ends up at the City Circle, where they will welcome us, play the anthem, and escort us into the Training Center, which will be our home/prison until the Games begin.

The tributes from District 1 ride out in a chariot pulled by snow-white horses. They look so beautiful, spray-painted silver, in tasteful tunics glittering with jewels. District 1 makes luxury items for the Capitol. You can hear the roar of the crowd. They are always favorites.

District 2 gets into position to follow them. In no time at all, we are approaching the door and I can see that between the overcast sky and evening hour the light is turning gray. The tributes from District 11 are just rolling out when Cinna appears with a lighted torch. "Here we go then," he says, and before we can react he sets our capes on fire. I gasp, waiting for the heat, but there is only a faint tickling sensation. Cinna climbs up before us and ignites our headdresses. He lets out a sigh of relief. "It works." Then he gently tucks a hand under my chin. "Remember, heads high. Smiles. They're going to love you!"

Cinna jumps off the chariot and has one last idea. He shouts something up at us, but the music drowns him out. He shouts again and gestures.

"What's he saying?" I ask Peeta. For the first time, I look at him and realize that ablaze with the fake flames, he is dazzling. And I must be, too.

"I think he said for us to hold hands," says Peeta. He grabs my right hand in his left, and we look to Cinna for confirmation. He nods and gives a thumbs-up, and that's the last thing I see before we enter the city.

The crowd's initial alarm at our appearance quickly changes to cheers and shouts of "District Twelve!" Every head is turned our way, pulling the focus from the three chariots ahead of us. At first, I'm frozen, but then I catch sight of us on a large television screen and am floored by how breathtaking we look. In the deepening twilight, the firelight illuminates our faces. We seem to be leaving a trail of fire off the flowing capes. Cinna was right about the minimal makeup, we both look more attractive but utterly recognizable.

Remember, heads high. Smiles. They're going to love you! I hear Cinna's voice in my head. I lift my chin a bit higher, put on my most winning smile, and wave with my free hand. I'm glad now I have Peeta to clutch for balance, he is so steady, solid as a rock. As I gain confidence, I actually blow a few kisses to the crowd. The people of the Capitol are going nuts, showering us with flowers, shouting our names, our first names, which they have bothered to find on the program.

The pounding music, the cheers, the admiration work their way into my blood, and I can't suppress my excitement. Cinna has given me a great advantage. No one will forget me. Not my look, not my name. Katniss. The girl who was on fire.

For the first time, I feel a flicker of hope rising up in me. Surely, there must be one sponsor willing to take me on! And with a little extra help, some food, the right weapon, why should I count myself out of the Games?

Someone throws me a red rose. I catch it, give it a

delicate sniff, and blow a kiss back in the general direction of the giver. A hundred hands reach up to catch my kiss, as if it were a real and tangible thing.

"Katniss! Katniss!" I can hear my name being called from all sides. Everyone wants my kisses.

It's not until we enter the City Circle that I realize I must have completely stopped the circulation in Peeta's hand. That's how tightly I've been holding it. I look down at our linked fingers as I loosen my grasp, but he regains his grip on me. "No, don't let go of me," he says. The firelight flickers off his blue eyes. "Please. I might fall out of this thing."

"Okay," I say. So I keep holding on, but I can't help feeling strange about the way Cinna has linked us together. It's not really fair to present us as a team and then lock us into the arena to kill each other.

The twelve chariots fill the loop of the City Circle. On the buildings that surround the Circle, every window is packed with the most prestigious citizens of the Capitol. Our horses pull our chariot right up to President Snow's mansion, and we come to a halt. The music ends with a flourish.

The president, a small, thin man with paper-white hair, gives the official welcome from a balcony above us. It is traditional to cut away to the faces of the tributes during the speech. But I can see on the screen that we are getting way more than our share of airtime. The darker it becomes, the more difficult it is to take your eyes off our flickering. When the national anthem plays, they do make an effort to do a quick cut around to each pair of tributes, but the camera holds on the District 12 chariot as it parades around the circle one final time and disappears into the Training Center.

The doors have only just shut behind us when we're engulfed by the prep teams, who are nearly unintelligible as they babble out praise. As I glance around, I notice a lot of the other tributes are shooting us dirty looks, which confirms what I've suspected, we've literally outshone them all. Then Cinna and Portia are there, helping us down from the chariot, carefully removing our flaming capes and headdresses. Portia extinguishes them with some kind of spray from a canister.

I realize I'm still glued to Peeta and force my stiff fingers to open. We both massage our hands.

"Thanks for keeping hold of me. I was getting a little shaky there," says Peeta.

"It didn't show," I tell him. "I'm sure no one noticed."

"I'm sure they didn't notice anything but you. You should wear flames more often," he says. "They suit you." And then he gives me a smile that seems so genuinely sweet with just the right touch of shyness that unexpected warmth rushes through me.

A warning bell goes off in my head. *Don't be so stupid. Peeta is planning how to kill you,* I remind myself. *He is luring you in to make you easy prey. The more likable he is, the more deadly he is.*

But because two can play at this game, I stand on tiptoe and kiss his cheek. Right on his bruise.

The Training Center has a tower designed exclusively for the tributes and their teams. This will be our home until the actual Games begin. Each district has an entire floor. You simply step onto an elevator and press the number of your district. Easy enough to remember.

I've ridden the elevator a couple of times in the Justice Building back in District 12. Once to receive the medal for my father's death and then yesterday to say my final good-byes to my friends and family. But that's a dark and creaky thing that moves like a snail and smells of sour milk. The walls of this elevator are made of crystal so that you can watch the people on the ground floor shrink to ants as you shoot up into the air. It's exhilarating and I'm tempted to ask Effie Trinket if we can ride it again, but somehow that seems childish.

Apparently, Effie Trinket's duties did not conclude at the station. She and Haymitch will be overseeing us right into the arena. In a way, that's a plus because at least she can be counted on to corral us around to places on time whereas we haven't seen Haymitch since he agreed to help us on the train. Probably passed out somewhere. Effie Trinket, on the other hand, seems to be flying high. We're the first team she's ever chaperoned that made a splash at the opening ceremonies. She's complimentary about not just our costumes but how we conducted ourselves. And, to hear her tell it, Effie knows everyone who's anyone in the Capitol and has been talking us up all day, trying to win us sponsors.

"I've been very mysterious, though," she says, her eyes squint half shut. "Because, of course, Haymitch hasn't bothered to tell me your strategies. But I've done my best with what I had to work with. How Katniss sacrificed herself for her sister. How you've both successfully struggled to overcome the barbarism of your district."

Barbarism? That's ironic coming from a woman helping to prepare us for slaughter. And what's she basing our success on? Our table manners?

"Everyone has their reservations, naturally. You being from the coal district. But I said, and this was very clever of me, I said, 'Well, if you put enough pressure on coal it turns to pearls!'" Effie beams at us so brilliantly that we have no choice but to respond enthusiastically to her cleverness even though it's wrong.

Coal doesn't turn to pearls. They grow in shellfish. Possibly she meant coal turns to diamonds, but that's untrue, too. I've heard they have some sort of machine in District 1 that can turn graphite into diamonds. But we don't mine graphite in District 12. That was part of District 13's job until they were destroyed.

I wonder if the people she's been plugging us to all day either know or care.

"Unfortunately, I can't seal the sponsor deals for you.

Only Haymitch can do that," says Effie grimly. "But don't worry, I'll get him to the table at gunpoint if necessary."

Although lacking in many departments, Effie Trinket has a certain determination I have to admire.

My quarters are larger than our entire house back home. They are plush, like the train car, but also have so many automatic gadgets that I'm sure I won't have time to press all the buttons. The shower alone has a panel with more than a hundred options you can choose regulating water temperature, pressure, soaps, shampoos, scents, oils, and massaging sponges. When you step out on a mat, heaters come on that blow-dry your body. Instead of struggling with the knots in my wet hair, I merely place my hand on a box that sends a current through my scalp, untangling, parting, and drying my hair almost instantly. It floats down around my shoulders in a glossy curtain.

I program the closet for an outfit to my taste. The windows zoom in and out on parts of the city at my command. You need only whisper a type of food from a gigantic menu into a mouthpiece and it appears, hot and steamy, before you in less than a minute. I walk around the room eating goose liver and puffy bread until there's a knock on the door. Effie's calling me to dinner.

Good. I'm starving.

Peeta, Cinna, and Portia are standing out on a balcony that overlooks the Capitol when we enter the dining room. I'm glad to see the stylists, particularly after I hear that Haymitch will be joining us. A meal presided over by just

Effie and Haymitch is bound to be a disaster. Besides, dinner isn't really about food, it's about planning out our strategies, and Cinna and Portia have already proven how valuable they are.

A silent young man dressed in a white tunic offers us all stemmed glasses of wine. I think about turning it down, but I've never had wine, except the homemade stuff my mother uses for coughs, and when will I get a chance to try it again? I take a sip of the tart, dry liquid and secretly think it could be improved by a few spoonfuls of honey.

Haymitch shows up just as dinner is being served. It looks as if he's had his own stylist because he's clean and groomed and about as sober as I've ever seen him. He doesn't refuse the offer of wine, but when he starts in on his soup, I realize it's the first time I've ever seen him eat. Maybe he really will pull himself together long enough to help us.

Cinna and Portia seem to have a civilizing effect on Haymitch and Effie. At least they're addressing each other decently. And they both have nothing but praise for our stylists' opening act. While they make small talk, I concentrate on the meal. Mushroom soup, bitter greens with tomatoes the size of peas, rare roast beef sliced as thin as paper, noodles in a green sauce, cheese that melts on your tongue served with sweet blue grapes. The servers, all young people dressed in white tunics like the one who gave us wine, move wordlessly to and from the table, keeping the platters and glasses full.

About halfway through my glass of wine, my head starts feeling foggy, so I change to water instead. I don't like the feeling and hope it wears off soon. How Haymitch can stand walking around like this full-time is a mystery.

I try to focus on the talk, which has turned to our interview costumes, when a girl sets a gorgeous-looking cake on the table and deftly lights it. It blazes up and then the flames flicker around the edges awhile until it finally goes out. I have a moment of doubt. "What makes it burn? Is it alcohol?" I say, looking up at the girl. "That's the last thing I wa — oh! I know you!"

I can't place a name or time to the girl's face. But I'm certain of it. The dark red hair, the striking features, the porcelain white skin. But even as I utter the words, I feel my insides contracting with anxiety and guilt at the sight of her, and while I can't pull it up, I know some bad memory is associated with her. The expression of terror that crosses her face only adds to my confusion and unease. She shakes her head in denial quickly and hurries away from the table.

When I look back, the four adults are watching me like hawks.

"Don't be ridiculous, Katniss. How could you possibly know an Avox?" snaps Effie. "The very thought."

"What's an Avox?" I ask stupidly.

"Someone who committed a crime. They cut her tongue so she can't speak," says Haymitch. "She's probably a traitor of some sort. Not likely you'd know her."

"And even if you did, you're not to speak to one of them unless it's to give an order," says Effie. "Of course, you don't really know her."

But I do know her. And now that Haymitch has mentioned the word *traitor* I remember from where. The disapproval is so high I could never admit it. "No, I guess not, I just —" I stammer, and the wine is not helping.

Peeta snaps his fingers. "Delly Cartwright. That's who it is. I kept thinking she looked familiar as well. Then I realized she's a dead ringer for Delly."

Delly Cartwright is a pasty-faced, lumpy girl with yellowish hair who looks about as much like our server as a beetle does a butterfly. She may also be the friendliest person on the planet — she smiles constantly at everybody in school, even me. I have never seen the girl with the red hair smile. But I jump on Peeta's suggestion gratefully. "Of course, that's who I was thinking of. It must be the hair," I say.

"Something about the eyes, too," says Peeta.

The energy at the table relaxes. "Oh, well. If that's all it is," says Cinna. "And yes, the cake has spirits, but all the alcohol has burned off. I ordered it specially in honor of your fiery debut."

We eat the cake and move into a sitting room to watch the replay of the opening ceremonies that's being broadcast. A few of the other couples make a nice impression, but none of them can hold a candle to us. Even our own party lets out an "Ahh!" as they show us coming out of the Remake Center.

"Whose idea was the hand holding?" asks Haymitch.

"Cinna's," says Portia.

"Just the perfect touch of rebellion," says Haymitch. "Very nice."

Rebellion? I have to think about that one a moment. But when I remember the other couples, standing stiffly apart, never touching or acknowledging each other, as if their fellow tribute did not exist, as if the Games had already begun, I know what Haymitch means. Presenting ourselves not as adversaries but as friends has distinguished us as much as the fiery costumes.

"Tomorrow morning is the first training session. Meet me for breakfast and I'll tell you exactly how I want you to play it," says Haymitch to Peeta and me. "Now go get some sleep while the grown-ups talk."

Peeta and I walk together down the corridor to our rooms. When we get to my door, he leans against the frame, not blocking my entrance exactly but insisting I pay attention to him. "So, Delly Cartwright. Imagine finding her lookalike here."

He's asking for an explanation, and I'm tempted to give him one. We both know he covered for me. So here I am in his debt again. If I tell him the truth about the girl, somehow that might even things up. How can it hurt really? Even if he repeated the story, it couldn't do me much harm. It was just something I witnessed. And he lied as much as I did about Delly Cartwright.

I realize I do want to talk to someone about the girl. Someone who might be able to help me figure out her story.

Gale would be my first choice, but it's unlikely I'll ever see Gale again. I try to think if telling Peeta could give him any possible advantage over me, but I don't see how. Maybe sharing a confidence will actually make him believe I see him as a friend.

Besides, the idea of the girl with her maimed tongue frightens me. She has reminded me why I'm here. Not to model flashy costumes and eat delicacies. But to die a bloody death while the crowds urge on my killer.

To tell or not to tell? My brain still feels slow from the wine. I stare down the empty corridor as if the decision lies there.

Peeta picks up on my hesitation. "Have you been on the roof yet?" I shake my head. "Cinna showed me. You can practically see the whole city. The wind's a bit loud, though."

I translate this into "No one will overhear us talking" in my head. You do have the sense that we might be under surveillance here. "Can we just go up?"

"Sure, come on," says Peeta. I follow him to a flight of stairs that lead to the roof. There's a small dome-shaped room with a door to the outside. As we step into the cool, windy evening air, I catch my breath at the view. The Capitol twinkles like a vast field of fireflies. Electricity in District 12 comes and goes, usually we only have it a few hours a day. Often the evenings are spent in candlelight. The only time you can count on it is when they're airing the Games or some important government message on television that it's mandatory to watch. But here there would be no shortage. Ever.

Peeta and I walk to a railing at the edge of the roof. I look straight down the side of the building to the street, which is buzzing with people. You can hear their cars, an occasional shout, and a strange metallic tinkling. In District 12, we'd all be thinking about bed right now.

"I asked Cinna why they let us up here. Weren't they worried that some of the tributes might decide to jump right over the side?" says Peeta.

"What'd he say?" I ask.

"You can't," says Peeta. He holds out his hand into seemingly empty space. There's a sharp zap and he jerks it back. "Some kind of electric field throws you back on the roof."

"Always worried about our safety," I say. Even though Cinna has shown Peeta the roof, I wonder if we're supposed to be up here now, so late and alone. I've never seen tributes on the Training Center roof before. But that doesn't mean we're not being taped. "Do you think they're watching us now?"

"Maybe," he admits. "Come see the garden."

On the other side of the dome, they've built a garden with flower beds and potted trees. From the branches hang hundreds of wind chimes, which account for the tinkling I heard. Here in the garden, on this windy night, it's enough to drown out two people who are trying not to be heard. Peeta looks at me expectantly.

I pretend to examine a blossom. "We were hunting in the woods one day. Hidden, waiting for game," I whisper.

"You and your father?" he whispers back.

"No, my friend Gale. Suddenly all the birds stopped singing at once. Except one. As if it were giving a warning call. And then we saw her. I'm sure it was the same girl. A boy was with her. Their clothes were tattered. They had dark circles under their eyes from no sleep. They were running as if their lives depended on it," I say.

For a moment I'm silent, as I remember how the sight of this strange pair, clearly not from District 12, fleeing through the woods immobilized us. Later, we wondered if we could have helped them escape. Perhaps we might have. Concealed them. If we'd moved quickly. Gale and I were taken by surprise, yes, but we're both hunters. We know how animals look at bay. We knew the pair was in trouble as soon as we saw them. But we only watched.

"The hovercraft appeared out of nowhere," I continue to Peeta. "I mean, one moment the sky was empty and the next it was there. It didn't make a sound, but they saw it. A net dropped down on the girl and carried her up, fast, so fast like the elevator. They shot some sort of spear through the boy. It was attached to a cable and they hauled him up as well. But I'm certain he was dead. We heard the girl scream once. The boy's name, I think. Then it was gone, the hovercraft. Vanished into thin air. And the birds began to sing again, as if nothing had happened."

"Did they see you?" Peeta asked.

"I don't know. We were under a shelf of rock," I reply.

But I do know. There was a moment, after the birdcall, but before the hovercraft, where the girl had seen us. She'd locked eyes with me and called out for help. But neither Gale or I had responded.

"You're shivering," says Peeta.

The wind and the story have blown all the warmth from my body. The girl's scream. Had it been her last?

Peeta takes off his jacket and wraps it around my shoulders. I start to take a step back, but then I let him, deciding for a moment to accept both his jacket and his kindness. A friend would do that, right?

"They were from here?" he asks, and he secures a button at my neck.

I nod. They'd had that Capitol look about them. The boy and the girl.

"Where do you suppose they were going?" he asks.

"I don't know that," I say. District 12 is pretty much the end of the line. Beyond us, there's only wilderness. If you don't count the ruins of District 13 that still smolder from the toxic bombs. They show it on television occasionally, just to remind us. "Or why they would leave here." Haymitch had called the Avoxes traitors. Against what? It could only be the Capitol. But they had everything here. No cause to rebel.

"I'd leave here," Peeta blurts out. Then he looks around nervously. It was loud enough to hear above the chimes. He laughs. "I'd go home now if they let me. But you have to admit, the food's prime."

He's covered again. If that's all you'd heard it would just

sound like the words of a scared tribute, not someone contemplating the unquestionable goodness of the Capitol.

"It's getting chilly. We better go in," he says. Inside the dome, it's warm and bright. His tone is conversational. "Your friend Gale. He's the one who took your sister away at the reaping?"

"Yes. Do you know him?" I ask.

"Not really. I hear the girls talk about him a lot. I thought he was your cousin or something. You favor each other," he says.

"No, we're not related," I say.

Peeta nods, unreadable. "Did he come to say good-bye to you?"

"Yes," I say, observing him carefully. "So did your father. He brought me cookies."

Peeta raises his eyebrows as if this is news. But after watching him lie so smoothly, I don't give this much weight. "Really? Well, he likes you and your sister. I think he wishes he had a daughter instead of a houseful of boys."

The idea that I might ever have been discussed, around the dinner table, at the bakery fire, just in passing in Peeta's house gives me a start. It must have been when the mother was out of the room.

"He knew your mother when they were kids," says Peeta.

Another surprise. But probably true. "Oh, yes. She grew up in town," I say. It seems impolite to say she never mentioned the baker except to compliment his bread.

We're at my door. I give back his jacket. "See you in the morning then."

"See you," he says, and walks off down the hall.

When I open my door, the redheaded girl is collecting my unitard and boots from where I left them on the floor before my shower. I want to apologize for possibly getting her in trouble earlier. But I remember I'm not supposed to speak to her unless I'm giving her an order.

"Oh, sorry," I say. "I was supposed to get those back to Cinna. I'm sorry. Can you take them to him?"

She avoids my eyes, gives a small nod, and heads out the door.

I'd set out to tell her I was sorry about dinner. But I know that my apology runs much deeper. That I'm ashamed I never tried to help her in the woods. That I let the Capitol kill the boy and mutilate her without lifting a finger.

Just like I was watching the Games.

I kick off my shoes and climb under the covers in my clothes. The shivering hasn't stopped. Perhaps the girl doesn't even remember me. But I know she does. You don't forget the face of the person who was your last hope. I pull the covers up over my head as if this will protect me from the redheaded girl who can't speak. But I can feel her eyes staring at me, piercing through walls and doors and bedding.

I wonder if she'll enjoy watching me die.

My slumbers are filled with disturbing dreams. The face of the redheaded girl intertwines with gory images from earlier Hunger Games, with my mother withdrawn and unreachable, with Prim emaciated and terrified. I bolt up screaming for my father to run as the mine explodes into a million deadly bits of light.

Dawn is breaking through the windows. The Capitol has a misty, haunted air. My head aches and I must have bitten into the side of my cheek in the night. My tongue probes the ragged flesh and I taste blood.

Slowly, I drag myself out of bed and into the shower. I arbitrarily punch buttons on the control board and end up hopping from foot to foot as alternating jets of icy cold and steaming hot water assault me. Then I'm deluged in lemony foam that I have to scrape off with a heavy bristled brush. Oh, well. At least my blood is flowing.

When I'm dried and moisturized with lotion, I find an outfit has been left for me at the front of the closet. Tight black pants, a long-sleeved burgundy tunic, and leather shoes. I put my hair in the single braid down my back. This is the first time since the morning of the reaping that I resemble myself. No fancy hair and clothes, no flaming capes. Just me. Looking like I could be headed for the woods. It calms me.

Haymitch didn't give us an exact time to meet for breakfast and no one has contacted me this morning, but I'm hungry so I head down to the dining room, hoping there will be food. I'm not disappointed. While the table is empty, a long board off to the side has been laid with at least twenty dishes. A young man, an Avox, stands at attention by the spread. When I ask if I can serve myself, he nods assent. I load a plate with eggs, sausages, batter cakes covered in thick orange preserves, slices of pale purple melon. As I gorge myself, I watch the sun rise over the Capitol. I have a second plate of hot grain smothered in beef stew. Finally, I fill a plate with rolls and sit at the table, breaking off bits and dipping them into hot chocolate, the way Peeta did on the train.

My mind wanders to my mother and Prim. They must be up. My mother getting their breakfast of mush. Prim milking her goat before school. Just two mornings ago, I was home. Can that be right? Yes, just two. And now how empty the house feels, even from a distance. What did they say last night about my fiery debut at the Games? Did it give them hope, or simply add to their terror when they saw the reality of twenty-four tributes circled together, knowing only one could live?

Haymitch and Peeta come in, bid me good morning, fill their plates. It makes me irritated that Peeta is wearing exactly the same outfit I am. I need to say something to

Cinna. This twins act is going to blow up in our faces once the Games begin. Surely, they must know this. Then I remember Haymitch telling me to do exactly what the stylists tell me to do. If it was anyone but Cinna, I might be tempted to ignore him. But after last night's triumph, I don't have a lot of room to criticize his choices.

I'm nervous about the training. There will be three days in which all the tributes practice together. On the last afternoon, we'll each get a chance to perform in private before the Gamemakers. The thought of meeting the other tributes face-to-face makes me queasy. I turn the roll I have just taken from the basket over and over in my hands, but my appetite is gone.

When Haymitch has finished several platters of stew, he pushes back his plate with a sigh. He takes a flask from his pocket and takes a long pull on it and leans his elbows on the table. "So, let's get down to business. Training. First off, if you like, I'll coach you separately. Decide now."

"Why would you coach us separately?" I ask.

"Say if you had a secret skill you might not want the other to know about," says Haymitch.

I exchange a look with Peeta. "I don't have any secret skills," he says. "And I already know what yours is, right? I mean, I've eaten enough of your squirrels."

I never thought about Peeta eating the squirrels I shot. Somehow I always pictured the baker quietly going off and frying them up for himself. Not out of greed. But because town families usually eat expensive butcher meat. Beef and chicken and horse.

"You can coach us together," I tell Haymitch. Peeta nods.

"All right, so give me some idea of what you can do," says Haymitch.

"I can't do anything," says Peeta. "Unless you count baking bread."

"Sorry, I don't. Katniss. I already know you're handy with a knife," says Haymitch.

"Not really. But I can hunt," I say. "With a bow and arrow."

"And you're good?" asks Haymitch.

I have to think about it. I've been putting food on the table for four years. That's no small task. I'm not as good as my father was, but he'd had more practice. I've better aim than Gale, but I've had more practice. He's a genius with traps and snares. "I'm all right," I say.

"She's excellent," says Peeta. "My father buys her squirrels. He always comments on how the arrows never pierce the body. She hits every one in the eye. It's the same with the rabbits she sells the butcher. She can even bring down deer."

This assessment of my skills from Peeta takes me totally by surprise. First, that he ever noticed. Second, that he's talking me up. "What are you doing?" I ask him suspiciously.

"What are you doing? If he's going to help you, he has to know what you're capable of. Don't underrate yourself," says Peeta.

I don't know why, but this rubs me the wrong way. "What about you? I've seen you in the market. You can lift hundred-pound bags of flour," I snap at him. "Tell him that. That's not nothing."

"Yes, and I'm sure the arena will be full of bags of flour for me to chuck at people. It's not like being able to use a weapon. You know it isn't," he shoots back.

"He can wrestle," I tell Haymitch. "He came in second in our school competition last year, only after his brother."

"What use is that? How many times have you seen someone wrestle someone to death?" says Peeta in disgust.

"There's always hand-to-hand combat. All you need is to come up with a knife, and you'll at least stand a chance. If I get jumped, I'm dead!" I can hear my voice rising in anger.

"But you won't! You'll be living up in some tree eating raw squirrels and picking off people with arrows. You know what my mother said to me when she came to say good-bye, as if to cheer me up, she says maybe District Twelve will finally have a winner. Then I realized, she didn't mean me, she meant you!" bursts out Peeta.

"Oh, she meant you," I say with a wave of dismissal.

"She said, 'She's a survivor, that one.' *She* is," says Peeta.

That pulls me up short. Did his mother really say that about me? Did she rate me over her son? I see the pain in Peeta's eyes and know he isn't lying.

Suddenly I'm behind the bakery and I can feel the chill of the rain running down my back, the hollowness in my belly. I sound eleven years old when I speak. "But only because someone helped me."

Peeta's eyes flicker down to the roll in my hands, and I know he remembers that day, too. But he just shrugs. "People will help you in the arena. They'll be tripping over each other to sponsor you."

"No more than you," I say.

Peeta rolls his eyes at Haymitch. "She has no idea. The effect she can have." He runs his fingernail along the wood grain in the table, refusing to look at me.

What on earth does he mean? People help me? When we were dying of starvation, no one helped me! No one except Peeta. Once I had something to barter with, things changed. I'm a tough trader. Or am I? What effect do I have? That I'm weak and needy? Is he suggesting that I got good deals because people pitied me? I try to think if this is true. Perhaps some of the merchants were a little generous in their trades, but I always attributed that to their long-standing relationship with my father. Besides, my game is first-class. No one pitied me!

I glower at the roll, sure he meant to insult me.

After about a minute of this, Haymitch says, "Well, then. Well, well, well. Katniss, there's no guarantee there'll be bows and arrows in the arena, but during your private session with the Gamemakers, show them what you can do. Until then, stay clear of archery. Are you any good at trapping?"

"I know a few basic snares," I mutter.

"That may be significant in terms of food," says Haymitch. "And, Peeta, she's right, never underestimate strength in the arena. Very often, physical power tilts the advantage to a player. In the Training Center, they will have weights, but don't reveal how much you can lift in front of the other tributes. The plan's the same for both of you. You go to group training. Spend the time trying to learn something you don't know. Throw a spear. Swing a mace. Learn to tie a decent knot. Save showing what you're best at until your private sessions. Are we clear?" says Haymitch.

Peeta and I nod.

"One last thing. In public, I want you by each other's side every minute," says Haymitch. We both start to object, but Haymitch slams his hand on the table. "Every minute! It's not open for discussion! You agreed to do as I said! You will be together, you will appear amiable to each other. Now get out. Meet Effie at the elevator at ten for training."

I bite my lip and stalk back to my room, making sure Peeta can hear the door slam. I sit on the bed, hating Haymitch, hating Peeta, hating myself for mentioning that day long ago in the rain.

It's such a joke! Peeta and I going along pretending to be friends! Talking up each other's strengths, insisting the other take credit for their abilities. Because, in fact, at some point, we're going to have to knock it off and accept we're bitter adversaries. Which I'd be prepared to do right now if it wasn't for Haymitch's stupid instruction that we stick together in training. It's my own fault, I guess, for telling him he didn't have to coach us separately. But that didn't mean I wanted to do everything with Peeta. Who, by the way, clearly doesn't want to be partnering up with me, either.

I hear Peeta's voice in my head. *She has no idea. The effect she can have.* Obviously meant to demean me. Right? But a tiny part of me wonders if this was a compliment. That he meant I was appealing in some way. It's weird, how much he's noticed me. Like the attention he's paid to my hunting. And apparently, I have not been as oblivious to him as I imagined, either. The flour. The wrestling. I have kept track of the boy with the bread.

It's almost ten. I clean my teeth and smooth back my hair again. Anger temporarily blocked out my nervousness about meeting the other tributes, but now I can feel my anxiety rising again. By the time I meet Effie and Peeta at the elevator, I catch myself biting my nails. I stop at once.

The actual training rooms are below ground level of our building. With these elevators, the ride is less than a minute. The doors open into an enormous gymnasium filled with various weapons and obstacle courses. Although it's not yet ten, we're the last ones to arrive. The other tributes are gathered in a tense circle. They each have a cloth square with their district number on it pinned to their shirts. While someone pins the number *12* on my back, I do a quick assessment. Peeta and I are the only two dressed alike.

As soon as we join the circle, the head trainer, a tall, athletic woman named Atala steps up and begins to explain the training schedule. Experts in each skill will remain at their stations. We will be free to travel from area to area as we choose, per our mentor's instructions. Some of the stations teach survival skills, others fighting techniques. We are forbidden to engage in any combative exercise with another tribute. There are assistants on hand if we want to practice with a partner.

When Atala begins to read down the list of the skill stations, my eyes can't help flitting around to the other tributes. It's the first time we've been assembled, on level ground, in simple clothes. My heart sinks. Almost all of the boys and at least half of the girls are bigger than I am, even though many of the tributes have never been fed properly. You can see it in their bones, their skin, the hollow look in their eyes. I may be smaller naturally, but overall my family's resourcefulness has given me an edge in that area. I stand straight, and while I'm thin, I'm strong. The meat and plants from the woods combined with the exertion it took to get them have given me a healthier body than most of those I see around me.

The exceptions are the kids from the wealthier districts, the volunteers, the ones who have been fed and trained throughout their lives for this moment. The tributes from 1, 2, and 4 traditionally have this look about them. It's technically against the rules to train tributes before they reach the Capitol but it happens every year. In District 12, we call them the Career Tributes, or just the Careers. And like as not, the winner will be one of them.

The slight advantage I held coming into the Training Center, my fiery entrance last night, seems to vanish in the presence of my competition. The other tributes were jealous of us, but not because we were amazing, because our stylists were. Now I see nothing but contempt in the glances of the Career Tributes. Each must have fifty to a

hundred pounds on me. They project arrogance and bru-
tality. When Atala releases us, they head straight for the
deadliest-looking weapons in the gym and handle them
with ease.

I'm thinking that it's lucky I'm a fast runner when Peeta
nudges my arm and I jump. He is still beside me, per
Haymitch's instructions. His expression is sober. "Where
would you like to start?"

I look around at the Career Tributes who are showing
off, clearly trying to intimidate the field. Then at the others, the underfed, the incompetent, shakily having their first
lessons with a knife or an ax.

"Suppose we tie some knots," I say.

"Right you are," says Peeta. We cross to an empty station where the trainer seems pleased to have students. You
get the feeling that the knot-tying class is not the Hunger
Games hot spot. When he realizes I know something about
snares, he shows us a simple, excellent trap that will leave a
human competitor dangling by a leg from a tree. We concentrate on this one skill for an hour until both of us have
mastered it. Then we move on to camouflage. Peeta genuinely seems to enjoy this station, swirling a combination of
mud and clay and berry juices around on his pale skin,
weaving disguises from vines and leaves. The trainer who
runs the camouflage station is full of enthusiasm at his work.

"I do the cakes," he admits to me.

"The cakes?" I ask. I've been preoccupied with watching
the boy from District 2 send a spear through a dummy's
heart from fifteen yards. "What cakes?"

"At home. The iced ones, for the bakery," he says.

He means the ones they display in the windows. Fancy cakes with flowers and pretty things painted in frosting. They're for birthdays and New Year's Day. When we're in the square, Prim always drags me over to admire them, although we'd never be able to afford one. There's little enough beauty in District 12, though, so I can hardly deny her this.

I look more critically at the design on Peeta's arm. The alternating pattern of light and dark suggests sunlight falling through the leaves in the woods. I wonder how he knows this, since I doubt he's ever been beyond the fence. Has he been able to pick this up from just that scraggly old apple tree in his backyard? Somehow the whole thing — his skill, those inaccessible cakes, the praise of the camouflage expert — annoys me.

"It's lovely. If only you could frost someone to death," I say.

"Don't be so superior. You can never tell what you'll find in the arena. Say it's actually a gigantic cake —" begins Peeta.

"Say we move on," I break in.

So the next three days pass with Peeta and me going quietly from station to station. We do pick up some valuable skills, from starting fires, to knife throwing, to making shelter. Despite Haymitch's order to appear mediocre, Peeta excels in hand-to-hand combat, and I sweep the edible plants test without blinking an eye. We steer clear of archery and weightlifting though, wanting to save those for our private sessions.

The Gamemakers appeared early on the first day. Twenty or so men and women dressed in deep purple robes. They sit in the elevated stands that surround the gymnasium, sometimes wandering about to watch us, jotting down notes, other times eating at the endless banquet that has been set for them, ignoring the lot of us. But they do seem to be keeping their eye on the District 12 tributes. Several times I've looked up to find one fixated on me. They consult with the trainers during our meals as well. We see them all gathered together when we come back.

Breakfast and dinner are served on our floor, but at lunch the twenty-four of us eat in a dining room off the gymnasium. Food is arranged on carts around the room and you serve yourself. The Career Tributes tend to gather rowdily around one table, as if to prove their superiority, that they have no fear of one another and consider the rest of us beneath notice. Most of the other tributes sit alone, like lost sheep. No one says a word to us. Peeta and I eat together, and since Haymitch keeps dogging us about it, try to keep up a friendly conversation during the meals.

It's not easy to find a topic. Talking of home is painful. Talking of the present unbearable. One day, Peeta empties our breadbasket and points out how they have been careful to include types from the districts along with the refined bread of the Capitol. The fish-shaped loaf tinted green with seaweed from District 4. The crescent moon roll dotted with seeds from District 11. Somehow, although it's made from the same stuff, it looks a lot more appetizing than the ugly drop biscuits that are the standard fare at home.

"And there you have it," says Peeta, scooping the breads back in the basket.

"You certainly know a lot," I say.

"Only about bread," he says. "Okay, now laugh as if I've said something funny."

We both give a somewhat convincing laugh and ignore the stares from around the room.

"All right, I'll keep smiling pleasantly and you talk," says Peeta. It's wearing us both out, Haymitch's direction to be friendly. Because ever since I slammed my door, there's been a chill in the air between us. But we have our orders.

"Did I ever tell you about the time I was chased by a bear?" I ask.

"No, but it sounds fascinating," says Peeta.

I try and animate my face as I recall the event, a true story, in which I'd foolishly challenged a black bear over the rights to a beehive. Peeta laughs and asks questions right on cue. He's much better at this than I am.

On the second day, while we're taking a shot at spear throwing, he whispers to me. "I think we have a shadow."

I throw my spear, which I'm not too bad at actually, if I don't have to throw too far, and see the little girl from District 11 standing back a bit, watching us. She's the twelve-year-old, the one who reminded me so of Prim in stature. Up close she looks about ten. She has bright, dark eyes and satiny brown skin and stands tilted up on her toes with her arms slightly extended to her sides, as if ready to take wing at the slightest sound. It's impossible not to think of a bird.

I pick up another spear while Peeta throws. "I think her name's Rue," he says softly.

I bite my lip. Rue is a small yellow flower that grows in the Meadow. Rue. Primrose. Neither of them could tip the scale at seventy pounds soaking wet.

"What can we do about it?" I ask him, more harshly than I intended.

"Nothing to do," he says back. "Just making conversation."

Now that I know she's there, it's hard to ignore the child. She slips up and joins us at different stations. Like me, she's clever with plants, climbs swiftly, and has good aim. She can hit the target every time with a slingshot. But what is a slingshot against a 220-pound male with a sword?

Back on the District 12 floor, Haymitch and Effie grill us throughout breakfast and dinner about every moment of the day. What we did, who watched us, how the other tributes size up. Cinna and Portia aren't around, so there's no one to add any sanity to the meals. Not that Haymitch and Effie are fighting anymore. Instead they seem to be of one mind, determined to whip us into shape. Full of endless directions about what we should do and not do in training. Peeta is more patient, but I become fed up and surly.

When we finally escape to bed on the second night, Peeta mumbles, "Someone ought to get Haymitch a drink."

I make a sound that is somewhere between a snort and a

laugh. Then catch myself. It's messing with my mind too much, trying to keep straight when we're supposedly friends and when we're not. At least when we get into the arena, I'll know where we stand. "Don't. Don't let's pretend when there's no one around."

"All right, Katniss," he says tiredly. After that, we only talk in front of people.

On the third day of training, they start to call us out of lunch for our private sessions with the Gamemakers. District by district, first the boy, then the girl tribute. As usual, District 12 is slated to go last. We linger in the dining room, unsure where else to go. No one comes back once they have left. As the room empties, the pressure to appear friendly lightens. By the time they call Rue, we are left alone. We sit in silence until they summon Peeta. He rises.

"Remember what Haymitch said about being sure to throw the weights." The words come out of my mouth without permission.

"Thanks. I will," he says. "You . . . shoot straight."

I nod. I don't know why I said anything at all. Although if I'm going to lose, I'd rather Peeta win than the others. Better for our district, for my mother and Prim.

After about fifteen minutes, they call my name. I smooth my hair, set my shoulders back, and walk into the gymnasium. Instantly, I know I'm in trouble. They've been here too long, the Gamemakers. Sat through twenty-three other demonstrations. Had too much wine, most of them. Want more than anything to go home.

There's nothing I can do but continue with the plan. I

walk to the archery station. Oh, the weapons! I've been itching to get my hands on them for days! Bows made of wood and plastic and metal and materials I can't even name. Arrows with feathers cut in flawless uniform lines. I choose a bow, string it, and sling the matching quiver of arrows over my shoulder. There's a shooting range, but it's much too limited. Standard bull's-eyes and human silhouettes. I walk to the center of the gymnasium and pick my first target. The dummy used for knife practice. Even as I pull back on the bow I know something is wrong. The string's tighter than the one I use at home. The arrow's more rigid. I miss the dummy by a couple of inches and lose what little attention I had been commanding. For a moment, I'm humiliated, then I head back to the bull's-eye. I shoot again and again until I get the feel of these new weapons.

Back in the center of the gymnasium, I take my initial position and skewer the dummy right through the heart. Then I sever the rope that holds the sandbag for boxing, and the bag splits open as it slams to the ground. Without pausing, I shoulder-roll forward, come up on one knee, and send an arrow into one of the hanging lights high above the gymnasium floor. A shower of sparks bursts from the fixture.

It's excellent shooting. I turn to the Gamemakers. A few are nodding approval, but the majority of them are fixated on a roast pig that has just arrived at their banquet table.

Suddenly I am furious, that with my life on the line, they don't even have the decency to pay attention to me. That I'm being upstaged by a dead pig. My heart starts to pound, I can feel my face burning. Without thinking, I pull an arrow from my quiver and send it straight at the Gamemakers' table. I hear shouts of alarm as people stumble back. The arrow skewers the apple in the pig's mouth and pins it to the wall behind it. Everyone stares at me in disbelief.

"Thank you for your consideration," I say. Then I give a slight bow and walk straight toward the exit without being dismissed.

As I stride toward the elevator, I fling my bow to one side and my quiver to the other. I brush past the gaping Avoxes who guard the elevators and hit the number twelve button with my fist. The doors slide together and I zip upward. I actually make it back to my floor before the tears start running down my cheeks. I can hear the others calling me from the sitting room, but I fly down the hall into my room, bolt the door, and fling myself onto my bed. Then I really begin to sob.

Now I've done it! Now I've ruined everything! If I'd stood even a ghost of chance, it vanished when I sent that arrow flying at the Gamemakers. What will they do to me now? Arrest me? Execute me? Cut my tongue and turn me into an Avox so I can wait on the future tributes of Panem? What was I thinking, shooting at the Gamemakers? Of course, I wasn't, I was shooting at that apple because I was so angry at being ignored. I wasn't trying to kill one of them. If I were, they'd be dead!

Oh, what does it matter? It's not like I was going to win the Games anyway. Who cares what they do to me? What really scares me is what they might do to my mother and Prim, how my family might suffer now because of my impulsiveness. Will they take their few belongings, or send my mother to prison and Prim to the community home, or kill them? They wouldn't kill them, would they? Why not? What do they care?

I should have stayed and apologized. Or laughed, like it was a big joke. Then maybe I would have found some leniency. But instead I stalked out of the place in the most disrespectful manner possible.

Haymitch and Effie are knocking on my door. I shout for them to go away and eventually they do. It takes at least an hour for me to cry myself out. Then I just lie curled up on the bed, stroking the silken sheets, watching the sun set over the artificial candy Capitol.

At first, I expect guards to come for me. But as time passes, it seems less likely. I calm down. They still need a girl tribute from District 12, don't they? If the Gamemakers want to punish me, they can do it publicly. Wait until I'm in the arena and sic starving wild animals on me. You can bet they'll make sure I don't have a bow and arrow to defend myself.

Before that though, they'll give me a score so low, no one in their right mind would sponsor me. That's what will happen tonight. Since the training isn't open to viewers, the Gamemakers announce a score for each player. It gives the audience a starting place for the betting that will continue throughout the Games. The number, which is between one and twelve, one being irredeemably bad and twelve being unattainably high, signifies the promise of the tribute. The mark is not a guarantee of which person will win. It's only an indication of the potential a tribute showed in training. Often, because of the variables in the actual arena, high-scoring tributes go down almost immediately. And a few years ago, the boy who won the Games only received a three. Still, the scores can help or hurt an individual tribute in terms of sponsorship. I had been hoping my shooting skills might get me a six or a seven, even if I'm not particularly powerful. Now I'm sure I'll have the lowest score of the twenty-four. If no one sponsors me, my odds of staying alive decrease to almost zero.

When Effie taps on the door to call me to dinner, I decide I may as well go. The scores will be televised tonight. It's not like I can hide what happened forever. I go to the bathroom and wash my face, but it's still red and splotchy.

Everyone's waiting at the table, even Cinna and Portia. I wish the stylists hadn't shown up because for some reason, I don't like the idea of disappointing them. It's as if I've thrown away all the good work they did on the opening ceremonies without a thought. I avoid looking at anyone as I take tiny spoonfuls of fish soup. The saltiness reminds me of my tears.

The adults begin some chitchat about the weather forecast, and I let my eyes meet Peeta's. He raises his eyebrows. A question. *What happened?* I just give my head a small shake. Then, as they're serving the main course, I hear Haymitch say, "Okay, enough small talk, just how bad were you today?"

Peeta jumps in. "I don't know that it mattered. By the time I showed up, no one even bothered to look at me. They were singing some kind of drinking song, I think. So,

I threw around some heavy objects until they told me I could go."

That makes me feel a bit better. It's not like Peeta attacked the Gamemakers, but at least he was provoked, too.

"And you, sweetheart?" says Haymitch.

Somehow Haymitch calling me sweetheart ticks me off enough that I'm at least able to speak. "I shot an arrow at the Gamemakers."

Everyone stops eating. "You what?" The horror in Effie's voice confirms my worse suspicions.

"I shot an arrow at them. Not exactly at them. In their direction. It's like Peeta said, I was shooting and they were ignoring me and I just . . . I just lost my head, so I shot an apple out of their stupid roast pig's mouth!" I say defiantly.

"And what did they say?" says Cinna carefully.

"Nothing. Or I don't know. I walked out after that," I say.

"Without being dismissed?" gasps Effie.

"I dismissed myself," I said. I remember how I promised Prim that I really would try to win and I feel like a ton of coal has dropped on me.

"Well, that's that," says Haymitch. Then he butters a roll.

"Do you think they'll arrest me?" I ask.

"Doubt it. Be a pain to replace you at this stage," says Haymitch.

"What about my family?" I say. "Will they punish them?"

"Don't think so. Wouldn't make much sense. See, they'd have to reveal what happened in the Training Center for it to have any worthwhile effect on the population. People would need to know what you did. But they can't since it's secret, so it'd be a waste of effort," says Haymitch. "More likely they'll make your life hell in the arena."

"Well, they've already promised to do that to us anyway," says Peeta.

"Very true," says Haymitch. And I realize the impossible has happened. They have actually cheered me up. Haymitch picks up a pork chop with his fingers, which makes Effie frown, and dunks it in his wine. He rips off a hunk of meat and starts to chuckle. "What were their faces like?"

I can feel the edges of my mouth tilting up. "Shocked. Terrified. Uh, ridiculous, some of them." An image pops into my mind. "One man tripped backward into a bowl of punch."

Haymitch guffaws and we all start laughing except Effie, although even she is suppressing a smile. "Well, it serves them right. It's their job to pay attention to you. And just because you come from District Twelve is no excuse to ignore you." Then her eyes dart around as if she's said something totally outrageous. "I'm sorry, but that's what I think," she says to no one in particular.

"I'll get a very bad score," I say.

"Scores only matter if they're very good, no one pays much attention to the bad or mediocre ones. For all they know, you could be hiding your talents to get a low score on purpose. People use that strategy," said Portia.

"I hope that's how people interpret the four I'll probably get," says Peeta. "If that. Really, is anything less impressive than watching a person pick up a heavy ball and throw it a couple of yards. One almost landed on my foot."

I grin at him and realize that I'm starving. I cut off a piece of pork, dunk it in mashed potatoes, and start eating. It's okay. My family is safe. And if they are safe, no real harm has been done.

After dinner, we go to the sitting room to watch the scores announced on television. First they show a photo of the tribute, then flash their score below it. The Career Tributes naturally get in the eight-to-ten range. Most of the other players average a five. Surprisingly, little Rue comes up with a seven. I don't know what she showed the judges, but she's so tiny it must have been impressive.

District 12 comes up last, as usual. Peeta pulls an eight so at least a couple of the Gamemakers must have been watching him. I dig my fingernails into my palms as my face comes up, expecting the worst. Then they're flashing the number eleven on the screen.

Eleven!

Effie Trinket lets out a squeal, and everybody is slapping me on the back and cheering and congratulating me. But it doesn't seem real.

"There must be a mistake. How . . . how could that happen?" I ask Haymitch.

"Guess they liked your temper," he says. "They've got a show to put on. They need some players with some heat."

"Katniss, the girl who was on fire," says Cinna and gives me a hug. "Oh, wait until you see your interview dress."

"More flames?" I ask.

"Of a sort," he says mischievously.

Peeta and I congratulate each other, another awkward moment. We've both done well, but what does that mean for the other? I escape to my room as quickly as possible and burrow down under the covers. The stress of the day, particularly the crying, has worn me out. I drift off, reprieved, relieved, and with the number eleven still flashing behind my eyelids.

At dawn, I lie in bed for a while, watching the sun come up on a beautiful morning. It's Sunday. A day off at home. I wonder if Gale is in the woods yet. Usually we devote all of Sunday to stocking up for the week. Rising early, hunting and gathering, then trading at the Hob. I think of Gale without me. Both of us can hunt alone, but we're better as a pair. Particularly if we're trying for bigger game. But also in the littler things, having a partner lightened the load, could even make the arduous task of filling my family's table enjoyable.

I had been struggling along on my own for about six months when I first ran into Gale in the woods. It was a Sunday in October, the air cool and pungent with dying things. I'd spent the morning competing with the squirrels for nuts and the slightly warmer afternoon wading in shallow ponds harvesting katniss. The only meat I'd shot was a squirrel that had practically run over my toes in its quest for acorns, but the animals would still be afoot when the snow buried my other food sources. Having strayed farther afield than usual, I was hurrying back home, lugging my burlap sacks, when I came across a dead rabbit. It was hanging by its neck in a thin wire a foot above my head. About fifteen yards away was another. I recognized the twitch-up snares because my father had used them. When the prey is caught, it's yanked into the air out of the reach of other hungry animals. I'd been trying to use snares all summer with no success, so I couldn't help dropping my sacks to examine this one. My fingers were just on the wire above one of the rabbits when a voice rang out. "That's dangerous."

I jumped back several feet as Gale materialized from behind a tree. He must have been watching me the whole time. He was only fourteen, but he cleared six feet and was as good as an adult to me. I'd seen him around the Seam and at school. And one other time. He'd lost his father in the same blast that killed mine. In January, I'd stood by while he received his medal of valor in the Justice Building, another oldest child with no father. I remembered his two little brothers clutching his mother, a woman whose swollen belly announced she was just days away from giving birth.

"What's your name?" he said, coming over and disengaging the rabbit from the snare. He had another three hanging from his belt.

"Katniss," I said, barely audible.

"Well, Catnip, stealing's punishable by death, or hadn't you heard?" he said.

"Katniss," I said louder. "And I wasn't stealing it. I just wanted to look at your snare. Mine never catch anything."

He scowled at me, not convinced. "So where'd you get the squirrel?"

"I shot it." I pulled my bow off my shoulder. I was still using the small version my father had made me, but I'd been practicing with the full-size one when I could. I was hoping that by spring I might be able to bring down some bigger game.

Gale's eyes fastened on the bow. "Can I see that?"

I handed it over. "Just remember, stealing's punishable by death."

That was the first time I ever saw him smile. It transformed him from someone menacing to someone you wished you knew. But it took several months before I returned that smile.

We talked hunting then. I told him I might be able to get him a bow if he had something to trade. Not food. I wanted knowledge. I wanted to set my own snares that caught a belt of fat rabbits in one day. He agreed something might be worked out. As the seasons went by, we grudgingly began to share our knowledge, our weapons, our secret places that were thick with wild plums or turkeys. He taught me snares and fishing. I showed him what plants to eat and eventually gave him one of our precious bows. And then one day, without either of us saying it, we became a team. Dividing the work and the spoils. Making sure that both our families had food.

Gale gave me a sense of security I'd lacked since my

father's death. His companionship replaced the long solitary hours in the woods. I became a much better hunter when I didn't have to look over my shoulder constantly, when someone was watching my back. But he turned into so much more than a hunting partner. He became my confidant, someone with whom I could share thoughts I could never voice inside the fence. In exchange, he trusted me with his. Being out in the woods with Gale . . . sometimes I was actually happy.

I call him my friend, but in the last year it's seemed too casual a word for what Gale is to me. A pang of longing shoots through my chest. If only he was with me now! But, of course, I don't want that. I don't want him in the arena where he'd be dead in a few days. I just . . . I just miss him. And I hate being so alone. Does he miss me? He must.

I think of the eleven flashing under my name last night. I know exactly what he'd say to me. "Well, there's some room for improvement there." And then he'd give me a smile and I'd return it without hesitating now.

I can't help comparing what I have with Gale to what I'm pretending to have with Peeta. How I never question Gale's motives while I do nothing but doubt the latter's. It's not a fair comparison really. Gale and I were thrown together by a mutual need to survive. Peeta and I know the other's survival means our own death. How do you sidestep that?

Effie's knocking at the door, reminding me there's another "big, big, big day!" ahead. Tomorrow night will be our televised interviews. I guess the whole team will have their hands full readying us for that.

I get up and take a quick shower, being a bit more careful about the buttons I hit, and head down to the dining room. Peeta, Effie, and Haymitch are huddled around the table talking in hushed voices. That seems odd, but hunger wins out over curiosity and I load up my plate with breakfast before I join them.

The stew's made with tender chunks of lamb and dried plums today. Perfect on the bed of wild rice. I've shoveled about halfway through the mound when I realize no one's talking. I take a big gulp of orange juice and wipe my mouth. "So, what's going on? You're coaching us on interviews today, right?"

"That's right," says Haymitch.

"You don't have to wait until I'm done. I can listen and eat at the same time," I say.

"Well, there's been a change of plans. About our current approach," says Haymitch.

"What's that?" I ask. I'm not sure what our current approach is. Trying to appear mediocre in front of the other tributes is the last bit of strategy I remember.

Haymitch shrugs. "Peeta has asked to be coached separately."

Betrayal. That's the first thing I feel, which is ludicrous. For there to be betrayal, there would have to have been trust first. Between Peeta and me. And trust has not been part of the agreement. We're tributes. But the boy who risked a beating to give me bread, the one who steadied me in the chariot, who covered for me with the redheaded Avox girl, who insisted Haymitch know my hunting skills . . . was there some part of me that couldn't help trusting him?

On the other hand, I'm relieved that we can stop the pretense of being friends. Obviously, whatever thin connection we'd foolishly formed has been severed. And high time, too. The Games begin in two days, and trust will only be a weakness. Whatever triggered Peeta's decision — and I suspect it had to do with my outperforming him in training — I should be nothing but grateful for it. Maybe he's finally accepted the fact that the sooner we openly acknowledge that we are enemies, the better.

"Good," I say. "So what's the schedule?"

"You'll each have four hours with Effie for presentation and four with me for content," says Haymitch. "You start with Effie, Katniss."

I can't imagine what Effie will have to teach me that could take four hours, but she's got me working down to the last minute. We go to my room and she puts me in a full-length gown and high-heeled shoes, not the ones I'll be wearing for the actual interview, and instructs me on walking. The shoes are the worst part. I've never worn high heels and can't get used to essentially wobbling around on the balls of my feet. But Effie runs around in them full-time, and I'm determined that if she can do it, so can I. The dress poses another problem. It keeps tangling around my shoes so, of course, I hitch it up, and then Effie swoops down on me like a hawk, smacking my hands and yelling, "Not above the ankle!" When I finally conquer walking, there's still sitting, posture — apparently I have a tendency to duck my head — eye contact, hand gestures, and smiling. Smiling is mostly about smiling more. Effie makes me say a hundred banal phrases starting with a smile, while smiling, or ending with a smile. By lunch, the muscles in my cheeks are twitching from overuse.

"Well, that's the best I can do," Effie says with a sigh. "Just remember, Katniss, you want the audience to like you."

"And you don't think they will?" I ask.

"Not if you glare at them the entire time. Why don't you save that for the arena? Instead, think of yourself among friends," says Effie.

"They're betting on how long I'll live!" I burst out. "They're not my friends!"

"Well, try and pretend!" snaps Effie. Then she composes herself and beams at me. "See, like this. I'm smiling at you even though you're aggravating me."

"Yes, it feels very convincing," I say. "I'm going to eat." I kick off my heels and stomp down to the dining room, hiking my skirt up to my thighs.

Peeta and Haymitch seem in pretty good moods, so I'm thinking the content session should be an improvement over the morning. I couldn't be more wrong. After lunch, Haymitch takes me into the sitting room, directs me to the couch, and then just frowns at me for a while.

"What?" I finally ask.

"I'm trying to figure out what to do with you," he says. "How we're going to present you. Are you going to be charming? Aloof? Fierce? So far, you're shining like a star. You volunteered to save your sister. Cinna made you look unforgettable. You've got the top training score. People are intrigued, but no one knows who you are. The impression you make tomorrow will decide exactly what I can get you in terms of sponsors," says Haymitch.

Having watched the tribute interviews all my life, I know there's truth to what he's saying. If you appeal to the crowd, either by being humorous or brutal or eccentric, you gain favor.

"What's Peeta's approach? Or am I not allowed to ask?" I say.

"Likable. He has a sort of self-deprecating humor naturally," says Haymitch. "Whereas when you open your mouth, you come across more as sullen and hostile."

"I do not!" I say.

"Please. I don't know where you pulled that cheery, wavy

girl on the chariot from, but I haven't seen her before or since," says Haymitch.

"And you've given me so many reasons to be cheery," I counter.

"But you don't have to please me. I'm not going to sponsor you. So pretend I'm the audience," says Haymitch. "Delight me."

"Fine!" I snarl. Haymitch takes the role of the interviewer and I try to answer his questions in a winning fashion. But I can't. I'm too angry with Haymitch for what he said and that I even have to answer the questions. All I can think is how unjust the whole thing is, the Hunger Games. Why am I hopping around like some trained dog trying to please people I hate? The longer the interview goes on, the more my fury seems to rise to the surface, until I'm literally spitting out answers at him.

"All right, enough," he says. "We've got to find another angle. Not only are you hostile, I don't know anything about you. I've asked you fifty questions and still have no sense of your life, your family, what you care about. They want to know about you, Katniss."

"But I don't want them to! They're already taking my future! They can't have the things that mattered to me in the past!" I say.

"Then lie! Make something up!" says Haymitch.

"I'm not good at lying," I say.

"Well, you better learn fast. You've got about as much charm as a dead slug," say Haymitch.

Ouch. That hurts. Even Haymitch must know he's been too harsh because his voice softens. "Here's an idea. Try acting humble."

"Humble," I echo.

"That you can't believe a little girl from District Twelve has done this well. The whole thing's been more than you ever could have dreamed of. Talk about Cinna's clothes. How nice the people are. How the city amazes you. If you won't talk about yourself, at least compliment the audience. Just keep turning it back around, all right. Gush."

The next hours are agonizing. At once, it's clear I cannot gush. We try me playing cocky, but I just don't have the arrogance. Apparently, I'm too "vulnerable" for ferocity. I'm not witty. Funny. Sexy. Or mysterious.

By the end of the session, I am no one at all. Haymitch started drinking somewhere around witty, and a nasty edge has crept into his voice. "I give up, sweetheart. Just answer the questions and try not to let the audience see how openly you despise them."

I have dinner that night in my room, ordering an outrageous number of delicacies, eating myself sick, and then taking out my anger at Haymitch, at the Hunger Games, at every living being in the Capitol by smashing dishes around my room. When the girl with the red hair comes in to turn down my bed, her eyes widen at the mess. "Just leave it!" I yell at her. "Just leave it alone!"

I hate her, too, with her knowing reproachful eyes that call me a coward, a monster, a puppet of the Capitol, both now and then. For her, justice must finally be happening. At least my death will help pay for the life of the boy in the woods.

But instead of fleeing the room, the girl closes the door behind her and goes to the bathroom. She comes back with a damp cloth and wipes my face gently then cleans the blood from a broken plate off my hands. Why is she doing this? Why am I letting her?

"I should have tried to save you," I whisper.

She shakes her head. Does this mean we were right to stand by? That she has forgiven me?

"No, it was wrong," I say.

She taps her lips with her fingers then points to my chest. I think she means that I would just have ended up an Avox, too. Probably would have. An Avox or dead.

I spend the next hour helping the redheaded girl clean the room. When all the garbage has been dropped down a disposal and the food cleaned away, she turns down my bed. I crawl in between the sheets like a five-year-old and let her tuck me in. Then she goes. I want her to stay until I fall asleep. To be there when I wake up. I want the protection of this girl, even though she never had mine.

In the morning, it's not the girl but my prep team who are hanging over me. My lessons with Effie and Haymitch are over. This day belongs to Cinna. He's my last hope. Maybe he can make me look so wonderful, no one will care what comes out of my mouth.

The team works on me until late afternoon, turning my skin to glowing satin, stenciling patterns on my arms, painting flame designs on my twenty perfect nails. Then Venia goes to work on my hair, weaving strands of red into a pattern that begins at my left ear, wraps around my head, and then falls in one braid down my right shoulder. They erase my face with a layer of pale makeup and draw my features back out. Huge dark eyes, full red lips, lashes that throw off bits of light when I blink. Finally, they cover my entire body in a powder that makes me shimmer in gold dust.

Then Cinna enters with what I assume is my dress, but I can't really see it because it's covered. "Close your eyes," he orders.

I can feel the silken inside as they slip it down over my naked body, then the weight. It must be forty pounds. I clutch Octavia's hand as I blindly step into my shoes, glad to find they are at least two inches lower than the pair Effie had me practice in. There's some adjusting and fidgeting. Then silence.

"Can I open my eyes?" I ask.

"Yes," says Cinna. "Open them."

The creature standing before me in the full-length mirror has come from another world. Where skin shimmers and eyes flash and apparently they make their clothes from jewels. Because my dress, oh, my dress is entirely covered in reflective precious gems, red and yellow and white with bits of blue that accent the tips of the flame design. The slightest movement gives the impression I am engulfed in tongues of fire.

I am not pretty. I am not beautiful. I am as radiant as the sun.

For a while, we all just stare at me. "Oh, Cinna," I finally whisper. "Thank you."

"Twirl for me," he says. I hold out my arms and spin in a circle. The prep team screams in admiration.

Cinna dismisses the team and has me move around in the dress and shoes, which are infinitely more manageable than Effie's. The dress hangs in such a way that I don't have to lift the skirt when I walk, leaving me with one less thing to worry about.

"So, all ready for the interview then?" asks Cinna. I can see by his expression that he's been talking to Haymitch. That he knows how dreadful I am.

"I'm awful. Haymitch called me a dead slug. No matter what we tried, I couldn't do it. I just can't be one of those people he wants me to be," I say.

Cinna thinks about this a moment. "Why don't you just be yourself?"

"Myself? That's no good, either. Haymitch says I'm sullen and hostile," I say.

"Well, you are . . . around Haymitch," says Cinna with a grin. "I don't find you so. The prep team adores you. You even won over the Gamemakers. And as for the citizens of the Capitol, well, they can't stop talking about you. No one can help but admire your spirit."

My spirit. This is a new thought. I'm not sure exactly what it means, but it suggests I'm a fighter. In a sort of brave way. It's not as if I'm never friendly. Okay, maybe I don't go around loving everybody I meet, maybe my smiles are hard to come by, but I do care for some people.

Cinna takes my icy hands in his warm ones. "Suppose, when you answer the questions, you think you're addressing a friend back home. Who would your best friend be?" asks Cinna.

"Gale," I say instantly. "Only it doesn't make sense, Cinna. I would never be telling Gale those things about me. He already knows them."

"What about me? Could you think of me as a friend?" asks Cinna.

Of all the people I've met since I left home, Cinna is by far my favorite. I liked him right off and he hasn't disappointed me yet. "I think so, but —"

"I'll be sitting on the main platform with the other stylists. You'll be able to look right at me. When you're asked a question, find me, and answer it as honestly as possible," says Cinna.

"Even if what I think is horrible?" I ask. Because it might be, really.

"Especially if what you think is horrible," says Cinna. "You'll try it?"

I nod. It's a plan. Or at least a straw to grasp at.

Too soon it's time to go. The interviews take place on a stage constructed in front of the Training Center. Once I leave my room, it will be only minutes until I'm in front of the crowd, the cameras, all of Panem.

As Cinna turns the doorknob, I stop his hand. "Cinna . . ." I'm completely overcome with stage fright.

"Remember, they already love you," he says gently. "Just be yourself."

We meet up with the rest of the District 12 crowd at the elevator. Portia and her gang have been hard at work. Peeta looks striking in a black suit with flame accents. While we look well together, it's a relief not to be dressed identically. Haymitch and Effie are all fancied up for the occasion. I avoid Haymitch, but accept Effie's compliments. Effie can be tiresome and clueless, but she's not destructive like Haymitch.

When the elevator opens, the other tributes are being lined up to take the stage. All twenty-four of us sit in a big arc throughout the interviews. I'll be last, or second to last since the girl tribute precedes the boy from each district. How I wish I could be first and get the whole thing out of the way! Now I'll have to listen to how witty, funny, humble, fierce, and charming everybody else is before I go up. Plus, the audience will start to get bored, just as the Gamemakers did. And I can't exactly shoot an arrow into the crowd to get their attention.

Right before we parade onto the stage, Haymitch comes up behind Peeta and me and growls, "Remember, you're still a happy pair. So act like it."

What? I thought we abandoned that when Peeta asked for separate coaching. But I guess that was a private, not a public thing. Anyway, there's not much chance for interaction now, as we walk single-file to our seats and take our places.

Just stepping on the stage makes my breathing rapid and shallow. I can feel my pulse pounding in my temples. It's a relief to get to my chair, because between the heels and my legs shaking, I'm afraid I'll trip. Although evening is falling, the City Circle is brighter than a summer's day. An elevated seating unit has been set up for prestigious guests, with the stylists commanding the front row. The cameras will turn to them when the crowd is reacting to their handiwork. A large balcony off a building to the right has been reserved for the Gamemakers. Television crews have claimed most of the other balconies. But the City Circle and the avenues that feed into it are completely packed with people. Standing room only. At homes and community halls around the country, every television set is turned on. Every citizen of Panem is tuned in. There will be no blackouts tonight.

Caesar Flickerman, the man who has hosted the interviews for more than forty years, bounces onto the stage. It's a little scary because his appearance has been virtually unchanged during all that time. Same face under a coating of pure white makeup. Same hairstyle that he dyes a different color for each Hunger Games. Same ceremonial suit, midnight blue dotted with a thousand tiny electric bulbs that twinkle like stars. They do surgery in the Capitol, to make people appear younger and thinner. In District 12, looking old is something of an achievement since so many people die early. You see an elderly person, you want to congratulate them on their longevity, ask the secret of survival. A plump person is envied because they aren't scraping by like the majority of us. But here it is different. Wrinkles aren't desirable. A round belly isn't a sign of success.

This year, Caesar's hair is powder blue and his eyelids and lips are coated in the same hue. He looks freakish but less frightening than he did last year when his color was crimson and he seemed to be bleeding. Caesar tells a few jokes to warm up the audience but then gets down to business.

The girl tribute from District 1, looking provocative in a see-through gold gown, steps up the center of the stage to join Caesar for her interview. You can tell her mentor didn't have any trouble coming up with an angle for her. With that flowing blonde hair, emerald green eyes, her body tall and lush . . . she's sexy all the way.

Each interview only lasts three minutes. Then a buzzer goes off and the next tribute is up. I'll say this for Caesar, he really does his best to make the tributes shine. He's friendly, tries to set the nervous ones at ease, laughs at lame jokes, and can turn a weak response into a memorable one by the way he reacts.

I sit like a lady, the way Effie showed me, as the districts slip by. 2, 3, 4. Everyone seems to be playing up some angle. The monstrous boy from District 2 is a ruthless killing machine. The fox-faced girl from District 5 sly and elusive. I spotted Cinna as soon as he took his place, but even his presence cannot relax me. 8, 9, 10. The crippled boy from 10 is very quiet. My palms are sweating like crazy, but the jeweled dress isn't absorbent and they skid right off if I try to dry them. 11.

Rue, who is dressed in a gossamer gown complete with wings, flutters her way to Caesar. A hush falls over the crowd at the sight of this magical wisp of a tribute. Caesar's very sweet with her, complimenting her seven in training, an excellent score for one so small. When he asks her what her greatest strength in the arena will be, she doesn't hesitate. "I'm very hard to catch," she says in a tremulous voice. "And if they can't catch me, they can't kill me. So don't count me out."

"I wouldn't in a million years," says Caesar encouragingly.

The boy tribute from District 11, Thresh, has the same dark skin as Rue, but the resemblance stops there. He's one of the giants, probably six and a half feet tall and built like an ox, but I noticed he rejected the invitations from the Career Tributes to join their crowd. Instead he's been very solitary, speaking to no one, showing little interest in training. Even so, he scored a ten and it's not hard to imagine he impressed the Gamemakers. He ignores Caesar's attempts at banter and answers with a yes or no or just remains silent.

If only I was his size, I could get away with sullen and hostile and it would be just fine! I bet half the sponsors are at least considering him. If I had any money, I'd bet on him myself.

And then they're calling Katniss Everdeen, and I feel

myself, as if in a dream, standing and making my way center stage. I shake Caesar's outstretched hand, and he has the good grace not to immediately wipe his off on his suit.

"So, Katniss, the Capitol must be quite a change from District Twelve. What's impressed you most since you arrived here?" asks Caesar.

What? What did he say? It's as if the words make no sense.

My mouth has gone as dry as sawdust. I desperately find Cinna in the crowd and lock eyes with him. I imagine the words coming from his lips. "What's impressed you most since you arrived here?" I rack my brain for something that made me happy here. *Be honest*, I think. *Be honest*.

"The lamb stew," I get out.

Caesar laughs, and vaguely I realize some of the audience has joined in.

"The one with the dried plums?" asks Caesar. I nod. "Oh, I eat it by the bucketful." He turns sideways to the audience in horror, hand on his stomach. "It doesn't show, does it?" They shout reassurances to him and applaud. This is what I mean about Caesar. He tries to help you out.

"Now, Katniss," he says confidentially, "When you came out in the opening ceremonies, my heart actually stopped. What did you think of that costume?"

Cinna raises one eyebrow at me. Be honest. "You mean after I got over my fear of being burned alive?" I ask.

Big laugh. A real one from the audience.

"Yes. Start then," says Caesar.

Cinna, my friend, I should tell him anyway. "I thought

Cinna was brilliant and it was the most gorgeous costume I'd ever seen and I couldn't believe I was wearing it. I can't believe I'm wearing this, either." I lift up my skirt to spread it out. "I mean, look at it!"

As the audience *ooh*s and *ah*s, I see Cinna make the tiniest circular motion with his finger. But I know what he's saying. *Twirl for me.*

I spin in a circle once and the reaction is immediate.

"Oh, do that again!" says Caesar, and so I lift up my arms and spin around and around letting the skirt fly out, letting the dress engulf me in flames. The audience breaks into cheers. When I stop, I clutch Caesar's arm.

"Don't stop!" he says.

"I have to, I'm dizzy!" I'm also giggling, which I think I've done maybe never in my lifetime. But the nerves and the spinning have gotten to me.

Caesar wraps a protective arm around me. "Don't worry, I've got you. Can't have you following in your mentor's footsteps."

Everyone's hooting as the cameras find Haymitch, who is by now famous for his head dive at the reaping, and he waves them away good-naturedly and points back to me.

"It's all right," Caesar reassures the crowd. "She's safe with me. So, how about that training score. E-le-ven. Give us a hint what happened in there."

I glance at the Gamemakers on the balcony and bite my lip. "Um . . . all I can say, is I think it was a first."

The cameras are right on the Gamemakers, who are chuckling and nodding.

"You're killing us," says Caesar as if in actual pain. "Details. Details."

I address the balcony. "I'm not supposed to talk about it, right?"

The Gamemaker who fell in the punch bowl shouts out, "She's not!"

"Thank you," I say. "Sorry. My lips are sealed."

"Let's go back then, to the moment they called your sister's name at the reaping," says Caesar. His mood is quieter now. "And you volunteered. Can you tell us about her?"

No. No, not all of you. But maybe Cinna. I don't think I'm imagining the sadness on his face. "Her name's Prim. She's just twelve. And I love her more than anything."

You could hear a pin drop in the City Circle now.

"What did she say to you? After the reaping?" Caesar asks.

Be honest. Be honest. I swallow hard. "She asked me to try really hard to win." The audience is frozen, hanging on my every word.

"And what did you say?" prompts Caesar gently.

But instead of warmth, I feel an icy rigidity take over my body. My muscles tense as they do before a kill. When I speak, my voice seems to have dropped an octave. "I swore I would."

"I bet you did," says Caesar, giving me a squeeze. The buzzer goes off. "Sorry we're out of time. Best of luck, Katniss Everdeen, tribute from District Twelve."

The applause continues long after I'm seated. I look to Cinna for reassurance. He gives me a subtle thumbs-up.

I'm still in a daze for the first part of Peeta's interview. He has the audience from the get-go, though; I can hear them laughing, shouting out. He plays up the baker's son thing, comparing the tributes to the breads from their districts. Then has a funny anecdote about the perils of the Capitol showers. "Tell me, do I still smell like roses?" he asks Caesar, and then there's a whole run where they take turns sniffing each other that brings down the house. I'm coming back into focus when Caesar asks him if he has a girlfriend back home.

Peeta hesitates, then gives an unconvincing shake of his head.

"Handsome lad like you. There must be some special girl. Come on, what's her name?" says Caesar.

Peeta sighs. "Well, there is this one girl. I've had a crush on her ever since I can remember. But I'm pretty sure she didn't know I was alive until the reaping."

Sounds of sympathy from the crowd. Unrequited love they can relate to.

"She have another fellow?" asks Caesar.

"I don't know, but a lot of boys like her," says Peeta.

"So, here's what you do. You win, you go home. She can't turn you down then, eh?" says Caesar encouragingly.

"I don't think it's going to work out. Winning . . . won't help in my case," says Peeta.

"Why ever not?" says Caesar, mystified.

Peeta blushes beet red and stammers out. "Because . . . because . . . she came here with me."

PART II
"THE GAMES"

For a moment, the cameras hold on Peeta's downcast eyes as what he says sinks in. Then I can see my face, mouth half open in a mix of surprise and protest, magnified on every screen as I realize, *Me! He means me!* I press my lips together and stare at the floor, hoping this will conceal the emotions starting to boil up inside of me.

"Oh, that is a piece of bad luck," says Caesar, and there's a real edge of pain in his voice. The crowd is murmuring in agreement, a few have even given agonized cries.

"It's not good," agrees Peeta.

"Well, I don't think any of us can blame you. It'd be hard not to fall for that young lady," says Caesar. "She didn't know?"

Peeta shakes his head. "Not until now."

I allow my eyes to flicker up to the screen long enough to see that the blush on my cheeks is unmistakable.

"Wouldn't you love to pull her back out here and get a response?" Caesar asks the audience. The crowd screams assent. "Sadly, rules are rules, and Katniss Everdeen's time has been spent. Well, best of luck to you, Peeta Mellark, and I think I speak for all of Panem when I say our hearts go with yours."

The roar of the crowd is deafening. Peeta has absolutely

wiped the rest of us off the map with his declaration of love for me. When the audience finally settles down, he chokes out a quiet "Thank you" and returns to his seat. We stand for the anthem. I have to raise my head out of the required respect and cannot avoid seeing that every screen is now dominated by a shot of Peeta and me, separated by a few feet that in the viewers' heads can never be breached. Poor tragic us.

But I know better.

After the anthem, the tributes file back into the Training Center lobby and onto the elevators. I make sure to veer into a car that does not contain Peeta. The crowd slows our entourages of stylists and mentors and chaperones, so we have only each other for company. No one speaks. My elevator stops to deposit four tributes before I am alone and then find the doors opening on the twelfth floor. Peeta has only just stepped from his car when I slam my palms into his chest. He loses his balance and crashes into an ugly urn filled with fake flowers. The urn tips and shatters into hundreds of tiny pieces. Peeta lands in the shards, and blood immediately flows from his hands.

"What was that for?" he says, aghast.

"You had no right! No right to go saying those things about me!" I shout at him.

Now the elevators open and the whole crew is there, Effie, Haymitch, Cinna, and Portia.

"What's going on?" says Effie, a note of hysteria in her voice. "Did you fall?"

"After she shoved me," says Peeta as Effie and Cinna help him up.

Haymitch turns on me. "Shoved him?"

"This was your idea, wasn't it? Turning me into some kind of fool in front of the entire country?" I answer.

"It was my idea," says Peeta, wincing as he pulls spikes of pottery from his palms. "Haymitch just helped me with it."

"Yes, Haymitch is very helpful. To you!" I say.

"You *are* a fool," Haymitch says in disgust. "Do you think he hurt you? That boy just gave you something you could never achieve on your own."

"He made me look weak!" I say.

"He made you look desirable! And let's face it, you can use all the help you can get in that department. You were about as romantic as dirt until he said he wanted you. Now they all do. You're all they're talking about. The star-crossed lovers from District Twelve!" says Haymitch.

"But we're not star-crossed lovers!" I say.

Haymitch grabs my shoulders and pins me against the wall. "Who cares? It's all a big show. It's all how you're perceived. The most I could say about you after your interview was that you were nice enough, although that in itself was a small miracle. Now I can say you're a heartbreaker. Oh, oh, oh, how the boys back home fall longingly at your feet. Which do you think will get you more sponsors?"

The smell of wine on his breath makes me sick. I shove his hands off my shoulders and step away, trying to clear my head.

Cinna comes over and puts his arm around me. "He's right, Katniss."

I don't know what to think. "I should have been told, so I didn't look so stupid."

"No, your reaction was perfect. If you'd known, it wouldn't have read as real," says Portia.

"She's just worried about her boyfriend," says Peeta gruffly, tossing away a bloody piece of the urn.

My cheeks burn again at the thought of Gale. "I don't have a boyfriend."

"Whatever," says Peeta. "But I bet he's smart enough to know a bluff when he sees it. Besides *you* didn't say you loved *me*. So what does it matter?"

The words are sinking in. My anger fading. I'm torn now between thinking I've been used and thinking I've been given an edge. Haymitch is right. I survived my interview, but what was I really? A silly girl spinning in a sparkling dress. Giggling. The only moment of any substance I had was when I talked about Prim. Compare that with Thresh, his silent, deadly power, and I'm forgettable. Silly and sparkly and forgettable. No, not entirely forgettable, I have my eleven in training.

But now Peeta has made me an object of love. Not just his. To hear him tell it I have many admirers. And if the audience really thinks we're in love . . . I remember how strongly they responded to his confession. Star-crossed lovers. Haymitch is right, they eat that stuff up in the Capitol. Suddenly I'm worried that I didn't react properly.

"After he said he loved me, did you think I could be in love with him, too?" I ask.

"I did," says Portia. "The way you avoided looking at the cameras, the blush."

The others chime in, agreeing.

"You're golden, sweetheart. You're going to have sponsors lined up around the block," says Haymitch.

I'm embarrassed about my reaction. I force myself to acknowledge Peeta. "I'm sorry I shoved you."

"Doesn't matter," he shrugs. "Although it's technically illegal."

"Are your hands okay?" I ask.

"They'll be all right," he says.

In the silence that follows, delicious smells of our dinner waft in from the dining room. "Come on, let's eat," says Haymitch. We all follow him to the table and take our places. But then Peeta is bleeding too heavily, and Portia leads him off for medical treatment. We start the cream and rose-petal soup without them. By the time we've finished, they're back. Peeta's hands are wrapped in bandages. I can't help feeling guilty. Tomorrow we will be in the arena. He has done me a favor and I have answered with an injury. Will I never stop owing him?

After dinner, we watch the replay in the sitting room. I seem frilly and shallow, twirling and giggling in my dress, although the others assure me I am charming. Peeta actually is charming and then utterly winning as the boy in love. And there I am, blushing and confused, made beautiful by

Cinna's hands, desirable by Peeta's confession, tragic by circumstance, and by all accounts, unforgettable.

When the anthem finishes and the screen goes dark, a hush falls on the room. Tomorrow at dawn, we will be roused and prepared for the arena. The actual Games don't start until ten because so many of the Capitol residents rise late. But Peeta and I must make an early start. There is no telling how far we will travel to the arena that has been prepared for this year's Games.

I know Haymitch and Effie will not be going with us. As soon as they leave here, they'll be at the Games Headquarters, hopefully madly signing up our sponsors, working out a strategy on how and when to deliver the gifts to us. Cinna and Portia will travel with us to the very spot from which we will be launched into the arena. Still final good-byes must be said here.

Effie takes both of us by the hand and, with actual tears in her eyes, wishes us well. Thanks us for being the best tributes it has ever been her privilege to sponsor. And then, because it's Effie and she's apparently required by law to say something awful, she adds "I wouldn't be at all surprised if I finally get promoted to a decent district next year!"

Then she kisses us each on the cheek and hurries out, overcome with either the emotional parting or the possible improvement of her fortunes.

Haymitch crosses his arms and looks us both over.

"Any final words of advice?" asks Peeta.

"When the gong sounds, get the hell out of there. You're neither of you up to the blood bath at the Cornucopia. Just clear out, put as much distance as you can between your-selves and the others, and find a source of water," he says. "Got it?"

"And after that?" I ask.

"Stay alive," says Haymitch. It's the same advice he gave us on the train, but he's not drunk and laughing this time. And we only nod. What else is there to say?

When I head to my room, Peeta lingers to talk to Portia. I'm glad. Whatever strange words of parting we exchange can wait until tomorrow. My covers are drawn back, but there is no sign of the redheaded Avox girl. I wish I knew her name. I should have asked it. She could write it down maybe. Or act it out. But perhaps that would only result in punishment for her.

I take a shower and scrub the gold paint, the makeup, the scent of beauty from my body. All that remains of the design-team's efforts are the flames on my nails. I decide to keep them as reminder of who I am to the audience. Katniss, the girl who was on fire. Perhaps it will give me something to hold on to in the days to come.

I pull on a thick, fleecy nightgown and climb into bed. It takes me about five seconds to realize I'll never fall asleep. And I need sleep desperately because in the arena every moment I give in to fatigue will be an invitation to death.

It's no good. One hour, two, three pass, and my eyelids refuse to get heavy. I can't stop trying to imagine exactly what terrain I'll be thrown into. Desert? Swamp? A frigid wasteland? Above all I am hoping for trees, which may afford me some means of concealment and food and shelter. Often there are trees because barren landscapes are dull and the Games resolve too quickly without them. But what will the climate be like? What traps have the Gamemakers hidden to liven up the slower moments? And then there are my fellow tributes . . .

The more anxious I am to find sleep, the more it eludes me. Finally, I am too restless to even stay in bed. I pace the floor, heart beating too fast, breathing too short. My room feels like a prison cell. If I don't get air soon, I'm going to start to throw things again. I run down the hall to the door to the roof. It's not only unlocked but ajar. Perhaps someone forgot to close it, but it doesn't matter. The energy field enclosing the roof prevents any desperate form of escape. And I'm not looking to escape, only to fill my lungs with air. I want to see the sky and the moon on the last night that no one will be hunting me.

The roof is not lit at night, but as soon as my bare feet reach its tiled surface I see his silhouette, black against the lights that shine endlessly in the Capitol. There's quite a commotion going on down in the streets, music and singing and car horns, none of which I could hear through the thick glass window panels in my room. I could slip away now, without him noticing me; he wouldn't hear me over the din. But the night air's so sweet, I can't bear returning to that stuffy cage of a room. And what difference does it make? Whether we speak or not?

My feet move soundlessly across the tiles. I'm only a

yard behind him when I say, "You should be getting some sleep."

He starts but doesn't turn. I can see him give his head a slight shake. "I didn't want to miss the party. It's for us, after all."

I come up beside him and lean over the edge of the rail. The wide streets are full of dancing people. I squint to make out their tiny figures in more detail. "Are they in costumes?"

"Who could tell?" Peeta answers. "With all the crazy clothes they wear here. Couldn't sleep, either?"

"Couldn't turn my mind off," I say.

"Thinking about your family?" he asks.

"No," I admit a bit guiltily. "All I can do is wonder about tomorrow. Which is pointless, of course." In the light from below, I can see his face now, the awkward way he holds his bandaged hands. "I really am sorry about your hands."

"It doesn't matter, Katniss," he says. "I've never been a contender in these Games anyway."

"That's no way to be thinking," I say.

"Why not? It's true. My best hope is to not disgrace myself and . . ." He hesitates.

"And what?" I say.

"I don't know how to say it exactly. Only . . . I want to die as myself. Does that make any sense?" he asks. I shake my head. How could he die as anyone but himself? "I don't want them to change me in there. Turn me into some kind of monster that I'm not."

I bite my lip, feeling inferior. While I've been ruminating on the availability of trees, Peeta has been struggling with how to maintain his identity. His purity of self. "Do you mean you won't kill anyone?" I ask.

"No, when the time comes, I'm sure I'll kill just like everybody else. I can't go down without a fight. Only I keep wishing I could think of a way to . . . to show the Capitol they don't own me. That I'm more than just a piece in their Games," says Peeta.

"But you're not," I say. "None of us are. That's how the Games work."

"Okay, but within that framework, there's still you, there's still me," he insists. "Don't you see?"

"A little. Only . . . no offense, but who cares, Peeta?" I say.

"I do. I mean, what else am I allowed to care about at this point?" he asks angrily. He's locked those blue eyes on mine now, demanding an answer.

I take a step back. "Care about what Haymitch said. About staying alive."

Peeta smiles at me, sad and mocking. "Okay. Thanks for the tip, sweetheart."

It's like a slap in the face. His use of Haymitch's patronizing endearment. "Look, if you want to spend the last hours of your life planning some noble death in the arena, that's your choice. I want to spend mine in District Twelve."

"Wouldn't surprise me if you do," says Peeta. "Give my mother my best when you make it back, will you?"

"Count on it," I say. Then I turn and leave the roof.

I spend the rest of the night slipping in and out of a doze, imagining the cutting remarks I will make to Peeta Mellark in the morning. Peeta Mellark. We will see how high and mighty he is when he's faced with life and death. He'll probably turn into one of those raging beast tributes, the kind who tries to eat someone's heart after they've killed them. There was a guy like that a few years ago from District 6 called Titus. He went completely savage and the Gamemakers had to have him stunned with electric guns to collect the bodies of the players he'd killed before he ate them. There are no rules in the arena, but cannibalism doesn't play well with the Capitol audience, so they tried to head it off. There was some speculation that the avalanche that finally took Titus out was specifically engineered to ensure the victor was not a lunatic.

I don't see Peeta in the morning. Cinna comes to me before dawn, gives me a simple shift to wear, and guides me to the roof. My final dressing and preparations will be done in the catacombs under the arena itself. A hovercraft appears out of thin air, just like the one did in the woods the day I saw the redheaded Avox girl captured, and a ladder drops down. I place my hands and feet on the lower rungs and instantly it's as if I'm frozen. Some sort of current glues me to the ladder while I'm lifted safely inside.

I expect the ladder to release me then, but I'm still stuck when a woman in a white coat approaches me carrying a syringe. "This is just your tracker, Katniss. The stiller you are, the more efficiently I can place it," she says.

Still? I'm a statue. But that doesn't prevent me from

feeling the sharp stab of pain as the needle inserts the metal tracking device deep under the skin on the inside of my forearm. Now the Gamemakers will always be able to trace my whereabouts in the arena. Wouldn't want to lose a tribute.

As soon as the tracker's in place, the ladder releases me. The woman disappears and Cinna is retrieved from the roof. An Avox boy comes in and directs us to a room where breakfast has been laid out. Despite the tension in my stomach, I eat as much as I can, although none of the delectable food makes any impression on me. I'm so nervous, I could be eating coal dust. The one thing that distracts me at all is the view from the windows as we sail over the city and then to the wilderness beyond. This is what birds see. Only they're free and safe. The very opposite of me.

The ride lasts about half an hour before the windows black out, suggesting that we're nearing the arena. The hovercraft lands and Cinna and I go back to the ladder, only this time it leads down into a tube underground, into the catacombs that lie beneath the arena. We follow instructions to my destination, a chamber for my preparation. In the Capitol, they call it the Launch Room. In the districts, it's referred to as the Stockyard. The place animals go before slaughter.

Everything is brand-new, I will be the first and only tribute to use this Launch Room. The arenas are historic sites, preserved after the Games. Popular destinations for Capitol residents to visit, to vacation. Go for a month, rewatch the

Games, tour the catacombs, visit the sites where the deaths took place. You can even take part in reenactments.

They say the food is excellent.

I struggle to keep my breakfast down as I shower and clean my teeth. Cinna does my hair in my simple trademark braid down my back. Then the clothes arrive, the same for every tribute. Cinna has had no say in my outfit, does not even know what will be in the package, but he helps me dress in the undergarments, simple tawny pants, light green blouse, sturdy brown belt, and thin, hooded black jacket that falls to my thighs. "The material in the jacket's designed to reflect body heat. Expect some cool nights," he says.

The boots, worn over skintight socks, are better than I could have hoped for. Soft leather not unlike my ones at home. These have a narrow flexible rubber sole with treads, though. Good for running.

I think I'm finished when Cinna pulls the gold mockingjay pin from his pocket. I had completely forgotten about it.

"Where did you get that?" I ask.

"Off the green outfit you wore on the train," he says. I remember now taking it off my mother's dress, pinning it to the shirt. "It's your district token, right?" I nod and he fastens it on my shirt. "It barely cleared the review board. Some thought the pin could be used as a weapon, giving you an unfair advantage. But eventually, they let it through," says Cinna. "They eliminated a ring from that District One girl, though. If you twisted the gemstone, a spike popped out. Poisoned one. She claimed she had no knowledge the ring transformed and there was no way to prove she did. But she lost her token. There, you're all set. Move around. Make sure everything feels comfortable."

I walk, run in a circle, swing my arms about. "Yes, it's fine. Fits perfectly."

"Then there's nothing to do but wait for the call," says Cinna. "Unless you think you could eat any more?"

I turn down food but accept a glass of water that I take tiny sips of as we wait on a couch. I don't want to chew on my nails or lips, so I find myself gnawing on the inside of my cheek. It still hasn't fully healed from a few days ago. Soon the taste of blood fills my mouth.

Nervousness seeps into terror as I anticipate what is to come. I could be dead, flat-out dead, in an hour. Not even. My fingers obsessively trace the hard little lump on my forearm where the woman injected the tracking device. I press on it, even though it hurts, I press on it so hard a small bruise begins to form.

"Do you want to talk, Katniss?" Cinna asks.

I shake my head but after a moment hold out my hand to him. Cinna encloses it in both of his. And this is how we sit until a pleasant female voice announces it's time to prepare for launch.

Still clenching one of Cinna's hands, I walk over and stand on the circular metal plate. "Remember what Haymitch said. Run, find water. The rest will follow," he says. I nod. "And remember this. I'm not allowed to bet, but if I could, my money would be on you."

"Truly?" I whisper.

"Truly," says Cinna. He leans down and kisses me on the forehead. "Good luck, girl on fire." And then a glass cylinder is lowering around me, breaking our handhold, cutting him off from me. He taps his fingers under his chin. Head high.

I lift my chin and stand as straight as I can. The cylinder begins to rise. For maybe fifteen seconds, I'm in darkness and then I can feel the metal plate pushing me out of the cylinder, into the open air. For a moment, my eyes are dazzled by the bright sunlight and I'm conscious only of a strong wind with the hopeful smell of pine trees.

Then I hear the legendary announcer, Claudius Templesmith, as his voice booms all around me.

"Ladies and gentlemen, let the Seventy-fourth Hunger Games begin!"

Sixty seconds. That's how long we're required to stand on our metal circles before the sound of a gong releases us. Step off before the minute is up, and land mines blow your legs off. Sixty seconds to take in the ring of tributes all equidistant from the Cornucopia, a giant golden horn shaped like a cone with a curved tail, the mouth of which is at least twenty feet high, spilling over with the things that will give us life here in the arena. Food, containers of water, weapons, medicine, garments, fire starters. Strewn around the Cornucopia are other supplies, their value decreasing the farther they are from the horn. For instance, only a few steps from my feet lies a three-foot square of plastic. Certainly it could be of some use in a downpour. But there in the mouth, I can see a tent pack that would protect from almost any sort of weather. If I had the guts to go in and fight for it against the other twenty-three tributes. Which I have been instructed not to do.

We're on a flat, open stretch of ground. A plain of hard-packed dirt. Behind the tributes across from me, I can see nothing, indicating either a steep downward slope or even a cliff. To my right lies a lake. To my left and back, sparse piney woods. This is where Haymitch would want me to go. Immediately.

I hear his instructions in my head. "Just clear out, put as much distance as you can between yourselves and the others, and find a source of water."

But it's tempting, so tempting, when I see the bounty waiting there before me. And I know that if I don't get it, someone else will. That the Career Tributes who survive the bloodbath will divide up most of these life-sustaining spoils. Something catches my eye. There, resting on a mound of blanket rolls, is a silver sheath of arrows and a bow, already strung, just waiting to be engaged. *That's mine,* I think. *It's meant for me.*

I'm fast. I can sprint faster than any of the girls in our school although a couple can beat me in distance races. But this forty-yard length, this is what I am built for. I know I can get it, I know I can reach it first, but then the question is how quickly can I get out of there? By the time I've scrambled up the packs and grabbed the weapons, others will have reached the horn, and one or two I might be able to pick off, but say there's a dozen, at that close range, they could take me down with the spears and the clubs. Or their own powerful fists.

Still, I won't be the only target. I'm betting many of the other tributes would pass up a smaller girl, even one who scored an eleven in training, to take out their more fierce adversaries.

Haymitch has never seen me run. Maybe if he had he'd tell me to go for it. Get the weapon. Since that's the very weapon that might be my salvation. And I only see one bow in that whole pile. I know the minute must be almost up and will have to decide what my strategy will be and I find myself positioning my feet to run, not away into the surrounding forests but toward the pile, toward the bow. When suddenly I notice Peeta, he's about five tributes to my right, quite a fair distance, still I can tell he's looking at me and I think he might be shaking his head. But the sun's in my eyes, and while I'm puzzling over it the gong rings out.

And I've missed it! I've missed my chance! Because those extra couple of seconds I've lost by not being ready are enough to change my mind about going in. My feet shuffle for a moment, confused at the direction my brain wants to take and then I lunge forward, scoop up the sheet of plastic and a loaf of bread. The pickings are so small and I'm so angry with Peeta for distracting me that I sprint in twenty yards to retrieve a bright orange backpack that could hold anything because I can't stand leaving with virtually nothing.

A boy, I think from District 9, reaches the pack at the same time I do and for a brief time we grapple for it and then he coughs, splattering my face with blood. I stagger back, repulsed by the warm, sticky spray. Then the boy slips to the ground. That's when I see the knife in his back. Already other tributes have reached the Cornucopia and are spreading out to attack. Yes, the girl from District 2, ten yards away, running toward me, one hand clutching a half-dozen knives. I've seen her throw in training. She never misses. And I'm her next target.

All the general fear I've been feeling condenses into an immediate fear of this girl, this predator who might kill me in seconds. Adrenaline shoots through me and I sling the pack over one shoulder and run full-speed for the woods. I can hear the blade whistling toward me and reflexively hike the pack up to protect my head. The blade lodges in the pack. Both straps on my shoulders now, I make for the trees. Somehow I know the girl will not pursue me. That she'll be drawn back into the Cornucopia before all the good stuff is gone. A grin crosses my face. *Thanks for the knife,* I think.

At the edge of the woods I turn for one instant to survey the field. About a dozen or so tributes are hacking away at one another at the horn. Several lie dead already on the ground. Those who have taken flight are disappearing into the trees or into the void opposite me. I continue running until the woods have hidden me from the other tributes then slow into a steady jog that I think I can maintain for a while. For the next few hours, I alternate between jogging and walking, putting as much distance as I can between myself and my competitors. I lost my bread during the struggle with the boy from District 9 but managed to stuff my plastic in my sleeve so as I walk I fold it neatly and tuck it into a pocket. I also free the knife — it's a fine one with a long sharp blade, serrated near the handle, which will make it handy for sawing through things — and slide it into my belt. I don't dare stop to examine the contents of the pack yet. I just keep moving, pausing only to check for pursuers.

I can go a long time. I know that from my days in the woods. But I will need water. That was Haymitch's second instruction, and since I sort of botched the first, I keep a sharp eye out for any sign of it. No luck.

The woods begin to evolve, and the pines are intermixed with a variety of trees, some I recognize, some completely foreign to me. At one point, I hear a noise and pull my knife, thinking I may have to defend myself, but I've only startled a rabbit. "Good to see you," I whisper. If there's one rabbit, there could be hundreds just waiting to be snared.

The ground slopes down. I don't particularly like this. Valleys make me feel trapped. I want to be high, like in the hills around District 12, where I can see my enemies approaching. But I have no choice but to keep going.

Funny though, I don't feel too bad. The days of gorging myself have paid off. I've got staying power even though I'm short on sleep. Being in the woods is rejuvenating. I'm glad for the solitude, even though it's an illusion, because I'm probably on-screen right now. Not consistently but off and on. There are so many deaths to show the first day that a tribute trekking through the woods isn't much to look at. But they'll show me enough to let people know I'm alive, uninjured and on the move. One of the heaviest days of betting is the opening, when the initial casualties come in. But that can't compare to what happens as the field shrinks to a handful of players.

It's late afternoon when I begin to hear the cannons. Each shot represents a dead tribute. The fighting must have finally stopped at the Cornucopia. They never collect the bloodbath bodies until the killers have dispersed. On the opening day, they don't even fire the cannons until the initial fighting's over because it's too hard to keep track of the fatalities. I allow myself to pause, panting, as I count the shots. One . . . two . . . three . . . on and on until they reach eleven. Eleven dead in all. Thirteen left to play. My fingernails scrape at the dried blood the boy from District 9 coughed into my face. He's gone, certainly. I wonder about Peeta. Has he lasted through the day? I'll know in a few hours. When they project the dead's images into the sky for the rest of us to see.

All of a sudden, I'm overwhelmed by the thought that Peeta may be already lost, bled white, collected, and in the process of being transported back to the Capitol to be cleaned up, redressed, and shipped in a simple wooden box back to District 12. No longer here. Heading home. I try hard to remember if I saw him once the action started. But the last image I can conjure up is Peeta shaking his head as the gong rang out.

Maybe it's better, if he's gone already. He had no confidence he could win. And I will not end up with the unpleasant task of killing him. Maybe it's better if he's out of this for good.

I slump down next to my pack, exhausted. I need to go through it anyway before night falls. See what I have to work with. As I unhook the straps, I can feel it's sturdily made although a rather unfortunate color. This orange will practically glow in the dark. I make a mental note to camouflage it first thing tomorrow.

I flip open the flap. What I want most, right at this moment, is water. Haymitch's directive to immediately find water was not arbitrary. I won't last long without it. For a few days, I'll be able to function with unpleasant symptoms of dehydration, but after that I'll deteriorate into helplessness and be dead in a week, tops. I carefully lay out the provisions. One thin black sleeping bag that reflects body heat. A pack of crackers. A pack of dried beef strips. A bottle of iodine. A box of wooden matches. A small coil of wire. A pair of sunglasses. And a half-gallon plastic bottle with a cap for carrying water that's bone dry.

No water. How hard would it have been for them to fill up the bottle? I become aware of the dryness in my throat and mouth, the cracks in my lips. I've been moving all day long. It's been hot and I've sweat a lot. I do this at home, but there are always streams to drink from, or snow to melt if it should come to it.

As I refill my pack I have an awful thought. The lake. The one I saw while I was waiting for the gong to sound. What if that's the only water source in the arena? That way they'll guarantee drawing us in to fight. The lake is a full day's journey from where I sit now, a much harder journey with nothing to drink. And then, even if I reach it, it's sure to be heavily guarded by some of the Career Tributes. I'm about to panic when I remember the rabbit I startled earlier today. It has to drink, too. I just have to find out where.

Twilight is closing in and I am ill at ease. The trees are too thin to offer much concealment. The layer of pine needles that muffles my footsteps also makes tracking animals harder when I need their trails to find water. And I'm still heading downhill, deeper and deeper into a valley that seems endless.

I'm hungry, too, but I don't dare break into my precious store of crackers and beef yet. Instead, I take my knife and go to work on a pine tree, cutting away the outer bark and scraping off a large handful of the softer inner bark. I slowly chew the stuff as I walk along. After a week of the finest food in the world, it's a little hard to choke down. But I've eaten plenty of pine in my life. I'll adjust quickly.

In another hour, it's clear I've got to find a place to camp. Night creatures are coming out. I can hear the occasional hoot or howl, my first clue that I'll be competing with natural predators for the rabbits. As to whether I'll be viewed as a source of food, it's too soon to tell. There could be any number of animals stalking me at this moment.

But right now, I decide to make my fellow tributes a priority. I'm sure many will continue hunting through the night. Those who fought it out at the Cornucopia will have food, an abundance of water from the lake, torches or flashlights, and weapons they're itching to use. I can only hope I've traveled far and fast enough to be out of range.

Before settling down, I take my wire and set two twitch-up snares in the brush. I know it's risky to be setting traps, but food will go so fast out here. And I can't set snares on the run. Still, I walk another five minutes before making camp.

I pick my tree carefully. A willow, not terribly tall but set in a clump of other willows, offering concealment in those long, flowing tresses. I climb up, sticking to the stronger branches close to the trunk, and find a sturdy fork for my bed. It takes some doing, but I arrange the sleeping bag in a relatively comfortable manner. I place my backpack in the foot of the bag, then slide in after it. As a precaution, I remove my belt, loop it all the way around the branch and my sleeping bag, and refasten it at my waist. Now if I roll over in my sleep, I won't go crashing to the ground. I'm small enough to tuck the top of the bag over my head, but I put on my hood as well. As night falls, the air is cooling quickly. Despite the risk I took in getting the backpack, I know now it was the right choice. This sleeping bag, radiating back and preserving my body heat, will be invaluable. I'm sure there are several other tributes whose biggest concern right now is how to stay warm whereas I may actually be able to get a few hours of sleep. If only I wasn't so thirsty . . .

Night has just come when I hear the anthem that proceeds the death recap. Through the branches I can see the seal of the Capitol, which appears to be floating in the sky. I'm actually viewing another screen, an enormous one that's transported by of one of their disappearing hovercraft. The anthem fades out and the sky goes dark for a moment. At home, we would be watching full coverage of each and every killing, but that's thought to give an unfair advantage to the living tributes. For instance, if I got my hands on the bow and shot someone, my secret would be revealed to all. No, here in the arena, all we see are the same photographs they showed when they televised our training scores. Simple head shots. But now instead of scores they post only district numbers. I take a deep breath as the faces of the eleven dead tributes begin and tick them off one by one on my fingers.

The first to appear is the girl from District 3. That means that the Career Tributes from 1 and 2 have all survived. No surprise there. Then the boy from 4. I didn't expect that one, usually all the Careers make it through the first day. The boy from District 5 . . . I guess the fox-faced girl made it. Both tributes from 6 and 7. The boy from 8. Both from 9. Yes, there's the boy who I fought for the backpack. I've run through my fingers, only one more dead tribute to go. Is it Peeta? No, there's the girl from District 10. That's it. The Capitol seal is back with a final musical flourish. Then darkness and the sounds of the forest resume.

I'm relieved Peeta's alive. I tell myself again that if I get killed, his winning will benefit my mother and Prim the most. This is what I tell myself to explain the conflicting emotions that arise when I think of Peeta. The gratitude that he gave me an edge by professing his love for me in the interview. The anger at his superiority on the roof. The dread that we may come face-to-face at any moment in this arena.

Eleven dead, but none from District 12. I try to work out who is left. Five Career Tributes. Foxface. Thresh and Rue. Rue . . . so she made it through the first day after all. I can't help feeling glad. That makes ten of us. The other three I'll figure out tomorrow. Now when it is dark, and I have traveled far, and I am nestled high in this tree, now I must try and rest.

I haven't really slept in two days, and then there's been

the long day's journey into the arena. Slowly, I allow my muscles to relax. My eyes to close. The last thing I think is it's lucky I don't snore. . . .

Snap! The sound of a breaking branch wakes me. How long have I been asleep? Four hours? Five? The tip of my nose is icy cold. *Snap! Snap!* What's going on? This is not the sound of a branch under someone's foot, but the sharp crack of one coming from a tree. *Snap! Snap!* I judge it to be several hundred yards to my right. Slowly, noiselessly, I turn myself in that direction. For a few minutes, there's nothing but blackness and some scuffling. Then I see a spark and a small fire begins to bloom. A pair of hands warms over flames, but I can't make out more than that.

I have to bite my lip not to scream every foul name I know at the fire starter. What are they thinking? A fire lit just at nightfall would have been one thing. Those who battled at the Cornucopia, with their superior strength and surplus of supplies, they couldn't possibly have been near enough to spot the flames then. But now, when they've probably been combing the woods for hours looking for victims. You might as well be waving a flag and shouting, "Come and get me!"

And here I am a stone's throw from the biggest idiot in the Games. Strapped in a tree. Not daring to flee since my general location has just been broadcast to any killer who cares. I mean, I know it's cold out here and not everybody has a sleeping bag. But then you grit your teeth and stick it out until dawn!

I lie smoldering in my bag for the next couple of hours,

really thinking that if I can get out of this tree, I won't have the least problem taking out my new neighbor. My instinct has been to flee, not fight. But obviously this person's a hazard. Stupid people are dangerous. And this one probably doesn't have much in the way of weapons while I've got this excellent knife.

The sky is still dark, but I can feel the first signs of dawn approaching. I'm beginning to think we — meaning the person whose death I'm now devising and I — we might actually have gone unnoticed. Then I hear it. Several pairs of feet breaking into a run. The fire starter must have dozed off. They're on her before she can escape. I know it's a girl now, I can tell by the pleading, the agonized scream that follows. Then there's laughter and congratulations from several voices. Someone cries out, "Twelve down and eleven to go!" which gets a round of appreciative hoots.

So they're fighting in a pack. I'm not really surprised. Often alliances are formed in the early stages of the Games. The strong band together to hunt down the weak then, when the tension becomes too great, begin to turn on one another. I don't have to wonder too hard who has made this alliance. It'll be the remaining Career Tributes from Districts 1, 2, and 4. Two boys and three girls. The ones who lunched together.

For a moment, I hear them checking the girl for supplies. I can tell by their comments they've found nothing good. I wonder if the victim is Rue but quickly dismiss the thought. She's much too bright to be building a fire like that.

"Better clear out so they can get the body before it starts

stinking." I'm almost certain that's the brutish boy from District 2. There are murmurs of assent and then, to my horror, I hear the pack heading toward me. They do not know I'm here. How could they? And I'm well concealed in the clump of trees. At least while the sun stays down. Then my black sleeping bag will turn from camouflage to trouble. If they just keep moving, they will pass me and be gone in a minute.

But the Careers stop in the clearing about ten yards from my tree. They have flashlights, torches. I can see an arm here, a boot there, through the breaks in the branches. I turn to stone, not even daring to breathe. Have they spotted me? No, not yet. I can tell from their words their minds are elsewhere.

"Shouldn't we have heard a cannon by now?"

"I'd say yes. Nothing to prevent them from going in immediately."

"Unless she isn't dead."

"She's dead. I stuck her myself."

"Then where's the cannon?"

"Someone should go back. Make sure the job's done."

"Yeah, we don't want to have to track her down twice."

"I said she's dead!"

An argument breaks out until one tribute silences the others. "We're wasting time! I'll go finish her and let's move on!"

I almost fall out of the tree. The voice belongs to Peeta.

Thank goodness, I had the foresight to belt myself in. I've rolled sideways off the fork and I'm facing the ground, held in place by the belt, one hand, and my feet straddling the pack inside my sleeping bag, braced against the trunk. There must have been some rustling when I tipped sideways, but the Careers have been too caught up in their own argument to catch it.

"Go on, then, Lover Boy," says the boy from District 2. "See for yourself."

I just get a glimpse of Peeta, lit by a torch, heading back to the girl by the fire. His face is swollen with bruises, there's a bloody bandage on one arm, and from the sound of his gait he's limping somewhat. I remember him shaking his head, telling me not to go into the fight for the supplies, when all along, all along he'd planned to throw himself into the thick of things. Just the opposite of what Haymitch had told him to do.

Okay, I can stomach that. Seeing all those supplies was tempting. But this . . . this other thing. This teaming up with the Career wolf pack to hunt down the rest of us. No one from District 12 would think of doing such a thing! Career tributes are overly vicious, arrogant, better fed, but only because they're the Capitol's lapdogs.

Universally, solidly hated by all but those from their own districts. I can imagine the things they're saying about him back home now. And Peeta had the gall to talk to me about disgrace?

Obviously, the noble boy on the rooftop was playing just one more game with me. But this will be his last. I will eagerly watch the night skies for signs of his death, if I don't kill him first myself.

The Career tributes are silent until he gets out of earshot, then use hushed voices.

"Why don't we just kill him now and get it over with?"

"Let him tag along. What's the harm? And he's handy with that knife."

Is he? That's news. What a lot of interesting things I'm learning about my friend Peeta today.

"Besides, he's our best chance of finding her."

It takes me a moment to register that the "her" they're referring to is me.

"Why? You think she bought into that sappy romance stuff?"

"She might have. Seemed pretty simpleminded to me. Every time I think about her spinning around in that dress, I want to puke."

"Wish we knew how she got that eleven."

"Bet you Lover Boy knows."

The sound of Peeta returning silences them.

"Was she dead?" asks the boy from District 2.

"No. But she is now," says Peeta. Just then, the cannon fires. "Ready to move on?"

The Career pack sets off at a run just as dawn begins to break, and birdsong fills the air. I remain in my awkward position, muscles trembling with exertion for a while longer, then hoist myself back onto my branch. I need to get down, to get going, but for a moment I lie there, digesting what I've heard. Not only is Peeta with the Careers, he's helping them find me. The simpleminded girl who has to be taken seriously because of her eleven. Because she can use a bow and arrow. Which Peeta knows better than anyone.

But he hasn't told them yet. Is he saving that information because he knows it's all that keeps him alive? Is he still pretending to love me for the audience? What is going on in his head?

Suddenly, the birds fall silent. Then one gives a high-pitched warning call. A single note. Just like the one Gale and I heard when the redheaded Avox girl was caught. High above the dying campfire a hovercraft materializes. A set of large metal teeth drops down. Slowly, gently, the dead trib-ute girl is lifted into the hovercraft. Then it vanishes. The birds resume their song.

"Move," I whisper to myself. I wriggle out of my sleeping bag, roll it up, and place it in the pack. I take a deep breath. While I've been concealed by darkness and the sleeping bag and the willow branches, it has probably been difficult for the cameras to get a good shot of me. I know they must be tracking me now though. The minute I hit the ground, I'm guaranteed a close-up.

The audience will have been beside themselves, know-ing I was in the tree, that I overheard the Careers talking, that I discovered Peeta was with them. Until I work out exactly how I want to play that, I'd better at least act on top of things. Not perplexed. Certainly not confused or frightened.

No, I need to look one step ahead of the game.

So as I slide out of the foliage and into the dawn light, I pause a second, giving the cameras time to lock on me. Then I cock my head slightly to the side and give a knowing smile. There! Let them figure out what that means!

I'm about to take off when I think of my snares. Maybe it's imprudent to check them with the others so close. But I have to. Too many years of hunting, I guess. And the lure of possible meat. I'm rewarded with one fine rabbit. In no time, I've cleaned and gutted the animal, leaving the head, feet, tail, skin, and innards, under a pile of leaves. I'm wishing for a fire — eating raw rabbit can give you rabbit fever, a lesson I learned the hard way — when I think of the dead tribute. I hurry back to her camp. Sure enough, the coals of her dying fire are still hot. I cut up the rabbit, fashion a spit out of branches, and set it over the coals.

I'm glad for the cameras now. I want sponsors to see I can hunt, that I'm a good bet because I won't be lured into traps as easily as the others will by hunger. While the rabbit cooks, I grind up part of a charred branch and set about camouflaging my orange pack. The black tones it down, but I feel a layer of mud would definitely help. Of course, to have mud, I'd need water. . . .

I pull on my gear, grab my spit, kick some dirt over the coals, and take off in the opposite direction the Careers went. I eat half the rabbit as I go, then wrap up the left-overs in my plastic for later. The meat stops the grumbling in my stomach but does little to quench my thirst. Water is my top priority now.

As I hike along, I feel certain I'm still holding the screen in the Capitol, so I'm careful to continue to hide my emotions. But what a good time Claudius Templesmith must be having with his guest commentators, dissecting Peeta's behavior, my reaction. What to make of it all? Has Peeta revealed his true colors? How does this affect the betting odds? Will we lose sponsors? Do we even *have* sponsors? Yes, I feel certain we do, or at least did.

Certainly Peeta has thrown a wrench into our star-crossed lover dynamic. Or has he? Maybe, since he hasn't spoken much about me, we can still get some mileage out of it. Maybe people will think it's something we plotted together if I seem like it amuses me now.

The sun rises in the sky and even through the canopy it seems overly bright. I coat my lips in some grease from the rabbit and try to keep from panting, but it's no use. It's only been a day and I'm dehydrating fast. I try and think of everything I know about finding water. It runs downhill, so, in fact, continuing down into this valley isn't a bad thing. If I could just locate a game trail or spot a particularly green patch of vegetation, these might help me along. But nothing seems to change. There's just the slight gradual slope, the birds, the sameness to the trees.

As the day wears on, I know I'm headed for trouble. What little urine I've been able to pass is a dark brown, my head is aching, and there's a dry patch on my tongue that refuses to moisten. The sun hurts my eyes so I dig out my sunglasses, but when I put them on they do something funny to my vision, so I just stuff them back in my pack.

It's late afternoon when I think I've found help. I spot a cluster of berry bushes and hurry to strip the fruit, to suck the sweet juices from the skins. But just as I'm holding them to my lips, I get a hard look at them. What I thought were blueberries have a slightly different shape, and when I break one open the insides are bloodred. I don't recognize these berries, perhaps they are edible, but I'm guessing this is some evil trick on the part of the Gamemakers. Even the plant instructor in the Training Center made a point of telling us to avoid berries unless you were 100 percent sure they weren't toxic. Something I already knew, but I'm so thirsty it takes her reminder to give me the strength to fling them away.

Fatigue is beginning to settle on me, but it's not the usual tiredness that follows a long hike. I have to stop and rest frequently, although I know the only cure for what ails me requires continued searching. I try a new tactic — climbing a tree as high as I dare in my shaky state — to look for any signs of water. But as far as I can see in any direction, there's the same unrelenting stretch of forest.

Determined to go on until nightfall, I walk until I'm stumbling over my own feet.

Exhausted, I haul myself up into a tree and belt myself in. I've no appetite, but I suck on a rabbit bone just to give my mouth something to do. Night falls, the anthem plays, and high in the sky I see the picture of the girl, who was apparently from District 8. The one Peeta went back to finish off.

My fear of the Career pack is minor compared to my burning thirst. Besides, they were heading away from me and by now they, too, will have to rest. With the scarcity of water, they may even have had to return to the lake for refills.

Maybe, that is the only course for me as well.

Morning brings distress. My heads throbs with every beat of my heart. Simple movements send stabs of pain through my joints. I fall, rather than jump from the tree. It takes several minutes for me to assemble my gear. Somewhere inside me, I know this is wrong. I should be acting with more caution, moving with more urgency. But my mind seems foggy and forming a plan is hard. I lean back against the trunk of my tree, one finger gingerly stroking the sandpaper surface of my tongue, as I assess my options. How can I get water?

Return to the lake. No good. I'd never make it.

Hope for rain. There's not a cloud in the sky.

Keep looking. Yes, this is my only chance. But then, another thought hits me, and the surge of anger that follows brings me to me senses.

Haymitch! He could send me water! Press a button and have it delivered to me in a silver parachute in minutes. I know I must have sponsors, at least one or two who could afford a pint of liquid for me. Yes, it's pricey, but these people, they're made of money. And they'll be betting on me as well. Perhaps Haymitch doesn't realize how deep my need is.

I say in a voice as loud as I dare. "Water." I wait, hopefully, for a parachute to descend from the sky. But nothing is forthcoming.

Something is wrong. Am I deluded about having sponsors? Or has Peeta's behavior made them all hang back? No, I don't believe it. There's someone out there who wants to buy me water only Haymitch is refusing to let it go through. As my mentor, he gets to control the flow of gifts from the sponsors. I know he hates me. He's made that clear enough. But enough to let me die? From this? He can't do that, can he? If a mentor mistreats his tributes, he'll be held accountable by the viewers, by the people back in District 12. Even Haymitch wouldn't risk that, would he? Say what you will about my fellow traders in the Hob, but I don't think they'd welcome him back there if he let me die this way. And then where would he get his liquor? So . . . what? Is he trying to make me suffer for defying him? Is he directing all the sponsors toward Peeta? Is he just too drunk to even notice what's going on at the moment? Somehow I don't believe that and I don't believe he's trying to kill me off by neglect, either. He has, in fact, in his own unpleasant way, genuinely been trying to prepare me for this. Then what is going on?

I bury my face in my hands. There's no danger of tears now, I couldn't produce one to save my life. What is

Haymitch doing? Despite my anger, hatred, and suspicions, a small voice in the back of my head whispers an answer.

Maybe he's sending you a message, it says. A message. Saying what? Then I know. There's only one good reason Haymitch could be withholding water from me. Because he knows I've almost found it.

I grit my teeth and pull myself to my feet. My backpack seems to have tripled in weight. I find a broken branch that will do for a walking stick and I start off. The sun's beating down, even more searing than the first two days. I feel like an old piece of leather, drying and cracking in the heat. Every step is an effort, but I refuse to stop. I refuse to sit down. If I sit, there's a good chance I won't be able to get up again, that I won't even remember my task.

What easy prey I am! Any tribute, even tiny Rue, could take me right now, merely shove me over and kill me with my own knife, and I'd have little strength to resist. But if anyone is in my part of the woods, they ignore me. The truth is, I feel a million miles from another living soul.

Not alone though. No, they've surely got a camera tracking me now. I think back to the years of watching tributes starve, freeze, bleed, and dehydrate to death. Unless there's a really good fight going on somewhere, I'm being featured.

My thoughts turn to Prim. It's likely she won't be watching me live, but they'll show updates at the school during lunch. For her sake, I try to look as least desperate as I can.

But by afternoon, I know the end is coming. My legs are shaking and my heart is too quick. I keep forgetting exactly what I'm doing. I've stumbled repeatedly and managed to regain my feet, but when the stick slides out from under me, I finally tumble to the ground unable to get up. I let my eyes close.

I have misjudged Haymitch. He has no intention of helping me at all.

This is all right, I think. *This is not so bad here.* The air is less hot, signifying evening's approach. There's a slight, sweet scent that reminds me of lilies. My fingers stroke the smooth ground, sliding easily across the top. *This is an okay place to die,* I think.

My fingertips make small swirling patterns in the cool, slippery earth. *I love mud,* I think. How many times I've tracked game with the help of its soft, readable surface. Good for bee stings, too. Mud. Mud. Mud! My eyes fly open and I dig my fingers into the earth. It is mud! My nose lifts in the air. And those are lilies! Pond lilies!

I crawl now, through the mud, dragging myself toward the scent. Five yards from where I fell, I crawl through a tangle of plants into a pond. Floating on the top, yellow flowers in bloom, are my beautiful lilies.

It's all I can do not to plunge my face into the water and gulp down as much as I can hold. But I have just enough sense left to abstain. With trembling hands, I get out my flask and fill it with water. I add what I remember to be the right number of drops of iodine for purifying it. The half an hour of waiting is agony, but I do it. At least,

I think it's a half an hour, but it's certainly as long as I can stand.

Slowly, easy now, I tell myself. I take one swallow and make myself wait. Then another. Over the next couple of hours, I drink the entire half gallon. Then a second. I prepare another before I retire to a tree where I continue sipping, eating rabbit, and even indulge in one of my precious crackers. By the time the anthem plays, I feel remarkably better. There are no faces tonight, no tributes died today. Tomorrow I'll stay here, resting, camouflaging my backpack with mud, catching some of those little fish I saw as I sipped, digging up the roots of the pond lilies to make a nice meal. I snuggle down in my sleeping bag, hanging on to my water bottle for dear life, which, of course, it is.

A few hours later, the stampede of feet shakes me from slumber. I look around in bewilderment. It's not yet dawn, but my stinging eyes can see it.

It would be hard to miss the wall of fire descending on me.

My first impulse is to scramble from the tree, but I'm belted in. Somehow my fumbling fingers release the buckle and I fall to the ground in a heap, still snarled in my sleeping bag. There's no time for any kind of packing. Fortunately, my backpack and water bottle are already in the bag. I shove in the belt, hoist the bag over my shoulder, and flee.

The world has transformed to flame and smoke. Burning branches crack from trees and fall in showers of sparks at my feet. All I can do is follow the others, the rabbits and deer, and I even spot a wild dog pack shooting through the woods. I trust their sense of direction because their instincts are sharper than mine. But they are much faster, flying through the underbrush so gracefully as my boots catch on roots and fallen tree limbs, that there's no way I can keep apace with them.

The heat is horrible, but worse than the heat is the smoke, which threatens to suffocate me at any moment. I pull the top of my shirt up over my nose, grateful to find it soaked in sweat, and it offers a thin veil of protection. And I run, choking, my bag banging against my back, my face cut with branches that materialize from the gray haze without warning, because I know I am supposed to run.

This was no tribute's campfire gone out of control, no accidental occurrence. The flames that bear down on me have an unnatural height, a uniformity that marks them as human-made, machine-made, Gamemaker-made. Things have been too quiet today. No deaths, perhaps no fights at all. The audience in the Capitol will be getting bored, claiming that these Games are verging on dullness. This is the one thing the Games must not do.

It's not hard to follow the Gamemakers' motivation. There is the Career pack and then there are the rest of us, probably spread far and thin across the arena. This fire is designed to flush us out, to drive us together. It may not be the most original device I've seen, but it's very, very effective.

I hurdle over a burning log. Not high enough. The tail end of my jacket catches on fire and I have to stop to rip it from my body and stamp out the flames. But I don't dare leave the jacket, scorched and smoldering as it is, I take the risk of shoving it in my sleeping bag, hoping the lack of air will quell what I haven't extinguished. This is all I have, what I carry on my back, and it's little enough to sur-vive with.

In a matter of minutes, my throat and nose are burning. The coughing begins soon after and my lungs begin to feel as if they are actually being cooked. Discomfort turns to distress until each breath sends a searing pain through my chest. I manage to take cover under a stone outcropping just as the vomiting begins, and I lose my meager supper and whatever water has remained in my stomach. Crouching on my hands and knees, I retch until there's nothing left to come up.

I know I need to keep moving, but I'm trembling and light-headed now, gasping for air. I allow myself about a spoonful of water to rinse my mouth and spit then take a few swallows from my bottle. *You get one minute,* I tell myself. *One minute to rest.* I take the time to reorder my supplies, wad up the sleeping bag, and messily stuff everything into the backpack. My minute's up. I know it's time to move on, but the smoke has clouded my thoughts. The swift-footed animals that were my compass have left me behind. I know I haven't been in this part of the woods before, there were no sizable rocks like the one I'm sheltering against on my earlier travels. Where are the Gamemakers driving me? Back to the lake? To a whole new terrain filled with new dangers? I had just found a few hours of peace at the pond when this attack began. Would there be any way I could travel parallel to the fire and work my way back there, to a source of water at least? The wall of fire must have an end and it won't burn indefinitely. Not because the Gamemakers couldn't keep it fueled but because, again, that would invite accusations of boredom from the audience. If I could get back behind the fire line, I could avoid meeting up with the Careers. I've just decided to try and loop back around, although it will require miles of travel away from the inferno and then a very circuitous route back, when the first fireball blasts into the rock about two feet from my head. I spring out from under my ledge, energized by renewed fear.

The game has taken a twist. The fire was just to get us moving, now the audience will get to see some real fun. When I hear the next hiss, I flatten on the ground, not taking time to look. The fireball hits a tree off to my left, engulfing it in flames. To remain still is death. I'm barely on my feet before the third ball hits the ground where I was lying, sending a pillar of fire up behind me. Time loses meaning now as I frantically try to dodge the attacks. I can't see where they're being launched from, but it's not a hovercraft. The angles are not extreme enough. Probably this whole segment of the woods has been armed with precision launchers that are concealed in trees or rocks. Somewhere, in a cool and spotless room, a Gamemaker sits at a set of controls, fingers on the triggers that could end my life in a second. All that is needed is a direct hit.

Whatever vague plan I had conceived regarding returning to my pond is wiped from my mind as I zigzag and dive and leap to avoid the fireballs. Each one is only the size of an apple, but packs tremendous power on contact. Every sense I have goes into overdrive as the need to survive takes over. There's no time to judge if a move is the correct one. When there's a hiss, I act or die.

Something keeps me moving forward, though. A lifetime of watching the Hunger Games lets me know that certain areas of the arena are rigged for certain attacks. And that if I can just get away from this section, I might be able to move out of reach of the launchers. I might also then fall straight into a pit of vipers, but I can't worry about that now.

How long I scramble along dodging the fireballs I can't say, but the attacks finally begin to abate. Which is good, because I'm retching again. This time it's an acidic substance that scalds my throat and makes its way into my nose as well. I'm forced to stop as my body convulses, trying desperately to rid itself of the poisons I've been sucking in during the attack. I wait for the next hiss, the next signal to bolt. It doesn't come. The force of the retching has squeezed tears out of my stinging eyes. My clothes are drenched in sweat. Somehow, through the smoke and vomit, I pick up the scent of singed hair. My hand fumbles to my braid and finds a fireball has seared off at least six inches of it. Strands of blackened hair crumble in my fingers. I stare at them, fascinated by the transformation, when the hissing registers.

My muscles react, only not fast enough this time. The fireball crashes into the ground at my side, but not before it skids across my right calf. Seeing my pants leg on fire sends me over the edge. I twist and scuttle backward on my hands and feet, shrieking, trying to remove myself from the horror. When I finally regain enough sense, I roll the leg back and forth on the ground, which stifles the worst of it. But then, without thinking, I rip away the remaining fabric with my bare hands.

I sit on the ground, a few yards from the blaze set off by the fireball. My calf is screaming, my hands covered in red welts. I'm shaking too hard to move. If the Gamemakers want to finish me off, now is the time.

I hear Cinna's voice, carrying images of rich fabric and

sparkling gems. "Katniss, the girl who was on fire." What a good laugh the Gamemakers must be having over that one. Perhaps, Cinna's beautiful costumes have even brought on this particular torture for me. I know he couldn't have foreseen this, must be hurting for me because, in fact, I believe he cares about me. But all in all, maybe showing up stark naked in that chariot would have been safer for me.

The attack is now over. The Gamemakers don't want me dead. Not yet anyway. Everyone knows they could destroy us all within seconds of the opening gong. The real sport of the Hunger Games is watching the tributes kill one another. Every so often, they do kill a tribute just to remind the players they can. But mostly, they manipulate us into confronting one another face-to-face. Which means, if I am no longer being fired at, there is at least one other tribute close at hand.

I would drag myself into a tree and take cover now if I could, but the smoke is still thick enough to kill me. I make myself stand and begin to limp away from the wall of flames that lights up the sky. It does not seem to be pursuing me any longer, except with its stinking black clouds.

Another light, daylight, begins to softly emerge. Swirls of smoke catch the sunbeams. My visibility is poor. I can see maybe fifteen yards in any direction. A tribute could easily be concealed from me here. I should draw my knife as a precaution, but I doubt my ability to hold it for long. The pain in my hands can in no way compete with that in my calf. I hate burns, have always hated them, even a small one gotten from pulling a pan of bread from the oven. It is the worst kind of pain to me, but I have never experienced anything like this.

I'm so weary I don't even notice I'm in the pool until I'm ankle-deep. It's spring-fed, bubbling up out of a crevice in some rocks, and blissfully cool. I plunge my hands into the shallow water and feel instant relief. Isn't that what my mother always says? The first treatment for a burn is cold water? That it draws out the heat? But she means minor burns. Probably she'd recommend it for my hands. But what of my calf? Although I have not yet had the courage to examine it, I'm guessing that it's an injury in a whole different class.

I lie on my stomach at the edge of the pool for a while, dangling my hands in the water, examining the little flames on my fingernails that are beginning to chip off. Good. I've had enough fire for a lifetime.

I bathe the blood and ash from my face. I try to recall all I know about burns. They are common injuries in the Seam where we cook and heat our homes with coal. Then there are the mine accidents. . . . A family once brought in an unconscious young man pleading with my mother to help him. The district doctor who's responsible for treating the miners had written him off, told the family to take him home to die. But they wouldn't accept this. He lay on our kitchen table, senseless to the world. I got a glimpse of the wound on his thigh, gaping, charred flesh, burned clear down to the bone, before I ran from the house. I went to the woods and hunted the entire day, haunted by the gruesome leg, memories of my father's death. What's funny was, Prim, who's scared of her own shadow, stayed and helped. My mother says healers are born, not made. They did their best, but the man died, just like the doctor said he would.

My leg is in need of attention, but I still can't look at it. What if it's as bad as the man's and I can see my bone? Then I remember my mother saying that if a burn's severe, the victim might not even feel pain because the nerves would be destroyed. Encouraged by this, I sit up and swing my leg in front of me.

I almost faint at the sight of my calf. The flesh is a brilliant red covered with blisters. I force myself to take deep, slow breaths, feeling quite certain the cameras are on my face. I can't show weakness at this injury. Not if I want help. Pity does not get you aid. Admiration at your refusal to give in does. I cut the remains of the pant leg off at the knee and examine the injury more closely. The burned area is about the size of my hand. None of the skin is blackened. I think it's not too bad to soak. Gingerly I stretch out my leg into the pool, propping the heel of my boot on a rock so the leather doesn't get too sodden, and sigh, because this does offer some relief. I know there are herbs, if I could find them, that would speed the healing, but I can't quite call them to mind. Water and time will probably be all I have to work with.

Should I be moving on? The smoke is slowly clearing but still too heavy to be healthy. If I do continue away from the fire, won't I be walking straight into the weapons of the Careers? Besides, every time I lift my leg from the water, the pain rebounds so intensely I have to slide it back in. My hands are slightly less demanding. They can handle small breaks from the pool. So I slowly put my gear back in order. First I fill my bottle with the pool water, treat it, and when enough time has passed, begin to rehydrate my body. After a time, I force myself to nibble on a cracker, which helps settle my stomach. I roll up my sleeping bag. Except for a few black marks, it's relatively unscathed. My jacket's another matter. Stinking and scorched, at least a foot of the back beyond repair. I cut off the damaged area leaving me with a garment that comes just to the bottom of my ribs. But the hood's intact and it's far better than nothing.

Despite the pain, drowsiness begins to take over. I'd take to a tree and try to rest, except I'd be too easy to spot. Besides, abandoning my pool seems impossible. I neatly arrange my supplies, even settle my pack on my shoulders, but I can't seem to leave. I spot some water plants with edible roots and make a small meal with my last piece of rabbit. Sip water. Watch the sun make its slow arc across the sky. Where would I go anyway that is any safer than here? I lean back on my pack, overcome by drowsiness. *If the Careers want me, let them find me,* I think before drifting into a stupor. *Let them find me.*

And find me, they do. It's lucky I'm ready to move on because when I hear the feet, I have less than a minute head start. Evening has begun to fall. The moment I awake, I'm up and running, splashing across the pool, flying into the underbrush. My leg slows me down, but I sense my pursuers are not as speedy as they were before the fire, either. I hear their coughs, their raspy voices calling to one another.

Still, they are closing in, just like a pack of wild dogs, and so I do what I have done my whole life in such circumstances. I pick a high tree and begin to climb. If running hurt, climbing is agonizing because it requires not only exertion but direct contact of my hands on the tree bark. I'm fast, though, and by the time they've reached the base of my trunk, I'm twenty feet up. For a moment, we stop and survey one another. I hope they can't hear the pounding of my heart.

This could be it, I think. What chance do I have against them? All six are there, the five Careers and Peeta, and my only consolation is they're pretty beat-up, too. Even so, look at their weapons. Look at their faces, grinning and snarling at me, a sure kill above them. It seems pretty hopeless. But then something else registers. They're bigger and stronger than I am, no doubt, but they're also heavier. There's a reason it's me and not Gale who ventures up to pluck the highest fruit, or rob the most remote bird nests. I must weigh at least fifty or sixty pounds less than the smallest Career.

Now I smile. "How's everything with you?" I call down cheerfully.

This takes them aback, but I know the crowd will love it.

"Well enough," says the boy from District 2. "Yourself?"

"It's been a bit warm for my taste," I say. I can almost

hear the laughter from the Capitol. "The air's better up here. Why don't you come on up?"

"Think I will," says the same boy.

"Here, take this, Cato," says the girl from District 1, and she offers him the silver bow and sheath of arrows. My bow! My arrows! Just the sight of them makes me so angry I want to scream, at myself, at that traitor Peeta for distracting me from having them. I try to make eye contact with him now, but he seems to be intentionally avoiding my gaze as he polishes his knife with the edge of his shirt.

"No," says Cato, pushing away the bow. "I'll do better with my sword." I can see the weapon, a short, heavy blade at his belt.

I give Cato time to hoist himself into the tree before I begin to climb again. Gale always says I remind him of a squirrel the way I can scurry up even the slenderest limbs. Part of it's my weight, but part of it's practice. You have to know where to place your hands and feet. I'm another thirty feet in the air when I hear the crack and look down to see Cato flailing as he and a branch go down. He hits the ground hard and I'm hoping he possibly broke his neck when he gets back to his feet, swearing like a fiend.

The girl with the arrows, Glimmer I hear someone call her — ugh, the names the people in District 1 give their children are so ridiculous — anyway Glimmer scales the tree until the branches begin to crack under her feet and then has the good sense to stop. I'm at least eighty feet high now. She tries to shoot me and it's immediately evident that she's incompetent with a bow. One of the arrows gets lodged in the tree near me though and I'm able to seize it. I wave it teasingly above her head, as if this was the sole purpose of retrieving it, when actually I mean to use it if I ever get the chance. I could kill them, every one of them, if those silver weapons were in my hands.

The Careers regroup on the ground and I can hear them growling conspiratorially among themselves, furious I have made them look foolish. But twilight has arrived and their window of attack on me is closing. Finally, I hear Peeta say harshly, "Oh, let her stay up there. It's not like she's going anywhere. We'll deal with her in the morning."

Well, he's right about one thing. I'm going nowhere. All the relief from the pool water has gone, leaving me to feel the full potency of my burns. I scoot down to a fork in the tree and clumsily prepare for bed. Put on my jacket. Lay out my sleeping bed. Belt myself in and try to keep from moaning. The heat of the bag's too much for my leg. I cut a slash in the fabric and hang my calf out in the open air. I drizzle water on the wound, my hands.

All my bravado is gone. I'm weak from pain and hunger but can't bring myself to eat. Even if I can last the night, what will the morning bring? I stare into the foliage trying to will myself to rest, but the burns forbid it. Birds are settling down for the night, singing lullabies to their young. Night creatures emerge. An owl hoots. The faint scent of a skunk cuts through the smoke. The eyes of some animal peer at me from the neighboring tree — a possum maybe — catching the firelight from the Careers' torches. Suddenly, I'm up on one elbow. Those are no possum's eyes, I know their glassy reflection too well. In fact, those are not animal eyes at all. In the last dim rays of light, I make her out, watching me silently from between the branches.

Rue.

How long has she been here? The whole time probably. Still and unobserved as the action unfolded beneath her. Perhaps she headed up her tree shortly before I did, hearing the pack was so close.

For a while we hold each other's gaze. Then, without even rustling a leaf, her little hand slides into the open and points to something above my head.

My eyes follow the line of her finger up into the foliage above me. At first, I have no idea what she's pointing to, but then, about fifteen feet up, I make out the vague shape in the dimming light. But of . . . of what? Some sort of animal? It looks about the size of a raccoon, but it hangs from the bottom of a branch, swaying ever so slightly. There's something else. Among the familiar evening sounds of the woods, my ears register a low hum. Then I know. It's a wasp nest.

Fear shoots through me, but I have enough sense to keep still. After all, I don't know what kind of wasp lives there. It could be the ordinary leave-us-alone-and-we'll-leave-you-alone type. But these are the Hunger Games, and ordinary isn't the norm. More likely they will be one of the Capitol's muttations, tracker jackers. Like the jabberjays, these killer wasps were spawned in a lab and strategically placed, like land mines, around the districts during the war. Larger than regular wasps, they have a distinctive solid gold body and a sting that raises a lump the size of a plum on contact. Most people can't tolerate more than a few stings. Some die at once. If you live, the hallucinations brought on by the venom have actually driven people to madness. And there's another thing, these wasps will hunt down anyone who disturbs their nest and attempt to kill them. That's where the tracker part of the name comes from.

After the war, the Capitol destroyed all the nests surrounding their city, but the ones near the districts were left untouched. Another reminder of our weakness, I suppose, just like the Hunger Games. Another reason to keep inside the fence of District 12. When Gale and I come across a tracker jacker nest, we immediately head in the opposite direction.

So is that what hangs above me? I look back to Rue for help, but she's melted into her tree.

Given my circumstances, I guess it doesn't matter what type of wasp nest it is. I'm wounded and trapped. Darkness has given me a brief reprieve, but by the time the sun rises, the Careers will have formulated a plan to kill me. There's no way they could do otherwise after I've made them look so stupid. That nest may be the sole option I have left. If I can drop it down on them, I may be able to escape. But I'll risk my life in the process.

Of course, I'll never be able to get in close enough to the actual nest to cut it free. I'll have to saw off the branch at the trunk and send the whole thing down. The serrated portion of my knife should be able to manage that. But can my hands? And will the vibration from the sawing raise the swarm? And what if the Careers figure out what I'm doing and move their camp? That would defeat the whole purpose.

I realize that the best chance I'll have to do the sawing without drawing notice will be during the anthem. That could begin any time. I drag myself out of my bag, make sure my knife is secured in my belt, and begin to make my way up the tree. This in itself is dangerous since the branches are becoming precariously thin even for me, but I persevere. When I reach the limb that supports the nest, the humming becomes more distinctive. But it's still oddly subdued if these are tracker jackers. *It's the smoke,* I think. *It's sedated them.* This was the one defense the rebels found to battle the wasps.

The seal of the Capitol shines above me and the anthem blares out. *It's now or never,* I think, and begin to saw. Blisters burst on my right hand as I awkwardly drag the knife back and forth. Once I've got a groove, the work requires less effort but is almost more than I can handle. I grit my teeth and saw away, occasionally glancing at the sky to register that there were no deaths today. That's all right. The audience will be sated seeing me injured and treed and the pack below me. But the anthem's running out and I'm only three quarters of the way through the wood when the music ends, the sky goes dark, and I'm forced to stop.

Now what? I could probably finish off the job by sense of feel but that may not be the smartest plan. If the wasps are too groggy, if the nest catches on its way down, if I try to escape, this could all be a deadly waste of time. Better, I think, to sneak up here at dawn and send the nest into my enemies.

In the faint light of the Careers' torches, I inch back down to my fork to find the best surprise I've ever had. Sitting on my sleeping bag is a small plastic pot attached to a silver parachute. My first gift from a sponsor! Haymitch must have had it sent in during the anthem. The pot easily fits in the palm of my hand. What can it be? Not food surely. I unscrew the lid and I know by the scent that it's medicine. Cautiously, I probe the surface of the ointment. The throbbing in my fingertip vanishes.

"Oh, Haymitch," I whisper. "Thank you." He has not abandoned me. Not left me to fend entirely for myself. The cost of this medicine must be astronomical. Probably not one but many sponsors have contributed to buy this one tiny pot. To me, it is priceless.

I dip two fingers in the jar and gently spread the balm over my calf. The effect is almost magical, erasing the pain on contact, leaving a pleasant cooling sensation behind. This is no herbal concoction that my mother grinds up out of woodland plants, it's high-tech medicine brewed up in the Capitol's labs. When my calf is treated, I rub a thin layer into my hands. After wrapping the pot in the parachute, I nestle it safely away in my pack. Now that the pain has eased, it's all I can do to reposition myself in my bag before I plunge into sleep.

A bird perched just a few feet from me alerts me that a new day is dawning. In the gray morning light, I examine my hands. The medicine has transformed all the angry red patches to a soft baby-skin pink. My leg still feels inflamed, but that burn was far deeper. I apply another coat of medicine and quietly pack up my gear. Whatever happens, I'm going to have to move and move fast. I also make myself eat a cracker and a strip of beef and drink a few cups of water.

Almost nothing stayed in my stomach yesterday, and I'm already starting to feel the effects of hunger.

Below me, I can see the Career pack and Peeta asleep on the ground. By her position, leaning up against the trunk of the tree, I'd guess Glimmer was supposed to be on guard, but fatigue overcame her.

My eyes squint as they try to penetrate the tree next to me, but I can't make out Rue. Since she tipped me off, it only seems fair to warn her. Besides, if I'm going to die today, it's Rue I want to win. Even if it means a little extra food for my family, the idea of Peeta being crowned victor is unbearable.

I call Rue's name in a hushed whisper and the eyes appear, wide and alert, at once. She points up to the nest again. I hold up my knife and make a sawing motion. She nods and disappears. There's a rustling in a nearby tree. Then the same noise again a bit farther off. I realize she's leaping from tree to tree. It's all I can do not to laugh out loud. Is this what she showed the Gamemakers? I imagine her flying around the training equipment never touching the floor. She should have gotten at least a ten.

Rosy streaks are breaking through in the east. I can't afford to wait any longer. Compared to the agony of last night's climb, this one is a cinch. At the tree limb that holds the nest, I position the knife in the groove and I'm about to draw the teeth across the wood when I see something moving. There, on the nest. The bright gold gleam of a tracker jacker lazily making its way across the papery gray surface. No question, it's acting a little subdued, but the wasp is up and moving and that means the others will be out soon as well. Sweat breaks out on the palms of my hands, beading up through the ointment, and I do my best to pat them dry on my shirt. If I don't get through this branch in a matter of seconds, the entire swarm could emerge and attack me.

There's no sense in putting it off. I take a deep breath, grip the knife handle and bear down as hard as I can. *Back, forth, back, forth!* The tracker jackers begin to buzz and I hear them coming out. *Back, forth, back, forth!* A stabbing pain shoots through my knee and I know one has found me and the others will be honing in. *Back, forth, back, forth.* And just as the knife cuts through, I shove the end of the branch as far away from me as I can. It crashes down through the lower branches, snagging temporarily on a few but then twisting free until it smashes with a thud on the ground. The nest bursts open like an egg, and a furious swarm of tracker jackers takes to the air.

I feel a second sting on the cheek, a third on my neck, and their venom almost immediately makes me woozy. I cling to the tree with one arm while I rip the barbed stingers out of my flesh. Fortunately, only these three tracker jackers had identified me before the nest went down. The rest of the insects have targeted their enemies on the ground.

It's mayhem. The Careers have woken to a full-scale tracker jacker attack. Peeta and a few others have the sense to drop everything and bolt. I can hear cries of "To the lake! To the lake!" and know they hope to evade the wasps by taking to the water. It must be close if they think they can outdistance the furious insects. Glimmer and another girl, the one from District 4, are not so lucky. They receive multiple stings before they're even out of my view. Glimmer appears to go completely mad, shrieking and trying to bat the wasps off with her bow, which is pointless. She calls to the others for help but, of course, no one returns. The girl from District 4 staggers out of sight, although I wouldn't bet on her making it to the lake. I watch Glimmer fall, twitch hysterically around on the ground for a few minutes, and then go still.

The nest is nothing but an empty shell. The wasps have vanished in pursuit of the others. I don't think they'll return, but I don't want to risk it. I scamper down the tree and hit the ground running in the opposite direction of the lake. The poison from the stingers makes me wobbly, but I find my way back to my own little pool and submerge myself in the water, just in case any wasps are still on my trail. After about five minutes, I drag myself onto the rocks. People have not exaggerated the effects of the tracker jacker stings. Actually, the one on my knee is closer to an orange than a plum in size. A foul-smelling green liquid oozes from the places where I pulled out the stingers.

The swelling. The pain. The ooze. Watching Glimmer twitching to death on the ground. It's a lot to handle before the sun has even cleared the horizon. I don't want to think about what Glimmer must look like now. Her body disfigured. Her swollen fingers stiffening around the bow . . .

The bow! Somewhere in my befuddled mind one thought connects to another and I'm on my feet, teetering through the trees back to Glimmer. The bow. The arrows. I must get them. I haven't heard the cannons fire yet, so perhaps Glimmer is in some sort of coma, her heart still struggling against the wasp venom. But once it stops and the cannon signals her death, a hovercraft will move in and retrieve her body, taking the only bow and sheath of arrows I've seen out of the Games for good. And I refuse to let them slip through my fingers again!

I reach Glimmer just as the cannon fires. The tracker jackers have vanished. This girl, so breathtakingly beautiful in her golden dress the night of the interviews, is unrecognizable. Her features eradicated, her limbs three times their normal size. The stinger lumps have begun to explode, spewing putrid green liquid around her. I have to break several of what used to be her fingers with a stone to free the bow. The sheath of arrows is pinned under her back. I try to roll over her body by pulling on one arm, but the flesh disintegrates in my hands and I fall back on the ground.

Is this real? Or have the hallucinations begun? I squeeze my eyes tight and try to breathe through my mouth, ordering myself not to become sick. Breakfast must stay down, it might be days before I can hunt again. A second cannon fires and I'm guessing the girl from District 4 has just died. I hear the birds fall silent and then one give the warning call, which means a hovercraft is about to appear. Confused, I think it's for Glimmer, although this doesn't quite make sense because I'm still in the picture, still fighting for the arrows. I lurch back onto my knees and the trees around me begin to spin in circles. In the middle of the sky, I spot the hovercraft. I throw myself over Glimmer's body as if to protect it but then I see the girl from District 4 being lifted into the air and vanishing.

"Do this!" I command myself. Clenching my jaw, I dig my hands under Glimmer's body, get a hold on what must be her rib cage, and force her onto her stomach. I can't help it, I'm hyperventilating now, the whole thing is so nightmarish and I'm losing my grasp on what's real. I tug on the silver sheath of arrows, but it's caught on something, her shoulder blade, something, and finally yank it free. I've just encircled the sheath with my arms when I hear the footsteps, several pairs, coming through the underbrush, and I realize the Careers have come back. They've come back to kill me or get their weapons or both.

But it's too late to run. I pull a slimy arrow from the sheath and try to position it on the bowstring but instead of one string I see three and the stench from the stings is so repulsive I can't do it. I can't do it. I can't do it.

I'm helpless as the first hunter crashes through the trees, spear lifted, poised to throw. The shock on Peeta's face makes no sense to me. I wait for the blow. Instead his arm drops to his side.

"What are you still doing here?" he hisses at me. I stare uncomprehendingly as a trickle of water drips off a sting under his ear. His whole body starts sparkling as if he's been dipped in dew. "Are you mad?" He's prodding me with the shaft of the spear now. "Get up! Get up!" I rise, but he's still pushing at me. What? What is going on? He shoves me away from him hard. "Run!" he screams. "Run!"

Behind him, Cato slashes his way through the brush. He's sparkling wet, too, and badly stung under one eye. I catch the gleam of sunlight on his sword and do as Peeta says. Holding tightly to my bow and arrows, banging into trees that appear out of nowhere, tripping and falling as I try to keep my balance. Back past my pool and into unfamiliar woods. The world begins to bend in alarming ways. A butterfly balloons to the size of a house then shatters into a million stars. Trees transform to blood and splash down over my boots. Ants begin to crawl out of the blisters on my hands and I can't shake them free. They're climbing up my arms, my neck. Someone's screaming, a long high-pitched scream that never breaks for breath. I have a vague idea it might be me. I trip and fall into a small pit lined with tiny orange bubbles that hum like the tracker jacker nest. Tucking my knees up to my chin, I wait for death.

Sick and disoriented, I'm able to form only one thought: *Peeta Mellark just saved my life.*

Then the ants bore into my eyes and I black out.

I enter a nightmare from which I wake repeatedly only to find a greater terror awaiting me. All the things I dread most, all the things I dread for others manifest in such vivid detail I can't help but believe they're real. Each time I wake, I think, *At last, this is over,* but it isn't. It's only the beginning of a new chapter of torture. How many ways do I watch Prim die? Relive my father's last moments? Feel my own body ripped apart? This is the nature of the tracker jacker venom, so carefully created to target the place where fear lives in your brain.

When I finally do come to my senses, I lie still, waiting for the next onslaught of imagery. But eventually I accept that the poison must have finally worked its way out of my system, leaving my body wracked and feeble. I'm still lying on my side, locked in the fetal position. I lift a hand to my eyes to find them sound, untouched by ants that never existed. Simply stretching out my limbs requires an enormous effort. So many parts of me hurt, it doesn't seem worthwhile taking inventory of them. Very, very slowly I manage to sit up. I'm in a shallow hole, not filled with the humming orange bubbles of my hallucination but with old, dead leaves. My clothing's damp, but I don't know whether pond water, dew, rain, or sweat is the cause. For a long time, all I can do is take tiny sips from my bottle and watch a beetle crawl up the side of a honeysuckle bush.

How long have I been out? It was morning when I lost reason. Now it's afternoon. But the stiffness in my joints suggests more than a day has passed, even two possibly. If so, I'll have no way of knowing which tributes survived that tracker jacker attack. Not Glimmer or the girl from District 4. But there was the boy from District 1, both tributes from District 2, and Peeta. Did they die from the stings? Certainly if they lived, their last days must have been as horrid as my own. And what about Rue? She's so small, it wouldn't take much venom to do her in. But then again . . . the tracker jackers would've had to catch her, and she had a good head start.

A foul, rotten taste pervades my mouth, and the water has little effect on it. I drag myself over to the honeysuckle bush and pluck a flower. I gently pull the stamen through the blossom and set the drop of nectar on my tongue. The sweetness spreads through my mouth, down my throat, warming my veins with memories of summer, and my home woods and Gale's presence beside me. For some reason, our discussion from that last morning comes back to me.

"We could do it, you know."

"What?"

"Leave the district. Run off. Live in the woods. You and I, we could make it."

And suddenly, I'm not thinking of Gale but of Peeta and . . . Peeta! *He saved my life!* I think. Because by the time we met up, I couldn't tell what was real and what the tracker jacker venom had caused me to imagine. But if he did, and my instincts tell me he did, what for? Is he simply working the Lover Boy angle he initiated at the interview? Or was he actually trying to protect me? And if he was, what was he doing with those Careers in the first place? None of it makes sense.

I wonder what Gale made of the incident for a moment and then I push the whole thing out of my mind because for some reason Gale and Peeta do not coexist well together in my thoughts.

So I focus on the one really good thing that's happened since I landed in the arena. I have a bow and arrows! A full dozen arrows if you count the one I retrieved in the tree. They bear no trace of the noxious green slime that came from Glimmer's body — which leads me to believe that might not have been wholly real — but they have a fair amount of dried blood on them. I can clean them later, but I do take a minute to shoot a few into a nearby tree. They are more like the weapons in the Training Center than my ones at home, but who cares? That I can work with.

The weapons give me an entirely new perspective on the Games. I know I have tough opponents left to face. But I am no longer merely prey that runs and hides or takes desperate measures. If Cato broke through the trees right now, I wouldn't flee, I'd shoot. I find I'm actually anticipating the moment with pleasure.

But first, I have to get some strength back in my body. I'm very dehydrated again and my water supply is dangerously low. The little padding I was able to put on by gorging myself during prep time in the Capitol is gone, plus several more pounds as well. My hip bones and ribs are more prominent than I remember them being since those awful months after my father's death. And then there are my wounds to contend with — burns, cuts, and bruises from smashing into the trees, and three tracker jacker stings, which are as sore and swollen as ever. I treat my burns with the ointment and try dabbing a bit on my stings as well, but it has no effect on them. My mother knew a treatment for them, some type of leaf that could draw out the poison, but she seldom had cause to use it, and I don't even remember its name let alone its appearance.

Water first, I think. *You can hunt along the way now.* It's easy to see the direction I came from by the path of destruction my crazed body made through the foliage. So I walk off in the other direction, hoping my enemies still lie locked in the surreal world of tracker jacker venom.

I can't move too quickly, my joints reject any abrupt motions. But I establish the slow hunter's tread I use when tracking game. Within a few minutes, I spot a rabbit and make my first kill with the bow and arrow. It's not my usual clean shot through the eye, but I'll take it. After about an hour, I find a stream, shallow but wide, and more than sufficient for my needs. The sun's hot and severe, so while I wait for my water to purify I strip down to my underclothes and wade into the mild current. I'm filthy from head to toe. I try splashing myself but eventually just lie down in the water for a few minutes, letting it wash off the soot and blood and skin that has started to peel off my burns. After rinsing out my clothes and hanging them on bushes to dry, I sit on the bank in the sun for a bit, untangling my hair with my fingers. My appetite returns and I eat a cracker and a strip of beef. With a handful of moss, I polish the blood from my silver weapons.

Refreshed, I treat my burns again, braid back my hair, and dress in the damp clothes, knowing the sun will dry them soon enough. Following the stream against its current seems the smartest course of action. I'm traveling uphill now, which I prefer, with a source of fresh water not only for myself but possible game. I easily take out a strange bird that must be some form of wild turkey. Anyway, it looks plenty edible to me. By late afternoon, I decide to build a small fire to cook the meat, betting that dusk will help conceal the smoke and I can quench the fire by nightfall. I clean the game, taking extra care with the bird, but there's nothing alarming about it. Once the feathers are plucked, it's no bigger than a chicken, but it's plump and firm. I've just placed the first lot over the coals when I hear the twig snap.

In one motion, I turn to the sound, bringing the bow and arrow to my shoulder. There's no one there. No one I can see anyway. Then I spot the tip of a child's boot just peeking out from behind the trunk of a tree. My shoulders relax and I grin. She can move through the woods like a shadow, you have to give her that. How else could she have followed me? The words come out of my mouth before I can stop them.

"You know, they're not the only ones who can form alliances," I say.

For a moment, no response. Then one of Rue's eyes edges around the trunk. "You want me for an ally?"

"Why not? You saved me with those tracker jackers. You're smart enough to still be alive. And I can't seem to shake you anyway," I say. She blinks at me, trying to decide. "You hungry?" I can see her swallow hard, her eye flickering to the meat. "Come on then, I've had two kills today."

Rue tentatively steps out into the open. "I can fix your stings."

"Can you?" I ask. "How?"

She digs in the pack she carries and pulls out a handful of leaves. I'm almost certain they're the ones my mother uses. "Where'd you find those?"

"Just around. We all carry them when we work in the orchards. They left a lot of nests there," says Rue. "There are a lot here, too."

"That's right. You're District Eleven. Agriculture," I say. "Orchards, huh? That must be how you can fly around the trees like you've got wings." Rue smiles. I've landed on one of the few things she'll admit pride in. "Well, come on, then. Fix me up."

I plunk down by the fire and roll up my pant leg to reveal the sting on my knee. To my surprise, Rue places the handful of leaves into her mouth and begins to chew them. My mother would use other methods, but it's not like we have a lot of options. After a minute or so, Rue presses a gloppy green wad of chewed leaves and spit on my knee.

"Ohhh." The sound comes out of my mouth before I can stop it. It's as if the leaves are actually leaching the pain right out of the sting.

Rue gives a giggle. "Lucky you had the sense to pull the stingers out or you'd be a lot worse."

"Do my neck! Do my cheek!" I almost beg.

Rue stuffs another handful of leaves in her mouth, and soon I'm laughing because the relief is so sweet. I notice a long burn on Rue's forearm. "I've got something for that." I set aside my weapons and anoint her arm with the burn medicine.

"You have good sponsors," she says longingly.

"Have you gotten anything yet?" I ask. She shakes her head. "You will, though. Watch. The closer we get to the end, the more people will realize how clever you are." I turn the meat over.

"You weren't joking, about wanting me for an ally?" she asks.

"No, I meant it," I say. I can almost hear Haymitch groaning as I team up with this wispy child. But I want her. Because she's a survivor, and I trust her, and why not admit it? She reminds me of Prim.

"Okay," she says, and holds out her hand. We shake. "It's a deal."

Of course, this kind of deal can only be temporary, but neither of us mentions that.

Rue contributes a big handful of some sort of starchy root to the meal. Roasted over the fire, they have the sharp sweet taste of a parsnip. She recognizes the bird, too, some wild thing they call a groosling in her district. She says sometimes a flock will wander into the orchard and they get a decent lunch that day. For a while, all conversation stops as we fill our stomachs. The groosling has delicious meat that's so fatty, the grease drips down your face when you bite into it.

"Oh," says Rue with a sigh. "I've never had a whole leg to myself before."

I'll bet she hasn't. I'll bet meat hardly ever comes her way. "Take the other," I say.

"Really?" she asks.

"Take whatever you want. Now that I've got a bow and arrows, I can get more. Plus I've got snares. I can show you how to set them," I say. Rue still looks uncertainly at the leg. "Oh, take it," I say, putting the drumstick in her hands. "It will only keep a few days anyway, and we've got the whole bird plus the rabbit." Once she's got hold of it, her appetite wins out and she takes a huge mouthful.

"I'd have thought, in District Eleven, you'd have a bit more to eat than us. You know, since you grow the food," I say.

Rue's eyes widen. "Oh, no, we're not allowed to eat the crops."

"They arrest you or something?" I ask.

"They whip you and make everyone else watch," says Rue. "The mayor's very strict about it."

I can tell by her expression that it's not that uncommon an occurrence. A public whipping's a rare thing in District 12, although occasionally one occurs. Technically, Gale and

I could be whipped on a daily basis for poaching in the woods — well, technically, we could get a whole lot worse — except all the officials buy our meat. Besides, our mayor, Madge's father, doesn't seem to have much taste for such events. Maybe being the least prestigious, poorest, most ridiculed district in the country has its advantages. Such as, being largely ignored by the Capitol as long as we produce our coal quotas.

"Do you get all the coal you want?" Rue asks.

"No," I answer. "Just what we buy and whatever we track in on our boots."

"They feed us a bit extra during harvest, so that people can keep going longer," says Rue.

"Don't you have to be in school?" I ask.

"Not during harvest. Everyone works then," says Rue.

It's interesting, hearing about her life. We have so little communication with anyone outside our district. In fact, I wonder if the Gamemakers are blocking out our conversation, because even though the information seems harmless, they don't want people in different districts to know about one another.

At Rue's suggestion, we lay out all our food to plan ahead. She's seen most of mine, but I add the last couple of crackers and beef strips to the pile. She's gathered quite a collection of roots, nuts, greens, and even some berries.

I roll an unfamiliar berry in my fingers. "You sure this is safe?"

"Oh, yes, we have them back home. I've been eating them for days," she says, popping a handful in her mouth. I tentatively bite into one, and it's as good as our blackberries. Taking Rue on as an ally seems a better choice all the time. We divide up our food supplies, so in case we're separated, we'll both be set for a few days. Apart from the food, Rue has a small water skin, a homemade slingshot, and an extra pair of socks. She also has a sharp shard of rock she uses as a knife. "I know it's not much," she says as if embarrassed, "but I had to get away from the Cornucopia fast."

"You did just right," I say. When I spread out my gear, she gasps a little when she sees the sunglasses.

"How did you get those?" she asks.

"In my pack. They've been useless so far. They don't block the sun and they make it harder to see," I say with a shrug.

"These aren't for sun, they're for darkness," exclaims Rue. "Sometimes, when we harvest through the night, they'll pass out a few pairs to those of us highest in the trees. Where the torchlight doesn't reach. One time, this boy Martin, he tried to keep his pair. Hid it in his pants. They killed him on the spot."

"They killed a boy for taking these?" I say.

"Yes, and everyone knew he was no danger. Martin wasn't right in the head. I mean, he still acted like a three-year-old. He just wanted the glasses to play with," says Rue.

Hearing this makes me feel like District 12 is some sort of safe haven. Of course, people keel over from starvation all the time, but I can't imagine the Peacekeepers murdering a simpleminded child. There's a little girl, one of Greasy

Sae's grandkids, who wanders around the Hob. She's not quite right, but she's treated as a sort of pet. People toss her scraps and things.

"So what do these do?" I ask Rue, taking the glasses.

"They let you see in complete darkness," says Rue. "Try them tonight when the sun goes down."

I give Rue some matches and she makes sure I have plenty of leaves in case my stings flare up again. We extinguish our fire and head upstream until it's almost nightfall.

"Where do you sleep?" I ask her. "In the trees?" She nods. "In just your jacket?"

Rue holds up her extra pair of socks. "I have these for my hands."

I think of how cold the nights have been. "You can share my sleeping bag if you want. We'll both easily fit." Her face lights up. I can tell this is more than she dared hope for.

We pick a fork high in a tree and settle in for the night just as the anthem begins to play. There were no deaths today.

"Rue, I only woke up today. How many nights did I miss?" The anthem should block out our words, but still I whisper. I even take the precaution of covering my lips with my hand. I don't want the audience to know what I'm planning to tell her about Peeta. Taking a cue from me, she does the same.

"Two," she says. "The girls from Districts One and Four are dead. There's ten of us left."

"Something strange happened. At least, I think it did. It

might have been the tracker jacker venom making me imagine things," I say. "You know the boy from my district? Peeta? I think he saved my life. But he was with the Careers."

"He's not with them now," she says. "I've spied on their base camp by the lake. They made it back before they collapsed from the stingers. But he's not there. Maybe he did save you and had to run."

I don't answer. If, in fact, Peeta did save me, I'm in his debt again. And this can't be paid back. "If he did, it was all probably just part of his act. You know, to make people think he's in love with me."

"Oh," says Rue thoughtfully. "I didn't think that was an act."

"Course it is," I say. "He worked it out with our mentor." The anthem ends and the sky goes dark. "Let's try out these glasses." I pull out the glasses and slip them on. Rue wasn't kidding. I can see everything from the leaves on the trees to a skunk strolling through the bushes a good fifty feet away. I could kill it from here if I had a mind to. I could kill anyone.

"I wonder who else got a pair of these," I say.

"The Careers have two pairs. But they've got everything down by the lake," Rue says. "And they're so strong."

"We're strong, too," I say. "Just in a different way."

"You are. You can shoot," she says. "What can I do?"

"You can feed yourself. Can they?" I ask.

"They don't need to. They have all those supplies," Rue says.

"Say they didn't. Say the supplies were gone. How long would they last?" I say. "I mean, it's the Hunger Games, right?"

"But, Katniss, they're not hungry," says Rue.

"No, they're not. That's the problem," I agree. And for the first time, I have a plan. A plan that isn't motivated by the need for flight and evasion. An offensive plan. "I think we're going to have to fix that, Rue."

Rue has decided to trust me wholeheartedly. I know this because as soon as the anthem finishes she snuggles up against me and falls asleep. Nor do I have any misgivings about her, as I take no particular precautions. If she'd wanted me dead, all she would have had to do was disappear from that tree without pointing out the tracker jacker nest. Needling me, at the very back of my mind, is the obvious. Both of us can't win these Games. But since the odds are still against either of us surviving, I manage to ignore the thought.

Besides, I'm distracted by my latest idea about the Careers and their supplies. Somehow Rue and I must find a way to destroy their food. I'm pretty sure feeding themselves will be a tremendous struggle. Traditionally, the Career tributes' strategy is to get hold of all the food early on and work from there. The years when they have not protected it well — one year a pack of hideous reptiles destroyed it, another a Gamemakers' flood washed it away — those are usually the years that tributes from other districts have won. That the Careers have been better fed growing up is actually to their disadvantage, because they don't know how to be hungry. Not the way Rue and I do.

But I'm too exhausted to begin any detailed plan tonight. My wounds recovering, my mind still a bit foggy from the venom, and the warmth of Rue at my side, her head cradled on my shoulder, have given me a sense of security. I realize, for the first time, how very lonely I've been in the arena. How comforting the presence of another human being can be. I give in to my drowsiness, resolving that tomorrow the tables will turn. Tomorrow, it's the Careers who will have to watch their backs.

The boom of the cannon jolts me awake. The sky's streaked with light, the birds already chattering. Rue perches in a branch across from me, her hands cupping something. We wait, listening for more shots, but there aren't any.

"Who do you think that was?" I can't help thinking of Peeta.

"I don't know. It could have been any of the others," says Rue. "I guess we'll know tonight."

"Who's left again?" I ask.

"The boy from District One. Both tributes from Two. The boy from Three. Thresh and me. And you and Peeta," says Rue. "That's eight. Wait, and the boy from Ten, the one with the bad leg. He makes nine."

There's someone else, but neither of us can remember who it is.

"I wonder how that last one died," says Rue.

"No telling. But it's good for us. A death should hold the crowd for a bit. Maybe we'll have time to do something before the Gamemakers decide things have been moving too slowly," I say. "What's in your hands?"

"Breakfast," says Rue. She holds them out revealing two big eggs.

"What kind are those?" I ask.

"Not sure. There's a marshy area over that way. Some kind of waterbird," she says.

It'd be nice to cook them, but neither of us wants to risk a fire. My guess is the tribute who died today was a victim of the Careers, which means they've recovered enough to be back in the Games. We each suck out the insides of an egg, eat a rabbit leg and some berries. It's a good breakfast anywhere.

"Ready to do it?" I say, pulling on my pack.

"Do what?" says Rue, but by the way she bounces up, you can tell she's up for whatever I propose.

"Today we take out the Careers' food," I say.

"Really? How?" You can see the glint of excitement in her eyes. In this way, she's exactly the opposite of Prim, for whom adventures are an ordeal.

"No idea. Come on, we'll figure out a plan while we hunt," I say.

We don't get much hunting done though because I'm too busy getting every scrap of information I can out of Rue about the Careers' base. She's only been in to spy on them briefly, but she's observant. They have set up their camp beside the lake. Their supply stash is about thirty yards away. During the day, they've been leaving another tribute, the boy from District 3, to watch over the supplies.

"The boy from District Three?" I ask. "He's working with them?"

"Yes, he stays at the camp full-time. He got stung, too, when they drew the tracker jackers in by the lake," says Rue. "I guess they agreed to let him live if he acted as their guard. But he's not very big."

"What weapons does he have?" I ask.

"Not much that I could see. A spear. He might be able to hold a few of us off with that, but Thresh could kill him easily," says Rue.

"And the food's just out in the open?" I say. She nods. "Something's not quite right about that whole setup."

"I know. But I couldn't tell what exactly," says Rue. "Katniss, even if you could get to the food, how would you get rid of it?"

"Burn it. Dump it in the lake. Soak it in fuel." I poke Rue in the belly, just like I would Prim. "Eat it!" She giggles. "Don't worry, I'll think of something. Destroying things is much easier than making them."

For a while, we dig roots, we gather berries and greens, we devise a strategy in hushed voices. And I come to know Rue, the oldest of six kids, fiercely protective of her siblings, who gives her rations to the younger ones, who forages in the meadows in a district where the Peacekeepers are far less obliging than ours. Rue, who when you ask her what she loves most in the world, replies, of all things, "Music."

"Music?" I say. In our world, I rank music somewhere between hair ribbons and rainbows in terms of usefulness. At least a rainbow gives you a tip about the weather. "You have a lot of time for that?"

"We sing at home. At work, too. That's why I love your

pin," she says, pointing to the mockingjay that I've again forgotten about.

"You have mockingjays?" I ask.

"Oh, yes. I have a few that are my special friends. We can sing back and forth for hours. They carry messages for me," she says.

"What do you mean?" I say.

"I'm usually up highest, so I'm the first to see the flag that signals quitting time. There's a special little song I do," says Rue. She opens her mouth and sings a little four-note run in a sweet, clear voice. "And the mockingjays spread it around the orchard. That's how everyone knows to knock off," she continues. "They can be dangerous though, if you get too near their nests. But you can't blame them for that."

I unclasp the pin and hold it out to her. "Here, you take it. It has more meaning for you than me."

"Oh, no," says Rue, closing my fingers back over the pin. "I like to see it on you. That's how I decided I could trust you. Besides, I have this." She pulls a necklace woven out of some kind of grass from her shirt. On it, hangs a roughly carved wooden star. Or maybe it's a flower. "It's a good luck charm."

"Well, it's worked so far," I say, pinning the mockingjay back on my shirt. "Maybe you should just stick with that."

By lunch, we have a plan. By early afternoon, we are poised to carry it out. I help Rue collect and place the wood for the first two campfires, the third she'll have time for on her own. We decide to meet afterward at the site where we ate our first meal together. The stream should help guide me back to it. Before I leave, I make sure Rue's well stocked with food and matches. I even insist she take my sleeping bag, in case it's not possible to rendezvous by nightfall.

"What about you? Won't you be cold?" she asks.

"Not if I pick up another bag down by the lake," I say. "You know, stealing isn't illegal here," I say with a grin.

At the last minute, Rue decides to teach me her mockingjay signal, the one she gives to indicate the day's work is done. "It might not work. But if you hear the mockingjays singing it, you'll know I'm okay, only I can't get back right away."

"Are there many mockingjays here?" I ask.

"Haven't you seen them? They've got nests everywhere," she says. I have to admit I haven't noticed.

"Okay, then. If all goes according to plan, I'll see you for dinner," I say.

Unexpectedly, Rue throws her arms around me. I only hesitate a moment before I hug her back.

"You be careful," she says to me.

"You, too," I say. I turn and head back to the stream, feeling somehow worried. About Rue being killed, about Rue not being killed and the two of us being left for last, about leaving Rue alone, about leaving Prim alone back home. No, Prim has my mother and Gale and a baker who has promised she won't go hungry. Rue has only me.

Once I reach the stream, I have only to follow it downhill to the place I initially picked it up after the tracker jacker attack. I have to be cautious as I move along the water though, because I find my thoughts preoccupied with unanswered questions, most of which concern Peeta. The cannon that fired early this morning, did that signify his death? If so, how did he die? At the hand of a Career? And was that in revenge for letting me live? I struggle again to remember that moment over Glimmer's body, when he burst through the trees. But just the fact that he was sparkling leads me to doubt everything that happened.

I must have been moving very slowly yesterday because I reach the shallow stretch where I took my bath in just a few hours. I stop to replenish my water and add a layer of mud to my backpack. It seems bent on reverting to orange no matter how many times I cover it.

My proximity to the Careers' camp sharpens my senses, and the closer I get to them, the more guarded I am, pausing frequently to listen for unnatural sounds, an arrow already fitted into the string of my bow. I don't see any other tributes, but I do notice some of the things Rue has mentioned. Patches of the sweet berries. A bush with the leaves that healed my stings. Clusters of tracker jacker nests in the vicinity of the tree I was trapped in. And here and there, the black-and-white flash of a mockingjay wing in the branches high over my head.

When I reach the tree with the abandoned nest at the foot, I pause a moment, to gather my courage. Rue has given specific instructions on how to reach the best spying place near the lake from this point. *Remember,* I tell myself. *You're the hunter now, not them.* I get a firmer grasp on my bow and go on. I make it to the copse Rue has told me about and again have to admire her cleverness. It's right at the edge of the wood, but the bushy foliage is so thick down low I can easily observe the Career camp without being spotted. Between us lies the flat expanse where the Games began.

There are four tributes. The boy from District 1, Cato and the girl from District 2, and a scrawny, ashen-skinned boy who must be from District 3. He made almost no impression on me at all during our time in the Capitol. I can remember almost nothing about him, not his costume, not his training score, not his interview. Even now, as he sits there fiddling with some kind of plastic box, he's easily ignored in the presence of his large and domineering companions. But he must be of some value or they wouldn't have bothered to let him live. Still, seeing him only adds to my sense of unease over why the Careers would possibly leave him as a guard, why they have allowed him to live at all.

All four tributes seem to still be recovering from the tracker jacker attack. Even from here, I can see the large swollen lumps on their bodies. They must not have had the sense to remove the stingers, or if they did, not known about the leaves that healed them. Apparently, whatever medicines they found in the Cornucopia have been ineffective.

The Cornucopia sits in its original position, but its insides have been picked clean. Most of the supplies, held in crates, burlap sacks, and plastic bins, are piled neatly in a pyramid in what seems a questionable distance from the camp. Others are sprinkled around the perimeter of the pyramid, almost mimicking the layout of supplies around the Cornucopia at the onset of the Games. A canopy of netting that, aside from discouraging birds, seems to be useless shelters the pyramid itself.

The whole setup is completely perplexing. The distance, the netting, and the presence of the boy from District 3. One thing's for sure, destroying those supplies is not going to be as simple as it looks. Some other factor is at play here, and I'd better stay put until I figure out what it is. My guess is the pyramid is booby-trapped in some manner. I think of concealed pits, descending nets, a thread that when broken sends a poisonous dart into your heart. Really, the possibilities are endless.

While I am mulling over my options, I hear Cato shout out. He's pointing up to the woods, far beyond me, and without turning I know that Rue must have set the first campfire. We'd made sure to gather enough green wood to make the smoke noticeable. The Careers begin to arm themselves at once.

An argument breaks out. It's loud enough for me to hear that it concerns whether or not the boy from District 3 should stay or accompany them.

"He's coming. We need him in the woods, and his job's done here anyway. No one can touch those supplies," says Cato.

"What about Lover Boy?" says the boy from District 1.

"I keep telling you, forget about him. I know where I cut him. It's a miracle he hasn't bled to death yet. At any rate, he's in no shape to raid us," says Cato.

So Peeta is out there in the woods, wounded badly. But I am still in the dark on what motivated him to betray the Careers.

"Come on," says Cato. He thrusts a spear into the hands of the boy from District 3, and they head off in the direction of the fire. The last thing I hear as they enter the woods is Cato saying, "When we find her, I kill her in my own way, and no one interferes."

Somehow I don't think he's talking about Rue. She didn't drop a nest of tracker jackers on him.

I stay put for a half an hour or so, trying to figure out what to do about the supplies. The one advantage I have with the bow and arrow is distance. I could send a flaming arrow into the pyramid easily enough — I'm a good enough shot to get it through those openings in the net — but there's no guarantee it would catch. More likely it'd just burn itself out and then what? I'd have achieved nothing and given them far too much information about myself. That I was here, that I have an accomplice, that I can use the bow and arrow with accuracy.

There's no alternative. I'm going to have to get in closer and see if I can't discover what exactly protects the supplies. In fact, I'm just about to reveal myself when a movement catches my eye. Several hundred yards to my right, I see someone emerge from the woods. For a second, I think it's Rue, but then I recognize Foxface — she's the one we couldn't remember this morning — creeping out onto the plain. When she decides it's safe, she runs for the pyramid, with quick, small steps. Just before she reaches the circle of supplies that have been littered around the pyramid, she stops, searches the ground, and carefully places her feet on a spot. Then she begins to approach the pyramid with strange little hops, sometimes landing on one foot, teetering slightly, sometimes risking a few steps. At one point, she launches up in the air, over a small barrel and lands poised on her tiptoes. But she overshot slightly, and her momentum throws her forward. I hear her give a sharp squeal as her hands hit the ground, but nothing happens. In a moment, she's regained her feet and continues until she has reached the bulk of the supplies.

So, I'm right about the booby trap, but it's clearly more complex than I had imagined. I was right about the girl, too. How wily is she to have discovered this path into the food and to be able to replicate it so neatly? She fills her pack, taking a few items from a variety of containers, crackers from a crate, a handful of apples from a burlap sack that hangs suspended from a rope off the side of a bin. But only a handful from each, not enough to tip off that the food is missing. Not enough to cause suspicion. And then she's doing her odd little dance back out of the circle and scampering into the woods again, safe and sound.

I realize I'm grinding my teeth in frustration. Foxface has confirmed what I'd already guessed. But what sort of trap have they laid that requires such dexterity? Has so many trigger points? Why did she squeal so as her hands made contact with the earth? You'd have thought . . . and slowly it begins to dawn on me . . . you'd have thought the very ground was going to explode.

"It's mined," I whisper. That explains everything. The Careers' willingness to leave their supplies, Foxface's reaction, the involvement of the boy from District 3, where they have the factories, where they make televisions and automobiles and explosives. But where did he get them? In the supplies? That's not the sort of weapon the Gamemakers usually provide, given that they like to see the tributes draw blood personally. I slip out of the bushes and cross to one of the round metal plates that lifted the tributes into the arena. The ground around it has been dug up and patted back down. The land mines were disabled after the sixty seconds we stood on the plates, but the boy from District 3 must have managed to reactivate them. I've never seen anyone in the Games do that. I bet it came as a shock even to the Gamemakers.

Well, hurray for the boy from District 3 for putting one over on them, but what am I supposed to do now? Obviously, I can't go strolling into that mess without blowing myself sky-high. As for sending in a burning arrow, that's more laughable than ever. The mines are set off by pressure. It doesn't have to be a lot, either. One year, a girl dropped her token, a small wooden ball, while she was at her plate, and they literally had to scrape bits of her off the ground.

My arm's pretty good, I might be able to chuck some rocks in there and set off what? Maybe one mine? That could start a chain reaction. Or could it? Would the boy from District 3 have placed the mines in such a way that a single mine would not disturb the others? Thereby protecting the supplies but ensuring the death of the invader. Even if I only blew up one mine, I'd draw the Careers back down on me for sure. And anyway, what am I thinking? There's that net, clearly strung to deflect any such attack. Besides, what I'd really need is to throw about thirty rocks in there at once, setting off a big chain reaction, demolishing the whole lot.

I glance back up at the woods. The smoke from Rue's second fire is wafting toward the sky. By now, the Careers have probably begun to suspect some sort of trick. Time is running out.

There is a solution to this, I know there is, if I can only focus hard enough. I stare at the pyramid, the bins, the crates, too heavy to topple over with an arrow. Maybe one contains cooking oil, and the burning arrow idea is reviving when I realize I could end up losing all twelve of my arrows and not get a direct hit on an oil bin, since I'd just be guessing. I'm genuinely thinking of trying to re-create Foxface's trip up to the pyramid in hopes of finding a new means of destruction when my eyes light on the burlap bag of apples. I could sever the rope in one shot, didn't I do as much in the Training Center? It's a big bag, but it still might only be good for one explosion. If only I could free the apples themselves . . .

I know what to do. I move into range and give myself three arrows to get the job done. I place my feet carefully, block out the rest of the world as I take meticulous aim. The first arrow tears through the side of the bag near the top, leaving a split in the burlap. The second widens it to a gaping hole. I can see the first apple teetering when I let the third arrow go, catching the torn flap of burlap and ripping it from the bag.

For a moment, everything seems frozen in time. Then the apples spill to the ground and I'm blown backward into the air.

The impact with the hard-packed earth of the plain knocks the wind out of me. My backpack does little to soften the blow. Fortunately my quiver has caught in the crook of my elbow, sparing both itself and my shoulder, and my bow is locked in my grasp. The ground still shakes with explosions. I can't hear them. I can't hear anything at the moment. But the apples must have set off enough mines, causing debris to activate the others. I manage to shield my face with my arms as shattered bits of matter, some of it burning, rain down around me. An acrid smoke fills the air, which is not the best remedy for someone trying to regain the ability to breathe.

After about a minute, the ground stops vibrating. I roll on my side and allow myself a moment of satisfaction at the sight of the smoldering wreckage that was recently the pyramid. The Careers aren't likely to salvage anything out of that.

I'd better get out of here, I think. *They'll be making a beeline for the place.* But once I'm on my feet, I realize escape may not be so simple. I'm dizzy. Not the slightly wobbly kind, but the kind that sends the trees swooping around you and causes the earth to move in waves under your feet.

I take a few steps and somehow wind up on my hands and knees. I wait a few minutes to let it pass, but it doesn't.

Panic begins to set in. I can't stay here. Flight is essential. But I can neither walk nor hear. I place a hand to my left ear, the one that was turned toward the blast, and it comes away bloody. Have I gone deaf from the explosion? The idea frightens me. I rely as much on my ears as my eyes as a hunter, maybe more at times. But I can't let my fear show. Absolutely, positively, I am live on every screen in Panem.

No blood trails, I tell myself, and manage to pull my hood up over my head, tie the cord under my chin with uncooperative fingers. That should help soak up the blood. I can't walk, but can I crawl? I move forward tentatively. Yes, if I go very slowly, I can crawl. Most of the woods will offer insufficient cover. My only hope is to make it back to Rue's copse and conceal myself in greenery. I can't get caught out here on my hands and knees in the open. Not only will I face death, it's sure to be a long and painful one at Cato's hand. The thought of Prim having to watch that keeps me doggedly inching my way toward the hideout.

Another blast knocks me flat on my face. A stray mine, set off by some collapsing crate. This happens twice more. I'm reminded of those last few kernels that burst when Prim and I pop corn over the fire at home.

To say I make it in the nick of time is an understatement. I have literally just dragged myself into the tangle of bushes at the base of the trees when there's Cato, barreling onto the plain, soon followed by his companions. His rage is so extreme it might be comical — so people really do tear out their hair and beat the ground with their fists — if I didn't know that it was aimed at me, at what I have done to him. Add to that my proximity, my inability to run or defend myself, and in fact, the whole thing has me terrified. I'm glad my hiding place makes it impossible for the cameras to get a close shot of me because I'm biting my nails like there's no tomorrow. Gnawing off the last bits of nail polish, trying to keep my teeth from chattering.

The boy from District 3 throws stones into the ruins and must have declared all the mines activated because the Careers are approaching the wreckage.

Cato has finished the first phase of his tantrum and takes out his anger on the smoking remains by kicking open various containers. The other tributes are poking around in the mess, looking for anything to salvage, but there's nothing. The boy from District 3 has done his job too well. This idea must occur to Cato, too, because he turns on the boy and appears to be shouting at him. The boy from District 3 only has time to turn and run before Cato catches him in a headlock from behind. I can see the muscles ripple in Cato's arms as he sharply jerks the boy's head to the side.

It's that quick. The death of the boy from District 3.

The other two Careers seem to be trying to calm Cato down. I can tell he wants to return to the woods, but they keep pointing at the sky, which puzzles me until I realize, *Of course. They think whoever set off the explosions is dead.*

They don't know about the arrows and the apples. They assume the booby trap was faulty, but that the tribute who blew up the supplies was killed doing it. If there was a cannon shot, it could have been easily lost in the subsequent explosions. The shattered remains of the thief removed by hovercraft. They retire to the far side of the lake to allow the Gamemakers to retrieve the body of the boy from District 3. And they wait.

I suppose a cannon goes off. A hovercraft appears and takes the dead boy. The sun dips below the horizon. Night falls. Up in the sky, I see the seal and know the anthem must have begun. A moment of darkness. They show the boy from District 3. They show the boy from District 10, who must have died this morning. Then the seal reappears. So, now they know. The bomber survived. In the seal's light, I can see Cato and the girl from District 2 put on their night-vision glasses. The boy from District 1 ignites a tree branch for a torch, illuminating the grim determination on all their faces. The Careers stride back into the woods to hunt.

The dizziness has subsided and while my left ear is still deafened, I can hear a ringing in my right, which seems a good sign. There's no point in leaving my hiding place, though. I'm about as safe as I can be, here at the crime scene. They probably think the bomber has a two- or three-hour lead on them. Still it's a long time before I risk moving.

The first thing I do is dig out my own glasses and put them on, which relaxes me a little, to have at least one of my hunter's senses working. I drink some water and wash the blood from my ear. Fearing the smell of meat will draw unwanted predators — fresh blood is bad enough — I make a good meal out of the greens and roots and berries Rue and I gathered today.

Where is my little ally? Did she make it back to the rendezvous point? Is she worried about me? At least, the sky has shown we're both alive.

I run through the surviving tributes on my fingers. The boy from 1, both from 2, Foxface, both from 11 and 12. Just eight of us. The betting must be getting really hot in the Capitol. They'll be doing special features on each of us now. Probably interviewing our friends and families. It's been a long time since a tribute from District 12 made it into the top eight. And now there are two of us. Although from what Cato said, Peeta's on his way out. Not that Cato is the final word on anything. Didn't he just lose his entire stash of supplies?

Let the Seventy-fourth Hunger Games begin, Cato, I think. *Let them begin for real.*

A cold breeze has sprung up. I reach for my sleeping bag before I remember I left it with Rue. I was supposed to pick up another one, but what with the mines and all, I forgot. I begin to shiver. Since roosting overnight in a tree isn't sensible anyway, I scoop out a hollow under the bushes and cover myself with leaves and pine needles. I'm still freezing. I lay my sheet of plastic over my upper body and position my backpack to block the wind. It's a little better. I begin to have more sympathy for the girl from District 8 that lit the fire that first night. But now it's me who needs to grit my teeth and tough it out until morning. More leaves, more pine needles. I pull my arms inside my jacket and tuck my knees up to my chest. Somehow, I drift off to sleep.

When I open my eyes, the world looks slightly fractured, and it takes a minute to realize that the sun must be well up and the glasses fragmenting my vision. As I sit up and remove them, I hear a laugh somewhere near the lake and freeze. The laugh's distorted, but the fact that it registered at all means I must be regaining my hearing. Yes, my right ear can hear again, although it's still ringing. As for my left ear, well, at least the bleeding has stopped.

I peer through the bushes, afraid the Careers have returned, trapping me here for an indefinite time. No, it's Foxface, standing in the rubble of the pyramid and laughing. She's smarter than the Careers, actually finding a few useful items in the ashes. A metal pot. A knife blade. I'm perplexed by her amusement until I realize that with the Careers' stores eliminated, she might actually stand a chance. Just like the rest of us. It crosses my mind to reveal myself and enlist her as a second ally against that pack. But I rule it out. There's something about that sly grin that makes me sure that befriending Foxface would ultimately get me a knife in the back. With that in mind, this might be an excellent time to shoot her. But she's heard something, not me, because her head turns away, toward the drop-off, and she sprints for the woods. I wait. No one, nothing shows up. Still, if Foxface thought it was dangerous, maybe it's time for me to get out of here, too. Besides, I'm eager to tell Rue about the pyramid.

Since I've no idea where the Careers are, the route back by the stream seems as good as any. I hurry, loaded bow in one hand, a hunk of cold groosling in the other, because I'm famished now, and not just for leaves and berries but for the fat and protein in the meat. The trip to the stream is uneventful. Once there, I refill my water and wash, taking particular care with my injured ear. Then I travel uphill using the stream as a guide. At one point, I find boot prints in the mud along the bank. The Careers have been here, but not for a while. The prints are deep because they were made in soft mud, but now they're nearly dry in the hot sun. I haven't been careful enough about my own tracks, counting on a light tread and the pine needles to conceal my prints. Now I strip off my boots and socks and go barefoot up the bed of the stream.

The cool water has an invigorating effect on my body, my spirits. I shoot two fish, easy pickings in this slow-moving stream, and go ahead and eat one raw even though I've just had the groosling. The second I'll save for Rue.

Gradually, subtly, the ringing in my right ear diminishes until it's gone entirely. I find myself pawing at my left ear periodically, trying to clean away whatever deadens its ability to collect sounds. If there's improvement, it's undetectable. I can't adjust to deafness in the ear. It makes me feel off-balanced and defenseless to my left. Blind even. My head keeps turning to the injured side, as my right ear tries to compensate for the wall of nothingness where yesterday there was a constant flow of information. The more time that passes, the less hopeful I am that this is an injury that will heal.

When I reach the site of our first meeting, I feel certain it's been undisturbed. There's no sign of Rue, not on the ground or in the trees. This is odd. By now she should have returned, as it's midday. Undoubtedly, she spent the night in a tree somewhere. What else could she do with no light and the Careers with their night-vision glasses tromping around the woods. And the third fire she was supposed to set — although I forgot to check for it last night — was the farthest from our site of all. She's probably just being cautious about making her way back. I wish she'd hurry, because I don't want to hang around here too long. I want to spend the afternoon traveling to higher ground, hunting as we go. But there's nothing really for me to do but wait.

I wash the blood out of my jacket and hair and clean my ever-growing list of wounds. The burns are much better but I use a bit of medicine on them anyway. The main thing to worry about now is keeping out infection. I go ahead and eat the second fish. It isn't going to last long in this hot sun, but it should be easy enough to spear a few more for Rue. If she would just show up.

Feeling too vulnerable on the ground with my lopsided hearing, I scale a tree to wait. If the Careers show up, this will be a fine place to shoot them from. The sun moves slowly. I do things to pass the time. Chew leaves and apply them to my stings that are deflated but still tender. Comb

229

through my damp hair with my fingers and braid it. Lace my boots back up. Check over my bow and remaining nine arrows. Test my left ear repeatedly for signs of life by rustling a leaf near it, but without good results.

Despite the groosling and the fish, my stomach's growling, and I know I'm going to have what we call a hollow day back in District 12. That's a day where no matter what you put in your belly, it's never enough. Having nothing to do but sit in a tree makes it worse, so I decide to give into it. After all, I've lost a lot of weight in the arena, I need some extra calories. And having the bow and arrows makes me far more confident about my future prospects.

I slowly peel and eat a handful of nuts. My last cracker. The groosling neck. That's good because it takes time to pick clean. Finally, a groosling wing and the bird is history. But it's a hollow day, and even with all that I start daydreaming about food. Particularly the decadent dishes served in the Capitol. The chicken in creamy orange sauce. The cakes and pudding. Bread with butter. Noodles in green sauce. The lamb and dried plum stew. I suck on a few mint leaves and tell myself to get over it. Mint is good because we drink mint tea after supper often, so it tricks my stomach into thinking eating time is over. Sort of.

Dangling up in the tree, with the sun warming me, a mouthful of mint, my bow and arrows at hand . . . this is the most relaxed I've been since I've entered the arena. If only Rue would show up, and we could clear out. As the shadows grow, so does my restlessness. By late afternoon, I've resolved to go looking for her. I can at least visit the spot where she set the third fire and see if there are any clues to her whereabouts.

Before I go, I scatter a few mint leaves around our old campfire. Since we gathered these some distance away, Rue will understand I've been here, while they'll mean nothing to the Careers.

In less than an hour, I'm at the place where we agreed to have the third fire and I know something has gone amiss. The wood has been neatly arranged, expertly interspersed with tinder, but it has never been lit. Rue set up the fire but never made it back here. Somewhere between the second column of smoke I spied before I blew up the supplies and this point, she ran into trouble.

I have to remind myself she's still alive. Or is she? Could the cannon shot announcing her death have come in the wee hours of the morning when even my good ear was too broken to pick it up? Will she appear in the sky tonight? No, I refuse to believe it. There could be a hundred other explanations. She could have lost her way. Run into a pack of predators or another tribute, like Thresh, and had to hide. Whatever happened, I'm almost certain she's stuck out there, somewhere between the second fire and the unlit one at my feet. Something is keeping her up a tree.

I think I'll go hunt it down.

It's a relief to be doing something after sitting around all afternoon. I creep silently through the shadows, letting them conceal me. But nothing seems suspicious. There's no sign of any kind of struggle, no disruption of the needles on the ground. I've stopped for just a moment when I hear it. I have to cock my head around to the side to be sure, but there it is again. Rue's four-note tune coming out of a mockingjay's mouth. The one that means she's all right.

I grin and move in the direction of the bird. Another just a short distance ahead, picks up on the handful of notes. Rue has been singing to them, and recently. Otherwise they'd have taken up some other song. My eyes lift up into the trees, searching for a sign of her. I swallow and sing softly back, hoping she'll know it's safe to join me. A mockingjay repeats the melody to me. And that's when I hear the scream.

It's a child's scream, a young girl's scream, there's no one in the arena capable of making that sound except Rue. And now I'm running, knowing this may be a trap, knowing the three Careers may be poised to attack me, but I can't help myself. There's another high-pitched cry, this time my name. "Katniss! Katniss!"

"Rue!" I shout back, so she knows I'm near. So, *they* know I'm near, and hopefully the girl who has attacked them with tracker jackers and gotten an eleven they still can't explain will be enough to pull their attention away from her. "Rue! I'm coming!"

When I break into the clearing, she's on the ground, hopelessly entangled in a net. She just has time to reach her hand through the mesh and say my name before the spear enters her body.

The boy from District 1 dies before he can pull out the spear. My arrow drives deeply into the center of his neck. He falls to his knees and halves the brief remainder of his life by yanking out the arrow and drowning in his own blood. I'm reloaded, shifting my aim from side to side, while I shout at Rue, "Are there more? Are there more?"

She has to say no several times before I hear it.

Rue has rolled to her side, her body curved in and around the spear. I shove the boy away from her and pull out my knife, freeing her from the net. One look at the wound and I know it's far beyond my capacity to heal. Beyond anyone's probably. The spearhead is buried up to the shaft in her stomach. I crouch before her, staring helplessly at the embedded weapon. There's no point in comforting words, in telling her she'll be all right. She's no fool. Her hand reaches out and I clutch it like a lifeline. As if it's me who's dying instead of Rue.

"You blew up the food?" she whispers.

"Every last bit," I say.

"You have to win," she says.

"I'm going to. Going to win for both of us now," I

promise. I hear a cannon and look up. It must be for the boy from District 1.

"Don't go." Rue tightens her grip on my hand.

"Course not. Staying right here," I say. I move in closer to her, pulling her head onto my lap. I gently brush the dark, thick hair back behind her ear.

"Sing," she says, but I barely catch the word.

Sing? I think. *Sing what?* I do know a few songs. Believe it or not, there was once music in my house, too. Music I helped make. My father pulled me in with that remarkable voice — but I haven't sung much since he died. Except when Prim is very sick. Then I sing her the same songs she liked as a baby.

Sing. My throat is tight with tears, hoarse from smoke and fatigue. But if this is Prim's, I mean, Rue's last request, I have to at least try. The song that comes to me is a simple lullaby, one we sing fretful, hungry babies to sleep with. It's old, very old I think. Made up long ago in our hills. What my music teacher calls a mountain air. But the words are easy and soothing, promising tomorrow will be more hopeful than this awful piece of time we call today.

I give a small cough, swallow hard, and begin:

> *Deep in the meadow, under the willow*
> *A bed of grass, a soft green pillow*
> *Lay down your head, and close your sleepy eyes*
> *And when again they open, the sun will rise.*

> *Here it's safe, here it's warm*
> *Here the daisies guard you from every harm*
> *Here your dreams are sweet and tomorrow brings*
> > *them true*
> *Here is the place where I love you.*

Rue's eyes have fluttered shut. Her chest moves but only slightly. My throat releases the tears and they slide down my cheeks. But I have to finish the song for her.

> *Deep in the meadow, hidden far away*
> *A cloak of leaves, a moonbeam ray*
> *Forget your woes and let your troubles lay*
> *And when again it's morning, they'll wash away.*

> *Here it's safe, here it's warm*
> *Here the daisies guard you from every harm*

The final lines are barely audible.

> *Here your dreams are sweet and tomorrow brings*
> > *them true*
> *Here is the place where I love you.*

Everything's still and quiet. Then, almost eerily, the mockingjays take up my song.

For a moment, I sit there, watching my tears drip down on her face. Rue's cannon fires. I lean forward and press my lips against her temple. Slowly, as if not to wake her, I lay her head back on the ground and release her hand.

They'll want me to clear out now. So they can collect the bodies. And there's nothing to stay for. I roll the boy from District 1 onto his face and take his pack, retrieve the arrow that ended his life. I cut Rue's pack from her back as well, knowing she'd want me to have it but leave the spear in her stomach. Weapons in bodies will be transported to the hovercraft. I've no use for a spear, so the sooner it's gone from the arena the better.

I can't stop looking at Rue, smaller than ever, a baby animal curled up in a nest of netting. I can't bring myself to leave her like this. Past harm, but seeming utterly defenseless. To hate the boy from District 1, who also appears so vulnerable in death, seems inadequate. It's the Capitol I hate, for doing this to all of us.

Gale's voice is in my head. His ravings against the Capitol no longer pointless, no longer to be ignored. Rue's death has forced me to confront my own fury against the cruelty, the injustice they inflict upon us. But here, even more strongly than at home, I feel my impotence. There's no way to take revenge on the Capitol. Is there?

Then I remember Peeta's words on the roof. *"Only I keep wishing I could think of a way to . . . to show the Capitol they don't own me. That I'm more than just a piece in their Games."* And for the first time, I understand what he means.

I want to do something, right here, right now, to shame

them, to make them accountable, to show the Capitol that whatever they do or force us to do there is a part of every tribute they can't own. That Rue was more than a piece in their Games. And so am I.

A few steps into the woods grows a bank of wildflowers. Perhaps they are really weeds of some sort, but they have blossoms in beautiful shades of violet and yellow and white. I gather up an armful and come back to Rue's side. Slowly, one stem at a time, I decorate her body in the flowers. Covering the ugly wound. Wreathing her face. Weaving her hair with bright colors.

They'll have to show it. Or, even if they choose to turn the cameras elsewhere at this moment, they'll have to bring them back when they collect the bodies and everyone will see her then and know I did it. I step back and take a last look at Rue. She could really be asleep in that meadow after all.

"Bye, Rue," I whisper. I press the three middle fingers of my left hand against my lips and hold them out in her direction. Then I walk away without looking back.

The birds fall silent. Somewhere, a mockingjay gives the warning whistle that precedes the hovercraft. I don't know how it knows. It must hear things that humans can't. I pause, my eyes focused on what's ahead, not what's happening behind me. It doesn't take long, then the general birdsong begins again and I know she's gone.

Another mockingjay, a young one by the look of it, lands on a branch before me and bursts out Rue's melody.

My song, the hovercraft, were too unfamiliar for this novice to pick up, but it has mastered her handful of notes. The ones that mean she's safe.

"Good and safe," I say as I pass under its branch. "We don't have to worry about her now." Good and safe.

I've no idea where to go. The brief sense of home I had that one night with Rue has vanished. My feet wander this way and that until sunset. I'm not afraid, not even watchful. Which makes me an easy target. Except I'd kill anyone I met on sight. Without emotion or the slightest tremor in my hands. My hatred of the Capitol has not lessened my hatred of my competitors in the least. Especially the Careers. They, at least, can be made to pay for Rue's death.

No one materializes though. There aren't many of us left and it's a big arena. Soon they'll be pulling out some other device to force us together. But there's been enough gore today. Perhaps we'll even get to sleep.

I'm about to haul my packs into a tree to make camp when a silver parachute floats down and lands in front of me. A gift from a sponsor. But why now? I've been in fairly good shape with supplies. Maybe Haymitch's noticed my despondency and is trying to cheer me up a bit. Or could it be something to help my ear?

I open the parachute and find a small loaf of bread. It's not the fine white Capitol stuff. It's made of dark ration grain and shaped in a crescent. Sprinkled with seeds. I flashback to Peeta's lesson on the various district breads in the Training Center. This bread came from District 11. I cautiously lift the still warm loaf. What must it have cost the people of District 11 who can't even feed themselves? How many would've had to do without to scrape up a coin to put in the collection for this one loaf? It had been meant for Rue, surely. But instead of pulling the gift when she died, they'd authorized Haymitch to give it to me. As a thank-you? Or because, like me, they don't like to let debts go unpaid? For whatever reason, this is a first. A district gift to a tribute who's not your own.

I lift my face and step into the last falling rays of sunlight. "My thanks to the people of District Eleven," I say. I want them to know I know where it came from. That the full value of their gift has been recognized.

I climb dangerously high into a tree, not for safety but to get as far away from today as I can. My sleeping bag is rolled neatly in Rue's pack. Tomorrow I'll sort through the supplies. Tomorrow I'll make a new plan. But tonight, all I can do is strap myself in and take tiny bites of the bread. It's good. It tastes of home.

Soon the seal's in the sky, the anthem plays in my right ear. I see the boy from District 1, Rue. That's all for tonight. *Six of us left,* I think. *Only six.* With the bread still locked in my hands, I fall asleep at once.

Sometimes when things are particularly bad, my brain will give me a happy dream. A visit with my father in the woods. An hour of sunlight and cake with Prim. Tonight it sends me Rue, still decked in her flowers, perched in a high sea of trees, trying to teach me to talk to the mockingjays. I see no sign of her wounds, no blood, just a bright, laughing girl. She sings songs I've never heard in a clear, melodic voice. On and on. Through the night. There's a drowsy in-between period when I can hear the last few strains of her music although she's lost in the leaves. When I fully awaken, I'm momentarily comforted. I try to hold on to the peaceful feeling of the dream, but it quickly slips away, leaving me sadder and lonelier than ever.

Heaviness infuses my whole body, as if there's liquid lead in my veins. I've lost the will to do the simplest tasks, to do anything but lie here, staring unblinkingly through the canopy of leaves. For several hours, I remain motionless. As usual, it's the thought of Prim's anxious face as she watches me on the screens back home that breaks me from my lethargy.

I give myself a series of simple commands to follow, like "Now you have to sit up, Katniss. Now you have to drink water, Katniss." I act on the orders with slow, robotic motions. "Now you have to sort the packs, Katniss."

Rue's pack holds my sleeping bag, her nearly empty water skin, a handful of nuts and roots, a bit of rabbit, her extra socks, and her slingshot. The boy from District 1 has several knives, two spare spearheads, a flashlight, a small leather pouch, a first-aid kit, a full bottle of water, and a pack of dried fruit. A pack of dried fruit! Out of all he might have chosen from. To me, this is a sign of extreme arrogance. Why bother to carry food when you have such a bounty back at camp? When you will kill your enemies so quickly you'll be home before you're hungry? I can only hope the other Careers traveled so lightly when it came to food and now find themselves with nothing.

Speaking of which, my own supply is running low. I finish off the loaf from District 11 and the last of the rabbit. How quickly the food disappears. All I have left are Rue's roots and nuts, the boy's dried fruit, and one strip of beef. *Now you have to hunt, Katniss,* I tell myself.

I obediently consolidate the supplies I want into my pack. After I climb down the tree, I conceal the boy's knives and spearheads in a pile of rocks so that no one else can use them. I've lost my bearings what with all the wandering around I did yesterday evening, but I try and head back in the general direction of the stream. I know I'm on course when I come across Rue's third, unlit fire. Shortly thereafter, I discover a flock of grooslings perched in the trees and take out three before they know what hit them. I return to Rue's signal fire and start it up, not caring about the excessive smoke. *Where are you, Cato?* I think as I roast the birds and Rue's roots. *I'm waiting right here.*

Who knows where the Careers are now? Either too far to reach me or too sure this is a trick or . . . is it possible? Too scared of me? They know I have the bow and arrows, of course, Cato saw me take them from Glimmer's body. But have they put two and two together yet? Figured out I blew up the supplies and killed their fellow Career? Possibly they think Thresh did this. Wouldn't he be more likely to revenge Rue's death than I would? Being from the same district? Not that he ever took any interest in her.

And what about Foxface? Did she hang around to watch me blow up the supplies? No. When I caught her laughing in the ashes the next morning, it was as if someone had given her a lovely surprise.

I doubt they think Peeta has lit this signal fire. Cato's sure he's as good as dead. I find myself wishing I could tell Peeta about the flowers I put on Rue. That I now understand what he was trying to say on the roof. Perhaps if he wins the Games, he'll see me on victor's night, when they replay the highlights of the Games on a screen over the stage where we did our interviews. The winner sits in a place of honor on the platform, surrounded by their support crew.

But I told Rue I'd be there. For both of us. And somehow that seems even more important than the vow I gave Prim.

I really think I stand a chance of doing it now. Winning. It's not just having the arrows or outsmarting the Careers a few times, although those things help. Something happened when I was holding Rue's hand, watching the life drain out of her. Now I am determined to avenge her, to make her loss unforgettable, and I can only do that by winning and thereby making myself unforgettable.

I overcook the birds hoping someone will show up to shoot, but no one does. Maybe the other tributes are out there beating one another senseless. Which would be fine. Ever since the bloodbath, I've been featured on screens more than I care.

Eventually, I wrap up my food and go back to the stream to replenish my water and gather some. But the heaviness from the morning drapes back over me and even though it's only early evening, I climb a tree and settle in for the night. My brain begins to replay the events from yesterday. I keep seeing Rue speared, my arrow piercing the boy's neck. I don't know why I should even care about the boy.

Then I realize . . . he was my first kill.

Along with other statistics they report to help people place their bets, every tribute has a list of kills. I guess technically I'd get credited for Glimmer and the girl from District 4, too, for dumping that nest on them. But the boy from District 1 was the first person I knew would die because of my actions. Numerous animals have lost their lives at my hands, but only one human. I hear Gale saying, "How different can it be, really?"

Amazingly similar in the execution. A bow pulled, an arrow shot. Entirely different in the aftermath. I killed a boy whose name I don't even know. Somewhere his family is weeping for him. His friends call for my blood. Maybe he had a girlfriend who really believed he would come back. . . .

But then I think of Rue's still body and I'm able to banish the boy from my mind. At least, for now.

It's been an uneventful day according to the sky. No deaths. I wonder how long we'll get until the next catastrophe drives us back together. If it's going to be tonight, I want to get some sleep first. I cover my good ear to block out the strains of the anthem, but then I hear the trumpets and sit straight up in anticipation.

For the most part, the only communication the tributes get from outside the arena is the nightly death toll. But occasionally, there will be trumpets followed by an announcement. Usually, this will be a call to a feast. When food is scarce, the Gamemakers will invite the players to a banquet, somewhere known to all like the Cornucopia, as an inducement to gather and fight. Sometimes there is a feast and sometimes there's nothing but a loaf of stale bread for the tributes to compete for. I wouldn't go in for the food, but this could be an ideal time to take out a few competitors.

Claudius Templesmith's voice booms down from over-head, congratulating the six of us who remain. But he is not inviting us to a feast. He's saying something very confusing. There's been a rule change in the Games. A rule change! That in itself is mind bending since we don't really have any rules to speak of except don't step off your circle for sixty seconds and the unspoken rule about not eating one another. Under the new rule, both tributes from the same district will be declared winners if they are the last two alive. Claudius pauses, as if he knows we're not getting it, and repeats the change again.

The news sinks in. Two tributes can win this year. If they're from the same district. Both can live. Both of us can live.

Before I can stop myself, I call out Peeta's name.

PART III
"THE VICTOR"

I clap my hands over my mouth, but the sound has already escaped. The sky goes black and I hear a chorus of frogs begin to sing. *Stupid!* I tell myself. *What a stupid thing to do!* I wait, frozen, for the woods to come alive with assailants. Then I remember there's almost no one left.

Peeta, who's been wounded, is now my ally. Whatever doubts I've had about him dissipate because if either of us took the other's life now we'd be pariahs when we returned to District 12. In fact, I know if I was watching I'd loathe any tribute who didn't immediately ally with their district partner. Besides, it just makes sense to protect each other. And in my case — being one of the star-crossed lovers from District 12 — it's an absolute requirement if I want any more help from sympathetic sponsors.

The star-crossed lovers . . . Peeta must have been playing that angle all along. Why else would the Gamemakers have made this unprecedented change in the rules? For two tributes to have a shot at winning, our "romance" must be so popular with the audience that condemning it would jeopardize the success of the Games. No thanks to me. All I've done is managed not to kill Peeta. But whatever he's done in the arena, he must have the audience convinced it was to keep me alive. Shaking his head to keep me from running to the Cornucopia. Fighting Cato to let me escape. Even hooking up with the Careers must have been a move to protect me. Peeta, it turns out, has never been a danger to me.

The thought makes me smile. I drop my hands and hold my face up to the moonlight so the cameras can be sure to catch it.

So, who is there left to be afraid of? Foxface? The boy tribute from her district is dead. She's operating alone, at night. And her strategy has been to evade, not attack. I don't really think that, even if she heard my voice, she'd do anything but hope someone else would kill me.

Then there's Thresh. All right, he's a distinct threat. But I haven't seen him, not once, since the Games began. I think about how Foxface grew alarmed when she heard a sound at the site of the explosion. But she didn't turn to the woods, she turned to whatever lies across from it. To that area of the arena that drops off into I don't know what. I feel almost certain that the person she ran from was Thresh and that is his domain. He'd never have heard me from there and, even if he did, I'm up too high for someone his size to reach.

So that leaves Cato and the girl from District 2, who are now surely celebrating the new rule. They're the only ones left who benefit from it besides Peeta and myself. Do I run from them now, on the chance they heard me call Peeta's name? *No,* I think. *Let them come.* Let them come with their night-vision glasses and their heavy, branch-breaking bodies.

Right into the range of my arrows. But I know they won't. If they didn't come in daylight to my fire, they won't risk what could be another trap at night. When they come, it will be on their own terms, not because I've let them know my whereabouts.

Stay put and get some sleep, Katniss, I instruct myself, although I wish I could start tracking Peeta now. *Tomorrow, you'll find him.*

I do sleep, but in the morning I'm extra-cautious, thinking that while the Careers might hesitate to attack me in a tree, they're completely capable of setting an ambush for me. I make sure to fully prepare myself for the day — eating a big breakfast, securing my pack, readying my weapons — before I descend. But all seems peaceful and undisturbed on the ground.

Today I'll have to be scrupulously careful. The Careers will know I'm trying to locate Peeta. They may well want to wait until I do before they move in. If he's as badly wounded as Cato thinks, I'd be in the position of having to defend us both without any assistance. But if he's that incapacitated, how has he managed to stay alive? And how on earth will I find him?

I try to think of anything Peeta ever said that might give me an indication as to where he's hiding out, but nothing rings a bell. So I go back to the last moment I saw him sparkling in the sunlight, yelling at me to run. Then Cato appeared, his sword drawn. And after I was gone, he wounded Peeta. But how did Peeta get away? Maybe he'd held out better against the tracker jacker poison than Cato.

Maybe that was the variable that allowed him to escape. But he'd been stung, too. So how far could he have gotten, stabbed and filled with venom? And how has he stayed alive all these days since? If the wound and the stingers haven't killed him, surely thirst would have taken him by now.

And that's when I get my first clue to his whereabouts. He couldn't have survived without water. I know that from my first few days here. He must be hidden somewhere near a source. There's the lake, but I find that an unlikely option since it's so close to the Careers' base camp. A few spring-fed pools. But you'd really be a sitting duck at one of those. And the stream. The one that leads from the camp Rue and I made all the way down near the lake and beyond. If he stuck to the stream, he could change his location and always be near water. He could walk in the current and erase any tracks. He might even be able to get a fish or two.

Well, it's a place to start, anyway.

To confuse my enemies' minds, I start a fire with plenty of green wood. Even if they think it's a ruse, I hope they'll decide I'm hidden somewhere near it. While in reality, I'll be tracking Peeta.

The sun burns off the morning haze almost immediately and I can tell the day will be hotter than usual. The water's cool and pleasant on my bare feet as I head downstream. I'm tempted to call out Peeta's name as I go but decide against it. I will have to find him with my eyes and one good ear or he will have to find me. But he'll know I'll be looking, right? He won't have so low of an opinion of me as to think I'd ignore the new rule and keep to myself. Would he? He's very hard to predict, which might be interesting under different circumstances, but at the moment only provides an extra obstacle.

It doesn't take long to reach the spot where I peeled off to go to the Careers' camp. There's been no sign of Peeta, but this doesn't surprise me. I've been up and down this stretch three times since the tracker jacker incident. If he were nearby, surely I'd have had some suspicion of it. The stream begins to curve to the left into a part of the woods that's new to me. Muddy banks covered in tangled water plants lead to large rocks that increase in size until I begin to feel somewhat trapped. It would be no small matter to escape the stream now. Fighting off Cato or Thresh as I climbed over this rocky terrain. In fact, I've just about decided I'm on the wrong track entirely, that a wounded boy would be unable to navigate getting to and from this water source, when I see the bloody streak going down the curve of a boulder. It's long dried now, but the smeary lines running side to side suggest someone — who perhaps was not fully in control of his mental faculties — tried to wipe it away.

Hugging the rocks, I move slowly in the direction of the blood, searching for him. I find a few more bloodstains, one with a few threads of fabric glued to it, but no sign of life. I break down and say his name in a hushed voice. "Peeta! Peeta!" Then a mockingjay lands on a scruffy tree and begins to mimic my tones so I stop. I give up and climb back down to the stream thinking, *He must have moved on. Somewhere farther down.*

My foot has just broken the surface of the water when I hear a voice.

"You here to finish me off, sweetheart?"

I whip around. It's come from the left, so I can't pick it up very well. And the voice was hoarse and weak. Still, it must have been Peeta. Who else in the arena would call me sweetheart? My eyes peruse the bank, but there's nothing. Just mud, the plants, the base of the rocks.

"Peeta?" I whisper. "Where are you?" There's no answer. Could I just have imagined it? No, I'm certain it was real and very close at hand, too. "Peeta?" I creep along the bank.

"Well, don't step on me."

I jump back. His voice was right under my feet. Still there's nothing. Then his eyes open, unmistakably blue in the brown mud and green leaves. I gasp and am rewarded with a hint of white teeth as he laughs.

It's the final word in camouflage. Forget chucking weights around. Peeta should have gone into his private session with the Gamemakers and painted himself into a tree. Or a boulder. Or a muddy bank full of weeds.

"Close your eyes again," I order. He does, and his mouth, too, and completely disappears. Most of what I judge to be his body is actually under a layer of mud and plants. His face and arms are so artfully disguised as to be invisible. I kneel beside him. "I guess all those hours decorating cakes paid off."

Peeta smiles. "Yes, frosting. The final defense of the dying."

"You're not going to die," I tell him firmly.

"Says who?" His voice is so ragged.

"Says me. We're on the same team now, you know," I tell him.

His eyes open. "So, I heard. Nice of you to find what's left of me."

I pull out my water bottle and give him a drink. "Did Cato cut you?" I ask.

"Left leg. Up high," he answers.

"Let's get you in the stream, wash you off so I can see what kind of wounds you've got," I say.

"Lean down a minute first," he says. "Need to tell you something." I lean over and put my good ear to his lips, which tickle as he whispers. "Remember, we're madly in love, so it's all right to kiss me anytime you feel like it."

I jerk my head back but end up laughing. "Thanks, I'll keep it in mind." At least, he's still able to joke around. But when I start to help him to the stream, all the levity disappears. It's only two feet away, how hard can it be? Very hard when I realize he's unable to move an inch on his own. He's so weak that the best he can do is not to resist. I try to drag him, but despite the fact that I know he's doing all he can to keep quiet, sharp cries of pain escape him. The mud and plants seem to have imprisoned him and I finally have to give a gigantic tug to break him from their clutches. He's still two feet from the water, lying there, teeth gritted, tears cutting trails in the dirt on his face.

"Look, Peeta, I'm going to roll you into the stream. It's very shallow here, okay?" I say.

"Excellent," he says.

I crouch down beside him. No matter what happens, I tell myself, don't stop until he's in the water. "On three," I say. "One, two, three!" I can only manage one full roll before I have to stop because of the horrible sound he's making. Now he's on the edge of the stream. Maybe this is better anyway.

"Okay, change of plans. I'm not going to put you all the way in," I tell him. Besides, if I get him in, who knows if I'd ever be able to get him out?

"No more rolling?" he asks.

"That's all done. Let's get you cleaned up. Keep an eye on the woods for me, okay?" I say. It's hard to know where to start. He's so caked with mud and matted leaves, I can't even see his clothes. If he's wearing clothes. The thought makes me hesitate a moment, but then I plunge in. Naked bodies are no big deal in the arena, right?

I've got two water bottles and Rue's water skin. I prop them against rocks in the stream so that two are always filling while I pour the third over Peeta's body. It takes a while, but I finally get rid of enough mud to find his clothes. I gently unzip his jacket, unbutton his shirt and ease them off him. His undershirt is so plastered into his wounds I have to cut it away with my knife and drench him again to work it loose. He's badly bruised with a long burn across his chest and four tracker jacker stings, if you count the one under his ear. But I feel a bit better. This much I can fix. I decide to take care of his upper body first, to alleviate some pain, before I tackle whatever damage Cato did to his leg.

Since treating his wounds seems pointless when he's lying in what's become a mud puddle, I manage to prop him up against a boulder. He sits there, uncomplaining, while I wash away all the traces of dirt from his hair and skin. His flesh is very pale in the sunlight and he no longer looks strong and stocky. I have to dig the stingers out of his tracker jacker lumps, which causes him to wince, but the minute I apply the leaves he sighs in relief. While he dries in the sun, I wash his filthy shirt and jacket and spread them over boulders. Then I apply the burn cream to his chest. This is when I notice how hot his skin is becoming. The layer of mud and the bottles of water have disguised the fact that he's burning with fever. I dig through the first-aid kit I got from the boy from District 1 and find pills that reduce your temperature. My mother actually breaks down and buys these on occasion when her home remedies fail.

"Swallow these," I tell him, and he obediently takes the medicine. "You must be hungry."

"Not really. It's funny, I haven't been hungry for days," says Peeta. In fact, when I offer him groosling, he wrinkles his nose at it and turns away. That's when I know how sick he is.

"Peeta, we need to get some food in you," I insist.

"It'll just come right back up," he says. The best I can do is to get him to eat a few bits of dried apple. "Thanks. I'm much better, really. Can I sleep now, Katniss?" he asks.

"Soon," I promise. "I need to look at your leg first." Trying to be as gentle as I can, I remove his boots, his socks, and then very slowly inch his pants off of him. I can see the tear Cato's sword made in the fabric over his thigh, but it in no way prepares me for what lies underneath. The deep inflamed gash oozing both blood and pus. The swelling of the leg. And worst of all, the smell of festering flesh.

I want to run away. Disappear into the woods like I did that day they brought the burn victim to our house. Go and hunt while my mother and Prim attend to what I have neither the skill nor the courage to face. But there's no one here but me. I try to capture the calm demeanor my mother assumes when handling particularly bad cases.

"Pretty awful, huh?" says Peeta. He's watching me closely.

"So-so." I shrug like it's no big deal. "You should see some of the people they bring my mother from the mines." I refrain from saying how I usually clear out of the house whenever she's treating anything worse than a cold. Come to think of it, I don't even much like to be around coughing. "First thing is to clean it well."

I've left on Peeta's undershorts because they're not in bad shape and I don't want to pull them over the swollen thigh and, all right, maybe the idea of him being naked makes me uncomfortable. That's another thing about my mother and Prim. Nakedness has no effect on them, gives them no cause for embarrassment. Ironically, at this point in the Games, my little sister would be of far more use to Peeta than I am. I scoot my square of plastic under him so I can wash down the rest of him. With each bottle I pour over him, the worse the wound looks. The rest of his lower body has fared pretty well, just one tracker jacker sting and a few small burns that I treat quickly. But the gash on his leg . . . what on earth can I do for that?

"Why don't we give it some air and then . . ." I trail off.

"And then you'll patch it up?" says Peeta. He looks almost sorry for me, as if he knows how lost I am.

"That's right," I say. "In the meantime, you eat these." I put a few dried pear halves in his hand and go back in the stream to wash the rest of his clothes. When they're flattened out and drying, I examine the contents of the first-aid kit. It's pretty basic stuff. Bandages, fever pills, medicine to calm stomachs. Nothing of the caliber I'll need to treat Peeta.

"We're going to have to experiment some," I admit. I know the tracker jacker leaves draw out infection, so I start with those. Within minutes of pressing the handful of chewed-up green stuff into the wound, pus begins running down the side of his leg. I tell myself this is a good thing and bite the inside of my cheek hard because my breakfast is threatening to make a reappearance.

"Katniss?" Peeta says. I meet his eyes, knowing my face must be some shade of green. He mouths the words. "How about that kiss?"

I burst out laughing because the whole thing is so revolting I can't stand it.

"Something wrong?" he asks a little too innocently.

"I . . . I'm no good at this. I'm not my mother. I've no idea what I'm doing and I hate pus," I say. "Euh!" I allow myself to let out a groan as I rinse away the first round of leaves and apply the second. "Euuuh!"

"How do you hunt?" he asks.

"Trust me. Killing things is much easier than this," I said. "Although for all I know, I am killing you."

"Can you speed it up a little?" he asks.

"No. Shut up and eat your pears," I say.

After three applications and what seems like a bucket of pus, the wound does look better. Now that the swelling has gone down, I can see how deep Cato's sword cut. Right down to the bone.

"What next, Dr. Everdeen?" he asks.

"Maybe I'll put some of the burn ointment on it. I think it helps with infection anyway. And wrap it up?" I say. I do and the whole thing seems a lot more manageable, covered in clean white cotton. Although, against the sterile bandage, the hem of his undershorts looks filthy and teeming with contagion. I pull out Rue's backpack. "Here, cover yourself with this and I'll wash your shorts."

"Oh, I don't care if you see me," says Peeta.

"You're just like the rest of my family," I say. "I care, all right?" I turn my back and look at the stream until the undershorts splash into the current. He must be feeling a bit better if he can throw.

"You know, you're kind of squeamish for such a lethal person," says Peeta as I beat the shorts clean between two rocks. "I wish I'd let you give Haymitch a shower after all."

I wrinkle my nose at the memory. "What's he sent you so far?"

"Not a thing," says Peeta. Then there's a pause as it hits him. "Why, did you get something?"

"Burn medicine," I say almost sheepishly. "Oh, and some bread."

"I always knew you were his favorite," says Peeta.

"Please, he can't stand being in the same room with me," I say.

"Because you're just alike," mutters Peeta. I ignore it though because this really isn't the time for me to be insulting Haymitch, which is my first impulse.

I let Peeta doze off while his clothes dry out, but by late afternoon, I don't dare wait any longer. I gently shake his shoulder. "Peeta, we've got to go now."

"Go?" He seems confused. "Go where?"

"Away from here. Downstream maybe. Somewhere we can hide you until you're stronger," I say. I help him dress, leaving his feet bare so we can walk in the water, and pull him upright. His face drains of color the moment he puts weight on his leg. "Come on. You can do this."

But he can't. Not for long anyway. We make it about fifty yards downstream, with him propped up by my shoulder, and I can tell he's going to black out. I sit him on the bank, push his head between his knees, and pat his back awkwardly as I survey the area. Of course, I'd love to get him up in a tree, but that's not going to happen. It could be worse though. Some of the rocks form small cavelike structures. I set my sights on one about twenty yards above the stream. When Peeta's able to stand, I half-guide, half-carry him up to the cave. Really, I'd like to look around for a better place, but this one will have to do because my ally is shot. Paper white, panting, and, even though it's only just cooling off, he's shivering.

I cover the floor of the cave with a layer of pine needles, unroll my sleeping bag, and tuck him into it. I get a couple of pills and some water into him when he's not noticing, but he refuses to eat even the fruit. Then he just lies there, his eyes trained on my face as I build a sort of blind out of vines to conceal the mouth of the cave. The result is unsatisfactory. An animal might not question it, but a human would see hands had manufactured it quickly enough. I tear it down in frustration.

"Katniss," he says. I go over to him and brush the hair back from his eyes. "Thanks for finding me."

"You would have found me if you could," I say. His forehead's burning up. Like the medicine's having no effect at all. Suddenly, out of nowhere, I'm scared he's going to die.

"Yes. Look, if I don't make it back —" he begins.

"Don't talk like that. I didn't drain all that pus for nothing," I say.

"I know. But just in case I don't —" he tries to continue.

"No, Peeta, I don't even want to discuss it," I say, placing my fingers on his lips to quiet him.

"But I —" he insists.

Impulsively, I lean forward and kiss him, stopping his words. This is probably overdue anyway since he's right, we are supposed to be madly in love. It's the first time I've ever kissed a boy, which should make some sort of impression I guess, but all I can register is how unnaturally hot his lips are from the fever. I break away and pull the edge of the sleeping bag up around him. "You're not going to die. I forbid it. All right?"

"All right," he whispers.

I step out in the cool evening air just as the parachute floats down from the sky. My fingers quickly undo the tie, hoping for some real medicine to treat Peeta's leg. Instead I find a pot of hot broth.

Haymitch couldn't be sending me a clearer message. One kiss equals one pot of broth. I can almost hear his snarl. "You're supposed to be in love, sweetheart. The boy's dying. Give me something I can work with!"

And he's right. If I want to keep Peeta alive, I've got to give the audience something more to care about. Star-crossed lovers desperate to get home together. Two hearts beating as one. Romance.

Never having been in love, this is going to be a real trick. I think of my parents. The way my father never failed to bring her gifts from the woods. The way my mother's face would light up at the sound of his boots at the door. The way she almost stopped living when he died.

"Peeta!" I say, trying for the special tone that my mother used only with my father. He's dozed off again, but I kiss him awake, which seems to startle him. Then he smiles as if he'd be happy to lie there gazing at me forever. He's great at this stuff.

I hold up the pot. "Peeta, look what Haymitch has sent you."

Getting the broth into Peeta takes an hour of coaxing, begging, threatening, and yes, kissing, but finally, sip by sip, he empties the pot. I let him drift off to sleep then and attend to my own needs, wolfing down a supper of groosling and roots while I watch the daily report in the sky. No new casualties. Still, Peeta and I have given the audience a fairly interesting day. Hopefully, the Gamemakers will allow us a peaceful night.

I automatically look around for a good tree to nest in before I realize that's over. At least for a while. I can't very well leave Peeta unguarded on the ground. I left the scene of his last hiding place on the bank of the stream untouched — how could I conceal it? — and we're a scant fifty yards downstream. I put on my glasses, place my weapons in readiness, and settle down to keep watch.

The temperature drops rapidly and soon I'm chilled to the bone. Eventually, I give in and slide into the sleeping bag with Peeta. It's toasty warm and I snuggle down gratefully until I realize it's more than warm, it's overly hot because the bag is reflecting back his fever. I check his forehead and find it burning and dry. I don't know what to do. Leave him in the bag and hope the excessive heat breaks the fever? Take him out and hope the night air cools him off? I end up just dampening a strip of bandage and placing it on his forehead. It seems weak, but I'm afraid to do anything too drastic.

I spend the night half-sitting, half-lying next to Peeta, refreshing the bandage, and trying not to dwell on the fact that by teaming up with him, I've made myself far more vulnerable than when I was alone. Tethered to the ground, on guard, with a very sick person to take care of. But I knew he was injured. And still I came after him. I'm just going to have to trust that whatever instinct sent me to find him was a good one.

When the sky turns rosy, I notice the sheen of sweat on Peeta's lip and discover the fever has broken. He's not back to normal, but it's come down a few degrees. Last night, when I was gathering vines, I came upon a bush of Rue's berries. I strip off the fruit and mash it up in the broth pot with cold water.

Peeta's struggling to get up when I reach the cave. "I woke up and you were gone," he says. "I was worried about you."

I have to laugh as I ease him back down. "You were worried about me? Have you taken a look at yourself lately?"

"I thought Cato and Clove might have found you. They like to hunt at night," he says, still serious.

"Clove? Which one is that?" I ask.

"The girl from District Two. She's still alive, right?" he says.

"Yes, there's just them and us and Thresh and Foxface," I say. "That's what I nicknamed the girl from Five. How do you feel?"

"Better than yesterday. This is an enormous improvement over the mud," he says. "Clean clothes and medicine and a sleeping bag . . . and you."

Oh, right, the whole romance thing. I reach out to touch his cheek and he catches my hand and presses it against his lips. I remember my father doing this very thing to my mother and I wonder where Peeta picked it up. Surely not from his father and the witch.

"No more kisses for you until you've eaten," I say.

We get him propped up against the wall and he obediently swallows the spoonfuls of the berry mush I feed him. He refuses the groosling again, though.

"You didn't sleep," Peeta says.

"I'm all right," I say. But the truth is, I'm exhausted.

"Sleep now. I'll keep watch. I'll wake you if anything happens," he says. I hesitate. "Katniss, you can't stay up forever."

He's got a point there. I'll have to sleep eventually. And probably better to do it now when he seems relatively alert and we have daylight on our side. "All right," I say. "But just for a few hours. Then you wake me."

It's too warm for the sleeping bag now. I smooth it out on the cave floor and lie down, one hand on my loaded bow in case I have to shoot at a moment's notice. Peeta sits beside me, leaning against the wall, his bad leg stretched out before him, his eyes trained on the world outside. "Go to sleep," he says softly. His hand brushes the loose strands of my hair off my forehead. Unlike the staged kisses and caresses so far, this gesture seems natural and comforting. I don't want him to stop and he doesn't. He's still stroking my hair when I fall asleep.

Too long. I sleep too long. I know from the moment I open my eyes that we're into the afternoon. Peeta's right beside me, his position unchanged. I sit up, feeling somehow defensive but better rested than I've been in days.

"Peeta, you were supposed to wake me after a couple of hours," I say.

"For what? Nothing's going on here," he says. "Besides I like watching you sleep. You don't scowl. Improves your looks a lot."

This, of course, brings on a scowl that makes him grin. That's when I notice how dry his lips are. I test his cheek. Hot as a coal stove. He claims he's been drinking, but the containers still feel full to me. I give him more fever pills and stand over him while he drinks first one, then a second quart of water. Then I tend to his minor wounds, the burns, the stings, which are showing improvement. I steel myself and unwrap the leg.

My heart drops into my stomach. It's worse, much worse. There's no more pus in evidence, but the swelling has increased and the tight shiny skin is inflamed. Then I see the red streaks starting to crawl up his leg. Blood poisoning. Unchecked, it will kill him for sure. My chewed-up leaves and ointment won't make a dent in it. We'll need strong anti-infection drugs from the Capitol. I can't imagine the cost of such potent medicine. If Haymitch pooled every donation from every sponsor, would he have enough? I doubt it. Gifts go up in price the longer the Games continue. What buys a full meal on day one buys a cracker on day twelve. And the kind of medicine Peeta needs would have been at a premium from the beginning.

"Well, there's more swelling, but the pus is gone," I say in an unsteady voice.

"I know what blood poisoning is, Katniss," says Peeta. "Even if my mother isn't a healer."

"You're just going to have to outlast the others, Peeta. They'll cure it back at the Capitol when we win," I say.

"Yes, that's a good plan," he says. But I feel this is mostly for my benefit.

"You have to eat. Keep your strength up. I'm going to make you soup," I say.

"Don't light a fire," he says. "It's not worth it."

"We'll see," I say. As I take the pot down to the stream, I'm struck by how brutally hot it is. I swear the Gamemakers are progressively ratcheting up the temperature in the day-time and sending it plummeting at night. The heat of the sun-baked stones by the stream gives me an idea though. Maybe I won't need to light a fire.

I settle down on a big flat rock halfway between the stream and the cave. After purifying half a pot of water, I place it in direct sunlight and add several egg-size hot stones to the water. I'm the first to admit I'm not much of a cook. But since soup mainly involves tossing everything in a pot and waiting, it's one of my better dishes. I mince groosling until it's practically mush and mash some of Rue's roots. Fortunately, they've both been roasted already so they mostly need to be heated up. Already, between the sunlight and the rocks, the water's warm. I put in the meat and roots, swap in fresh rocks, and go find something green to spice it up a little. Before long, I discover a tuft of chives growing at the base of some rocks. Perfect. I chop them very fine and add them to the pot, switch out the rocks again, put on the lid, and let the whole thing stew.

I've seen very few signs of game around, but I don't feel comfortable leaving Peeta alone while I hunt, so I rig half a dozen snares and hope I get lucky. I wonder about the other tributes, how they're managing now that their main source of food has been blown up. At least three of them, Cato, Clove, and Foxface, had been relying on it. Probably not Thresh though. I've got a feeling he must share some of Rue's knowledge on how to feed yourself from the earth. Are they fighting each other? Looking for us? Maybe one of them has located us and is just waiting for the right moment to attack. The idea sends me back to the cave.

Peeta's stretched out on top of the sleeping bag in the shade of the rocks. Although he brightens a bit when I come in, it's clear he feels miserable. I put cool cloths on his head, but they warm up almost as soon as they touch his skin.

"Do you want anything?" I ask.

"No," he says. "Thank you. Wait, yes. Tell me a story."

"A story? What about?" I say. I'm not much for story-telling. It's kind of like singing. But once in a while, Prim wheedles one out of me.

"Something happy. Tell me about the happiest day you can remember," says Peeta.

Something between a sigh and a huff of exasperation leaves my mouth. A happy story? This will require a lot more effort than the soup. I rack my brains for good memories. Most of them involve Gale and me out hunting and somehow I don't think these will play well with either Peeta or the audience. That leaves Prim.

"Did I ever tell you about how I got Prim's goat?" I ask. Peeta shakes his head, and looks at me expectantly. So I begin. But carefully. Because my words are going out all over Panem. And while people have no doubt put two and two together that I hunt illegally, I don't want to hurt Gale or Greasy Sae or the butcher or even the Peacekeepers back home who are my customers by publicly announcing they're breaking the law, too.

Here's the real story of how I got the money for Prim's goat, Lady. It was a Friday evening, the day before Prim's tenth birthday in late May. As soon as school ended, Gale and I hit the woods, because I wanted to get enough to trade for a present for Prim. Maybe some new cloth for a dress or a hairbrush. Our snares had done well enough and the woods were flush with greens, but this was really no more than our average Friday-night haul. I was disappointed as we headed back, even though Gale said we'd be sure to do better tomorrow. We were resting a moment by a stream when we saw him. A young buck, probably a yearling by his size. His antlers were just growing in, still small and coated in velvet. Poised to run but unsure of us, unfamiliar with humans. Beautiful.

Less beautiful perhaps when the two arrows caught him, one in the neck, the other in the chest. Gale and I had shot at the same time. The buck tried to run but stumbled, and Gale's knife slit his throat before he knew what had happened. Momentarily, I'd felt a pang at killing something so fresh and innocent. And then my stomach rumbled at the thought of all that fresh and innocent meat.

A deer! Gale and I have only brought down three in all. The first one, a doe that had injured her leg somehow, almost didn't count. But we knew from that experience not to go dragging the carcass into the Hob. It had caused chaos with people bidding on parts and actually trying to hack off pieces themselves. Greasy Sae had intervened and sent us with our deer to the butcher, but not before it'd been badly damaged, hunks of meat taken, the hide riddled with holes. Although everybody paid up fairly, it had lowered the value of the kill.

This time, we waited until dark fell and slipped under a hole in the fence close to the butcher. Even though we were known hunters, it wouldn't have been good to go carrying a 150-pound deer through the streets of District 12 in daylight like we were rubbing it in the officials' faces.

The butcher, a short, chunky woman named Rooba, came to the back door when we knocked. You don't haggle with Rooba. She gives you one price, which you can take or leave, but it's a fair price. We took her offer on the deer and she threw in a couple of venison steaks we could pick up after the butchering. Even with the money divided in two, neither Gale nor I had held so much at one time in our lives. We decided to keep it a secret and surprise our families with the meat and money at the end of the next day.

This is where I really got the money for the goat, but I tell Peeta I sold an old silver locket of my mother's. That can't hurt anyone. Then I pick up the story in the late afternoon of Prim's birthday.

Gale and I went to the market on the square so that I could buy dress materials. As I was running my fingers over a length of thick blue cotton cloth, something caught my eye. There's an old man who keeps a small herd of goats on the other side of the Seam. I don't know his real name, everyone just calls him the Goat Man. His joints are swollen and twisted in painful angles, and he's got a hacking cough that proves he spent years in the mines. But he's lucky. Somewhere along the way he saved up enough for these goats and now has something to do in his old age besides slowly starve to death. He's filthy and impatient, but the goats are clean and their milk is rich if you can afford it.

One of the goats, a white one with black patches, was lying down in a cart. It was easy to see why. Something, probably a dog, had mauled her shoulder and infection had set in. It was bad, the Goat Man had to hold her up to milk her. But I thought I knew someone who could fix it.

"Gale," I whispered. "I want that goat for Prim."

Owning a nanny goat can change your life in District 12. The animals can live off almost anything, the Meadow's a perfect feeding place, and they can give four quarts of milk a day. To drink, to make into cheese, to sell. It's not even against the law.

"She's hurt pretty bad," said Gale. "We better take a closer look."

We went over and bought a cup of milk to share, then stood over the goat as if idly curious.

"Let her be," said the man.

"Just looking," said Gale.

"Well, look fast. She goes to the butcher soon. Hardly anyone will buy her milk, and then they only pay half price," said the man.

"What's the butcher giving for her?" I asked.

The man shrugged. "Hang around and see." I turned and saw Rooba coming across the square toward us. "Lucky thing you showed up," said the Goat Man when she arrived. "Girl's got her eye on your goat."

"Not if she's spoken for," I said carelessly.

Rooba looked me up and down then frowned at the goat. "She's not. Look at that shoulder. Bet you half the carcass will be too rotten for even sausage."

"What?" said the Goat Man. "We had a deal."

"We had a deal on an animal with a few teeth marks.

Not that thing. Sell her to the girl if she's stupid enough to take her," said Rooba. As she marched off, I caught her wink.

The Goat Man was mad, but he still wanted that goat off his hands. It took us half an hour to agree on the price. Quite a crowd had gathered by then to hand out opinions. It was an excellent deal if the goat lived; I'd been robbed if she died. People took sides in the argument, but I took the goat.

Gale offered to carry her. I think he wanted to see the look on Prim's face as much as I did. In a moment of complete giddiness, I bought a pink ribbon and tied it around her neck. Then we hurried back to my house.

You should have seen Prim's reaction when we walked in with that goat. Remember this is a girl who wept to save that awful old cat, Buttercup. She was so excited she started crying and laughing all at once. My mother was less sure, seeing the injury, but the pair of them went to work on it, grinding up herbs and coaxing brews down the animal's throat.

"They sound like you," says Peeta. I had almost forgotten he was there.

"Oh, no, Peeta. They work magic. That thing couldn't have died if it tried," I say. But then I bite my tongue, realizing what that must sound like to Peeta, who is dying, in my incompetent hands.

"Don't worry. I'm not trying," he jokes. "Finish the story."

"Well, that's it. Only I remember that night, Prim insisted on sleeping with Lady on a blanket next to the fire. And just before they drifted off, the goat licked her cheek, like it was giving her a good night kiss or something," I say. "It was already mad about her."

"Was it still wearing the pink ribbon?" he asks.

"I think so," I say. "Why?"

"I'm just trying to get a picture," he says thoughtfully. "I can see why that day made you happy."

"Well, I knew that goat would be a little gold mine," I say.

"Yes, of course I was referring to that, not the lasting joy you gave the sister you love so much you took her place in the reaping," says Peeta drily.

"The goat *has* paid for itself. Several times over," I say in a superior tone.

"Well, it wouldn't dare do anything else after you saved its life," says Peeta. "I intend to do the same thing."

"Really? What did you cost me again?" I ask.

"A lot of trouble. Don't worry. You'll get it all back," he says.

"You're not making sense," I say. I test his forehead. The fever's going nowhere but up. "You're a little cooler though."

The sound of the trumpets startles me. I'm on my feet and at the mouth of the cave in a flash, not wanting to miss a syllable. It's my new best friend, Claudius Templesmith, and as I expected, he's inviting us to a feast. Well, we're not that hungry and I actually wave his offer away in indifference when he says, "Now hold on. Some of you may already be declining my invitation. But this is no ordinary feast. Each of you needs something desperately."

I do need something desperately. Something to heal Peeta's leg.

"Each of you will find that something in a backpack, marked with your district number, at the Cornucopia at dawn. Think hard about refusing to show up. For some of you, this will be your last chance," says Claudius.

There's nothing else, just his words hanging in the air. I jump as Peeta grips my shoulder from behind. "No," he says. "You're not risking your life for me."

"Who said I was?" I say.

"So, you're not going?" he asks.

"Of course, I'm not going. Give me some credit. Do you think I'm running straight into some free-for-all against Cato and Clove and Thresh? Don't be stupid," I say, helping him back to bed. "I'll let them fight it out, we'll see who's in the sky tomorrow night and work out a plan from there."

"You're such a bad liar, Katniss. I don't know how you've survived this long." He begins to mimic me. "*I knew that goat would be a little gold mine. You're a little cooler though. Of course, I'm not going.*" He shakes his head. "Never gamble at cards. You'll lose your last coin," he says.

Anger flushes my face. "All right, I am going, and you can't stop me!"

"I can follow you. At least partway. I may not make it to the Cornucopia, but if I'm yelling your name, I bet someone can find me. And then I'll be dead for sure," he says.

"You won't get a hundred yards from here on that leg," I say.

"Then I'll drag myself," says Peeta. "You go and I'm going, too."

He's just stubborn enough and maybe just strong enough to do it. Come howling after me in the woods. Even if a tribute doesn't find him, something else might. He can't defend himself. I'd probably have to wall him up in the cave just to go myself. And who knows what the exertion will do to him?

"What am I supposed to do? Sit here and watch you die?" I say. He must know that's not an option. That the audience would hate me. And frankly, I would hate myself, too, if I didn't even try.

"I won't die. I promise. If you promise not to go," he says.

We're at something of a stalemate. I know I can't argue him out of this one, so I don't try. I pretend, reluctantly, to go along. "Then you have to do what I say. Drink your water, wake me when I tell you, and eat every bite of the soup no matter how disgusting it is!" I snap at him.

"Agreed. Is it ready?" he asks.

"Wait here," I say. The air's gone cold even though the sun's still up. I'm right about the Gamemakers messing with the temperature. I wonder if the thing someone needs desperately is a good blanket. The soup is still nice and warm in its iron pot. And actually doesn't taste too bad.

Peeta eats without complaint, even scraping out the pot to show his enthusiasm. He rambles on about how delicious it is, which should be encouraging if you don't know what fever does to people. He's like listening to Haymitch before the alcohol has soaked him into incoherence. I give him another dose of fever medicine before he goes off his head completely.

As I go down to the stream to wash up, all I can think is that he's going to die if I don't get to that feast. I'll keep him going for a day or two, and then the infection will reach his heart or his brain or his lungs and he'll be gone. And I'll be here all alone. Again. Waiting for the others.

I'm so lost in thought that I almost miss the parachute, even though it floats right by me. Then I spring after it, yanking it from the water, tearing off the silver fabric to retrieve the vial. Haymitch has done it! He's gotten the medicine — I don't know how, persuaded some gaggle of romantic fools to sell their jewels — and I can save Peeta! It's such a tiny vial though. It must be very strong to cure someone as ill as Peeta. A ripple of doubt runs through me. I uncork the vial and take a deep sniff. My spirits fall at the sickly sweet scent. Just to be sure, I place a drop on the tip of my tongue. There's no question, it's sleep syrup. It's a common medicine in District 12. Cheap, as medicine goes, but very addictive. Almost everyone's had a dose at one time or another. We have some in a bottle at home. My mother gives it to hysterical patients to knock them out to stitch up a bad wound or quiet their minds or just to help someone in pain get through the night. It only takes a little. A vial this size could knock Peeta out for a full day, but what good is that? I'm so furious I'm about to throw Haymitch's last offering into the stream when it hits me. A full day? That's more than I need.

I mash up a handful of berries so the taste won't be as noticeable and add some mint leaves for good measure. Then I head back up to the cave. "I've brought you a treat. I found a new patch of berries a little farther downstream."

Peeta opens his mouth for the first bite without hesitation. He swallows then frowns slightly. "They're very sweet."

"Yes, they're sugar berries. My mother makes jam from them. Haven't you ever had them before?" I say, poking the next spoonful in his mouth.

"No," he says, almost puzzled. "But they taste familiar. Sugar berries?"

"Well, you can't get them in the market much, they only grow wild," I say. Another mouthful goes down. Just one more to go.

"They're sweet as syrup," he says, taking the last spoonful. "Syrup." His eyes widen as he realizes the truth. I clamp my hand over his mouth and nose hard, forcing him to swallow instead of spit. He tries to make himself vomit the stuff up, but it's too late, he's already losing consciousness. Even as he fades away, I can see in his eyes what I've done is unforgivable.

I sit back on my heels and look at him with a mixture of sadness and satisfaction. A stray berry stains his chin and I wipe it away. "Who can't lie, Peeta?" I say, even though he can't hear me.

It doesn't matter. The rest of Panem can.

21

In the remaining hours before nightfall, I gather rocks and do my best to camouflage the opening of the cave. It's a slow and arduous process, but after a lot of sweating and shifting things around, I'm pretty pleased with my work. The cave now appears to be part of a larger pile of rocks, like so many in the vicinity. I can still crawl in to Peeta through a small opening, but it's undetectable from the outside. That's good, because I'll need to share that sleeping bag again tonight. Also, if I don't make it back from the feast, Peeta will be hidden but not entirely imprisoned. Although I doubt he can hang on much longer without medicine. If I die at the feast, District 12 isn't likely to have a victor.

I make a meal out of the smaller, bonier fish that inhabit the stream down here, fill every water container and purify it, and clean my weapons. I've nine arrows left in all. I debate leaving the knife with Peeta so he'll have some protection while I'm gone, but there's really no point. He was right about camouflage being his final defense. But I still might have use for the knife. Who knows what I'll encounter?

Here are some things I'm fairly certain of. That at least

Cato, Clove, and Thresh will be on hand when the feast starts. I'm not sure about Foxface since direct confrontation isn't her style or her forte. She's even smaller than I am and unarmed, unless she's picked up some weapons recently. She'll probably be hanging somewhere nearby, seeing what she can scavenge. But the other three . . . I'm going to have my hands full. My ability to kill at a distance is my greatest asset, but I know I'll have to go right into the thick of things to get that backpack, the one with the number *12* on it that Claudius Templesmith mentioned.

I watch the sky, hoping for one less opponent at dawn, but nobody appears tonight. Tomorrow there will be faces up there. Feasts always result in fatalities.

I crawl into the cave, secure my glasses, and curl up next to Peeta. Luckily I had that good long sleep today. I have to stay awake. I don't really think anyone will attack our cave tonight, but I can't risk missing the dawn.

So cold, so bitterly cold tonight. As if the Gamemakers have sent an infusion of frozen air across the arena, which may be exactly what they've done. I lie next to Peeta in the bag, trying to absorb every bit of his fever heat. It's strange to be so physically close to someone who's so distant. Peeta might as well be back in the Capitol, or in District 12, or on the moon right now, he'd be no harder to reach. I've never felt lonelier since the Games began.

Just accept it will be a bad night, I tell myself. I try not to, but I can't help thinking of my mother and Prim, wondering if they'll sleep a wink tonight. At this late stage in the Games, with an important event like the feast, school will probably be canceled. My family can either watch on that static-filled old clunker of a television at home or join the crowds in the square to watch on the big, clear screens. They'll have privacy at home but support in the square. People will give them a kind word, a bit of food if they can spare it. I wonder if the baker has sought them out, especially now that Peeta and I are a team, and made good on his promise to keep my sister's belly full.

Spirits must be running high in District 12. We so rarely have anyone to root for at this point in the Games. Surely, people are excited about Peeta and me, especially now that we're together. If I close my eyes, I can imagine their shouts at the screens, urging us on. I see their faces — Greasy Sae and Madge and even the Peacekeepers who buy my meat — cheering for us.

And Gale. I know him. He won't be shouting and cheering. But he'll be watching, every moment, every twist and turn, and willing me to come home. I wonder if he's hoping that Peeta makes it as well. Gale's not my boyfriend, but would he be, if I opened that door? He talked about us running away together. Was that just a practical calculation of our chances of survival away from the district? Or something more?

I wonder what he makes of all this kissing.

Through a crack in the rocks, I watch the moon cross the sky. At what I judge to be about three hours before dawn, I begin final preparations. I'm careful to leave Peeta with water and the medical kit right beside him. Nothing else will be of much use if I don't return, and even these would only prolong his life a short time. After some debate, I strip him of his jacket and zip it on over my own. He doesn't need it. Not now in the sleeping bag with his fever, and during the day, if I'm not there to remove it, he'll be roasting in it. My hands are already stiff from cold, so I take Rue's spare pair of socks, cut holes for my fingers and thumbs, and pull them on. It helps anyway. I fill her small pack with some food, a water bottle, and bandages, tuck the knife in my belt, get my bow and arrows. I'm about to leave when I remember the importance of sustaining the star-crossed lover routine and I lean over and give Peeta a long, lingering kiss. I imagine the teary sighs emanating from the Capitol and pretend to brush away a tear of my own. Then I squeeze through the opening in the rocks out into the night.

My breath makes small white clouds as it hits the air. It's as cold as a November night at home. One where I've slipped into the woods, lantern in hand, to join Gale at some prearranged place where we'll sit bundled together, sipping herb tea from metal flasks wrapped in quilting, hoping game will pass our way as the morning comes on. *Oh, Gale*, I think. *If only you had my back now . . .*

I move as fast as I dare. The glasses are quite remarkable, but I still sorely miss having the use of my left ear. I don't know what the explosion did, but it damaged something deep and irreparable. Never mind. If I get home, I'll be so stinking rich, I'll be able to pay someone to do my hearing.

The woods always look different at night. Even with the glasses, everything has an unfamiliar slant to it. As if the daytime trees and flowers and stones had gone to bed and sent slightly more ominous versions of themselves to take their places. I don't try anything tricky, like taking a new route. I make my way back up the stream and follow the same path back to Rue's hiding place near the lake. Along the way, I see no sign of another tribute, not a puff of breath, not a quiver of a branch. Either I'm the first to arrive or the others positioned themselves last night. There's still more than an hour, maybe two, when I wriggle into the underbrush and wait for the blood to begin to flow.

I chew a few mint leaves, my stomach isn't up for much more. Thank goodness, I have Peeta's jacket as well as my own. If not, I'd be forced to move around to stay warm. The sky turns a misty morning gray and still there's no sign of the other tributes. It's not surprising really. Everyone has distinguished themselves either by strength or deadliness or cunning. Do they suppose, I wonder, that I have Peeta with me? I doubt Foxface and Thresh even know he was wounded. All the better if they think he's covering me when I go in for the backpack.

But where is it? The arena has lightened enough for me to remove my glasses. I can hear the morning birds singing. Isn't it time? For a second, I'm panicked that I'm at the wrong location. But no, I'm certain I remember Claudius Templesmith specifying the Cornucopia. And there it is. And here I am. So where's my feast?

Just as the first ray of sun glints off the gold Cornucopia, there's a disturbance on the plain. The ground before the mouth of the horn splits in two and a round table with a snowy white cloth rises into the arena. On the table sit four backpacks, two large black ones with the numbers *2* and *11*, a medium-size green one with the number *5*, and a tiny orange one — really I could carry it around my wrist — that must be marked with a *12*.

The table has just clicked into place when a figure darts out of the Cornucopia, snags the green backpack, and speeds off. Foxface! Leave it to her to come up with such a clever and risky idea! The rest of us are still poised around the plain, sizing up the situation, and she's got hers. She's got us trapped, too, because no one wants to chase her down, not while their own pack sits so vulnerable on the table. Foxface must have purposefully left the other packs alone, knowing that to steal one without her number would definitely bring on a pursuer. That should have been my strategy! By the time I've worked through the emotions of surprise, admiration, anger, jealousy, and frustration, I'm watching that reddish mane of hair disappear into the trees well out of shooting range. Huh. I'm always dreading the others, but maybe Foxface is the real opponent here.

She's cost me time, too, because by now it's clear that I must get to the table next. Anyone who beats me to it will easily scoop up my pack and be gone. Without hesitation, I sprint for the table. I can sense the emergence of danger before I see it. Fortunately, the first knife comes whizzing in on my right side so I can hear it and I'm able to deflect it with my bow. I turn, drawing back the bowstring and send an arrow straight at Clove's heart. She turns just enough to avoid a fatal hit, but the point punctures her upper left arm. Unfortunately, she throws with her right, but it's enough to slow her down a few moments, having to pull the arrow from her arm, take in the severity of the wound. I keep moving, positioning the next arrow automatically, as only someone who has hunted for years can do.

I'm at the table now, my fingers closing over the tiny orange backpack. My hand slips between the straps and I yank it up on my arm, it's really too small to fit on any other part of my anatomy, and I'm turning to fire again when the second knife catches me in the forehead. It slices above my right eyebrow, opening a gash that sends a gush running down my face, blinding my eye, filling my mouth with the sharp, metallic taste of my own blood. I stagger backward but still manage to send my readied arrow in the general direction of my assailant. I know as it leaves my hands it will miss. And then Clove slams into me, knocking me flat on my back, pinning my shoulders to the ground with her knees.

This is it, I think, and hope for Prim's sake it will be fast. But Clove means to savor the moment. Even feels she has time. No doubt Cato is somewhere nearby, guarding her, waiting for Thresh and possibly Peeta.

"Where's your boyfriend, District Twelve? Still hanging on?" she asks.

Well, as long as we're talking I'm alive. "He's out there now. Hunting Cato," I snarl at her. Then I scream at the top of my lungs. "Peeta!"

Clove jams her fist into my windpipe, very effectively cutting off my voice. But her head's whipping from side to side, and I know for a moment she's at least considering I'm telling the truth. Since no Peeta appears to save me, she turns back to me.

"Liar," she says with a grin. "He's nearly dead. Cato knows where he cut him. You've probably got him strapped up in some tree while you try to keep his heart going. What's in the pretty little backpack? That medicine for Lover Boy? Too bad he'll never get it."

Clove opens her jacket. It's lined with an impressive array of knives. She carefully selects an almost dainty-looking number with a cruel, curved blade. "I promised Cato if he let me have you, I'd give the audience a good show."

I'm struggling now in an effort to unseat her, but it's no use. She's too heavy and her lock on me too tight.

"Forget it, District Twelve. We're going to kill you. Just like we did your pathetic little ally . . . what was her name? The one who hopped around in the trees? Rue? Well, first Rue, then you, and then I think we'll just let nature take care of Lover Boy. How does that sound?" Clove asks. "Now, where to start?"

She carelessly wipes away the blood from my wound with her jacket sleeve. For a moment, she surveys my face, tilting it from side to side as if it's a block of wood and she's deciding exactly what pattern to carve on it. I attempt to bite her hand, but she grabs the hair on the top of my head, forcing me back to the ground. "I think . . ." she almost purrs. "I think we'll start with your mouth." I clamp my teeth together as she teasingly traces the outline of my lips with the tip of the blade.

I won't close my eyes. The comment about Rue has filled me with fury, enough fury I think to die with some dignity. As my last act of defiance, I will stare her down as long as I can see, which will probably not be an extended period of time, but I will stare her down, I will not cry out, I will die, in my own small way, undefeated.

"Yes, I don't think you'll have much use for your lips anymore. Want to blow Lover Boy one last kiss?" she asks. I work up a mouthful of blood and saliva and spit it in her face. She flushes with rage. "All right then. Let's get started."

I brace myself for the agony that's sure to follow. But as I feel the tip open the first cut at my lip, some great force yanks Clove from my body and then she's screaming. I'm too stunned at first, too unable to process what has happened. Has Peeta somehow come to my rescue? Have the Gamemakers sent in some wild animal to add to the fun? Has a hovercraft inexplicably plucked her into the air?

But when I push myself up on my numb arms, I see it's none of the above. Clove is dangling a foot off the ground, imprisoned in Thresh's arms. I let out a gasp, seeing him like that, towering over me, holding Clove like a rag doll. I remember him as big, but he seems more massive, more powerful than I even recall. If anything, he seems to have gained weight in the arena. He flips Clove around and flings her onto the ground.

When he shouts, I jump, never having heard him speak

above a mutter. "What'd you do to that little girl? You kill her?"

Clove is scrambling backward on all fours, like a frantic insect, too shocked to even call for Cato. "No! No, it wasn't me!"

"You said her name. I heard you. You kill her?" Another thought brings a fresh wave of rage to his features. "You cut her up like you were going to cut up this girl here?"

"No! No, I —" Clove sees the stone, about the size of a small loaf of bread in Thresh's hand and loses it. "Cato!" she screeches. "Cato!"

"Clove!" I hear Cato's answer, but he's too far away, I can tell that much, to do her any good. What was he doing? Trying to get Foxface or Peeta? Or had he been lying in wait for Thresh and just badly misjudged his location?

Thresh brings the rock down hard against Clove's temple. It's not bleeding, but I can see the dent in her skull and I know that she's a goner. There's still life in her now though, in the rapid rise and fall of her chest, the low moan escaping her lips.

When Thresh whirls around on me, the rock raised, I know it's no good to run. And my bow is empty, the last loaded arrow having gone in Clove's direction. I'm trapped in the glare of his strange golden brown eyes. "What'd she mean? About Rue being your ally?"

"I — I — we teamed up. Blew up the supplies. I tried to save her, I did. But he got there first. District One," I say. Maybe if he knows I helped Rue, he won't choose some slow, sadistic end for me.

"And you killed him?" he demands.

"Yes. I killed him. And buried her in flowers," I say. "And I sang her to sleep."

Tears spring in my eyes. The tension, the fight goes out of me at the memory. And I'm overwhelmed by Rue, and the pain in my head, and my fear of Thresh, and the moaning of the dying girl a few feet away.

"To sleep?" Thresh says gruffly.

"To death. I sang until she died," I say. "Your district . . . they sent me bread." My hand reaches up but not for an arrow that I know I'll never reach. Just to wipe my nose. "Do it fast, okay, Thresh?"

Conflicting emotions cross Thresh's face. He lowers the rock and points at me, almost accusingly. "Just this one time, I let you go. For the little girl. You and me, we're even then. No more owed. You understand?"

I nod because I do understand. About owing. About hating it. I understand that if Thresh wins, he'll have to go back and face a district that has already broken all the rules to thank me, and he is breaking the rules to thank me, too. And I understand that, for the moment, Thresh is not going to smash in my skull.

"Clove!" Cato's voice is much nearer now. I can tell by the pain in it that he sees her on the ground.

"You better run now, Fire Girl," says Thresh.

I don't need to be told twice. I flip over and my feet dig into the hard-packed earth as I run away from Thresh and Clove and the sound of Cato's voice. Only when I reach the woods do I turn back for an instant. Thresh and both large backpacks are vanishing over the edge of the plain into the area I've never seen. Cato kneels beside Clove, spear in hand, begging her to stay with him. In a moment, he will realize it's futile, she can't be saved. I crash into the trees, repeatedly swiping away the blood that's pouring into my eye, fleeing like the wild, wounded creature I am. After a few minutes, I hear the cannon and I know that Clove has died, that Cato will be on one of our trails. Either Thresh's or mine. I'm seized with terror, weak from my head wound, shaking. I load an arrow, but Cato can throw that spear almost as far as I can shoot.

Only one thing calms me down. Thresh has Cato's backpack containing the thing he needs desperately. If I had to bet, Cato headed out after Thresh, not me. Still I don't slow down when I reach the water. I plunge right in, boots still on, and flounder downstream. I pull off Rue's socks that I've been using for gloves and press them into my forehead, trying to staunch the flow of blood, but they're soaked in minutes.

Somehow I make it back to the cave. I squeeze through the rocks. In the dappled light, I pull the little orange backpack from my arm, cut open the clasp, and dump the contents on the ground. One slim box containing one hypodermic needle. Without hesitating, I jam the needle into Peeta's arm and slowly press down on the plunger.

My hands go to my head and then drop to my lap, slick with blood.

The last thing I remember is an exquisitely beautiful green-and-silver moth landing on the curve of my wrist.

The sound of rain drumming on the roof of our house gently pulls me toward consciousness. I fight to return to sleep though, wrapped in a warm cocoon of blankets, safe at home. I'm vaguely aware that my head aches. Possibly I have the flu and this is why I'm allowed to stay in bed, even though I can tell I've been asleep a long time. My mother's hand strokes my cheek and I don't push it away as I would in wakefulness, never wanting her to know how much I crave that gentle touch. How much I miss her even though I still don't trust her. Then there's a voice, the wrong voice, not my mother's, and I'm scared.

"Katniss," it says. "Katniss, can you hear me?"

My eyes open and the sense of security vanishes. I'm not home, not with my mother. I'm in a dim, chilly cave, my bare feet freezing despite the cover, the air tainted with the unmistakable smell of blood. The haggard, pale face of a boy slides into view, and after an initial jolt of alarm, I feel better. "Peeta."

"Hey," he says. "Good to see your eyes again."

"How long have I been out?" I ask.

"Not sure. I woke up yesterday evening and you were lying next to me in a very scary pool of blood," he says. "I think it's stopped finally, but I wouldn't sit up or anything."

I gingerly lift my hand to my head and find it bandaged. This simple gesture leaves me weak and dizzy. Peeta holds a bottle to my lips and I drink thirstily.

"You're better," I say.

"Much better. Whatever you shot into my arm did the trick," he says. "By this morning, almost all the swelling in my leg was gone."

He doesn't seem angry about my tricking him, drugging him, and running off to the feast. Maybe I'm just too beat-up and I'll hear about it later when I'm stronger. But for the moment, he's all gentleness.

"Did you eat?" I ask.

"I'm sorry to say I gobbled down three pieces of that groosling before I realized it might have to last a while. Don't worry, I'm back on a strict diet," he says.

"No, it's good. You need to eat. I'll go hunting soon," I say.

"Not too soon, all right?" he says. "You just let me take care of you for a while."

I don't really seem to have much choice. Peeta feeds me bites of groosling and raisins and makes me drink plenty of water. He rubs some warmth back into my feet and wraps them in his jacket before tucking the sleeping bag back up around my chin.

"Your boots and socks are still damp and the weather's not helping much," he says. There's a clap of thunder, and I see lightning electrify the sky through an opening in the rocks. Rain drips through several holes in the ceiling, but Peeta has built a sort of canopy over my head and upper body by wedging the square of plastic into the rocks above me.

"I wonder what brought on this storm? I mean, who's the target?" says Peeta.

"Cato and Thresh," I say without thinking. "Foxface will be in her den somewhere, and Clove . . . she cut me and then . . ." My voice trails off.

"I know Clove's dead. I saw it in the sky last night," he says. "Did you kill her?"

"No. Thresh broke her skull with a rock," I say.

"Lucky he didn't catch you, too," says Peeta.

The memory of the feast returns full-force and I feel sick. "He did. But he let me go." Then, of course, I have to tell him. About things I've kept to myself because he was too sick to ask and I wasn't ready to relive anyway. Like the explosion and my ear and Rue's dying and the boy from District 1 and the bread. All of which leads to what happened with Thresh and how he was paying off a debt of sorts.

"He let you go because he didn't want to owe you anything?" asks Peeta in disbelief.

"Yes. I don't expect you to understand it. You've always had enough. But if you'd lived in the Seam, I wouldn't have to explain," I say.

"And don't try. Obviously I'm too dim to get it," he says.

"It's like the bread. How I never seem to get over owing you for that," I say.

"The bread? What? From when we were kids?" he says. "I think we can let that go. I mean, you just brought me back from the dead."

"But you didn't know me. We had never even spoken. Besides, it's the first gift that's always the hardest to pay back. I wouldn't even have been here to do it if you hadn't helped me then," I say. "Why did you, anyway?"

"Why? You know why," Peeta says. I give my head a slight, painful shake. "Haymitch said you would take a lot of convincing."

"Haymitch?" I ask. "What's he got to do with it?"

"Nothing," Peeta says. "So, Cato and Thresh, huh? I guess it's too much to hope that they'll simultaneously destroy each other?"

But the thought only upsets me. "I think we would like Thresh. I think he'd be our friend back in District Twelve," I say.

"Then let's hope Cato kills him, so we don't have to," says Peeta grimly.

I don't want Cato to kill Thresh at all. I don't want anyone else to die. But this is absolutely not the kind of thing that victors go around saying in the arena. Despite my best efforts, I can feel tears starting to pool in my eyes.

Peeta looks at me in concern. "What is it? Are you in a lot of pain?"

I give him another answer, because it is equally true but can be taken as a brief moment of weakness instead of a terminal one. "I want to go home, Peeta," I say plaintively, like a small child.

"You will. I promise," he says, and bends over to give me a kiss.

"I want to go home now," I say.

"Tell you what. You go back to sleep and dream of home. And you'll be there for real before you know it," he says. "Okay?"

"Okay," I whisper. "Wake me if you need me to keep watch."

"I'm good and rested, thanks to you and Haymitch. Besides, who knows how long this will last?" he says.

What does he mean? The storm? The brief respite it brings us? The Games themselves? I don't know, but I'm too sad and tired to ask.

It's evening when Peeta wakes me again. The rain has turned to a downpour, sending streams of water through our ceiling where earlier there had been only drips. Peeta has placed the broth pot under the worst one and repositioned the plastic to deflect most of it from me. I feel a bit better, able to sit up without getting too dizzy, and I'm absolutely famished. So is Peeta. It's clear he's been waiting for me to wake up to eat and is eager to get started.

There's not much left. Two pieces of groosling, a small mishmash of roots, and a handful of dried fruit.

"Should we try and ration it?" Peeta asks.

"No, let's just finish it. The groosling's getting old anyway, and the last thing we need is to get sick off spoiled food," I say, dividing the food into two equal piles. We try and eat slowly, but we're both so hungry we're done in a couple of minutes. My stomach is in no way satisfied.

"Tomorrow's a hunting day," I say.

"I won't be much help with that," Peeta says. "I've never hunted before."

"I'll kill and you cook," I say. "And you can always gather."

"I wish there was some sort of bread bush out there," says Peeta.

"The bread they sent me from District Eleven was still warm," I say with a sigh. "Here, chew these." I hand him a couple of mint leaves and pop a few in my own mouth.

It's hard to even see the projection in the sky, but it's clear enough to know there were no more deaths today. So Cato and Thresh haven't had it out yet.

"Where did Thresh go? I mean, what's on the far side of the circle?" I ask Peeta.

"A field. As far as you can see it's full of grasses as high as my shoulders. I don't know, maybe some of them are grain. There are patches of different colors. But there are no paths," says Peeta.

"I bet some of them are grain. I bet Thresh knows which ones, too," I say. "Did you go in there?"

"No. Nobody really wanted to track Thresh down in that grass. It has a sinister feeling to it. Every time I look at that field, all I can think of are hidden things. Snakes, and rabid animals, and quicksand," Peeta says. "There could be anything in there."

I don't say so but Peeta's words remind me of the

warnings they give us about not going beyond the fence in District 12. I can't help, for a moment, comparing him with Gale, who would see that field as a potential source of food as well as a threat. Thresh certainly did. It's not that Peeta's soft exactly, and he's proved he's not a coward. But there are things you don't question too much, I guess, when your home always smells like baking bread, whereas Gale questions everything. What would Peeta think of the irreverent banter that passes between us as we break the law each day? Would it shock him? The things we say about Panem? Gale's tirades against the Capitol?

"Maybe there is a bread bush in that field," I say. "Maybe that's why Thresh looks better fed now than when we started the Games."

"Either that or he's got very generous sponsors," says Peeta. "I wonder what we'd have to do to get Haymitch to send us some bread."

I raise my eyebrows before I remember he doesn't know about the message Haymitch sent us a couple of nights ago. One kiss equals one pot of broth. It's not the sort of thing I can blurt out, either. To say my thoughts aloud would be tipping off the audience that the romance has been fabricated to play on their sympathies and that would result in no food at all. Somehow, believably, I've got to get things back on track. Something simple to start with. I reach out and take his hand.

"Well, he probably used up a lot of resources helping me knock you out," I say mischievously.

"Yeah, about that," says Peeta, entwining his fingers in mine. "Don't try something like that again."

"Or what?" I ask.

"Or . . . or . . ." He can't think of anything good. "Just give me a minute."

"What's the problem?" I say with a grin.

"The problem is we're both still alive. Which only reinforces the idea in your mind that you did the right thing," says Peeta.

"I did do the right thing," I say.

"No! Just don't, Katniss!" His grip tightens, hurting my hand, and there's real anger in his voice. "Don't die for me. You won't be doing me any favors. All right?"

I'm startled by his intensity but recognize an excellent opportunity for getting food, so I try to keep up. "Maybe I did it for myself, Peeta, did you ever think of that? Maybe you aren't the only one who . . . who worries about . . . what it would be like if . . ."

I fumble. I'm not as smooth with words as Peeta. And while I was talking, the idea of actually losing Peeta hit me again and I realized how much I don't want him to die. And it's not about the sponsors. And it's not about what will happen back home. And it's not just that I don't want to be alone. It's him. I do not want to lose the boy with the bread.

"If what, Katniss?" he says softly.

I wish I could pull the shutters closed, blocking out this moment from the prying eyes of Panem. Even if it means losing food. Whatever I'm feeling, it's no one's business but mine.

"That's exactly the kind of topic Haymitch told me to steer clear of," I say evasively, although Haymitch never said anything of the kind. In fact, he's probably cursing me out right now for dropping the ball during such an emotionally charged moment. But Peeta somehow catches it.

"Then I'll just have to fill in the blanks myself," he says, and moves in to me.

This is the first kiss that we're both fully aware of. Neither of us hobbled by sickness or pain or simply unconscious. Our lips neither burning with fever or icy cold. This is the first kiss where I actually feel stirring inside my chest. Warm and curious. This is the first kiss that makes me want another.

But I don't get it. Well, I do get a second kiss, but it's just a light one on the tip of my nose because Peeta's been distracted. "I think your wound is bleeding again. Come on, lie down, it's bedtime anyway," he says.

My socks are dry enough to wear now. I make Peeta put his jacket back on. The damp cold seems to cut right down to my bones, so he must be half frozen. I insist on taking the first watch, too, although neither of us think it's likely anyone will come in this weather. But he won't agree unless I'm in the bag, too, and I'm shivering so hard that it's pointless to object. In stark contrast to two nights ago, when I felt Peeta was a million miles away, I'm struck by his immediacy now. As we settle in, he pulls my head down to use his arm as a pillow; the other rests protectively over me even when he goes to sleep. No one has held me like this in such a long time. Since my father died and I stopped trusting my mother, no one else's arms have made me feel this safe.

With the aid of the glasses, I lie watching the drips of water splatter on the cave floor. Rhythmic and lulling. Several times, I drift off briefly and then snap awake, guilty and angry with myself. After three or four hours, I can't help it, I have to rouse Peeta because I can't keep my eyes open. He doesn't seem to mind.

"Tomorrow, when it's dry, I'll find us a place so high in the trees we can both sleep in peace," I promise as I drift off.

But tomorrow is no better in terms of weather. The deluge continues as if the Gamemakers are intent on washing us all away. The thunder's so powerful it seems to shake the ground. Peeta's considering heading out anyway to scavenge for food, but I tell him in this storm it would be pointless. He won't be able to see three feet in front of his face and he'll only end up getting soaked to the skin for his troubles. He knows I'm right, but the gnawing in our stomachs is becoming painful.

The day drags on turning into evening and there's no break in the weather. Haymitch is our only hope, but nothing is forthcoming, either from lack of money — everything will cost an exorbitant amount — or because he's dissatisfied with our performance. Probably the latter. I'd be the first to admit we're not exactly riveting today. Starving, weak from injuries, trying not to reopen wounds. We're sitting huddled together wrapped in the sleeping bag, yes, but mostly to keep warm. The most exciting thing either of us does is nap.

I'm not really sure how to ramp up the romance. The kiss last night was nice, but working up to another will take some forethought. There are girls in the Seam, some of the merchant girls, too, who navigate these waters so easily. But I've never had much time or use for it. Anyway, just a kiss isn't enough anymore clearly because if it was we'd have gotten food last night. My instincts tell me Haymitch isn't just looking for physical affection, he wants something more personal. The sort of stuff he was trying to get me to tell about myself when we were practicing for the interview. I'm rotten at it, but Peeta's not. Maybe the best approach is to get him talking.

"Peeta," I say lightly. "You said at the interview you'd had a crush on me forever. When did forever start?"

"Oh, let's see. I guess the first day of school. We were five. You had on a red plaid dress and your hair . . . it was in two braids instead of one. My father pointed you out when we were waiting to line up," Peeta says.

"Your father? Why?" I ask.

"He said, 'See that little girl? I wanted to marry her mother, but she ran off with a coal miner,'" Peeta says.

"What? You're making that up!" I exclaim.

"No, true story," Peeta says. "And I said, 'A coal miner? Why did she want a coal miner if she could've had you?' And he said, 'Because when he sings . . . even the birds stop to listen.'"

"That's true. They do. I mean, they did," I say. I'm

stunned and surprisingly moved, thinking of the baker telling this to Peeta. It strikes me that my own reluctance to sing, my own dismissal of music might not really be that I think it's a waste of time. It might be because it reminds me too much of my father.

"So that day, in music assembly, the teacher asked who knew the valley song. Your hand shot right up in the air. She stood you up on a stool and had you sing it for us. And I swear, every bird outside the windows fell silent," Peeta says.

"Oh, please," I say, laughing.

"No, it happened. And right when your song ended, I knew — just like your mother — I was a goner," Peeta says. "Then for the next eleven years, I tried to work up the nerve to talk to you."

"Without success," I add.

"Without success. So, in a way, my name being drawn in the reaping was a real piece of luck," says Peeta.

For a moment, I'm almost foolishly happy and then confusion sweeps over me. Because we're supposed to be making up this stuff, playing at being in love, not actually being in love. But Peeta's story has a ring of truth to it. That part about my father and the birds. And I did sing the first day of school, although I don't remember the song. And that red plaid dress . . . there was one, a hand-me-down to Prim that got washed to rags after my father's death.

It would explain another thing, too. Why Peeta took a beating to give me the bread on that awful hollow day. So, if those details are true . . . could it all be true?

"You have a . . . remarkable memory," I say haltingly.

"I remember everything about you," says Peeta, tucking a loose strand of hair behind my ear. "You're the one who wasn't paying attention."

"I am now," I say.

"Well, I don't have much competition here," he says.

I want to draw away, to close those shutters again, but I know I can't. It's as if I can hear Haymitch whispering in my ear, "Say it! Say it!"

I swallow hard and get the words out. "You don't have much competition anywhere." And this time, it's me who leans in.

Our lips have just barely touched when the clunk outside makes us jump. My bow comes up, the arrow ready to fly, but there's no other sound. Peeta peers through the rocks and then gives a whoop. Before I can stop him, he's out in the rain, then handing something in to me. A silver parachute attached to a basket. I rip it open at once and inside there's a feast — fresh rolls, goat cheese, apples, and best of all, a tureen of that incredible lamb stew on wild rice. The very dish I told Caesar Flickerman was the most impressive thing the Capitol had to offer.

Peeta wriggles back inside, his face lit up like the sun. "I guess Haymitch finally got tired of watching us starve."

"I guess so," I answer.

But in my head I can hear Haymitch's smug, if slightly exasperated, words, "Yes, *that's* what I'm looking for, sweetheart."

Every cell in my body wants me to dig into the stew and cram it, handful by handful into my mouth. But Peeta's voice stops me. "We better take it slow on that stew. Remember the first night on the train? The rich food made me sick and I wasn't even starving then."

"You're right. And I could just inhale the whole thing!" I say regretfully. But I don't. We are quite sensible. We each have a roll, half an apple, and an egg-size serving of stew and rice. I make myself eat the stew in tiny spoonfuls — they even sent us silverware and plates — savoring each bite. When we finish, I stare longingly at the dish. "I want more."

"Me, too. Tell you what. We wait an hour, if it stays down, then we get another serving," Peeta says.

"Agreed," I say. "It's going to be a long hour."

"Maybe not that long," says Peeta. "What was that you were saying just before the food arrived? Something about me . . . no competition . . . best thing that ever happened to you . . ."

"I don't remember that last part," I say, hoping it's too dim in here for the cameras to pick up my blush.

"Oh, that's right. That's what *I* was thinking," he says. "Scoot over, I'm freezing."

I make room for him in the sleeping bag. We lean back against the cave wall, my head on his shoulder, his arms wrapped around me. I can feel Haymitch nudging me to keep up the act. "So, since we were five, you never even noticed any other girls?" I ask him.

"No, I noticed just about every girl, but none of them made a lasting impression but you," he says.

"I'm sure that would thrill your parents, you liking a girl from the Seam," I say.

"Hardly. But I couldn't care less. Anyway, if we make it back, you won't be a girl from the Seam, you'll be a girl from the Victor's Village," he says.

That's right. If we win, we'll each get a house in the part of town reserved for Hunger Games' victors. Long ago, when the Games began, the Capitol had built a dozen fine houses in each district. Of course, in ours only one is occupied. Most of the others have never been lived in at all.

A disturbing thought hits me. "But then, our only neighbor will be Haymitch!"

"Ah, that'll be nice," says Peeta, tightening his arms around me. "You and me and Haymitch. Very cozy. Picnics, birthdays, long winter nights around the fire retelling old Hunger Games tales."

"I told you, he hates me!" I say, but I can't help laughing at the image of Haymitch becoming my new pal.

"Only sometimes. When he's sober, I've never heard him say one negative thing about you," says Peeta.

"He's never sober!" I protest.

"That's right. Who am I thinking of? Oh, I know. It's Cinna who likes you. But that's mainly because you didn't try to run when he set you on fire," says Peeta. "On the other hand, Haymitch . . . well, if I were you, I'd avoid Haymitch completely. He hates you."

"I thought you said I was his favorite," I say.

"He hates me more," says Peeta. "I don't think people in general are his sort of thing."

I know the audience will enjoy our having fun at Haymitch's expense. He has been around so long, he's practically an old friend to some of them. And after his head-dive off the stage at the reaping, everybody knows him. By this time, they'll have dragged him out of the control room for interviews about us. No telling what sort of lies he's made up. He's at something of a disadvantage because most mentors have a partner, another victor to help them whereas Haymitch has to be ready to go into action at any moment. Kind of like me when I was alone in the arena. I wonder how he's holding up, with the drinking, the attention, and the stress of trying to keep us alive.

It's funny. Haymitch and I don't get along well in person, but maybe Peeta is right about us being alike because he seems able to communicate with me by the timing of his gifts. Like how I knew I must be close to water when he withheld it and how I knew the sleep syrup just wasn't something to ease Peeta's pain and how I know now that I have to play up the romance. He hasn't made much effort to connect with Peeta really. Perhaps he thinks a bowl of broth would just be a bowl of broth to Peeta, whereas I'll see the strings attached to it.

A thought hits me, and I'm amazed the question's taken so long to surface. Maybe it's because I've only recently begun to view Haymitch with a degree of curiosity. "How do you think he did it?"

"Who? Did what?" Peeta asks.

"Haymitch. How do you think he won the Games?" I say.

Peeta considers this quite a while before he answers. Haymitch is sturdily built, but no physical wonder like Cato or Thresh. He's not particularly handsome. Not in the way that causes sponsors to rain gifts on you. And he's so surly, it's hard to imagine anyone teaming up with him. There's only one way Haymitch could have won, and Peeta says it just as I'm reaching this conclusion myself.

"He outsmarted the others," says Peeta.

I nod, then let the conversation drop. But secretly I'm wondering if Haymitch sobered up long enough to help Peeta and me because he thought we just might have the wits to survive. Maybe he wasn't always a drunk. Maybe, in the beginning, he tried to help the tributes. But then it got unbearable. It must be hell to mentor two kids and then watch them die. Year after year after year. I realize that if I get out of here, that will become my job. To mentor the girl from District 12. The idea is so repellent, I thrust it from my mind.

About half an hour has passed before I decide I have to eat again. Peeta's too hungry himself to put up an argument. While I'm dishing up two more small servings of lamb stew and rice, we hear the anthem begin to play. Peeta presses his eyes against a crack in the rocks to watch the sky.

"There won't be anything to see tonight," I say, far more interested in the stew than the sky. "Nothing's happened or we would've heard a cannon."

"Katniss," Peeta says quietly.

"What? Should we split another roll, too?" I ask.

"Katniss," he repeats, but I find myself wanting to ignore him.

"I'm going to split one. But I'll save the cheese for tomorrow," I say. I see Peeta staring at me. "What?"

"Thresh is dead," says Peeta.

"He can't be," I say.

"They must have fired the cannon during the thunder and we missed it," says Peeta.

"Are you sure? I mean, it's pouring buckets out there. I don't know how you can see anything," I say. I push him away from the rocks and squint out into the dark, rainy sky. For about ten seconds, I catch a distorted glimpse of Thresh's picture and then he's gone. Just like that.

I slump down against the rocks, momentarily forgetting about the task at hand. Thresh dead. I should be happy, right? One less tribute to face. And a powerful one, too. But I'm not happy. All I can think about is Thresh letting me go, letting me run because of Rue, who died with that spear in her stomach. . . .

"You all right?" asks Peeta.

I give a noncommittal shrug and cup my elbows in my hands, hugging them close to my body. I have to bury the real pain because who's going to bet on a tribute who keeps sniveling over the deaths of her opponents. Rue was one thing. We were allies. She was so young. But no one will understand my sorrow at Thresh's murder. The word pulls me up short. Murder! Thankfully, I didn't say it aloud. That's not going to win me any points in the arena. What I do say is, "It's just . . . if we didn't win . . . I wanted Thresh to. Because he let me go. And because of Rue."

"Yeah, I know," says Peeta. "But this means we're one step closer to District Twelve." He nudges a plate of food into my hands. "Eat. It's still warm."

I take a bite of the stew to show I don't really care, but it's like glue in my mouth and takes a lot of effort to swallow. "It also means Cato will be back hunting us."

"And he's got supplies again," says Peeta.

"He'll be wounded, I bet," I say.

"What makes you say that?" Peeta asks.

"Because Thresh would have never gone down without a fight. He's so strong, I mean, he was. And they were in his territory," I say.

"Good," says Peeta. "The more wounded Cato is the better. I wonder how Foxface is making out."

"Oh, she's fine," I say peevishly. I'm still angry she thought of hiding in the Cornucopia and I didn't. "Probably be easier to catch Cato than her."

"Maybe they'll catch each other and we can just go

home," says Peeta. "But we better be extra careful about the watches. I dozed off a few times."

"Me, too," I admit. "But not tonight."

We finish our food in silence and then Peeta offers to take the first watch. I burrow down in the sleeping bag next to him, pulling my hood up over my face to hide it from the cameras. I just need a few moments of privacy where I can let any emotion cross my face without being seen. Under the hood, I silently say good-bye to Thresh and thank him for my life. I promise to remember him and, if I can, do something to help his family and Rue's, if I win. Then I escape into sleep, comforted by a full belly and the steady warmth of Peeta beside me.

When Peeta wakes me later, the first thing I register is the smell of goat cheese. He's holding out half a roll spread with the creamy white stuff and topped with apple slices. "Don't be mad," he says. "I had to eat again. Here's your half."

"Oh, good," I say, immediately taking a huge bite. The strong fatty cheese tastes just like the kind Prim makes, the apples are sweet and crunchy. "Mm."

"We make a goat cheese and apple tart at the bakery," he says.

"Bet that's expensive," I say.

"Too expensive for my family to eat. Unless it's gone very stale. Of course, practically everything we eat is stale," says Peeta, pulling the sleeping bag up around him. In less than a minute, he's snoring.

Huh. I always assumed the shopkeepers live a soft life.

And it's true, Peeta has always had enough to eat. But there's something kind of depressing about living your life on stale bread, the hard, dry loaves that no one else wanted. One thing about us, since I bring our food home on a daily basis, most of it is so fresh you have to make sure it isn't going to make a run for it.

Somewhere during my shift, the rain stops not gradually but all at once. The downpour ends and there's only the residual drippings of water from branches, the rush of the now overflowing stream below us. A full, beautiful moon emerges, and even without the glasses I can see outside. I can't decide if the moon is real or merely a projection of the Gamemakers. I know it was full shortly before I left home. Gale and I watched it rise as we hunted into the late hours.

How long have I been gone? I'm guessing it's been about two weeks in the arena, and there was that week of preparation in the Capitol. Maybe the moon has completed its cycle. For some reason, I badly want it to be my moon, the same one I see from the woods around District 12. That would give me something to cling to in the surreal world of the arena where the authenticity of everything is to be doubted.

Four of us left.

For the first time, I allow myself to truly think about the possibility that I might make it home. To fame. To wealth. To my own house in the Victor's Village. My mother and Prim would live there with me. No more fear of hunger. A new kind of freedom. But then . . . what? What would my life be like on a daily basis? Most of it has been consumed with the acquisition of food. Take that away and I'm not really sure who I am, what my identity is. The idea scares me some. I think of Haymitch, with all his money. What did his life become? He lives alone, no wife or children, most of his waking hours drunk. I don't want to end up like that.

"But you won't be alone," I whisper to myself. I have my mother and Prim. Well, for the time being. And then . . . I don't want to think about then, when Prim has grown up, my mother passed away. I know I'll never marry, never risk bringing a child into the world. Because if there's one thing being a victor doesn't guarantee, it's your children's safety. My kids' names would go right into the reaping balls with everyone else's. And I swear I'll never let that happen.

The sun eventually rises, its light slipping through the cracks and illuminating Peeta's face. Who will he transform into if we make it home? This perplexing, good-natured boy who can spin out lies so convincingly the whole of Panem believes him to be hopelessly in love with me, and I'll admit it, there are moments when he makes me believe it myself? *At least, we'll be friends,* I think. Nothing will change the fact that we've saved each other's lives in here. And beyond that, he will always be the boy with the bread. *Good friends.* Anything beyond that though . . . and I feel Gale's gray eyes watching me watching Peeta, all the way from District 12.

Discomfort causes me to move. I scoot over and shake Peeta's shoulder. His eyes open sleepily and when they focus on me, he pulls me down for a long kiss.

"We're wasting hunting time," I say when I finally break away.

"I wouldn't call it wasting," he says, giving a big stretch as he sits up. "So do we hunt on empty stomachs to give us an edge?"

"Not us," I say. "We stuff ourselves to give us staying power."

"Count me in," Peeta says. But I can see he's surprised when I divide the rest of the stew and rice and hand a heaping plate to him. "All this?"

"We'll earn it back today," I say, and we both plow into our plates. Even cold, it's one of the best things I've ever tasted. I abandon my fork and scrape up the last dabs of gravy with my finger. "I can feel Effie Trinket shuddering at my manners."

"Hey, Effie, watch this!" says Peeta. He tosses his fork over his shoulder and literally licks his plate clean with his tongue making loud, satisfied sounds. Then he blows a kiss out to her in general and calls, "We miss you, Effie!"

I cover his mouth with my hand, but I'm laughing. "Stop! Cato could be right outside our cave."

He grabs my hand away. "What do I care? I've got you to protect me now," says Peeta, pulling me to him.

"Come on," I say in exasperation, extricating myself from his grasp but not before he gets in another kiss.

Once we're packed up and standing outside our cave, our mood shifts to serious. It's as though for the last few days, sheltered by the rocks and the rain and Cato's preoccupation with Thresh, we were given a respite, a holiday of sorts. Now, although the day is sunny and warm, we both sense we're really back in the Games. I hand Peeta my knife, since whatever weapons he once had are long gone, and he slips it into his belt. My last seven arrows — of the twelve I sacrificed three in the explosion, two at the feast — rattle a bit too loosely in the quiver. I can't afford to lose any more.

"He'll be hunting us by now," says Peeta. "Cato isn't one to wait for his prey to wander by."

"If he's wounded —" I begin.

"It won't matter," Peeta breaks in. "If he can move, he's coming."

With all the rain, the stream has overrun its banks by several feet on either side. We stop there to replenish our water. I check the snares I set days ago and come up empty. Not surprising with the weather. Besides, I haven't seen many animals or signs of them in this area.

"If we want food, we better head back up to my old hunting grounds," I say.

"Your call. Just tell me what you need me to do," Peeta says.

"Keep an eye out," I say. "Stay on the rocks as much as possible, no sense in leaving him tracks to follow. And listen for both of us." It's clear, at this point, that the explosion destroyed the hearing in my left ear for good.

I'd walk in the water to cover our tracks completely, but I'm not sure Peeta's leg could take the current. Although the drugs have erased the infection, he's still pretty weak. My forehead hurts along the knife cut, but after three days the bleeding has stopped. I wear a bandage around my head though, just in case physical exertion should bring it back.

As we head up alongside the stream, we pass the place where I found Peeta camouflaged in the weeds and mud. One good thing, between the downpour and the flooded banks, all signs of his hiding place have been wiped out. That means that, if need be, we can come back to our cave. Otherwise, I wouldn't risk it with Cato after us.

The boulders diminish to rocks that eventually turn to pebbles, and then, to my relief, we're back on pine needles and the gentle incline of the forest floor. For the first time, I realize we have a problem. Navigating the rocky terrain with a bad leg — well, you're naturally going to make some noise. But even on the smooth bed of needles, Peeta is loud. And I mean *loud* loud, as if he's stomping his feet or something. I turn and look at him.

"What?" he asks.

"You've got to move more quietly," I say. "Forget about Cato, you're chasing off every rabbit in a ten-mile radius."

"Really?" he says. "Sorry, I didn't know."

So, we start up again and he's a tiny bit better, but even with only one working ear, he's making me jump.

"Can you take your boots off?" I suggest.

"Here?" he asks in disbelief, as if I'd asked him to walk barefoot on hot coals or something. I have to remind myself that he's still not used to the woods, that it's the scary, forbidden place beyond the fences of District 12. I think of Gale, with his velvet tread. It's eerie how little sound he makes, even when the leaves have fallen and it's a challenge to move at all without chasing off the game. I feel certain he's laughing back home.

"Yes," I say patiently. "I will, too. That way we'll both be quieter." Like I was making any noise. So we both strip off our boots and socks and, while there's some improvement, I could swear he's making an effort to snap every branch we encounter.

Needless to say, although it takes several hours to reach my old camp with Rue, I've shot nothing. If the stream would settle down, fish might be an option, but the current is still too strong. As we stop to rest and drink water, I try to work out a solution. Ideally, I'd dump Peeta now with some simple root-gathering chore and go hunt, but then he'd be left with only a knife to defend himself against Cato's spears and superior strength. So what I'd really like is to try and conceal him somewhere safe, then go hunt, and come back and collect him. But I have a feeling his ego isn't going to go for that suggestion.

"Katniss," he says. "We need to split up. I know I'm chasing away the game."

"Only because your leg's hurt," I say generously, because really, you can tell that's only a small part of the problem.

"I know," he says. "So, why don't you go on? Show me some plants to gather and that way we'll both be useful."

"Not if Cato comes and kills you." I tried to say it in a nice way, but it still sounds like I think he's a weakling.

Surprisingly, he just laughs. "Look, I can handle Cato. I fought him before, didn't I?"

Yeah, and that turned out great. You ended up dying in a mud bank. That's what I want to say, but I can't. He did save my life by taking on Cato after all. I try another tactic. "What if you climbed up in a tree and acted as a lookout while I hunted?" I say, trying to make it sound like very important work.

"What if you show me what's edible around here and go get us some meat?" he says, mimicking my tone. "Just don't go far, in case you need help."

I sigh and show him some roots to dig. We do need food, no question. One apple, two rolls, and a blob of cheese the size of a plum won't last long. I'll just go a short distance and hope Cato is a long way off.

I teach him a bird whistle — not a melody like Rue's but a simple two-note whistle — which we can use to communicate that we're all right. Fortunately, he's good at this. Leaving him with the pack, I head off.

I feel like I'm eleven again, tethered not to the safety of the fence but to Peeta, allowing myself twenty, maybe thirty yards of hunting space. Away from him though, the woods come alive with animal sounds. Reassured by his periodic whistles, I allow myself to drift farther away, and soon have two rabbits and a fat squirrel to show for it. I decide it's enough. I can set snares and maybe get some fish. With Peeta's roots, this will be enough for now.

As I travel the short distance back, I realize we haven't exchanged signals in a while. When my whistle receives no response, I run. In no time, I find the pack, a neat pile of roots beside it. The sheet of plastic has been laid on the ground where the sun can reach the single layer of berries that covers it. But where is he?

"Peeta!" I call out in a panic. "Peeta!" I turn to the rustle of brush and almost send an arrow through him. Fortunately, I pull my bow at the last second and it sticks in an oak trunk to his left. He jumps back, flinging a handful of berries into the foliage.

My fear comes out as anger. "What are you doing? You're supposed to be here, not running around in the woods!"

"I found some berries down by the stream," he says, clearly confused by my outburst.

"I whistled. Why didn't you whistle back?" I snap at him.

"I didn't hear. The water's too loud, I guess," he says. He crosses and puts his hands on my shoulders. That's when I feel that I'm trembling.

"I thought Cato killed you!" I almost shout.

"No, I'm fine." Peeta wraps his arms around me, but I don't respond. "Katniss?"

I push away, trying to sort out my feelings. "If two people agree on a signal, they stay in range. Because if one of them doesn't answer, they're in trouble, all right?"

"All right!" he says.

"All right. Because that's what happened with Rue, and I watched her die!" I say. I turn away from him, go to the pack and open a fresh bottle of water, although I still have some in mine. But I'm not ready to forgive him. I notice the food. The rolls and apples are untouched, but someone's definitely picked away part of the cheese. "And you ate without me!" I really don't care, I just want something else to be mad about.

"What? No, I didn't," Peeta says.

"Oh, and I suppose the apples ate the cheese," I say.

"I don't know what ate the cheese," Peeta says slowly and distinctly, as if trying not to lose his temper, "but it wasn't me. I've been down by the stream collecting berries. Would you care for some?"

I would actually, but I don't want to relent too soon. I do walk over and look at them. I've never seen this type before. No, I have. But not in the arena. These aren't Rue's berries, although they resemble them. Nor do they match any I learned about in training. I lean down and scoop up a few, rolling them between my fingers.

My father's voice comes back to me. "Not these, Katniss. Never these. They're nightlock. You'll be dead before they reach your stomach."

Just then, the cannon fires. I whip around, expecting Peeta to collapse to the ground, but he only raises his eyebrows. The hovercraft appears a hundred yards or so away. What's left of Foxface's emaciated body is lifted into the air. I can see the red glint of her hair in the sunlight.

I should have known the moment I saw the missing cheese. . . .

Peeta has me by the arm, pushing me toward a tree. "Climb. He'll be here in a second. We'll stand a better chance fighting him from above."

I stop him, suddenly calm. "No, Peeta, she's your kill, not Cato's."

"What? I haven't even seen her since the first day," he says. "How could I have killed her?"

In answer, I hold out the berries.

It takes a while to explain the situation to Peeta. How Foxface stole the food from the supply pile before I blew it up, how she tried to take enough to stay alive but not enough that anyone would notice it, how she wouldn't question the safety of berries we were preparing to eat ourselves.

"I wonder how she found us," says Peeta. "My fault, I guess, if I'm as loud as you say."

We were about as hard to follow as a herd of cattle, but I try to be kind. "And she's very clever, Peeta. Well, she was. Until you outfoxed her."

"Not on purpose. Doesn't seem fair somehow. I mean, we would have both been dead, too, if she hadn't eaten the berries first." He checks himself. "No, of course, we wouldn't. You recognized them, didn't you?"

I give a nod. "We call them nightlock."

"Even the name sounds deadly," he says. "I'm sorry, Katniss. I really thought they were the same ones you'd gathered."

"Don't apologize. It just means we're one step closer to home, right?" I ask.

"I'll get rid of the rest," Peeta says. He gathers up the sheet of blue plastic, careful to trap the berries inside, and goes to toss them into the woods.

"Wait!" I cry. I find the leather pouch that belonged to the boy from District 1 and fill it with a few handfuls of berries from the plastic. "If they fooled Foxface, maybe they can fool Cato as well. If he's chasing us or something, we can act like we accidentally drop the pouch and if he eats them —"

"Then hello District Twelve," says Peeta.

"That's it," I say, securing the pouch to my belt.

"He'll know where we are now," says Peeta. "If he was anywhere nearby and saw that hovercraft, he'll know we killed her and come after us."

Peeta's right. This could be just the opportunity Cato's been waiting for. But even if we run now, there's the meat to cook and our fire will be another sign of our whereabouts. "Let's make a fire. Right now." I begin to gather branches and brush.

"Are you ready to face him?" Peeta asks.

"I'm ready to eat. Better to cook our food while we have the chance. If he knows we're here, he knows. But he also knows there's two of us and probably assumes we were hunting Foxface. That means you're recovered. And the fire means we're not hiding, we're inviting him here. Would you show up?" I ask.

"Maybe not," he says.

Peeta's a whiz with fires, coaxing a blaze out of the damp wood. In no time, I have the rabbits and squirrel roasting, the roots, wrapped in leaves, baking in the coals. We take turns gathering greens and keeping a careful watch for Cato, but as I anticipated, he doesn't make an appearance.

When the food's cooked, I pack most of it up, leaving us each a rabbit's leg to eat as we walk.

I want to move higher into the woods, climb a good tree, and make camp for the night, but Peeta resists. "I can't climb like you, Katniss, especially with my leg, and I don't think I could ever fall asleep fifty feet above the ground."

"It's not safe to stay in the open, Peeta," I say.

"Can't we go back to the cave?" he asks. "It's near water and easy to defend."

I sigh. Several more hours of walking — or should I say crashing — through the woods to reach an area we'll just have to leave in the morning to hunt. But Peeta doesn't ask for much. He's followed my instructions all day and I'm sure if things were reversed, he wouldn't make me spend the night in a tree. It dawns on me that I haven't been very nice to Peeta today. Nagging him about how loud he was, screaming at him over disappearing. The playful romance we had sustained in the cave has disappeared out in the open, under the hot sun, with the threat of Cato looming over us. Haymitch has probably just about had it with me. And as for the audience . . .

I reach up and give him a kiss. "Sure. Let's go back to the cave."

He looks pleased and relieved. "Well, that was easy."

I work my arrow out of the oak, careful not to damage the shaft. These arrows are food, safety, and life itself now.

We toss a bunch more wood on the fire. It should be sending off smoke for a few more hours, although I doubt Cato assumes anything at this point. When we reach the stream, I see the water has dropped considerably and moves at its old leisurely pace, so I suggest we walk back in it. Peeta's happy to oblige and since he's a lot quieter in water than on land, it's a doubly good idea. It's a long walk back to the cave though, even going downward, even with the rabbit to give us a boost. We're both exhausted by our hike today and still way too underfed. I keep my bow loaded, both for Cato and any fish I might see, but the stream seems strangely empty of creatures.

By the time we reach our destination, our feet are dragging and the sun sits low on the horizon. We fill up our water bottles and climb the little slope to our den. It's not much, but out here in the wilderness, it's the closest thing we have to a home. It will be warmer than a tree, too, because it provides some shelter from the wind that has begun to blow steadily in from the west. I set a good dinner out, but halfway through Peeta begins to nod off. After days of inactivity, the hunt has taken its toll. I order him into the sleeping bag and set aside the rest of his food for when he wakes. He drops off immediately. I pull the sleeping bag up to his chin and kiss his forehead, not for the audience, but for me. Because I'm so grateful that he's still here, not dead by the stream as I'd thought. So glad that I don't have to face Cato alone.

Brutal, bloody Cato who can snap a neck with a twist of his arm, who had the power to overcome Thresh, who has had it out for me since the beginning. He probably has had a special hatred for me ever since I outscored him in training. A boy like Peeta would simply shrug that off. But

I have a feeling it drove Cato to distraction. Which is not that hard. I think of his ridiculous reaction to finding the supplies blown up. The others were upset, of course, but he was completely unhinged. I wonder now if Cato might not be entirely sane.

The sky lights up with the seal, and I watch Foxface shine in the sky and then disappear from the world forever. He hasn't said it, but I don't think Peeta felt good about killing her, even if it was essential. I can't pretend I'll miss her, but I have to admire her. My guess is if they had given us some sort of test, she would have been the smartest of all the tributes. If, in fact, we had been setting a trap for her, I bet she'd have sensed it and avoided the berries. It was Peeta's own ignorance that brought her down. I've spent so much time making sure I don't underestimate my opponents that I've forgotten it's just as dangerous to overestimate them as well.

That brings me back to Cato. But while I think I had a sense of Foxface, who she was and how she operated, he's a little more slippery. Powerful, well trained, but smart? I don't know. Not like she was. And utterly lacking in the control Foxface demonstrated. I believe Cato could easily lose his judgment in a fit of temper. Not that I can feel superior on that point. I think of the moment I sent the arrow flying into the apple in the pig's mouth when I was so enraged. Maybe I do understand Cato better than I think.

Despite the fatigue in my body, my mind's alert, so I let Peeta sleep long past our usual switch. In fact, a soft gray day has begun when I shake his shoulder. He looks out, almost in alarm. "I slept the whole night. That's not fair, Katniss, you should have woken me."

I stretch and burrow down into the bag. "I'll sleep now. Wake me if anything interesting happens."

Apparently nothing does, because when I open my eyes, bright hot afternoon light gleams through the rocks. "Any sign of our friend?" I ask.

Peeta shakes his head. "No, he's keeping a disturbingly low profile."

"How long do you think we'll have before the Gamemakers drive us together?" I ask.

"Well, Foxface died almost a day ago, so there's been plenty of time for the audience to place bets and get bored. I guess it could happen at any moment," says Peeta.

"Yeah, I have a feeling today's the day," I say. I sit up and look out at the peaceful terrain. "I wonder how they'll do it."

Peeta remains silent. There's not really any good answer.

"Well, until they do, no sense in wasting a hunting day. But we should probably eat as much as we can hold just in case we run into trouble," I say.

Peeta packs up our gear while I lay out a big meal. The rest of the rabbits, roots, greens, the rolls spread with the last bit of cheese. The only thing I leave in reserve is the squirrel and the apple.

By the time we're done, all that's left is a pile of rabbit bones. My hands are greasy, which only adds to my growing feeling of grubbiness. Maybe we don't bathe daily in the Seam, but we keep cleaner than I have of late. Except for my feet, which have walked in the stream, I'm covered in a layer of grime.

Leaving the cave has a sense of finality about it. I don't think there will be another night in the arena somehow. One way or the other, dead or alive, I have the feeling I'll escape it today. I give the rocks a pat good-bye and we head down to the stream to wash up. I can feel my skin, itching for the cool water. I may do my hair and braid it back wet. I'm wondering if we might even be able to give our clothes a quick scrub when we reach the stream. Or what used to be the stream. Now there's only a bone-dry bed. I put my hand down to feel it.

"Not even a little damp. They must have drained it while we slept," I say. A fear of the cracked tongue, aching body and fuzzy mind brought on by my previous dehydration creeps into my consciousness. Our bottles and skin are fairly full, but with two drinking and this hot sun it won't take long to deplete them.

"The lake," says Peeta. "That's where they want us to go."

"Maybe the ponds still have some," I say hopefully.

"We can check," he says, but he's just humoring me. I'm humoring myself because I know what I'll find when we return to the pond where I soaked my leg. A dusty, gaping mouth of a hole. But we make the trip anyway just to confirm what we already know.

"You're right. They're driving us to the lake," I say. Where there's no cover. Where they're guaranteed a bloody fight to the death with nothing to block their view. "Do you want to go straightaway or wait until the water's tapped out?"

"Let's go now, while we've had food and rest. Let's just go end this thing," he says.

I nod. It's funny. I feel almost as if it's the first day of the Games again. That I'm in the same position. Twenty-one tributes are dead, but I still have yet to kill Cato. And really, wasn't he always the one to kill? Now it seems the other tributes were just minor obstacles, distractions, keeping us from the real battle of the Games. Cato and me.

But no, there's the boy waiting beside me. I feel his arms wrap around me.

"Two against one. Should be a piece of cake," he says.

"Next time we eat, it will be in the Capitol," I answer.

"You bet it will," he says.

We stand there a while, locked in an embrace, feeling each other, the sunlight, the rustle of the leaves at our feet. Then without a word, we break apart and head for the lake.

I don't care now that Peeta's footfalls send rodents scurrying, make birds take wing. We have to fight Cato and I'd just as soon do it here as on the plain. But I doubt I'll have that choice. If the Gamemakers want us in the open, then in the open we will be.

We stop to rest for a few moments under the tree where the Careers trapped me. The husk of the tracker jacker nest, beaten to a pulp by the heavy rains and dried in the burning sun, confirms the location. I touch it with the tip of my boot, and it dissolves into dust that is quickly carried off by the breeze. I can't help looking up in the tree where Rue secretly perched, waiting to save my life. Tracker jackers. Glimmer's bloated body. The terrifying hallucinations . . .

"Let's move on," I say, wanting to escape the darkness that surrounds this place. Peeta doesn't object.

Given our late start to the day, when we reach the plain it's already early evening. There's no sign of Cato. No sign of anything except the gold Cornucopia glowing in the slanting sun rays. Just in case Cato decided to pull a Foxface on us, we circle the Cornucopia to make sure it's empty. Then obediently, as if following instructions, we cross to the lake and fill our water containers.

I frown at the shrinking sun. "We don't want to fight him after dark. There's only the one pair of glasses."

Peeta carefully squeezes drops of iodine into the water. "Maybe that's what he's waiting for. What do you want to do? Go back to the cave?"

"Either that or find a tree. But let's give him another half an hour or so. Then we'll take cover," I answer.

We sit by the lake, in full sight. There's no point in hiding now. In the trees at the edge of the plain, I can see the mockingjays flitting about. Bouncing melodies back and forth between them like brightly colored balls. I open my mouth and sing out Rue's four-note run. I can feel them pause curiously at the sound of my voice, listening for more. I repeat the notes in the silence. First one mockingjay trills the tune back, then another. Then the whole world comes alive with the sound.

"Just like your father," says Peeta.

My fingers find the pin on my shirt. "That's Rue's song," I say. "I think they remember it."

The music swells and I recognize the brilliance of it. As the notes overlap, they complement one another, forming a lovely, unearthly harmony. It was this sound then, thanks to Rue, that sent the orchard workers of District 11 home each night. Does someone start it at quitting time, I wonder, now that she is dead?

For a while, I just close my eyes and listen, mesmerized by the beauty of the song. Then something begins to disrupt the music. Runs cut off in jagged, imperfect lines. Dissonant notes intersperse with the melody. The mockingjays' voices rise up in a shrieking cry of alarm.

We're on our feet, Peeta wielding his knife, me poised to shoot, when Cato smashes through the trees and bears down on us. He has no spear. In fact, his hands are empty, yet he runs straight for us. My first arrow hits his chest and inexplicably falls aside.

"He's got some kind of body armor!" I shout to Peeta.

Just in time, too, because Cato is upon us. I brace myself, but he rockets right between us with no attempt to check his speed. I can tell from his panting, the sweat pouring off his purplish face, that he's been running hard a long time. Not toward us. From something. But what?

My eyes scan the woods just in time to see the first creature leap onto the plain. As I'm turning away, I see another half dozen join it. Then I am stumbling blindly after Cato with no thought of anything but to save myself.

Muttations. No question about it. I've never seen these mutts, but they're no natural-born animals. They resemble huge wolves, but what wolf lands and then balances easily on its hind legs? What wolf waves the rest of the pack forward with its front paw as though it had a wrist? These things I can see at a distance. Up close, I'm sure their more menacing attributes will be revealed.

Cato has made a beeline for the Cornucopia, and without question I follow him. If he thinks it's the safest place, who am I to argue? Besides, even if I could make it to the trees, it would be impossible for Peeta to outrun them on that leg — Peeta! My hands have just landed on the metal at the pointed tail of the Cornucopia when I remember I'm part of a team. He's about fifteen yards behind me, hobbling as fast as he can, but the mutts are closing in on him fast. I send an arrow into the pack and one goes down, but there are plenty to take its place.

Peeta's waving me up the horn, "Go, Katniss! Go!"

He's right. I can't protect either of us on the ground. I start climbing, scaling the Cornucopia on my hands and feet. The pure gold surface has been designed to resemble the woven horn that we fill at harvest, so there are little ridges and seams to get a decent hold on. But after a day in the arena sun, the metal feels hot enough to blister my hands.

Cato lies on his side at the very top of the horn, twenty feet above the ground, gasping to catch his breath as he gags over the edge. Now's my chance to finish him off. I stop midway up the horn and load another arrow, but just as I'm about to let it fly, I hear Peeta cry out. I twist around and see he's just reached the tail, and the mutts are right on his heels.

"Climb!" I yell. Peeta starts up hampered by not only the leg but the knife in his hand. I shoot my arrow down the throat of the first mutt that places its paws on the metal. As it dies the creature lashes out, inadvertently opening gashes on a few of its companions. That's when I get a look at the claws. Four inches and clearly razor-sharp.

Peeta reaches my feet and I grab his arm and pull him along. Then I remember Cato waiting at the top and whip around, but he's doubled over with cramps and apparently more preoccupied with the mutts than us. He coughs out something unintelligible. The snuffling, growling sound coming from the mutts isn't helping.

"What?" I shout at him.

"He said, 'Can they climb it?'" answers Peeta, drawing my focus back to the base of the horn.

The mutts are beginning to assemble. As they join together, they raise up again to stand easily on their back legs giving them an eerily human quality. Each has a thick coat, some with fur that is straight and sleek, others curly, and the colors vary from jet black to what I can only describe as blond. There's something else about them, something that makes the hair rise up on the back of my neck, but I can't put my finger on it.

They put their snouts on the horn, sniffing and tasting the metal, scraping paws over the surface and then making high-pitched yipping sounds to one another. This must be how they communicate because the pack backs up as if to make room. Then one of them, a good-size mutt with silky waves of blond fur takes a running start and leaps onto the horn. Its back legs must be incredibly powerful because it lands a mere ten feet below us, its pink lips pulled back in a snarl. For a moment it hangs there, and in that moment I realize what else unsettled me about the mutts. The green eyes glowering at me are unlike any dog or wolf, any canine I've ever seen. They are unmistakably human. And that revelation has barely registered when I notice the collar with the number *1* inlaid with jewels and the whole horrible thing hits me. The blonde hair, the green eyes, the number . . . it's Glimmer.

A shriek escapes my lips and I'm having trouble holding the arrow in place. I have been waiting to fire, only too aware of my dwindling supply of arrows. Waiting to see if the creatures can, in fact, climb. But now, even though the mutt has begun to slide backward, unable to find any purchase on the metal, even though I can hear the slow screeching of the claws like nails on a blackboard, I fire into its throat. Its body twitches and flops onto the ground with a thud.

"Katniss?" I can feel Peeta's grip on my arm.

"It's her!" I get out.

"Who?" asks Peeta.

My head snaps from side to side as I examine the pack, taking in the various sizes and colors. The small one with the red coat and amber eyes . . . Foxface! And there, the ashen hair and hazel eyes of the boy from District 9 who died as we struggled for the backpack! And worst of all, the smallest mutt, with dark glossy fur, huge brown eyes and a collar that reads *11* in woven straw. Teeth bared in hatred. Rue . . .

"What is it, Katniss?" Peeta shakes my shoulder.

"It's them. It's all of them. The others. Rue and Foxface and . . . all of the other tributes," I choke out.

I hear Peeta's gasp of recognition. "What did they do to them? You don't think . . . those could be their real eyes?"

Their eyes are the least of my worries. What about their brains? Have they been given any of the real tributes memories? Have they been programmed to hate our faces particularly because we have survived and they were so callously murdered? And the ones we actually killed . . . do they believe they're avenging their own deaths?

Before I can get this out, the mutts begin a new assault on the horn. They've split into two groups at the sides of the horn and are using those powerful hindquarters to launch themselves at us. A pair of teeth ring together just inches from my hand and then I hear Peeta cry out, feel the yank on his body, the heavy weight of boy and mutt pulling me over the side. If not for the grip on my arm, he'd be on the ground, but as it is, it takes all my strength to keep us both on the curved back of the horn. And more tributes are coming.

"Kill it, Peeta! Kill it!" I'm shouting, and although I can't quite see what's happening, I know he must have stabbed the thing because the pull lessens. I'm able to haul him back onto the horn where we drag ourselves toward the top where the lesser of two evils awaits.

Cato has still not regained his feet, but his breathing is slowing and I know soon he'll be recovered enough to come for us, to hurl us over the side to our deaths. I arm my bow, but the arrow ends up taking out a mutt that can only be Thresh. Who else could jump so high? I feel a moment's relief because we must finally be up above the mutt line and I'm just turning back to face Cato when Peeta's jerked from my side. I'm sure the pack has got him until his blood splatters my face.

Cato stands before me, almost at the lip of the horn, holding Peeta in some kind of headlock, cutting off his air. Peeta's clawing at Cato's arm, but weakly, as if confused over whether it's more important to breathe or try and stem the gush of blood from the gaping hole a mutt left in his calf.

I aim one of my last two arrows at Cato's head, knowing it'll have no effect on his trunk or limbs, which I can now see are clothed in a skintight, flesh-colored mesh. Some high-grade body armor from the Capitol. Was that what was in his pack at the feast? Body armor to defend against my arrows? Well, they neglected to send a face guard.

Cato just laughs. "Shoot me and he goes down with me."

He's right. If I take him out and he falls to the mutts, Peeta is sure to die with him. We've reached a stalemate. I can't shoot Cato without killing Peeta, too. He can't kill Peeta without guaranteeing an arrow in his brain. We stand like statues, both of us seeking an out.

My muscles are strained so tightly, they feel they might snap at any moment. My teeth clenched to the breaking point. The mutts go silent and the only thing I can hear is the blood pounding in my good ear.

Peeta's lips are turning blue. If I don't do something quickly, he'll die of asphyxiation and then I'll have lost him and Cato will probably use his body as a weapon against me. In fact, I'm sure this is Cato's plan because while he's stopped laughing, his lips are set in a triumphant smile.

As if in a last-ditch effort, Peeta raises his fingers, dripping with blood from his leg, up to Cato's arm. Instead of trying to wrestle his way free, his forefinger veers off and makes a deliberate X on the back of Cato's hand. Cato realizes what it means exactly one second after I do. I can tell by the way the smile drops from his lips. But it's one second too late because, by that time, my arrow is piercing his hand. He cries out and reflexively releases Peeta who slams back against him. For a horrible moment, I think they're both going over. I dive forward just catching hold of Peeta as Cato loses his footing on the blood-slick horn and plummets to the ground.

We hear him hit, the air leaving his body on impact, and then the mutts attack him. Peeta and I hold on to each other, waiting for the cannon, waiting for the competition to finish, waiting to be released. But it doesn't happen. Not yet. Because this is the climax of the Hunger Games, and the audience expects a show.

I don't watch, but I can hear the snarls, the growls, the howls of pain from both human and beast as Cato takes on the mutt pack. I can't understand how he can be surviving until I remember the body armor protecting him from ankle to neck and I realize what a long night this could be. Cato must have a knife or sword or something, too, something he had hidden in his clothes, because on occasion there's the death scream of a mutt or the sound of metal on metal as the blade collides with the golden horn. The combat moves around the side of the Cornucopia, and I know Cato must be attempting the one maneuver that could save his life — to make his way back around to the tail of the horn and rejoin us. But in the end, despite his remarkable strength and skill, he is simply overpowered.

I don't know how long it has been, maybe an hour or so, when Cato hits the ground and we hear the mutts dragging him, dragging him back into the Cornucopia. *Now they'll finish him off,* I think. But there's still no cannon.

Night falls and the anthem plays and there's no picture of Cato in the sky, only the faint moans coming through the metal beneath us. The icy air blowing across the plain reminds me that the Games are not over and may not be for who knows how long, and there is still no guarantee of victory.

I turn my attention to Peeta and discover his leg is bleeding as badly as ever. All our supplies, our packs, remain down by the lake where we abandoned them when we fled from the mutts. I have no bandage, nothing to staunch the flow of blood from his calf. Although I'm shaking in the biting wind, I rip off my jacket, remove my shirt, and zip back into the jacket as swiftly as possible. That brief exposure sets my teeth chattering beyond control.

Peeta's face is gray in the pale moonlight. I make him lie down before I probe his wound. Warm, slippery blood runs over my fingers. A bandage will not be enough. I've seen my mother tie a tourniquet a handful of times and try to replicate it. I cut free a sleeve from my shirt, wrap it twice around his leg just under his knee, and tie a half knot. I don't have a stick, so I take my remaining arrow and insert it in the knot, twisting it as tightly at I dare. It's risky business — Peeta may end up losing his leg — but when I weigh this against him losing his life, what alternative do I have? I bandage the wound in the rest of my shirt and lie down with him.

"Don't go to sleep," I tell him. I'm not sure if this is exactly medical protocol, but I'm terrified that if he drifts off he'll never wake again.

"Are you cold?" he asks. He unzips his jacket and I press against him as he fastens it around me. It's a bit warmer, sharing our body heat inside my double layer of jackets, but the night is young. The temperature will continue to drop.

Even now I can feel the Cornucopia, which burned so when I first climbed it, slowly turning to ice.

"Cato may win this thing yet," I whisper to Peeta.

"Don't you believe it," he says, pulling up my hood, but he's shaking harder than I am.

The next hours are the worst in my life, which if you think about it, is saying something. The cold would be torture enough, but the real nightmare is listening to Cato, moaning, begging, and finally just whimpering as the mutts work away at him. After a very short time, I don't care who he is or what he's done, all I want is for his suffering to end.

"Why don't they just kill him?" I ask Peeta.

"You know why," he says, and pulls me closer to him.

And I do. No viewer could turn away from the show now. From the Gamemakers' point of view, this is the final word in entertainment.

It goes on and on and on and eventually completely consumes my mind, blocking out memories and hopes of tomorrow, erasing everything but the present, which I begin to believe will never change. There will never be anything but cold and fear and the agonized sounds of the boy dying in the horn.

Peeta begins to doze off now, and each time he does, I find myself yelling his name louder and louder because if he goes and dies on me now, I know I'll go completely insane. He's fighting it, probably more for me than for him, and it's hard because unconsciousness would be its own form of escape. But the adrenaline pumping through my body would never allow me to follow him, so I can't let him go. I just can't.

The only indication of the passage of time lies in the heavens, the subtle shift of the moon. So Peeta begins pointing it out to me, insisting I acknowledge its progress and sometimes, for just a moment I feel a flicker of hope before the agony of the night engulfs me again.

Finally, I hear him whisper that the sun is rising. I open my eyes and find the stars fading in the pale light of dawn. I can see, too, how bloodless Peeta's face has become. How little time he has left. And I know I have to get him back to the Capitol.

Still, no cannon has fired. I press my good ear against the horn and can just make out Cato's voice.

"I think he's closer now. Katniss, can you shoot him?" Peeta asks.

If he's near the mouth, I may be able to take him out. It would be an act of mercy at this point.

"My last arrow's in your tourniquet," I say.

"Make it count," says Peeta, unzipping his jacket, letting me loose.

So I free the arrow, tying the tourniquet back as tightly as my frozen fingers can manage. I rub my hands together, trying to regain circulation. When I crawl to the lip of the horn and hang over the edge, I feel Peeta's hands grip me for support.

It takes a few moments to find Cato in the dim light, in the blood. Then the raw hunk of meat that used to be my enemy makes a sound, and I know where his mouth is. And I think the word he's trying to say is *please*.

Pity, not vengeance, sends my arrow flying into his skull. Peeta pulls me back up, bow in hand, quiver empty.

"Did you get him?" he whispers.

The cannon fires in answer.

"Then we won, Katniss," he says hollowly.

"Hurray for us," I get out, but there's no joy of victory in my voice.

A hole opens in the plain and as if on cue, the remaining mutts bound into it, disappearing as the earth closes above them.

We wait, for the hovercraft to take Cato's remains, for the trumpets of victory that should follow, but nothing happens.

"Hey!" I shout into air. "What's going on?" The only response is the chatter of waking birds.

"Maybe it's the body. Maybe we have to move away from it," says Peeta.

I try to remember. Do you have to distance yourself from the dead tribute on the final kill? My brain is too muddled to be sure, but what else could be the reason for the delay?

"Okay. Think you could make it to the lake?" I ask.

"Think I better try," says Peeta. We inch down to the tail of the horn and fall to the ground. If the stiffness in my limbs is this bad, how can Peeta even move? I rise first, swinging and bending my arms and legs until I think I can help him up. Somehow, we make it back to the lake. I scoop up a handful of the cold water for Peeta and bring a second to my lips.

A mockingjay gives the long, low whistle, and tears of relief fill my eyes as the hovercraft appears and takes Cato's body away. Now they will take us. Now we can go home.

But again there's no response.

"What are they waiting for?" says Peeta weakly. Between the loss of the tourniquet and the effort it took to get to the lake, his wound has opened up again.

"I don't know," I say. Whatever the holdup is, I can't watch him lose any more blood. I get up to find a stick but almost immediately come across the arrow that bounced off Cato's body armor. It will do as well as the other arrow. As I stoop to pick it up, Claudius Templesmith's voice booms into the arena.

"Greetings to the final contestants of the Seventy-fourth Hunger Games. The earlier revision has been revoked. Closer examination of the rule book has disclosed that only one winner may be allowed," he says. "Good luck and may the odds be ever in your favor."

There's a small burst of static and then nothing more. I stare at Peeta in disbelief as the truth sinks in. They never intended to let us both live. This has all been devised by the Gamemakers to guarantee the most dramatic showdown in history. And like a fool, I bought into it.

"If you think about it, it's not that surprising," he says softly. I watch as he painfully makes it to his feet. Then he's moving toward me, as if in slow motion, his hand is pulling the knife from his belt —

Before I am even aware of my actions, my bow is loaded with the arrow pointed straight at his heart. Peeta raises his eyebrows and I see the knife has already left his hand on its way to the lake where it splashes in the water. I drop my weapons and take a step back, my face burning in what can only be shame.

"No," he says. "Do it." Peeta limps toward me and thrusts the weapons back in my hands.

"I can't," I say. "I won't."

"Do it. Before they send those mutts back or something. I don't want to die like Cato," he says.

"Then you shoot me," I say furiously, shoving the weapons back at him. "You shoot me and go home and live with it!" And as I say it, I know death right here, right now would be the easier of the two.

"You know I can't," Peeta says, discarding the weapons. "Fine, I'll go first anyway." He leans down and rips the bandage off his leg, eliminating the final barrier between his blood and the earth.

"No, you can't kill yourself," I say. I'm on my knees, desperately plastering the bandage back onto his wound.

"Katniss," he says. "It's what I want."

"You're not leaving me here alone," I say. Because if he dies, I'll never go home, not really. I'll spend the rest of my life in this arena trying to think my way out.

"Listen," he says, pulling me to my feet. "We both know

they have to have a victor. It can only be one of us. Please, take it. For me." And he goes on about how he loves me, what life would be without me but I've stopped listening because his previous words are trapped in my head, thrashing desperately around.

We both know they have to have a victor.

Yes, they have to have a victor. Without a victor, the whole thing would blow up in the Gamemakers' faces. They'd have failed the Capitol. Might possibly even be executed, slowly and painfully while the cameras broadcast it to every screen in the country.

If Peeta and I were both to die, or they thought we were . . .

My fingers fumble with the pouch on my belt, freeing it. Peeta sees it and his hand clamps on my wrist. "No, I won't let you."

"Trust me," I whisper. He holds my gaze for a long moment then lets me go. I loosen the top of the pouch and pour a few spoonfuls of berries into his palm. Then I fill my own. "On the count of three?"

Peeta leans down and kisses me once, very gently. "The count of three," he says.

We stand, our backs pressed together, our empty hands locked tight.

"Hold them out. I want everyone to see," he says.

I spread out my fingers, and the dark berries glisten in the sun. I give Peeta's hand one last squeeze as a signal, as a good-bye, and we begin counting. "One." Maybe I'm wrong. "Two." Maybe they don't care if we both die. "Three!" It's too late to change my mind. I lift my hand to my mouth, taking one last look at the world. The berries have just passed my lips when the trumpets begin to blare.

The frantic voice of Claudius Templesmith shouts above them. "Stop! Stop! Ladies and gentlemen, I am pleased to present the victors of the Seventy-fourth Hunger Games, Katniss Everdeen and Peeta Mellark! I give you — the tributes of District Twelve!"

I spew the berries from my mouth, wiping my tongue with the end of my shirt to make sure no juice remains. Peeta pulls me to the lake where we both flush our mouths with water and then collapse into each other's arms.

"You didn't swallow any?" I ask him.

He shakes his head. "You?"

"Guess I'd be dead by now if I did," I say. I can see his lips moving in reply, but I can't hear him over the roar of the crowd in the Capitol that they're playing live over the speakers.

The hovercraft materializes overhead and two ladders drop, only there's no way I'm letting go of Peeta. I keep one arm around him as I help him up, and we each place a foot on the first rung of the ladder. The electric current freezes us in place, and this time I'm glad because I'm not really sure Peeta can hang on for the whole ride. And since my eyes were looking down, I can see that while our muscles are immobile, nothing is preventing the blood from draining out of Peeta's leg. Sure enough, the minute the door closes behind us and the current stops, he slumps to the floor unconscious.

My fingers are still gripping the back of his jacket so tightly that when they take him away it tears leaving me with a fistful of black fabric. Doctors in sterile white, masked and gloved, already prepped to operate, go into action. Peeta's so pale and still on a silver table, tubes and wires springing out of him every which way, and for a moment I forget we're out of the Games and I see the doctors as just one more threat, one more pack of mutts designed to kill him. Petrified, I lunge for him, but I'm caught and thrust back into another room, and a glass door seals between us. I pound on the glass, screaming my head off. Everyone ignores me except for some Capitol attendant who appears behind me and offers me a beverage.

I slump down on the floor, my face against the door, staring uncomprehendingly at the crystal glass in my hand. Icy cold, filled with orange juice, a straw with a frilly white collar. How wrong it looks in my bloody, filthy hand with its dirt-caked nails and scars. My mouth waters at the smell, but I place it carefully on the floor, not trusting anything so clean and pretty.

Through the glass, I see the doctors working feverishly on Peeta, their brows creased in concentration. I see the flow of liquids, pumping through the tubes, watch a wall of dials and lights that mean nothing to me. I'm not sure, but I think his heart stops twice.

It's like being home again, when they bring in the hopelessly mangled person from the mine explosion, or the woman in her third day of labor, or the famished child struggling against pneumonia and my mother and Prim, they wear that same look on their faces. Now is the time to run away to the woods, to hide in the trees until the patient is long gone and in another part of the Seam the hammers make the coffin. But I'm held here both by the hovercraft walls and the same force that holds the loved ones of the dying. How often I've seen them, ringed around our kitchen table and I thought, *Why don't they leave? Why do they stay to watch?*

And now I know. It's because you have no choice.

I startle when I catch someone staring at me from only a few inches away and then realize it's my own face reflecting back in the glass. Wild eyes, hollow cheeks, my hair in a tangled mat. Rabid. Feral. Mad. No wonder everyone is keeping a safe distance from me.

The next thing I know we've landed back on the roof of the Training Center and they're taking Peeta but leaving me behind the door. I start hurling myself against the glass, shrieking and I think I just catch a glimpse of pink hair — it must be Effie, it has to be Effie coming to my rescue — when the needle jabs me from behind.

When I wake, I'm afraid to move at first. The entire ceiling glows with a soft yellow light allowing me to see that I'm in a room containing just my bed. No doors, no windows are visible. The air smells of something sharp and antiseptic. My right arm has several tubes that extend into the wall behind me. I'm naked, but the bedclothes are soothing against my skin. I tentatively lift my left hand above the cover. Not only has it been scrubbed clean, the nails are filed in perfect ovals, the scars from the burns are less prominent. I touch my cheek, my lips, the puckered scar above my eyebrow, and am just running my fingers through my silken hair when I freeze. Apprehensively I ruffle the hair by my left ear. No, it wasn't an illusion. I can hear again.

I try and sit up, but some sort of wide restraining band around my waist keeps me from rising more than a few inches. The physical confinement makes me panic and I'm trying to pull myself up and wriggle my hips through the band when a portion of the wall slides open and in steps the redheaded Avox girl carrying a tray. The sight of her calms me and I stop trying to escape. I want to ask her a million questions, but I'm afraid any familiarity would cause her harm. Obviously I am being closely monitored. She sets the tray across my thighs and presses something that raises me to a sitting position. While she adjusts my pillows, I risk one question. I say it out loud, as clearly as my rusty voice will allow, so nothing will seem secretive. "Did Peeta make it?" She gives me a nod, and as she slips a spoon into my hand, I feel the pressure of friendship.

I guess she did not wish me dead after all. And Peeta has made it. Of course, he did. With all their expensive equipment here. Still, I hadn't been sure until now.

As the Avox leaves, the door closes noiselessly after her and I turn hungrily to the tray. A bowl of clear broth, a small serving of applesauce, and a glass of water. *This is it?* I think grouchily. Shouldn't my homecoming dinner be a little more spectacular? But I find it's an effort to finish the spare meal before me. My stomach seems to have shrunk to the size of a chestnut, and I have to wonder how long I've been out because I had no trouble eating a fairly sizable breakfast that last morning in the arena. There's usually a lag of a few days between the end of the competition and the presentation of the victor so that they can put the starving, wounded, mess of a person back together again. Somewhere, Cinna and Portia will be creating our wardrobes for the public appearances. Haymitch and Effie will be arranging the banquet for our sponsors, reviewing the questions for our final interviews. Back home, District 12 is probably in chaos as they try and organize the homecoming celebrations for Peeta and me, given that the last one was close to thirty years ago.

Home! Prim and my mother! Gale! Even the thought of Prim's scruffy old cat makes me smile. Soon I will be home!

I want to get out of this bed. To see Peeta and Cinna, to find out more about what's been going on. And why shouldn't I? I feel fine. But as I start to work my way out of the band, I feel a cold liquid seeping into my vein from one of the tubes and almost immediately lose consciousness.

This happens on and off for an indeterminate amount of time. My waking, eating, and, even though I resist the impulse to try and escape the bed, being knocked out again. I seem to be in a strange, continual twilight. Only a few things register. The redheaded Avox girl has not returned since the feeding, my scars are disappearing, and do I imagine it? Or do I hear a man's voice yelling? Not in the Capitol accent, but in the rougher cadences of home. And I can't help having a vague, comforting feeling that someone is looking out for me.

Then finally, the time arrives when I come to and there's nothing plugged into my right arm. The restraint around my middle has been removed and I am free to move about. I start to sit up but am arrested by the sight of my hands. The skin's perfection, smooth and glowing. Not only are the scars from the arena gone, but those accumulated over years of hunting have vanished without a trace. My forehead feels like satin, and when I try to find the burn on my calf, there's nothing.

I slip my legs out of bed, nervous about how they will bear my weight, and find them strong and steady. Lying at the foot of the bed is an outfit that makes me flinch. It's what all of us tributes wore in the arena. I stare at it as if it had teeth until I remember that, of course, this is what I will wear to greet my team.

I'm dressed in less than a minute and fidgeting in front of the wall where I know there's a door even if I can't see it when suddenly it slides open. I step into a wide, deserted hall that appears to have no other doors on it. But it must. And behind one of them must be Peeta. Now that I'm conscious and moving, I'm growing more and more anxious about him. He must be all right or the Avox girl wouldn't have said so. But I need to see him for myself.

"Peeta!" I call out, since there's no one to ask. I hear my name in response, but it's not his voice. It's a voice that provokes first irritation and then eagerness. Effie.

I turn and see them all waiting in a big chamber at the

end of the hall — Effie, Haymitch, and Cinna. My feet take off without hesitation. Maybe a victor should show more restraint, more superiority, especially when she knows this will be on tape, but I don't care. I run for them and surprise even myself when I launch into Haymitch's arms first. When he whispers in my ear, "Nice job, sweetheart," it doesn't sound sarcastic. Effie's somewhat teary and keeps patting my hair and talking about how she told everyone we were pearls. Cinna just hugs me tight and doesn't say anything. Then I notice Portia is absent and get a bad feeling.

"Where's Portia? Is she with Peeta? He is all right, isn't he? I mean, he's alive?" I blurt out.

"He's fine. Only they want to do your reunion live on air at the ceremony," says Haymitch.

"Oh. That's all," I say. The awful moment of thinking Peeta's dead again passes. "I guess I'd want to see that myself."

"Go on with Cinna. He has to get you ready," says Haymitch.

It's a relief to be alone with Cinna, to feel his protective arm around my shoulders as he guides me away from the cameras, down a few passages and to an elevator that leads to the lobby of the Training Center. The hospital then is far underground, even beneath the gym where the tributes practiced tying knots and throwing spears. The windows of the lobby are darkened, and a handful of guards stand on duty. No one else is there to see us cross to the tribute elevator. Our footsteps echo in the emptiness. And when we ride up to the twelfth floor, the faces of all the tributes who will never return flash across my mind and there's a heavy, tight place in my chest.

When the elevator doors open, Venia, Flavius, and Octavia engulf me, talking so quickly and ecstatically I can't make out their words. The sentiment is clear though. They are truly thrilled to see me and I'm happy to see them, too, although not like I was to see Cinna. It's more in the way one might be glad to see an affectionate trio of pets at the end of a particularly difficult day.

They sweep me into the dining room and I get a real meal — roast beef and peas and soft rolls — although my portions are still being strictly controlled. Because when I ask for seconds, I'm refused.

"No, no, no. They don't want it all coming back up on the stage," says Octavia, but she secretly slips me an extra roll under the table to let me know she's on my side.

We go back to my room and Cinna disappears for a while as the prep team gets me ready.

"Oh, they did a full body polish on you," says Flavius enviously. "Not a flaw left on your skin."

But when I look at my naked body in the mirror, all I can see is how skinny I am. I mean, I'm sure I was worse when I came out of the arena, but I can easily count my ribs.

They take care of the shower settings for me, and they go to work on my hair, nails, and makeup when I'm done. They chatter so continuously that I barely have to reply, which is good, since I don't feel very talkative. It's funny, because even though they're rattling on about the Games, it's all about where they were or what they were doing or how they felt when a specific event occurred. "I was still in bed!" "I had just had my eyebrows dyed!" "I swear I nearly fainted!" Everything is about them, not the dying boys and girls in the arena.

We don't wallow around in the Games this way in District 12. We grit our teeth and watch because we must and try to get back to business as soon as possible when they're over. To keep from hating the prep team, I effectively tune out most of what they're saying.

Cinna comes in with what appears to be an unassuming yellow dress across his arms.

"Have you given up the whole 'girl on fire' thing?" I ask.

"You tell me," he says, and slips it over my head. I immediately notice the padding over my breasts, adding curves that hunger has stolen from my body. My hands go to my chest and I frown.

"I know," says Cinna before I can object. "But the Gamemakers wanted to alter you surgically. Haymitch had a huge fight with them over it. This was the compromise." He stops me before I can look at my reflection. "Wait, don't forget the shoes." Venia helps me into a pair of flat leather sandals and I turn to the mirror.

I am still the "girl on fire." The sheer fabric softly glows. Even the slight movement in the air sends a ripple up my body. By comparison, the chariot costume seems garish, the interview dress too contrived. In this dress, I give the illusion of wearing candlelight.

"What do you think?" asks Cinna.

"I think it's the best yet," I say. When I manage to pull my eyes away from the flickering fabric, I'm in for something of a shock. My hair's loose, held back by a simple hairband. The makeup rounds and fills out the sharp angles of my face. A clear polish coats my nails. The sleeveless dress is gathered at my ribs, not my waist, largely eliminating any help the padding would have given my figure. The hem falls just to my knees. Without heels, you can see my true stature. I look, very simply, like a girl. A young one. Fourteen at the most. Innocent. Harmless. Yes, it is shocking that Cinna has pulled this off when you remember I've just won the Games.

This is a very calculated look. Nothing Cinna designs is arbitrary. I bite my lip trying to figure out his motivation.

"I thought it'd be something more . . . sophisticated-looking," I say.

"I thought Peeta would like this better," he answers carefully.

Peeta? No, it's not about Peeta. It's about the Capitol and the Gamemakers and the audience. Although I do not yet understand Cinna's design, it's a reminder the Games are not quite finished. And beneath his benign reply, I sense a warning. Of something he can't even mention in front of his own team.

We take the elevator to the level where we trained. It's

customary for the victor and his or her support team to rise from beneath the stage. First the prep team, followed by the escort, the stylist, the mentor, and finally the victor. Only this year, with two victors who share both an escort and a mentor, the whole thing has had to be rethought. I find myself in a poorly lit area under the stage. A brand-new metal plate has been installed to transport me upward. You can still see small piles of sawdust, smell fresh paint. Cinna and the prep team peel off to change into their own costumes and take their positions, leaving me alone. In the gloom, I see a makeshift wall about ten yards away and assume Peeta's behind it.

The rumbling of the crowd is loud, so I don't notice Haymitch until he touches my shoulder. I spring away, startled, still half in the arena, I guess.

"Easy, just me. Let's have a look at you," Haymitch says. I hold out my arms and turn once. "Good enough."

It's not much of a compliment. "But what?" I say.

Haymitch's eyes shift around my musty holding space, and he seems to make a decision. "But nothing. How about a hug for luck?"

Okay, that's an odd request from Haymitch but, after all, we are victors. Maybe a hug for luck is in order. Only, when I put my arms around his neck, I find myself trapped in his embrace. He begins talking, very fast, very quietly in my ear, my hair concealing his lips.

"Listen up. You're in trouble. Word is the Capitol's furious about you showing them up in the arena. The one thing they can't stand is being laughed at and they're the joke of Panem," says Haymitch.

I feel dread coursing through me now, but I laugh as though Haymitch is saying something completely delightful because nothing is covering my mouth. "So, what?"

"Your only defense can be you were so madly in love you weren't responsible for your actions." Haymitch pulls back and adjusts my hairband. "Got it, sweetheart?" He could be talking about anything now.

"Got it," I say. "Did you tell Peeta this?"

"Don't have to," says Haymitch. "He's already there."

"But you think I'm not?" I say, taking the opportunity to straighten a bright red bow tie Cinna must have wrestled him into.

"Since when does it matter what I think?" says Haymitch. "Better take our places." He leads me to the metal circle. "This is your night, sweetheart. Enjoy it." He kisses me on the forehead and disappears into the gloom.

I tug on my skirt, willing it to be longer, wanting it to cover the knocking in my knees. Then I realize it's point-less. My whole body's shaking like a leaf. Hopefully, it will be put down to excitement. After all, it's my night.

The damp, moldy smell beneath the stage threatens to choke me. A cold, clammy sweat breaks out on my skin and I can't rid myself of the feeling that the boards above my head are about to collapse, to bury me alive under the rubble. When I left the arena, when the trumpets played, I was supposed to be safe. From then on. For the rest of my life. But if what Haymitch says is true, and he's got no reason to lie, I've never been in such a dangerous place in my life.

It's so much worse than being hunted in the arena. There, I could only die. End of story. But out here Prim, my mother, Gale, the people of District 12, everyone I care about back home could be punished if I can't pull off the girl-driven-crazy-by-love scenario Haymitch has suggested.

So I still have a chance, though. Funny, in the arena, when I poured out those berries, I was only thinking of outsmarting the Gamemakers, not how my actions would reflect on the Capitol. But the Hunger Games are their weapon and you are not supposed to be able to defeat it. So now the Capitol will act as if they've been in control the whole time. As if they orchestrated the whole event, right down to the double suicide. But that will only work if I play along with them.

And Peeta . . . Peeta will suffer, too, if this goes wrong. But what was it Haymitch said when I asked if he had told Peeta the situation? That he had to pretend to be desperately in love?

"Don't have to. He's already there."

Already thinking ahead of me in the Games again and well aware of the danger we're in? Or . . . already desperately in love? I don't know. I haven't even begun to separate out my feelings about Peeta. It's too complicated. What I did as part of the Games. As opposed to what I did out of anger at the Capitol. Or because of how it would be viewed back in District 12. Or simply because it was the only decent thing to do. Or what I did because I cared about him.

These are questions to be unraveled back home, in the peace and quiet of the woods, when no one is watching. Not here with every eye upon me. But I won't have that luxury for who knows how long. And right now, the most dangerous part of the Hunger Games is about to begin.

The anthem booms in my ears, and then I hear Caesar Flickerman greeting the audience. Does he know how crucial it is to get every word right from now on? He must. He will want to help us. The crowd breaks into applause as the prep teams are presented. I imagine Flavius, Venia, and Octavia bouncing around and taking ridiculous, bobbing bows. It's a safe bet they're clueless. Then Effie's introduced. How long she's waited for this moment. I hope she's able to enjoy it because as misguided as Effie can be, she has a very keen instinct about certain things and must at least suspect we're in trouble. Portia and Cinna receive huge cheers, of course, they've been brilliant, had a dazzling debut. I now understand Cinna's choice of dress for me for tonight. I'll need to look as girlish and innocent as possible. Haymitch's appearance brings a round of stomping that goes on at least five minutes. Well, he's accomplished a first. Keeping not only one but two tributes alive. What if he hadn't warned me in time? Would I have acted differently? Flaunted the moment with the berries in the Capitol's face? No, I don't think so. But I could easily have been a lot less convincing than I need to be now. Right now. Because I can feel the plate lifting me up to the stage.

Blinding lights. The deafening roar rattles the metal

under my feet. Then there's Peeta just a few yards away. He looks so clean and healthy and beautiful, I can hardly recognize him. But his smile is the same whether in mud or in the Capitol and when I see it, I take about three steps and fling myself into his arms. He staggers back, almost losing his balance, and that's when I realize the slim, metal contraption in his hand is some kind of cane. He rights himself and we just cling to each other while the audience goes insane. He's kissing me and all the time I'm thinking, *Do you know? Do you know how much danger we're in?* After about ten minutes of this, Caesar Flickerman taps on his shoulder to continue the show, and Peeta just pushes him aside without even glancing at him. The audience goes berserk. Whether he knows or not, Peeta is, as usual, playing the crowd exactly right.

Finally, Haymitch interrupts us and gives us a good-natured shove toward the victor's chair. Usually, this is a single, ornate chair from which the winning tribute watches a film of the highlights of the Games, but since there are two of us, the Gamemakers have provided a plush red velvet couch. A small one, my mother would call it a love seat, I think. I sit so close to Peeta that I'm practically on his lap, but one look from Haymitch tells me it isn't enough. Kicking off my sandals, I tuck my feet to the side and lean my head against Peeta's shoulder. His arm goes around me automatically, and I feel like I'm back in the cave, curled up against him, trying to keep warm. His shirt is made of the same yellow material as my dress, but Portia's put him in long black pants. No sandals, either, but a pair of sturdy black boots he keeps solidly planted on the stage. I wish Cinna had given me a similar outfit, I feel so vulnerable in this flimsy dress. But I guess that was the point.

Caesar Flickerman makes a few more jokes, and then it's time for the show. This will last exactly three hours and is required viewing for all of Panem. As the lights dim and the seal appears on the screen, I realize I'm unprepared for this. I do not want to watch my twenty-two fellow tributes die. I saw enough of them die the first time. My heart starts pounding and I have a strong impulse to run. How have the other victors faced this alone? During the highlights, they periodically show the winner's reaction up on a box in the corner of the screen. I think back to earlier years . . . some are triumphant, pumping their fists in the air, beating their chests. Most just seem stunned. All I know is that the only thing keeping me on this love seat is Peeta — his arm around my shoulder, his other hand claimed by both of mine. Of course, the previous victors didn't have the Capitol looking for a way to destroy them.

Condensing several weeks into three hours is quite a feat, especially when you consider how many cameras were going at once. Whoever puts together the highlights has to choose what sort of story to tell. This year, for the first time, they tell a love story. I know Peeta and I won, but a disproportionate amount of time is spent on us, right from the beginning. I'm glad though, because it supports the whole crazy-in-love thing that's my defense for defying the Capitol, plus it means we won't have as much time to linger over the deaths.

The first half hour or so focuses on the pre-arena events, the reaping, the chariot ride through the Capitol, our training scores, and our interviews. There's this sort of upbeat soundtrack playing under it that makes it twice as awful because, of course, almost everyone on-screen is dead.

Once we're in the arena, there's detailed coverage of the bloodbath and then the filmmakers basically alternate between shots of tributes dying and shots of us. Mostly Peeta really, there's no question he's carrying this romance thing on his shoulders. Now I see what the audience saw, how he misled the Careers about me, stayed awake the entire night under the tracker jacker tree, fought Cato to let me escape and even while he lay in that mud bank, whispered my name in his sleep. I seem heartless in comparison — dodging fireballs, dropping nests, and blowing up supplies — until I go hunting for Rue. They play her death in full, the spearing, my failed rescue attempt, my arrow through the boy from District 1's throat, Rue drawing her last breath in my arms. And the song. I get to sing every note of the song. Something inside me shuts down and I'm too numb to feel anything. It's like watching complete strangers in another Hunger Games. But I do notice they omit the part where I covered her in flowers.

Right. Because even that smacks of rebellion.

Things pick up for me once they've announced two tributes from the same district can live and I shout out Peeta's name and then clap my hands over my mouth. If I've seemed indifferent to him earlier, I make up for it now, by finding him, nursing him back to health, going to the feast for the medicine, and being very free with my kisses. Objectively, I can see the mutts and Cato's death are as gruesome as ever, but again, I feel it happens to people I have never met.

And then comes the moment with the berries. I can hear the audience hushing one another, not wanting to miss anything. A wave of gratitude to the filmmakers sweeps over me when they end not with the announcement of our victory, but with me pounding on the glass door of the hovercraft, screaming Peeta's name as they try to revive him.

In terms of survival, it's my best moment all night.

The anthem's playing yet again and we rise as President Snow himself takes the stage followed by a little girl carrying a cushion that holds the crown. There's just one crown, though, and you can hear the crowd's confusion — whose head will he place it on? — until President Snow gives it a twist and it separates into two halves. He places the first around Peeta's brow with a smile. He's still smiling when he settles the second on my head, but his eyes, just inches from mine, are as unforgiving as a snake's.

That's when I know that even though both of us would have eaten the berries, I am to blame for having the idea. I'm the instigator. I'm the one to be punished.

Much bowing and cheering follows. My arm is about to fall off from waving when Caesar Flickerman finally bids the audience good night, reminding them to tune in tomorrow for the final interviews. As if they have a choice.

Peeta and I are whisked to the president's mansion for the Victory Banquet, where we have very little time to eat as Capitol officials and particularly generous sponsors elbow one another out of the way as they try to get their picture with us. Face after beaming face flashes by, becoming increasingly intoxicated as the evening wears on. Occasionally, I catch a glimpse of Haymitch, which is reassuring, or President Snow, which is terrifying, but I keep laughing and thanking people and smiling as my picture is taken. The one thing I never do is let go of Peeta's hand.

The sun is just peeking over the horizon when we straggle back to the twelfth floor of the Training Center. I think now I'll finally get a word alone with Peeta, but Haymitch sends him off with Portia to get something fitted for the interview and personally escorts me to my door.

"Why can't I talk to him?" I ask.

"Plenty of time for talk when we get home," says Haymitch. "Go to bed, you're on air at two."

Despite Haymitch's running interference, I'm determined to see Peeta privately. After I toss and turn for a few hours, I slip into the hall. My first thought is to check the roof, but it's empty. Even the city streets far below are deserted after the celebration last night. I go back to bed for a while and then decide to go directly to his room, but when I try to turn the knob, I find my own bedroom door has been locked from the outside. I suspect Haymitch initially, but then there's a more insidious fear that the Capitol may be monitoring and confining me. I've been unable to escape since the Hunger Games began, but this feels different, much more personal. This feels like I've been imprisoned for a crime and I'm awaiting sentencing. I quickly get back in bed and pretend to sleep until Effie Trinket comes to alert me to the start of another "big, big, big day!"

I have about five minutes to eat a bowl of hot grain and stew before the prep team descends. All I have to say is, "The crowd loved you!" and it's unnecessary to speak for the next couple of hours. When Cinna comes in, he shoos them out and dresses me in a white, gauzy dress and pink shoes. Then he personally adjusts my makeup until I seem to radiate a soft, rosy glow. We make idle chitchat, but I'm afraid to ask him anything of real importance because after the incident with the door, I can't shake the feeling that I'm being watched constantly.

The interview takes place right down the hall in the sitting room. A space has been cleared and the love seat has been moved in and surrounded by vases of red and pink roses. There are only a handful of cameras to record the event. No live audience at least.

Caesar Flickerman gives me a warm hug when I come in. "Congratulations, Katniss. How are you faring?"

"Fine. Nervous about the interview," I say.

"Don't be. We're going to have a fabulous time," he says, giving my cheek a reassuring pat.

"I'm not good at talking about myself," I say.

"Nothing you say will be wrong," he says.

And I think, *Oh, Caesar, if only that were true. But actually, President Snow may be arranging some sort of "accident" for me as we speak.*

Then Peeta's there looking handsome in red and white,

pulling me off to the side. "I hardly get to see you. Haymitch seems bent on keeping us apart."

Haymitch is actually bent on keeping us alive, but there are too many ears listening, so I just say, "Yes, he's gotten very responsible lately."

"Well, there's just this and we go home. Then he can't watch us all the time," says Peeta.

I feel a sort of shiver run through me and there's no time to analyze why, because they're ready for us. We sit somewhat formally on the love seat, but Caesar says, "Oh, go ahead and curl up next to him if you want. It looked very sweet." So I tuck my feet up and Peeta pulls me in close to him.

Someone counts backward and just like that, we're being broadcast live to the entire country. Caesar Flickerman is wonderful, teasing, joking, getting choked up when the occasion presents itself. He and Peeta already have the rapport they established that night of the first interview, that easy banter, so I just smile a lot and try to speak as little as possible. I mean, I have to talk some, but as soon as I can I redirect the conversation back to Peeta.

Eventually though, Caesar begins to pose questions that insist on fuller answers. "Well, Peeta, we know, from our days in the cave, that it was love at first sight for you from what, age five?" Caesar says.

"From the moment I laid eyes on her," says Peeta.

"But, Katniss, what a ride for you. I think the real excitement for the audience was watching you fall for him.

When did you realize you were in love with him?" asks Caesar.

"Oh, that's a hard one . . ." I give a faint, breathy laugh and look down at my hands. Help.

"Well, I know when it hit me. The night when you shouted out his name from that tree," says Caesar.

Thank you, Caesar! I think, and then go with his idea. "Yes, I guess that was it. I mean, until that point, I just tried not to think about what my feelings might be, honestly, because it was so confusing and it only made things worse if I actually cared about him. But then, in the tree, everything changed," I say.

"Why do you think that was?" urges Caesar.

"Maybe . . . because for the first time . . . there was a chance I could keep him," I say.

Behind a cameraman, I see Haymitch give a sort of huff with relief and I know I've said the right thing. Caesar pulls out a handkerchief and has to take a moment because he's so moved. I can feel Peeta press his forehead into my temple and he asks, "So now that you've got me, what are you going to do with me?"

I turn in to him. "Put you somewhere you can't get hurt." And when he kisses me, people in the room actually sigh.

For Caesar, this is a natural place to segue into all the ways we did get hurt in the arena, from burns, to stings, to wounds. But it's not until we get around to the mutts that I forget I'm on camera. When Caesar asks Peeta how his "new leg" is working out.

"New leg?" I say, and I can't help reaching out and pulling up the bottom of Peeta's pants. "Oh, no," I whisper, taking in the metal-and-plastic device that has replaced his flesh.

"No one told you?" asks Caesar gently. I shake my head.

"I haven't had the chance," says Peeta with a slight shrug.

"It's my fault," I say. "Because I used that tourniquet."

"Yes, it's your fault I'm alive," says Peeta.

"He's right," says Caesar. "He'd have bled to death for sure without it."

I guess this is true, but I can't help feeling upset about it to the extent that I'm afraid I might cry and then I remember everyone in the country is watching me so I just bury my face in Peeta's shirt. It takes them a couple of minutes to coax me back out because it's better in the shirt, where no one can see me, and when I do come out, Caesar backs off questioning me so I can recover. In fact, he pretty much leaves me alone until the berries come up.

"Katniss, I know you've had a shock, but I've got to ask. The moment when you pulled out those berries. What was going on in your mind . . . hm?" he says.

I take a long pause before I answer, trying to collect my thoughts. This is the crucial moment where I either challenged the Capitol or went so crazy at the idea of losing Peeta that I can't be held responsible for my actions. It seems to call for a big, dramatic speech, but all I get out is one almost inaudible sentence. "I don't know, I just . . . couldn't bear the thought of . . . being without him."

"Peeta? Anything to add?" asks Caesar.

"No. I think that goes for both of us," he says.

Caesar signs off and it's over. Everyone's laughing and crying and hugging, but I'm still not sure until I reach Haymitch. "Okay?" I whisper.

"Perfect," he answers.

I go back to my room to collect a few things and find there's nothing to take but the mockingjay pin Madge gave me. Someone returned it to my room after the Games. They drive us through the streets in a car with blackened windows, and the train's waiting for us. We barely have time to say good-bye to Cinna and Portia, although we'll see them in a few months, when we tour the districts for a round of victory ceremonies. It's the Capitol's way of reminding people that the Hunger Games never really go away. We'll be given a lot of useless plaques, and everyone will have to pretend they love us.

The train begins moving and we're plunged into night until we clear the tunnel and I take my first free breath since the reaping. Effie is accompanying us back and Haymitch, too, of course. We eat an enormous dinner and settle into silence in front of the television to watch a replay of the interview. With the Capitol growing farther away every second, I begin to think of home. Of Prim and my mother. Of Gale. I excuse myself to change out of my dress and into a plain shirt and pants. As I slowly, thoroughly wash the makeup from my face and put my hair in its braid, I begin transforming back into myself. Katniss Everdeen. A girl who lives in the Seam. Hunts in the woods. Trades in the Hob. I stare in the mirror as I try to remember who I am and who I am not. By the time I join the others, the pressure of Peeta's arm around my shoulders feels alien.

When the train makes a brief stop for fuel, we're allowed to go outside for some fresh air. There's no longer any need to guard us. Peeta and I walk down along the track, hand in hand, and I can't find anything to say now that we're alone. He stops to gather a bunch of wildflowers for me. When he presents them, I work hard to look pleased. Because he can't know that the pink-and-white flowers are the tops of wild onions and only remind me of the hours I've spent gathering them with Gale.

Gale. The idea of seeing Gale in a matter of hours makes my stomach churn. But why? I can't quite frame it in my mind. I only know that I feel like I've been lying to someone who trusts me. Or more accurately, to two people. I've been getting away with it up to this point because of the Games. But there will be no Games to hide behind back home.

"What's wrong?" Peeta asks.

"Nothing," I answer. We continue walking, past the end of the train, out where even I'm fairly sure there are no cameras hidden in the scrubby bushes along the track. Still no words come.

Haymitch startles me when he lays a hand on my back. Even now, in the middle of nowhere, he keeps his voice down. "Great job, you two. Just keep it up in the district until the cameras are gone. We should be okay." I watch him head back to the train, avoiding Peeta's eyes.

"What's he mean?" Peeta asks me.

"It's the Capitol. They didn't like our stunt with the berries," I blurt out.

"What? What are you talking about?" he says.

"It seemed too rebellious. So, Haymitch has been coaching me through the last few days. So I didn't make it worse," I say.

"Coaching you? But not me," says Peeta.

"He knew you were smart enough to get it right," I say.

"I didn't know there was anything to get right," says Peeta. "So, what you're saying is, these last few days and then I guess . . . back in the arena . . . that was just some strategy you two worked out."

"No. I mean, I couldn't even talk to him in the arena, could I?" I stammer.

"But you knew what he wanted you to do, didn't you?" says Peeta. I bite my lip. "Katniss?" He drops my hand and I take a step, as if to catch my balance.

"It was all for the Games," Peeta says. "How you acted."

"Not all of it," I say, tightly holding onto my flowers.

"Then how much? No, forget that. I guess the real question is what's going to be left when we get home?" he says.

"I don't know. The closer we get to District Twelve, the more confused I get," I say. He waits, for further explanation, but none's forthcoming.

"Well, let me know when you work it out," he says, and the pain in his voice is palpable.

I know my ears are healed because, even with the rumble of the engine, I can hear every step he takes back to the train. By the time I've climbed aboard, Peeta has disappeared into his room for the night. I don't see him the next morning, either. In fact, the next time he turns up, we're pulling into District 12. He gives me a nod, his face expressionless.

I want to tell him that he's not being fair. That we were strangers. That I did what it took to stay alive, to keep us both alive in the arena. That I can't explain how things are with Gale because I don't know myself. That it's no good loving me because I'm never going to get married anyway and he'd just end up hating me later instead of sooner. That if I do have feelings for him, it doesn't matter because I'll never be able to afford the kind of love that leads to a family, to children. And how can he? How can he after what we've just been through?

I also want to tell him how much I already miss him. But that wouldn't be fair on my part.

So we just stand there silently, watching our grimy little station rise up around us. Through the window, I can see the platform's thick with cameras. Everyone will be eagerly watching our homecoming.

Out of the corner of my eye, I see Peeta extend his hand. I look at him, unsure. "One more time? For the audience?" he says. His voice isn't angry. It's hollow, which is worse. Already the boy with the bread is slipping away from me.

I take his hand, holding on tightly, preparing for the cameras, and dreading the moment when I will finally have to let go.

END OF BOOK ONE